Creating a Legacy

By Steven F. Deslippe

Acknowledgments

As always, I would like to thank those individuals who have been a part of my everyday life; my friends who have stuck by me throughout the years, and my family whose love is felt every day — even though there have been many times when I have intentionally stranded myself on an island of solitude.

A special thanks to Tina Rosekrans (www.editthisone.com) for taking the time to proofread, make suggestions and edit this novel. Without her help, this novel more than likely would never see the light of day and it would probably just stay on my computer for no one else to read.

In closing, I would also like to acknowledge those whose written or visual work has not only allowed my imagination to run wild but has encouraged, then inspired me to keep moving forward with this monumental challenge I long ago chose to undertake — Steve Perry, Stephanie (S.D.) Perry, Nyx Smith, Diane Carey, William Shatner, Stieg Larsson, Sherrilyn Kenyon, Laura K. Hamilton, Kevin J. Anderson, Kristine Kathryn Rusch, David R. George III, Dayton Ward, Michael A. Martin, David Alan Mack, Una McCormack, Keith R.A. DeCandido, Jana Oliver, Kristen Beyer & Christopher L. Bennett.

*** This book is dedicated to the memory of my
incredible grandmother. You will be forever loved
and missed. ***

R.I.P.

Mary Alice Barron
Dec. 06, 1923 – Jan. 15, 2016

*** Not one grandchild ever left her home without first stealing one or
two of her 'world-famous' chocolate chip cookies or other delicious
pastries. ***

A little insight into this book…

This book is the result of a decision I made to expand and split the original draft of 'Creating a Legacy' into two novels. A good portion of that draft thus became the previous novel, 'Staying the Course', which left me well short of the number of words necessary for a standard length novel. Therefore, the expanded result of what is now book #4 goes much more in-depth into Louie's state of mind, Sabastian's journey down the path he was born to walk, and Maxwell's determination to ensure that his longtime enemy fulfills his fated destiny.

Prologue

From the moment he took possession of the Apollo's Stone, he knew what he wanted to do — but that didn't mean that he should. Invading the dreams of the enemy or showing up in an ethereal form to haunt them was one thing, but using this otherworldly object to selfishly visit his son would undoubtedly be considered deliberate abuse of the otherworldly power bestowed upon him.

Seeing Sabastian in person for the first time in twenty-five years was on the top of his afterlife bucket list, but some fears were lingering within Maxwell that he just could not dispel. The more he thought about it, the more convinced he had become that an unexpected ethereal appearance by him would have a negative effect on his son and end up changing his fated destiny. Just because they shared some DNA, did not mean that Sabastian would welcome him with open arms. Yes, it was unlikely that his son held any kind of real animosity toward him, but there was still that possibility. After all, Maxwell hadn't been there to protect his family, as he should have.

It would also be stupid of him to do something that in turn, would piss off Nefieti. Just because there appeared to be an understanding between them, didn't mean that he could take advantage of the privilege he had been given in order to satisfy a personal want. As the old saying goes, just because you can, doesn't mean that you should. The last thing Maxwell wanted was to give the angel a reason to banish him to the Amaranthine — that godforsaken place. If only the Apollo's Stone could show him the future, then at least he would know whether or not an appearance would do any sort of damage. He had a lot of thinking to do. He also knew that he could not procrastinate for too long. More than likely, Louie Mazotti had plans in place for his son to walk the same path as he. What was impossible to predict, was when he would place him upon it.

He claimed a seat in the living area of his manifested apartment and held the Apollo's Stone in his hand. Within only a few seconds, a virtual window had opened up right in front of him and

Maxwell could see his son. Sabastian looked different this day; he didn't look like his normal, jovial self. He didn't look like he was depressed, just uncertain. It was almost as if a giant weight had suddenly been placed upon his shoulders.

At that moment, his fatherly instincts were urging him to go to his son — but he resisted. Sabastian was a grown man and there was no reason for Maxwell to have to make an appearance every single time he needed a Band-Aid placed upon his knee. And there was certainly no reason for him, whatsoever, to show up whenever his son faced some sort of adversity. Up until now, his boy had done just fine all on his own.

Sure, it wasn't fair that his fatherly rights had been taken away from him. He should have been there, right by his son's side during every evolutionary step he took. But he hadn't been; that's just the way the cards had been dealt. That being said, Maxwell couldn't help but beam with pride. His own legacy had inspired Sabastian. It wasn't much of a consolation, but it would have to suffice.

"When are you going to go to him?"

Maxwell hadn't even realized that his wife had been standing behind him and looking over his shoulder, watching him watch over their son. "This isn't a good time. Sabastian appears to have a lot on his mind right now. My sudden appearance might end up making things worse."

"That's nonsense! Now would be as good a time as any to go. Our son appears to have a serious dilemma that I know you can help him work through."

Maxwell smiled as Sylvia maneuvered herself around from behind and sat across his lap — she then leaned in and gave her husband a loving kiss. "He is you and I. There is not an ounce of hate in him. There may be some lingering anger, but I believe that is just because of what had happened to him when he was a baby."

"But that's what I am afraid of, dear. I am afraid that Sabastian might be holding onto a grudge because I made my job a priority and not my family."

Sylvia took both of her soft, dainty hands and placed them on either side of Maxwell's face. She then looked him in the eyes and spoke with the utmost of confidence, "Believe me when I say,

Sabastian's anger is not because of you… it is directed toward everyone who is responsible for what has taken place. That is why he has chosen to continue on with what you had started. All that he needs from you is your support. Once he knows that he has your blessing, he will continue on down the path that he was born to walk. And when all is said and done, he will leave behind a legacy that easily will mirror yours."

Maxwell allowed the live image of his son to disappear. He then set the Apollo's Stone down onto the end table that was beside his chair, wrapped his arms around his wife's waist, and planted a loving, tender kiss on her lips. Her words; her ability to make him understand and look at situations from a completely different perspective was one of the things that had made Maxwell fall in love with her all those years ago.

He could have just stayed there for the remainder of eternity and kissed his wife, but their son needed him. Sabastian had a potential situation headed his way and it was Maxwell's responsibility to not only warn him but also prepare him for it.

After Sylvia vacated his lap and stepped aside to give him some space, he picked the Apollo's Stone up again. The next thing Maxwell knew, he was no longer in his manifested apartment. He hadn't yet used his thoughts or allowed his emotions to trigger the stone's powers, so it left him confused as to how he was able to get where he now was.

A slight sense of déjà-vu quickly enveloped him as he sat in a chair across from a rather large white desk. After quickly looking at his surroundings, he determined that this place looked more like an interrogation room than what it actually was — someone's office. For a handful of seconds, he thought that Christopher White was going to come storming up behind him and chew his ass out for something. His mind, however, erased that notion, as it reminded him that his old boss was not yet dead.

This space, with its semi-gloss white walls and arched ceiling, didn't feel as sterile as it should. In fact, it strangely felt warm and inviting. But that didn't mean what was about to transpire in this room would allow Maxwell to stay comfortably at ease, so he just kept to himself, kept his mouth closed, and patiently waited. Soon, it was easy to assume, someone of importance would be joining him.

Less than a minute after his arrival, he heard a door open up. Though he was curious, he didn't turn around; he instead decided to just play it cool until whoever had entered, made their presence known. Once they did, Maxwell would then quickly assess this individual and determine whether or not they would receive one of his famous wisecracks. He had, after all, been brought here against his will.

He had several clever comments ready and waiting, but the moment he became aware of who was now occupying the room with him, Maxwell somehow lost his ability to form a comprehensive sentence. It wasn't that he all of a sudden became a mute; it was because he never in a million centuries imagined that the face now looking at him would be exactly the same as those minions that had marched right toward him during his brief few moments spent in the Amaranthine.

Because he knew where this 'creature' was from, Maxwell's mind immediately drew an unfounded conclusion — this grey-skinned troll had come to escort him right back to that place. Nefieti had made it very clear to him that at any time, he could easily be sent back to that misery-filled expanse if he said or did something that the angel didn't like.

For a few brief seconds, Maxwell reviewed what he had recently done, but he just could not think of anything that might warrant his banishment from the Netherworld. So he hesitantly asked, "Um… Why have I been brought here?"

The minion didn't respond to his question. Instead, he/she reached over and effortlessly removed the Apollo's Stone from Maxwell's hand. From there, this subordinate, spawned from somewhere within the depths of hell, walked over to the other side of the desk and patiently waited beside the yellow and black, high-back office chair; the only item in the entire room that didn't seem to match the rest of the insipid decor.

"Am I in shit?"

Again, the creature did not reply to Maxwell's question; a commanding voice from behind him though, did. "No.., but you are here because of a concern."

Like before, Maxwell did not turn around. He sat still and waited. There was no uncertainty this time, however, as the owner of the voice was not at all a mystery to him. "Pertaining to what?"

Nefieti walked around behind his desk and took a seat. As he did this, he thanked his trusted servant, Beezel, for retrieving the stone. Without having to be told, the minion then left the office, leaving Maxwell and the angel alone. "I am concerned about you not staying focused on what you have been brought here to do."

"When it comes to Louie Mazotti, I never lose my focus. Unfortunately, I have only been able to figure out how to make an appearance in an ethereal state, not a corporeal one."

"Learning that takes some time. But that is not what I was referring to."

"Then what?"

"I am led to believe that you are contemplating using the Apollo's Stone for something other than what it was given to you for."

It utterly annoyed Maxwell when people were somehow able to make an accurate assumption when no indication at all was given for them to come to such a conclusion. Although the angel hadn't specifically come out and said it, he knew exactly what the immortal being was referring to. "What makes you think that?"

"You do have a reputation for not always following the rules."

"Yes, but I also get the job done. I will make sure that Louie reaches the end of his destined path. You just need to be patient."

"I am. What bothers me though, is that some selfishness and guilt exists within your soul."

"What the hell are you talking about, Angel?"

Nefieti held the Apollo's Stone in his hand and immediately, the image of Sabastian could be seen. He was in his apartment, beer in hand, and looked rather disheartened. "I know that you love your son very much and that you regret making the decision that led to his life becoming much different than you would have wanted. But I gave you this stone for one specific reason, and changing your son's destiny was not it."

"Again.., what are you talking about? Other than what it was given to me for, I have only used the stone to keep watch over him."

"That may be so.., but it has become apparent to me that you fully intend to visit Sabastian. This, I cannot allow. You cannot warn him of what's to come."

Apparently, any sort of privacy did not exist in the afterlife — and Maxwell was not at all happy about that. His thoughts and contemplations were none of the angel's business. "I was only considering a visit."

"That's bullshit and you know it. You were just about to go to him when I summoned you here."

Maxwell paused; he could not deny the angel's allegation. That though, he would never admit to.

Unexpectedly, he now found himself backed into a corner. The only way he knew how to get out of it was to implore the same tactic he would, back when he was a police officer — the manipulation of the truth. But unlike then, he had to choose his words carefully so that they were not perceived as being a blatant lie. "Only if I were to see that my son was veering from the path he was born to walk, would I then go to him. As his father, I have a responsibility to ensure that his destiny is fulfilled."

Sabastian's image disappeared, the Apollo's Stone resorted back to an inert state, and Nefieti sat there perturbed. "First off... you're dead. That means you can't ever be a part of your son's life. And.., I didn't get the memo, telling me that you had become an honorary Fate."

Although sarcastic in nature, the angel's words were also meant to remind Maxwell who was in charge of the Netherworld.

"Your given task is to ensure that Louie Mazotti does not stray from his chosen path; not to ensure that your son stays on the one you believe is his. If you cannot complete the given assignment without being compromised by your emotions, then your lent services will come to an abrupt end. Upon that taking place, your wife's soul will be returned to heaven and you would go straight to the Amaranthine; and not just for another cup of coffee."

"Wait! Did you not say to me when I was first brought here that Purgatory had been my initial destination? If anything, that is where I should be sent to."

Nefieti looked at Maxwell in a manner in which he could not misinterpret. "I have been granted the liberty of deciding what to do with you, should you fail. Just be thankful that Lucifer's Kingdom is not one of the other two options available."

Maxwell could not even begin to speculate what those were, nor did he want to find this out firsthand. He actually liked where he was and if heaven weren't in the cards, he'd rather stay right where he was if it was at all possible.

After a moment of thought, Maxwell felt that he should at least try and explain himself. That way, Nefieti would not wonder whether or not he was an honorable man. "It's just... Sabastian is in a very difficult position right now. He seems uncertain of what he should be doing. Like any father, I only want to make sure that he does the right thing. You can't blame me for that."

"No, but... You need to be just like any other parent sitting in the stands and watching their kid participating in a sporting activity. Encourage and cheer him on. When he fails, he will learn from it; and with every victory earned, his confidence will grow. Just because he may want you there, does not mean he needs you there."

As much as Maxwell hated it, he had to acknowledge that Nefieti was right. Maybe, somewhere on down the road, he could find some creative way to let Sabastian know that he is proud of him, but altering the events that are destined to occur, even in the slightest of ways, was not for him to do. He needed to step aside and allow his son's life to take shape the way it is supposed to and be content with the outcome — no matter what that might be. "Ok. I promise to leave things well enough alone."

"Good."

The Apollo's Stone suddenly reappeared in Maxwell's hand. He then looked at Nefieti with an odd expression and said, "Why didn't you just flash the stone out of my hand instead of having your minion take it from me?"

"His name is Beezel... and it's only right that I allow him to feel useful once in a while."

Maxwell couldn't fault the angel for that. The immortal had a good heart, even though he was certain that he could/would be a bastard if he was ever crossed. That was something that he had to be conscious of never doing. "Am I going to have to wait until my son dies before I see him again?"

The angel did not reply; he instead produced an odd smile that was hard to interpret. The next thing Maxwell knew, he was back in his manifested apartment. Sylvia hadn't moved from the spot she had been in. She looked at her husband and said, "Where did you go?"

"Nefieti summoned me. How long was I gone?"

"About five seconds."

Had he still been alive, that would have seemed impossible. Not now though, as Maxwell was well aware that, just like the entire universe, time was not constant in the Netherworld.

Over the next few minutes, he proceeded to explain to his wife everything that had happened to him. By the time he was done, Sylvia was sitting back across his lap and feeling content. "We just have to have faith in our son that he will fulfill his destiny all on his own."

"I know, it's just.., I am uncertain that the dilemma he is currently facing will be one that he can figure out without having us give him some sort of guidance."

"He is us. He will be fine."

For a moment, Maxwell kept to himself and sunk into deep thought. Yes, he did promise that he would not interfere with his son's life, but he never promised that someone else wouldn't.

Within a few days, another aperture was scheduled to open up — and he was getting pretty good at using the Apollo's Stone. Out of everyone that Maxwell had ever known, there was only one person that wouldn't hesitate to do him a favor. He just needed to figure out how to summon him to the Netherworld, because unlike his wife and son, he didn't have the same kind of unconditional, deep-rooted love for him.

1

"The things you do for yourself are gone when you are gone, but the things you do for others remain as your legacy." (Quote from Kalu Ndukwe Kalu)

This mission should have been no different than any other that Sabastian and the rest of his S.N.A.F.U. brethren had been on. But right from the start, it just did not feel right. Maybe it had something to do with the fact that they had been placed on a plane in the middle of the night without any advance warning or any explanation. Now, they were hunkered down in a makeshift command post in one of the most hostile places in the world today — Mogadishu, Somalia.

The only thing they had been told was that the individual who sat right at the top of the Union's most wanted list, Asad Kaheen, was believed to be somewhere in the area. He was the despot leader of the largest known group of Somalia pirates, and not only were they responsible for a recent raid and pillaging of a Union cargo ship that had been en route to India, but he had callously ordered the execution of its entire crew of twenty-seven.

Sabastian and the rest of his brethren all agreed that Asad, a man with a reputation for having no regard for human life, had to be found and captured. But what bothered nearly everyone was that no credible Intel had been provided to them beforehand — they were here based solely upon suspicion and hearsay. As of late, all of their missions seemed to be like this.

Having to search door to door for information wasn't anything new for them, but having to walk the streets of an unstable country while wearing the military uniform of another, wasn't something that any of them would prefer to do. Besides the fact that it would add more uncertainty to the unnerving existence that the citizens of this country already had to deal with on a near-daily basis, it would only be a matter of minutes before word spread of their arrival. At that point, it was all but guaranteed that a pirate or an insurgent, singularly or in a group, would search them out and then open fire on the first Union soldier they saw.

Like in Tijuana, Captain Swilling had placed Sabastian in charge of the unit. And as he did then, his intent was to do the dirty work himself instead of delegating the rather huge responsibility to any of the other members of the unit. So he removed his military uniform, changed into some civilian clothes in order to look like an out of the country visitor, and then started toward the exit of the building.

Several of his fellow soldiers immediately objected to what Sabastian intended to do. Their reasoning was simple — Somalia wasn't Mexico. Asad Kaheen and his pirates were unpredictable and far more unstable than what the A.R.M. was. As far as they were concerned, it was not wise to allow their appointed leader to do something that anyone else in the unit, could.

He understood his brethren's concern, but what he wanted to do was what any commanding officer does — they lead by example. The success of this mission fell squarely on his shoulders. As well, it was his responsibility to ensure that everyone made it home safely.

However, in order to appease his brethren, Sabastian decided to take along with him one person; the unit's newest recruit. This was the man's first mission. In fact, Sabastian couldn't even remember what his name was. But this new recruit had to learn what this unit was all about somehow, so throwing the newbie into the fire seemed like the logical thing for him to do.

Although there were still some emphatic objections given, nothing was going to change his mind so, before any insubordination took place, the two of them promptly left their command post. The moment they hit the street, they started to canvas the area.

Three blocks on every side of them they searched; unfortunately, not one single lead had been procured. No one single place they had come across seemed like a possible hideout for Asad Kaheen, nor had anyone they talked to been willing to share what they knew. It was easy for Sabastian to understand why.

Although unsuccessful, he surprisingly wasn't feeling defeated. Certainly, they weren't going to give up. However, after an hour spent in the city, he and his fellow soldier both agreed to temporarily put an end to their search and return to where everyone else was waiting for

*them. Later on, after coming up with a different game plan, they'd try
again.*

*No sooner had they stepped foot across the back door
threshold, just like when Sabastian had first arrived in this country,
something didn't seem right. The further that he walked into their
command post, the more he felt an uneasiness surround him. At first,
he thought that maybe this was being triggered because of the
discontent he was admittedly holding onto for being where they were
and for not having any legitimate reason to support it. Common sense
though, allowed him to promptly realize that an answer more than
likely wasn't there. Whatever it was that had caused this, he had never
experienced anything like it before. It deeply seeped its way into his
bones and took up residence in his spine.*

*Once they had made it up to the third floor where the rest of
their platoon was waiting, Sabastian understood why that took place.
His internal warning had gone off. Even if he had recognized it at the
time, it would not have prepared him for what he was now looking at.*

*Right there in front of him, the scene was unfathomable. His
first thought was that he was hallucinating — but his eyes were not
being lied to. There, every single one of his brethren was on the floor,
twisted, bent, mangled, and lying in an amalgamated pool of each
other's blood. All of them had been mercilessly slaughtered.*

*Where he stood was one of the very few spaces left on the floor
that had not been stained in red. His body wanted to give out;
Sabastian all but felt like submitting to its want. Though unfounded,
he honestly believed that it was his fault. He was the unit's leader —
and he had failed them.*

*How was it even possible that this kind of carnage could occur
to twenty-eight of the world's most elite soldiers? Putting on the
Union uniform meant not only a willingness to fight for their country
but that they would freely accept death if it came as a result. But to
see not one dead enemy amongst the bodies made what Sabastian was
looking at, impossible to even fathom.*

*He lowered himself to the ground, sat cross-legged, and
covered his face. This was something that he could never unsee. The
horror of this was never going to leave his thoughts. Emotionally
broken, he just cowered there and allowed guilt to consume him.*

"Don't let what you can't control be the reason that you give up."

Intentionally, Sabastian let those spoken words go right through one ear and then out the other. He didn't want to acknowledge that the harsh world even existed, nor did he wish to leave the bubble he had just created that now isolated him from it. But his self-imposed exile away from the bloodshed spread out in front of him couldn't last forever. He simply had no other choice but to be a man, not a coward, and find a way to deal with what had just happened.

Reluctantly, he removed his hands from his face and looked at the newbie, the not-as-young-as-he-had-previously-thought soldier, and said, "This is entirely my fault. I am responsible for this. I failed them all. I don't know why, but they are all dead because of me."

"You are wrong, Lieutenant. This," the newbie pointed to the slaughter with his right hand, "is simply a cruel example of the many adversities that you will have to face and then overcome throughout your life."

"What are you talking about? My brethren are all dead! Can you not see this?"

"I see what you see. And it is your fears right now that are making this appear. You are the one that is in control; not the one who intends to take your life. If you allow that individual the opportunity to do that, you may as well just save them the time and cut your own throat."

This newbie was not making any sort of sense. Sabastian stood up and actually contemplated grabbing the man by his collar and then dragging him right into the middle of his dead brethren so that he could see firsthand exactly what had happened here. But for some reason, he didn't. Instead, he just looked into the man's eyes and saw a trust; one that would normally be earned only after years of friendship.

"From birth, you were destined to take a specific path. And now that you have stepped onto it, it's up to you to walk it with nothing but a belief that success will be achieved. Doing so will all but guarantee you to make it right to the end. And yes, Sabastian.., enemy after enemy after enemy will attempt to prevent you from fulfilling your

destiny. So long as you stay true to who you are, what you are fated to become, will occur."

He still wasn't quite sure what this newbie was talking about; he hated it when people would not just come out and say what they meant — then again, he was guilty of that himself on occasion. After a few seconds of thought, Sabastian made a decision that would probably be considered irrational to everyone. To him, however, it was the only course of action for him to take. As far as he was concerned, it was now his responsibility to ensure that the honor of each one of his fallen brethren was defended.

He brushed passed the newbie, rifle in hand, and headed toward the building's exit; revenge was on his mind.

"Where are you going now?"

Sabastian turned and faced the newbie; the man stood there with his arms spread out wide. At that moment, his face morphed in confusion. There were no longer any dead soldiers on the ground. The entire room was empty. No blood, no bodies. It was just he and the newbie. "What the hell..?"

"Adversity is always going to be a part of your life. It is up to you to find the best possible way to face it. You, Sabastian, are not only a highly trained soldier, but you were born to take on a task that very few are given. You are a special individual that has the same drive and determination as someone else that I had once known; someone whom I had the utmost respect for."

"A mentor?"

"A brother.., just like all your fellow S.N.A.F.U. soldiers are your brothers."

Suddenly, Sabastian was no longer in Somalia. Instead, he was in Detroit, standing at the foot of the monument of Joe Lewis; an erected symbol against racial and individual injustice. "What's going on here?"

"Is it not obvious? This is about your fight. The path you have already started to walk; it will eventually lead you right back here."

Sabastian was now all but certain that this strange experience was being manifested by his own subconscious. In spite of that, he could not deny what this newbie was saying to him. Though probably not in this exact spot, he knew that he would one day return here. Detroit is where his roots were. As they say, you can try and deny your past, but one day it will rear its ugly head. It seemed appropriate that this was where it was all going to end — one day. "Nothing is set in stone."

"Ah, but it is. Even if you were to try and take a completely different path than the one you were born to walk, fate will ensure that you will end up right here at some point. It can't be avoided. How prepared you are when this happens, will be a determining factor on whether or not your existence will continue on afterward."

Once again, this newbie was right. Fate simply will not allow him to turn a blind eye — and postponing the inevitable will only make things more difficult when it comes time for him to face what awaits him. "My father never let anyone or anything, let alone a fear of the unknown influence his decisions. So I won't either."

"That's good to hear." With a smile on his face, the 'newbie' turned his back to Sabastian and then started walking toward Hart Plaza.

"Hey! Who are you, anyway? Are you like one of those ghosts of Christmas past?"

The 'newbie' could not help but expunge an odd laugh. He then turned back around, faced Sabastian, and said, "No, I am not... My name is Joshua.

Sabastian woke from his strange dream; one that had actually caused him a little bit of anxiety. More than likely, his subconscious had done this to him intentionally so that he would come to the realization that, even though there were other options on the table, there was only one for him to choose.

If for some reason Louie were to offer him an outrageous amount of money to leave well enough alone, or even propose that the both of them sign a declaration stating the war was over, there still was no guarantee that the bastard would adhere either of those. Besides, the moment Sabastian decided to step onto the same path his father had walked, an obligation was bestowed upon him — and it was one he knew he had to fulfill. Otherwise, the tarnish that was thickly layered over the Banks family name would never get removed.

He hadn't planned on waking up this early, but there was no use in him attempting to go back to sleep; his mind was still racing a mile a minute, trying to fully comprehend the unsettling, as well as enlightening dream he just had. He could have just left his room and started off his day at that point, but Jerrelle was sound asleep on his couch and they weren't supposed to leave for the gym for another two hours. Therefore, he just sat up in his bed, pulled back the curtains so that the rising sun could illuminate his bedroom, and reviewed in his mind what he had experienced. He was nowhere near an expert when it came to dissecting and then understanding what one's dreams meant, but Sabastian did know what some things represented — like death.

The intent of such a dream could just be a wakeup call. Or, it could be a representation of what you have and are willing to sacrifice. It could also signify that there is a certain aspect or quality missing in your life. As well, it could indicate that an important part of you has died. It was quite possible that bits and pieces of each meaning applied to him. However, Sabastian was also smart enough to not take dreams of death literally.

After about an hour spent trying to interpret what message his dream was trying to convey, he decided to give it a rest — he hadn't even gotten close to obtaining an acceptable answer. What he was convinced of though, was that he was numerous decades away from knocking on death's door. So long as he didn't do something stupid, he should live a long and prosperous life. An epic journey, he believed, now awaited him; it was one that was going to commence right after he flat out refused to do what the enemy had suggested to him yesterday.

After quietly chastising himself for even contemplating it, Sabastian left his bedroom, snuck past a still sleeping Jerrelle, and made his way to the kitchen. With only the overhead stove light on he made a fresh cup of sim-caf. After pouring himself a cup, he took up a seat at the kitchen table. Two sips were all he had taken before he again, gave himself another internal reprimanded. Never before had he thrown in the towel, yet the belief unbecoming of a coward had somehow altered who he really was. For seven years, he had been a Union Soldier; he was not afraid of anything. Thankfully, that crazy notion had been brief and had not resulted in him doing something he later would regret.

Sabastian knew that he could not let Louie Mazotti's arrogance influence his emotions and dictate his actions. Undoubtedly, he was now facing one of the most important decisions in his relatively short life. He certainly did not want to rush into it. Therefore, he decided that the best course of action for him to take was to 'sleep on it' for a few days. It was going to be difficult to not do something impulsively, but time had to be taken. Although doing this came with no guarantee that a mistake wouldn't be made, it unquestionably was going to help reduce the chances of that occurring.

Just because he was now firmly on the path he was born to walk, didn't mean that he could amble on down it carelessly. He had to be smart. Only one calculated move at a time could be made. By being patient and imploring that type of strategy, Sabastian would be able to slowly inch that Sicilian bastard right on over to the edge of the precipice without him even knowing. No need would be there for him to push Louie beyond it; the man would surely end up stepping over the edge himself.

Over the past month, Sabastian had dealt with more bullshit than he had in his entire twenty-five years of existence — though he did have to admit that some of it was caused by his own innate desire to right what had wronged his family. He didn't know for sure, but that yearning may have in turn, been responsible for the unsettling dream he had.

He doubted that any sort of clarity would ever come to him. However, he decided to approach his reverie in a pragmatic way. If it had indeed been a foresight into what could happen to those who mattered to him the most, then he needed to make sure that he was wary of what possible consequences could come as a result of whatever action he took. If anything were to happen to any of his family or friends, Sabastian would probably lose his mind. Both of his parents were dead — as was Terrance Burelli. His circle was already broken. In no way shape or form could he let Louie Mazotti take any more segments from it. The madness had to stop now. It was obvious that the road the bastard traveled, led straight to the front door of

8

Lucifer's Kingdom — how fast he got there, however, was the only thing left to determine.

By the time his sim-caf was finished, Jerrelle had awoken and was ready to hit the gym. The cool air from their morning walk had an energetic effect on her; for Sabastian, it just added more aggravation to his current frame of mind. He knew that he had to find a way to deal with it before he walked through the doors of the gym; otherwise he was going to overdo his morning workout. It wouldn't be the first time he'd done such a thing, but he'd rather not spend tomorrow useless and on the couch with an entire body of aching muscles and stiff joints.

A half an hour on the treadmill, and a half an hour session with the heavy bag, was all that it should have taken for Sabastian to get in his necessary workout and to give his mind the time it needed to sort itself out and return to normal. But that hadn't happened. It was almost as if his brain had decided to place a bet with his body to see which one would give in first.

"Is something bothering you, Sab?"

He didn't answer his friend. He just walked right past Jerrelle and made his way over to the Smith Machine, set the weight where he wanted it, and then began his series of squats.

With a towel draped over her right shoulder and a visible sheen of sweat coating her face, Jerrelle approached Sabastian, stood only a few feet from him, and watched him squat. After a few seconds of focused observation, she said, "Now I know something is bothering you."

He completed two more reps, placed the bar back onto the rack, and then grabbed his workout towel. It wasn't until Sabastian wiped the sweat from his hands and forehead that he responded to Jerrelle's statement, "Louie is bothering me."

"Yeah… he annoys me too."

"That is not what I mean. The fuckin' bastard thinks that he is far superior to me."

"He is!"

Sabastian promptly gave Jerrelle a bemused look.

"He has decades of experience; especially when it comes to playing games. He is using that to get inside your head. He's trying to get you to think that you will never rise to his level. To him, you are

9

nothing more than an overzealous kid who's trying to step out from his father's shadow."

"Yeah well... I may admittedly be a bit wet behind the ears, but I learn fast and I don't make the same mistake twice. Time; that's all it is going to take before he finds out the hard way that I am a significant threat to him and his organization."

With her help, Jerrelle had no doubt about that declaration becoming a reality.

Deciding at that moment their topic of conversation needed to cease, because he could foresee it becoming like gasoline being tossed on an open flame and fuel the angst that still existed within him, Sabastian walked away from his friend and headed over to the linear leg press machine.

Not adjusting the machine upon his arrival to a weight that he could ordinarily handle, Sabastian started his reps. As Jerrelle approached, she could easily see by his struggles that her friend was only focused on his frustrations and was trying to purposely punish himself for allowing the enemy to get under his skin. "You are not honestly thinking about accepting Louie's offer, are you?"

Sabastian let the weight and the machine slam down; he couldn't believe what she had just asked him. However, he quickly realized that it would be an outright lie to not admit that he had indeed been mulling over that very thing. "I was contemplating..."

At that moment, Jerrelle all but wanted to slap her friend in midsentence for what she immediately assumed was going to be a foolish admission.

"...but as of this morning, that all changed."

"Good! The bastard deserves the worst possible fate any miscreant could be given."

"That, he does." Sabastian got off the leg press and walked right on over to the stair stepper. Again, Jerrelle followed him over there.

"Listen, Sab. I've decided to go back home to Detroit tonight. Before I can even consider accepting your offer to move here, I have to address a few things that I have been purposely avoiding. If I don't deal with them now, somewhere on down the road I could end up doing something that I will surely regret. I hope you understand."

"Of course. Take whatever time you need." Sabastian took a moment to ponder. After making what he now knew was the right decision, he said, "I will meet you there at the end of the week. Don't kill yourself beforehand, as I will need your help to take down the asshole and anyone else who is associated with him."

"Oh, I'll be ready.., even if five days isn't enough time for me to do what I want to do." Jerrelle gave Sabastian a friendly pat on the shoulder and then left, leaving him to finish abusing his body on the stair stepper. She honestly didn't blame her friend for staying behind and working out longer; she had been guilty of doing that herself in the past whenever she had a lot of built-up frustration. For Sabastian's sake though, she hoped that common sense would prevail and get him to realize that he had exercised enough, otherwise he was going to regret it the next day.

Fifteen minutes, and after hundreds of steps were climbed, Sabastian went over to the vending machines. Before he continued on with his workout, he thought it was best that he first take a short break and replenish the lost nutrients in his body. Right as he was about halfway there, his unfocused mind got distracted. Exiting from the hallway that led to the locker rooms was what might be considered to most men as being an unattainable fantasy. It wasn't that the gym didn't currently have any beautiful looking women inside, but in his eyes, she was near flawless. *'Oh, I'd like to replenish my body by drinking her up instead,'* Sabastian crudely thought. Yes, it was inappropriate, but it was hard for him not to stare at her tight, perfectly shaped rear end as she walked across the gym floor toward the treadmills.

Sabastian wasn't normally the kind of person who would drool over someone of the opposite sex. He also wasn't some hard up horndog hoping to claim a rare victory, or even the irresistible stud that most average men only dreamed about being — but there definitely was an allure about this woman that certainly garnered everyone's attention.

Until just recently, he had never remembered mentally objectifying a woman. It wasn't until he had changed his military status to reserve and begun his mission to restore the honor of his family's name that he had done such a thing: in Japan when his 'yet-to-

11

be-revealed' cousin first approached him in that hotel lounge, when he sat down in that café to look over some photos of the enemy and studied the waitress as she walked away after taking his order — and then recently, when he spent those few hours lying on the beach in Puerto Rico.

Without even having to try, this woman had caused his hormones to rise to a dangerous level. At approximately five and a half feet tall, she could not be ignored — by either sex. Her long reddish-brown hair was braided in a ponytail and it hung down her back a good two feet. Of course, the outfit that she chose to work out in only accentuated even more just how perfect her lightly tanned body was. Her blue/green eyes were absolutely captivating, and her smile was infectious. But those were not the only distinctive features she had that stood out. More than anything, it was the natural twins that demanded your attention. They were not too big, nor were they too small. For Sabastian, breasts like hers were not only the ideal size to admire but to enjoy for the rest of his natural life. If only he had that opportunity.

His fleeting, one-track mind had caused him to completely forget that he had wanted to get himself a Gatorade. Like a stray puppy dog looking for a home, Sabastian not-so-subtly followed the 'goddess' over toward the treadmills. Halfway there though, it actually dawned on him that he had already spent thirty minutes on one of those machines. So, as unobvious as he could be, he detoured right past them and went over to the free weight rack that was stationed against the outside wall of the gym and parallel to the line of treadmills — he had yet to work out his upper body anyway.

Within only a few seconds, Sabastian realized that his impromptu decision had unintentionally put him in her direct line of sight. The 'goddess' was certainly going to notice him. It definitely wasn't what he wanted, as he knew that he was already going to have a difficult time not looking at her while she worked out.

Try as he might, Sabastian found it impossible to not watch her. He just could not resist scrutinizing and memorizing every inch of her anatomy — and it didn't take long for him to get caught stealing more than just a harmless gaze.

Immediately, he felt embarrassed. But that soon went away when the 'goddess'' facial expression wasn't one of annoyance, as would be expected. Instead, she warmly smiled and said hello. This caused Sabastian to accidentally drop the dumbbell that was in his left hand. It slammed onto the floor and sounded much louder than it should. Humiliation promptly enveloped him. At the same time, a light chuckle came from the 'goddess'.

'You're not some shy, ugly smuck who could never get a date with someone as beautiful as she,' Sabastian said to himself. *'Be a man, be courteous, and at least return her a smile.'* After doing that, he bent over to retrieve the dropped dumbbell. Just as he was about to place it back in its spot on the weight rack, she asked, "Are you by chance, Sabastian Banks?"

He did not at all expect that question to be asked; it left him dumbfounded. And because it had, he failed to pay attention to what he was doing. The weight in his hand was not quite lined up with the rack. Like before, he dropped the dumbbell. This time, it was intentional; he expected it to end up in its rightful place. Instead, it made a loud noise when it hit the side of the rack, and then another one when it landed on the floor. "Um..," Sabastian felt like an idiot, "yes, I am. How did you know who I was?"

The 'goddess' slowed down her treadmill to a steady walking pace. After allowing a few seconds to pass so that her heart rate could decrease to a more normal level, she replied, "Well.., it's kind of a strange story. You see... I have this problem that so far, no one has been able to help me with. They've all reached the same dead ends. I'm desperate. I don't have anyone else to turn to."

Sabastian never expected that he would be sought out for help. Like the other times he had been recognized, he assumed that this woman might have known his father or someone else who had. "Um.., what makes you think that I can help you?"

"I don't know if you can or not but... while I was flying home to Chicago from a photo shoot that I had in Seattle last week, I ended up seated next to this guy whom I conversed with throughout the entire trip. When I happened to mention to him my problem, he told me that he knew of someone who knew you from the military. That person had apparently told him that you were the kind of person who always put other people ahead of yourself and wouldn't hesitate to help out anyone who needed it or asked for it. And then once he told me that you were now a private detective, I knew that I had to contact you. I know that I could have just called your agency, but luckily I have another shoot scheduled five days from now in Corpus Christi. San Antonio is only a couple of hours away from there, so I decided to come here beforehand. I really didn't know what to expect once I got here, or if you'd even want to help me, but... I know this is a long shot, but I am truly beginning to lose all hope."

Sabastian listened intently to what this woman was saying to him. He wasn't so much paying attention to her words, as much as he was trying to determine whether or not she was being completely forthcoming. Chicago was a long way and there had to be numerous other private detectives between there and here who could help her. Besides, he had yet to even take on his first case and was unsure if he was even capable of being a good detective. "Why did you come to the gym looking for me?"

"I didn't specifically. When I got into town late last night, I went straight to my hotel and to bed. Whenever I travel somewhere, I always hit the gym first thing in the morning for a workout before I do anything else. I fully intended to go to your agency afterward, but... Not thinking that luck would be on my side this morning, I asked the lady at the reception desk if she happened to know who you were... and she said that she did. She then informed me that you were actually here right now working out and she graciously pointed you out to me."

"I don't wish to come across as being cynical, but you've come a long way in search of help that you could have probably gotten from someone else who is a lot closer to you than I."

"I know that. Do you see any blonde roots in my hair? Like I have said, no one so far has been able to help me. I just figured that with the military background you have and the pedigree that your father had, and that I was going to be in the neighborhood..."

"Just so you know, I have only just recently taken over the family business. I haven't even had the opportunity to work on my first case yet." Although he was a little leery when it came to the validity of this woman's story, it had not yet gotten to the point where he felt compelled to deny her request. There was something about this woman that held Sabastian's attention — and it wasn't her incredible looks. Even if she was keeping something important from him, he believed that she possessed an honest soul. However, just because she had apparently traveled a long way to find him, didn't mean that Sabastian was going to automatically offer her his services. "So... what exactly is it that you need my help with?"

"I want to find someone whom I lost touch with about five years ago who meant a lot to me."

"Locating people is not that hard. Any private detective or locating service should have been able to do that for you."

"None of them so far have been able to. Everyone I have asked for help has failed. That is why I am here now."

"What is her name?"

"Her name is Amy Amylia."

"And who is she to you?"

"Since high school, she's been my best friend. We were so close; she became the sister that I had always wanted. Unfortunately, life happens and she moved away."

Sabastian could relate to that as Richard Atwater had become as close to him as any brother would be. Had their paths not crossed, his life surely would be a lot different than it was today. It was even possible that the discovering of who he really was may not have happened at all.

"Like you, her father was in the military and right after our senior year, he was killed in a peacekeeping mission in Cambodia. Stricken by grief, her mother decided it was best that she move the two of them back to her home state of New York. About a year after that, we lost touch with each other."

Silence hung between them for a few minutes. This should be an easy case for anyone who knew how to look for lost individuals. Also, with the numerous social media platforms out there, it was very easy to get a post to go viral. Still, that wasn't a guaranteed method.

"Have you ever had this feeling deep down inside your gut telling you that something isn't quite right, or even wrong?"

"I have.., plenty of times." Case in point, right after Sabastian read the article about his father's murder.

"And that is what I have now. It is why I am so desperate to find Amy. That is why I chose to come all the way here to see you. I need your help." The 'goddess' stopped her treadmill, stepped off it, and moved right in front of Sabastian. The heat that radiated from her body, and the sweat that dripped off of it, only intensified the hormones that he had, up until that moment, been able to keep in check. Now, they were desperately trying to break loose.

"If I do agree to help you, chances are that I will find the same dead ends that the others did."

"That may be, but… something tells me you won't stop at them."

Sabastian smiled; she was right. He didn't give up easily. "Why don't you finish your workout, go back to your hotel and shower, and then meet me at my agency in a couple of hours. We can talk more then. It is only four blocks down the street, east from here."

"Thank you for agreeing to do that for me." She then extended her sweaty hand.

Sabastian reciprocated the gesture; he found it extremely hard to act like a gentleman. The sweat he could ignore; the softness of her hand sent confusing signals to his brain. When he released his light grip, she smiled again, then turned and walked toward where the rowing machines were. "Hey, Um… You never told me your name?"

"It's Lizanne… Lizanne Kinsworth. See you in a little while, Sabastian."

Again, he couldn't divert his eyes. That walk of hers did more to hypnotize him than any swinging pocket watch could. *'Whatever man wins her heart will be the luckiest individual to have ever walked the face of this earth… and he sure as hell better not fuck that up because I would be the first one in line to go that extra mile in order to make sure that she always stays a very happy woman.'*

After the angel on his shoulder smacked him on the side of his head, bringing him back to reality, Sabastian bent over and picked up the weight that he had dropped, twice, placed it back on the rack, grabbed his towel from there, and left. He didn't bother going back to the dressing room to get his street clothes from his locker; he'd get them when he returned to the gym sometime tomorrow. He wasn't at all lazy, but he was certain that Lizanne would easily distract him

16

again as she continued with her work out. So he just left and went home straight away.

All the way to his apartment, his mind refused to wander away from the ingrained image of her beauty instead of it trying to determine whether or not she was being completely forthcoming. The moment he crossed the threshold to his home though, a realization hit him like an unsuspecting pie in the face. He had screwed up. He should have been more skeptical. He should not have taken her at face value. What he should have done instead was what any good detective does and asked her some more in-depth, personal questions; even ones that would have made her feel a bit uncomfortable.

His raging hormones seemed like the perfect excuse to use for his blunder. Had they not unexpectedly come to life, Sabastian might have been able to see right through any holes in her story. Seven years, right before he officially joined the military, on the night of his high school prom, was the last time he had wrinkled the sheets. Perhaps, all that he really needed was a good series of unabated escapades to satisfy his libido. Maybe then, the next time he was faced with a similar situation, he would be able to determine whether or not he was being fed a lie.

He could also place the blame on his inexperience, as he was only in the beginning stages of his new career. But that would be a cop-out. Besides, the one thing he learned way back at the start of his military training was that all mistakes needed to be owned up to and excuses were never to be given — which was what he chose to do.

As he dropped his apartment keys onto the kitchen table, he noticed that Jerrelle was already gone. Had she still been there, she certainly would have sensed that something had taken place at the gym — Sabastian after all, radiated of more than just some residual sweat.

As he removed his sweaty shirt on the way toward his bathroom, the doubt that had been lingering within his thoughts could no longer wait for clarification. Just because he was still unsure of Lizanne's given reason for coming to San Antonio, five days before she needed to be in the state, didn't mean that she wasn't telling him the truth. Unfortunately, his mind refused to let it go; it was repetitively pestering him to find an acceptable explanation.

17

Knowing that he'd probably end up drawing an unfounded conclusion if he didn't find a way to push aside his mind's want until he at least had some more information, he sat on the edge of his tub, turned on the tap just enough so that it rhythmically dripped, closed his eyes, and concentrated on what he was hearing. After successfully meditating for about fifteen minutes, he took his much need shower. While doing so, he reminded himself that accusations should never be given unless proof was in your hand. Lizanne deserved the benefit of the doubt. The last thing he wanted to do was make a false accusation and then be viewed as an asshole because of it. What he also needed to do, once he got to the agency, was ensure that his focus stayed linear. The reason for this was so that he did not impulsively commit to something before he was one hundred percent certain. His already complicated life didn't need to become even more so.

Twice now, the enemy had appeared to him — and unfairly, there was nothing that he could do about it. After Maxwell's death, Louie just assumed that he would be gone forever. Never did he expect that his old adversary would find a way to return from beyond the grave and become even more of a pain in the ass.

Before his rival first reappeared, ghosts were something that Louie never believed in. Now, he did. If what he had so far experienced ended up being explained as a simple manifestation generated by his own complex mind, then logic dictated that there had to be a way to stop these unsettling occurrences from continuing. Even if it was something else that was responsible for Maxwell Bank's visits, Louie still needed to find a way to prevent them from ever happening again. As it was, he already had enough on his plate and he didn't need to have to contend with what in all actuality, shouldn't be possible.

To deal with the impossible, it was only logical to look toward the unconventional for a solution. The problem Louie had was that he had no idea as to what kind of options there were available for him to use in order to prevent his nemesis from showing up again. Hypnosis, ghost hunters, voodoo, and exorcism — any of them might work. Or maybe, he needed to think outside of the box and find some eccentric individual who could arrange some sort of inter-dimensional transference so that he could then face the man one last time on an even playing field.

Before he could even contemplate pursuing any one of those avenues, he had to take care of his daily responsibilities. One of those was the first of a weekly meeting he had decided to start having with his new executive manager. "So that this organization does not have a repeat performance where we will have to deal with an employee who chooses not to adhere to the necessary discretion that is expected of them, we need to develop a method of assuring that any chance of this organization being stabbed in the back, never happens again."

"I agree, sir," Connie Yale said. "I think that maybe our human resources department should develop an employee code of conduct book, outlining what is expected from them, as well as any possible disciplinary action that may be taken if the employee fails to adhere to anything that we state as being part of our policy."

"That sounds good. But can you please make sure that they leave out the possibility of death as being one of the consequences?"

Although Connie knew that Louie's comment had a touch of intended humor behind it, she also knew that he was serious when it came to such a result taking place. Jason Hernandez was proof of that. "We should also draft a letter for which each employee will have to sign; a letter which states that an individual's employment can be terminated without just cause if it is even suspected that they have violated the outlined policy."

"That's a good idea. Just make sure that there's enough grey area within the wording so that it cannot be determined whether or not an individual's human rights are being infringed upon."

"I will. And then once I have obtained a working draft, I will submit it to you for review."

"Excellent!"

"Is there anything else that you need from me today, sir?"

"Actually.., there is, Ms. Yale. But first, I have a question." Louie paused for a moment, trying to figure out how to say what he wanted to say without sounding too strange. "I'm curious. Do you believe in ghosts?"

To Connie, that query came straight out of left field; a question for which she could just humor her boss and reply 'yes' — but doing

19

so would simply be giving an answer that he more than likely expected to get. So instead, she decided to just be brutally honest with her response. "We believe what we want to believe. For example.., there are those who closely follow, and live their lives in accordance with the teachings of what I personally deem as being the greatest piece of literary fiction ever to be written. That of course, is the Holy Bible. Ghosts.., just like angels, Jesus, God, and the Devil; they all are derived from ancient stories that have been told, inaccurately translated, reinterpreted over and over again, and are considered to be factual. To coincide with that, there are things in and about this world, no matter how deeply we look, even with modern science at our disposal, an irrefutable proof will never be found. Because we are taught by those who came before us, then we, in turn, teach our children, and so on and so on, the truth has no choice at some point but to become skewed. That is one of the main reasons why those who have a steadfast belief will adamantly refuse to listen to the other side of the anarchists' argument."

Louie sat there and smiled. Instead of just giving a straightforward answer, Connie enlightened him even more about who she was as a person. That's why he liked her, and that was another reason why he had chosen her for the position she now held. She wasn't afraid to speak her mind, is intelligent, very respectful, and is also an insightful individual. And whether or not it was intended, her opinion on the subject also just told him that she was either an Atheist or Agnostic. "The reason I asked you that was… I am actually beginning to believe that I am being haunted. I'm not sure if it is this office, or if it is just me. But I have had some rather strange, unexplained experiences lately."

"I see. And.., how can I help to put your mind at ease, sir?"

"I am aware that you have lived in this city your entire life and that you spent the majority of your youth living in a relatively lower class, rundown neighborhoods; the type of places where strange individuals, I have to assume, call home."

"You could say that. There were plenty of those where I grew up."

"I envy and respect you for not allowing those individuals or your surroundings to influence the path you chose to take in life. If you had, then you would not be here right now."

"I can't think of another place I'd rather be than here, sir."

Louie's smile continued with Connie's declaration. Maybe, in a few years, once the casino and hotel get to where he wanted them to be, he'd promote her again and bring her officially into the organization. Until then, he was going to get to know her on a more professional basis and ask for her opinion on a variety of subjects whenever a fresh perspective was needed. "I don't know if you know of anyone from your past that could help me or not, but I am looking for a way to 'exorcize my demons'."

"From my past, I'd have to say I do not. I do remember though, there use to be this man who would come into the old Greektown Casino and sit at the hotel bar, back when I first became an assistant manager there. Even though the man was a known alcoholic, he swore that this demon doctor he went to was able to stop the ghost of his ex-wife from haunting him."

"Do you know what this man's name was?"

"I do… but he died a few years ago in a car accident."

"Let me guess… drinking and driving?"

"Yep!"

"Do you know what this demon doctor's name is?"

"I believe his name is Cain. And if I remember correctly, he supposedly lives somewhere within the Dead Zone."

Although that area of the city is nowhere near as bad as it once was, most people still tended to stay away from there. "Does this Cain also have a last name?"

"I'm sure he does, but I am unaware of what it is."

"No last name and the man lives within the Dead Zone. This wasn't what I was hoping for."

"Where did you expect a man like that to live? West Bloomfield?"

"I suppose not." Louie got up from his desk chair and went over to his wet bar. He had a lot to think about before he went looking for this demon doctor and a stiff drink at that moment was what he needed to help him concentrate. He returned to his desk a few minutes later with a glass of Walker's Club on the rocks. After taking a healthy sip, he said, "I'm sure that there are other people out there who claim to be able to exorcise ghosts."

"I'm sure there is... but this goes right back to what I said earlier. It is what you believe. Those people who say they have the ability to banish a ghost back to where ever it came from, are the same ones who not only believe themselves that the ghost is real, but have the ability to make others believe that it is as well. That is why it works."

"So... you think this ghost that I believe I am seeing is nothing but a figment of my imagination?"

"I believe that there is something in the back of your mind that is manifesting this apparent apparition. You don't need a demon doctor or an exorcist or any other carnival whack-job to help you get rid of it. You just need to figure out what is ingrained in your thoughts that is causing this to appear in the first place."

Louie had a feeling that he knew what the root of his problem was — but he also knew that Sabastian Banks wasn't the only reason that Maxwell was now haunting him. Still, he could not dismiss his executive manager's opinion, as there was a lot of validity to it. "Thank you very much for your input on this."

"You're welcome, sir."

After a few more inconsequential words were exchanged, Connie Yale left Louie's office, leaving him alone to ponder his thoughts and enjoy his drink. Right after the last of his Walker's Club was finished, he arrived at a decision. It might not be the smartest one he had ever made, but he was going to do it anyway, so he exited his office and headed to the elevator — the old Dead Zone was to be his destination.

Thinking that it would not be the wisest move on his part to take the organization's BMW to where he intended to go, Louie called himself a cab and then asked to be taken to the Dead Zone. After being dropped off about a half a block away, only because the cab driver refused to go anywhere near it, Louie took a few relaxing breaths to help calm the reservations he still had. Once he felt he was as ready as he was ever going to be, he made his way toward that renowned area of the inner city.

He had no idea as to where he needed to go, nor had he come with any protection other than his nine millimeter. He could have; should have brought Zhin or Nicoli along, but then he'd have to admit to them that he believed Maxwell Banks was haunting him.

At first glance, this area of the city didn't appear to be as dangerous as its past reputation suggested. Of course, everything isn't always, as it seems. Just because it looked safe, didn't mean that the average Joe or Jane should take a carefree stroll through it alone.

Louie had not even walked half a block into it before an unnerving chill invaded his spine. Even so, that still wasn't enough to dissuade him from doing what he had come here to do. So onward he went. No more than a minute later; odd, strange, and even indiscernible noises began to around him. What he was hearing, promptly reminded him to stay on full alert.

Because his focus had to be divided equally, there was now a chance that his objective, finding the demon doctor, might not be achieved. He had been in numerous uncertain situations throughout his tenure with the D.U.O., so he felt confident that he could handle just about anything. Strangely though, his nerves were feeling rather unsettled — but he wasn't about to chicken out. As long as he didn't panic, everything should be fine.

After walking two more blocks, Louie spotted what looked to be a bum on the street; she was sitting on the ground, nestled up against the wall in the mouth of an adjoining alleyway and wrapped in a tattered, dirty wool blanket. The weird thing was, it was summer and near ninety degrees outside.

Assuming that this person was probably a resident of the Dead Zone, Louie walked up to her and said, "Excuse me. I am looking for someone who resides in the area. Do you happen to know who the demon doctor, Cain is?"

The bum looked up a Louie, produced a near-toothless grin, and then said, "If I did, why would I tell you?"

"Because I can help you if you help me."

"You can't help me," the bum said cynically. There is nothing that can be done. I've been living on the street for nearly a decade. I have half a kidney left and have been suffering from Crohn's disease for most of my life."

"Well.., maybe I can make it more comfortable." Louie reached into his wallet and removed one hundred Union dollars. He then attempted to hand it to the unfortunate woman.

"Just because I have nothing, doesn't mean that you can insult me."

That statement took Louie by surprise. Only after a few minutes of uncertain silence had passed was he then able to decipher what her response really meant. This woman did have the information he sought. He also felt like an idiot. His offer was the same as an actual slap in the face, so he opened his wallet back up and removed another two hundred. Instead of giving it to her though, he just held it visibly in his hand; he first wanted to hear what she was going to say before he handed it over.

"I do know of him. What's odd though is that you don't seem like the typical individual that would seek out Cain. You must be far more desperate than them to risk your own life in order to have your problem solved."

Her words caused Louie to pause. He knew that an element of danger might find him before he located the man he sought, but he didn't expect that it would come from the demon doctor himself. "How dangerous can the man be?"

The homeless woman stood up, unevenly folded her blanket, set it down on the large cardboard box that sat just off to the side, that she more than likely used for shelter when needed, and looked at Louie in a manner in which he could not misinterpret her seriousness. "Very! But it's your life."

It was, and he was willing to do what was necessary to get rid of his 'ghost' problem. "I've survived many precarious situations before. I'll be fine." Louie then extended his hand in an attempt to hand the woman the three hundred Union dollars; she did not reach out to take it. Her not doing so, caused him to pause. His only thought at that moment was that this woman probably had difficulty fully trusting someone, even if that person's intentions were genuine.

It was clearly obvious that life had dealt her a series of very bad hands. Chances were that throughout her time living on the

24

streets, she had been taken advantage of or even abused. It was unfortunate, as Louie was fairly certain that at one time, she had been a very good-looking woman — almost comparable to Madelyn. "So.., where can I find Cain?"

"Two blocks down. He lives in what used to be Qwon's Oriental Textile Factory."

"Thank you." Louie again tried to hand her the money; she did not take it. This time though, she said, "Just place it on top of my blanket."

"Why?"

"Do you know how dirty money is? Hundreds, maybe even thousands of people have touched those bills? The germs on them are worse than using the top edge of the dumpster as my dinner plate."

To Louie, that didn't make any sense. It wasn't as if she knew what hygiene was — but he didn't care. He got what he wanted, so he placed the money where he was asked to and then headed down the street to the old textile factory.

Once he arrived, a bit of anxiety consumed him. That statement from the woman, 'You must be far more desperate than them to risk your own life', started to repeat in his head. Louie wasn't scared of anyone, let alone someone who was more than likely entrenched within the occult lifestyle. Whatever was to come, he was confident that it would be nothing that he couldn't handle.

The moment he crossed the threshold of the old building's entrance, something washed against his face. It was cold; dead skin cold. It was as if he had passed right through an invisible barrier. The air was stale, the lighting was very dull, and the place smelled heavily of dust and patchouli.

He walked down the hall until he came upon a room that was easy for Louie to identify. Inside there were about a dozen large spools of fabric, cutting and sewing machines, large wooden work tables, plastic empty storage bins, and cardboard shipping boxes. The only things that didn't really belong there were the two groups of lit church candles on either side of the throne-like carved, oak chair that sat at the far end of the room. Lying on the ground next to it, right by its master's feet, was a mostly white wolf — Louie hoped that the animal was tame.

25

"Mr. Mazotti. Please come on in."

Those words came from the individual who occupied the chair; Louie could only assume that he was the demon doctor, seeing that the man already knew his name. "You must be Cain?"

"That I am."

"Well then… I have come here to ask something of you."

"Yes.., there is a deceased individual from your past that refuses to leave you alone."

If Louie didn't believe in things like ghosts, otherworldly beings, telepathy, a clairvoyant, fortunetellers, visionaries, and other strange individuals with claims of special abilities, that all changed the moment Cain addressed him upon his arrival. Knowing exactly why he was here, on the other hand, was probably easy for him to assume. If Louie himself were to guess, most of the man's visitors were probably for that very same thing. "Well.., my skepticism seems no longer to be warranted. It appears as if you do have some kind of special talent; a gift that unfairly gives you the advantage over others."

"It is a blessing as much as it is a curse. That is why I live here and very rarely leave. Most of society has a difficult time understanding what I am, and those that do, would rather exploit my abilities then embrace them. As for you, you once were a part of the majority. But now, what you have recently experienced has forced you to open up your mind and consider what you have always thought to be impossible, might not actually be. Welcome to the club."

"I'd prefer not to be a member. Can you help me put an end to my problem?"

Cain did not reply to Louie's request. He instead, accepted a chalice of something from a young, female child who had suddenly appeared from out of the shadows. She wasn't dressed normally. One piece of black material, with a hole in the middle of it for her head to fit through, was draped over her shoulders — it was then subsequently tied at the waist with a piece of gold, braided cording. This garment, more than likely was 'made' from the available fabric within this old factory.

The young girl, no more than twelve, had unkempt, long dark hair, and her pale face stayed stoic. She didn't even acknowledge Louie's presence. She just stood there and waited to be excused.

When she was, she bowed to Cain as if he was her master and then left the room as ingenuously as she had appeared.

After taking a sip of the odd red-hued brew, Cain looked at Louie and said, "The ethereal being that haunts you is one that I must stay far away from."

"Why is that? It is only a ghost."

"A ghost is an entity that has stayed behind to complete a task that it must before it leaves this world for the afterlife. The individual that haunts you is no ghost. When he appears, it is for an intended purpose."

"What are you talking about?" Louie hadn't realized it, but his curiosity had actually taken him closer to Cain so that he could get a better look at the man — his doing this is what also caused the demon doctor's watchdog to stir. "Everyone has a price. Whatever amount of money that you require to get rid of my 'ghost' problem, I am willing to pay it."

"You, Mr. Louie Mazotti, are what people like me label as being a 'hot target'. Your soul has already reached a certain level of blackness. And because it has, it is now desired. There are beings beyond this world that want a soul just like yours once its host has died. All that I can say, without any repercussions coming my way, is that your essence has already been claimed, and that entity is the one that has made arrangements to allow your deceased adversary to make appearances in order to ensure that you do not somehow stray from your fated path."

Louie did not like what he was hearing. In fact, he took two more steps toward Cain in order for him to see just how serious he was that Maxwell's ethereal visits needed to end. His presumptuousness, however, quickly evolved into an apparent error on his part as the lying wolf rose up on all fours and then slowly, with obvious intent, started walking right toward Louie. Only a command from Cain stopped him from going any further than the three feet he already had gone.

"I sympathize and understand your desire, but there is a line that even I will not cross. If I were to, then I would end up in the same place that already has a reservation booked in your name. And as much as I like the dark, the color red, and the smell of burning sulfur, I can't stand the extreme heat. Now, if you'll excuse me.., it's time for me to feed Cujo."

"You have a rare ability that other people, I'm sure, would love to have, yet you are afraid of what might happen if you piss off the wrong person."

"Only a fool would knowingly do something like that."

"Well… then you must be a fool because you've just pissed me off." Louie removed the gun he had tucked in the backside of his pants. "You have now left me with no other choice." He cocked his weapon, aimed it at Cain, and stated, "I came here because I need to get rid of the ghost of my enemy, and that is what you are going to do for me whether you want to or not." Louie then lowered his gun a few inches and aimed it at Cain's pet. He was just about to pull the trigger when his gun disintegrated into tiny metal shards.

"No one comes into my lair and issues a threat!"

As if the magical leash that held Cujo in place had suddenly been unhooked, the wolf sprang forward. Louie's first thought was to turn and hightail it out of there, but he knew that the Demon Doctor's pet would catch him long before he got to the front door. Instead, he readied a fist, hoping that one good hard shot to the wolf's nose would at least stun it long enough so that he could then escape. But right before the beast was about to latch its jaws onto him, it dropped dead. The next thing Louie knew, there was a red dot on Cain's forehead.

"You ok?"

He turned around and couldn't have been any happier to see who was there, standing at the entrance to the room, with a Ruger mini rifle in hand. Had he not stupidly decided to do this alone, what had just taken place would not have even occurred. Nicoli's decision to follow him to the old textile factory, not only had saved his hide from being torn to shreds, but it proved where the man's allegiance now lied. No longer did Louie need to contemplate. The ex-Liberation member had just earned his keep.

"Just say the word. I don't have a problem giving this nut-bar a third eye."

"That won't be necessary, Nicoli." Louie then took a few steps closer to Cain and looked at him in an unyielding manner. He then, with unequivocal conviction, said, "You use whatever ability you have and you tell whoever it is that supposedly has claimed my soul that I will not give it up without a fight. And if and when I ever meet them, they will then be the ones who will be sorry for doing to me what they are."

Cain could not help but expunge a comical laugh, knowing whom Louie had just made an open threat to. At the conclusion of his short-lived bit of amusement, he rose up from his throne and took a step forward; the red dot did not leave his forehead. "And if I don't?"

"Then a dead pet is the least of your worries," Nicoli stated.

"All threats are empty to me. You see.., I only deal with the dearly departed. Unlike most individuals, I am very patient. Like taxes, death is guaranteed. Your day will come, Mr. Nemchieve. And when your soul is set free, I will be the first one in line to fuck with it."

All of the candles suddenly went out. At the same time, the immediate area that surrounded Louie and Nicoli was swallowed up in something, almost like a black hole, and separating them from the rest of reality.

With an air of confidence in his stride, Cain walked right up to the slightly distorted barrier, took one last sip out of his chalice, made it disappear into thin air, and then said, "Because of who you are and what you've done, what actually awaits you once your time on this earth is over, Louie, I can honestly say, you wholeheartedly deserve. And you, Nicoli..; I'll introduce myself to your essence sometime within the next… couple of years. So, until our paths cross next..." The room was then enveloped in complete darkness — but only for a few seconds. When the little ambiance that had initially been there, returned, the demon doctor, as was the 'bubble' that had encased them, was gone.

Nicoli had no worries whatsoever. As far as he was concerned, the wolf deserved to die because it was about to attack his boss. But if and when the Demon Doctor's divination came, whatever form of revenge the man planned on employing, he believed he'd have no problem dealing with — even after he was dead. To him, Cain appeared to be nothing more than a proficient illusionist.

Unlike his associate, Louie felt some anxiety. Like everything else he thought was impossible, prophecies were simply a bunch of words meant to instill fear in those who were weak-minded. What the

Demon Doctor had said though, just before he disappeared, got him thinking. He knew that his final destination was Hell, but Louie honestly thought that it wasn't going to be anywhere near as bad as what has always been alleged. Now, he was starting to worry as to what exactly awaited him in the afterlife.

His demise, he believed, was still a long ways away. For that reason, it did not make any sense to him to worry about what might be. He needed to continue on living in the here and now. So Louie pushed aside that unsettling thought and, along with Nicoli, headed to the front door.

From the moment the two of them left the old textile factory until they left the Dead Zone, not a word was spoken. It wasn't until they both got into the organization's parked S.U.V. that Louie asked Nicoli. "How did you know where I was?"

"You weren't in your office. I inquired on your whereabouts with your new executive manager. She told me about your conversation."

"Everything?"

"Just enough for me to know that you were doing something alone that you should not. Your personal agendas are none of my business, but the next time you feel the need to go unprotected to an area as historically dangerous as this one, I will put a bullet in each of your legs so that you don't."

If Louie didn't know any better, he'd swear that Nicoli actually cared. But the reality of it was that he was only worried about his paycheck. And since he already had alienated himself from one faction, the chances of him getting in deep with another were not that good. That was why he had tracked Louie down; he was protecting his own interests. "I will not do anything like that again."

"Good! Now that that is settled, let's get out of here and get a beer."

A beer sounded good. The only problem with alcohol was that one usually led to another and then another — and lately, that was usually followed by an unwanted visit from Maxwell Banks.

Roughly a half an hour after he stepped out of his shower, Sabastian arrived at the agency. The first thing he did was walk over to the kitchen nook. There, he grabbed a bottle of water and exchanged morning pleasantries with Savanna and Baylor before heading to his office.

After claiming his desk chair, he took a moment to organize his thoughts. Preferably, he would have loved to have a cup of English tea with lemon rum, but he didn't want to take a chance that the little amount of alcohol in his tea would become all that was needed for him to not act professional or say something to Lizanne that would be deemed inappropriate.

After he took a few healthy swigs of his water, Sabastian leaned back in his chair, looked at the framed family picture on the corner of the desk, and thought to himself, *'I hope that I make the right decisions. I don't want to do anything that could jeopardize the lives of those who mean the world to me, Dad. I need your guidance and strength to help me to deal with whatever obstacles might lie ahead.'*

As he took another sip of his water, he turned on his computer. Sabastian hadn't really kept up with all of his e-mails and v-mails over the last week or so, so while he was waiting for Lizanne to arrive, he thought that this would be as good a time as any to do just that. Surprisingly, he found that he only had a half a dozen unread messages awaiting him. One of them contained a few interesting video links from his favorite website, 'Today's Military'. One was from Richard Atwater, letting him know that he had been given a promotion for the great job they had done in Puerto Rico — that brought a smile to Sabastian's face, knowing that his friend had deserved it. One message was from his grandmother, Edith Burelli; a lengthy letter about a whole lot of really nothing important, except that she missed him, loved him, and could not wait to see him again. Two messages were junk that had somehow gotten past the spam filter, and the last message was from Governor White.

"Sabastian,

I was going through my attic at home and came across a shoebox that had a few old photos in it of your father when he was working as a Detroit police officer. I thought you'd like a copy of them.

31

BTW, I haven't heard anything new pertaining to the D.U.O. that may be of importance. When I do, I'll be sure to let you know.

Take care,

Governor Christopher White

PS... I think you'll get a kick out of the one photo of me hovering over your father's desk and screaming at him and his partner."

Sabastian opened up the attachment and an instant smile came to his face. The governor had sent him six photos of his father in which he looked to be roughly the same age as he was now — his resemblance to him was uncanny. And even his father's unique mannerisms that could be seen in the pictures were almost identical to the ones that Sabastian knew he had.

One by one, he scrutinized each of the photos. These weren't just pictures taken for the sake of having a memory; each photo in itself told a story. And the governor was right — the photo of his father getting reamed out was priceless.

The more he looked at it, the more Sabastian had to smile. Christopher White looked like he was furious with his father and his partner — for what, he could only imagine. A screwup, an insensitive or inappropriate joke told at the wrong moment, a lack of progress — any one of those could have been the reason why this photo told such a unique tale. *'Even my dad's partner looks uneasy in the picture. Hey, what the..?'*

"Well, you seem to be in a much better mood than you have been lately."

Sabastian's uncertain train of thought got interrupted because of his uncle's words. "I am. Governor White just sent me some old photos of my father, back when he was a police officer." Happily, he showed them to Sydney, which also brought an instant smile to his face. "If I load these pictures onto a memory stick, could you take

32

them to a photo lab and have them printed out so that I can hang them on the walls here in the office?"

"Savanna has a good digital printer at her desk. You could just use it."

"I know but… it's not the same. I want as close to a real copy of these as I can get."

He wasn't about to get into a debate with his nephew — even though he felt that there was no difference in quality between a digital printer and a copy made from a photo lab. "Ok.., but the only place I can think of to get that done is clear across town, so I'll have to do it when I get some free time."

After loading a copy of the photos onto a stick, Sabastian handed it over to Sydney. Almost right afterward, the picture that he had been looking at right before his uncle came into the office, started to haunt him — in a bizarre way. He didn't know why, as he had never seen a photo of his father's partner before, yet Sabastian clearly remembered seeing his face last night in his disturbing dream. "Uncle Sydney.., can I ask you a question?"

"Always."

"My father's old partner…"

"Joshua Brampton."

"Yes. What was he like?"

"I don't know as I never had the pleasure of meeting him. But your father did tell me that he considered him to be his brother from another mother. They were that close."

A gentle knock resonated from the doorframe; they each looked toward the office entrance and saw that Savanna was standing there. "Um.., I believe that we have our first client. She's waiting in the lobby area to see you."

"Ah, that would be Lizanne. I was expecting her."

"You know her?" Savanna asked.

"No. She approached me about an hour ago while I was at the gym concerning a long lost friend of hers. I told her to come by here later this morning so that we could talk some more about it."

Sabastian got up out of his chair, walked passed his uncle, and then followed Savanna into the lobby area where Lizanne was waiting. Again, he found it hard to ignore her beauty, but he knew that he had to — he wasn't in the gym, a bar, or on the street, so he couldn't behave like a famished man who hadn't eaten in three days, salivating over a piece of prime rib.

Lizanne was dressed for success. She had on a tailored, dark brown business suit jacket with a knee-length matching skirt. Under the jacket, she wore a lightly tanned blouse, had on a pair of gold earrings that dangled a few inches below her lobes, and she carried over her shoulder a dainty, synth-leather coordinating purse. Even dressed the way she was, she was still the most stunning woman that Sabastian had ever seen. "Would you please follow me into my office, Ms. Kinsworth?"

"Of course, Mr. Banks."

Being the gentleman that he was, Sabastian stepped aside and let Lizanne walk in ahead of him. Well, actually, he just wanted to take another look at that perfect posterior of hers. Even in a business suit, she still had the finest backside that he had ever seen.

As he was about to close his office door, he heard both Savanna and Sydney make a few surprising comments under their breath. Smiling, he looked at the abnormal expressions that both had on their faces. Yes, he had visually undressed Lizanne as she made her way into his office, but he didn't care that they had noticed — any single straight man would have done the exact same thing. Maybe, once this was all over, he would make an honest effort to pursue a potential relationship with her.

Once their privacy was attained, Sabastian pulled back the chair that was in front of his desk and slid it forward as Lizanne sat down. He then took a few methodical, relaxing breaths, walked around to the other side, sat down in his chair, and produced a warming smile. He not only had to control his hormones but this meeting as well — and for that to happen, he felt that he had to get an answer to a question that had been bombarding his thoughts earlier. "Before we begin, there is something that I would like to know."

"And what would that be?"

"I am finding it difficult to accept the fact that you came here, all the way from Chicago, in search of me, solely based upon the word of a stranger that you met who apparently knows someone who knows me. There are, after all, hundreds of private detectives throughout the Union."

"And as I already said to you at the gym.., those that I have so far asked for help have failed me. They are all nothing but old, fat, retired police officers that only give a shit about a paycheck. None of them care about their clients.., especially if the case turns out to be a difficult one. And that is what has happened concerning my friend, Amy. Locating her whereabouts has become much more difficult than I ever expected."

"If they cannot find her, what makes you think that I can?"

"You are not old and fat. You are young, have a military background instead of a police background... And you care."

"You only assume that to be the case. You really don't know anything about me."

"I was told that your time in the military was spent serving in our Union's most elite unit; a group whose sole purpose is to ensure that our country is safe from any potential threat. That fact alone tells me that you are a very caring, dedicated, and a strong-willed individual who fights for what is right and will not stop until his mission is complete. Am I wrong?"

"No, you're not."

"And that is why I came all the way to San Antonio to ask for your help."

Sabastian could actually accept some of her reasoning, but there was still one thing that bothered him. It might be considered irrelevant to anyone else who would find themselves in a similar situation, but to him, this was very important. "What was the name of the person you met and what did he say his friend's name was who apparently knew me?"

Lizanne knew that there was a chance she might be exposed as a fraud. When trying to pull the wool over someone's eyes, it's nearly impossible to not slip up somewhere along the way. Now, she was nervous — but she could not let Sabastian see the panic that was now starting to grow inside of her. She needed to gather herself in order to assure that the task she had been given was completed.

She had never expected the receptionist at the gym to point him out to her when she made her initial inquiry. She only wanted to get a little insight from someone into what kind of person Sabastian was before she met him. Her intent this morning had been to just get in a short workout and then head over to his agency, but when she realized that he was noticeably staring at her, she was uncertain what to do.

Introducing herself at that moment was the only thing that she could think of. Right after that, she had forgotten most of what her rehearsed narrative was to be. Because of this, she had been forced to improvise and think up a lie on the spot, which was something she had never been all that good at. Now, she had to do everything that she could think of to extricate herself from the deep hole she had stupidly fallen into without looking like a complete fool in the process.

"I'm sorry; I should have been completely honest with you back at the gym. It's just…"

'It's just?' Now, Sabastian was a bit confused. He was also curious. What exactly did this woman want? Whatever it was, he hoped that it didn't entice him into taking an ill-advised path. After all, she had just admitted that she had not been straight with him. Despite that, his gut was still telling him that she was genuinely a good person. In fact, it was quite possible that her worrying and uncertainty may have been the cause of her unintentional misleading.

"This is very difficult for me, but… if you could please be a little patient, I'll try to explain." She took a deep breath, gathered her thoughts, and then began the rectification of her lie — with the lie that she now fully remembered. "When I was ten years old, I was kidnapped by an individual who was part of a black market child trafficking operation. With your father's help, the police were able to shut it down. I distinctly remember the detectives mentioning during my debriefing that if it wasn't for your father stumbling upon it and bringing it to their attention, then I undoubtedly would have ended up in some backwater country as some pedophile's personal toy. Anyway.., when I read that article about your father's unfortunate death, it triggered all those bad memories I had. It hurt me deeply to read about what had happened to him. I mean, I didn't know him, but he was directly responsible for my life being saved." Lizanne paused for a moment to gather her thoughts, as an untimely mistake now could ruin everything. "The guy I met on the plane; I'm sorry I don't remember his name, but it was he that told me a friend of his worked for the San Antonio Police Department, and they had told him that Maxwell Banks' son had miraculously turned up alive after all these years. When I heard this, I took this as being a sign of hope. I know that I am placing everything on blind faith, but I am willing to believe that you are cut from the same cloth as your father. If anyone can find my friend, Amy, it's you."

'Hum,' Sabastian thought. "Excuse me for one moment." He got up from behind his desk, left his office, and then headed for the sim-caf machine. While there, he mentally reviewed everything that Lizanne had just said to him. Once he was sure that he had it straight, he compared it to everything she had said to him at the gym. *'Her revised story did seem somewhat plausible, as there are a few documented instances in which my father had helped to rescue young children from traffickers, but it also varies quite a bit from her original one. Then again, reliving those painful memories from her childhood may have indirectly been the cause of her not being completely accurate with what she had initially told me.'*

"Ok… where do I go from here?" Sabastian said under his breath as he poured his sim-caf. *'Is her new story the honest truth? I'm just not too sure if I should agree to help find her missing friend. I wish I were better at reading people. The last thing that I want to do is to commit to this then regret doing so.'*

Sabastian returned to his office. With him, he carried a fresh cup of sim-caf for himself and one for Lizanne He handed the cup to her; she smiled in appreciation of his kind gesture. As he was about to reclaim his chair, he said, "You are aware that I am just learning how to be a private detective and there is a very good chance that if I take on your case, I might not be able to find your friend."

"Yes… you mentioned that to me at the gym. Your efforts nevertheless, I'm sure, will be more honorable than the ones that I got from the others that I have asked for help."

"You also have to be ready and willing to accept the possibility that she may not want you to know where she is. Or, she might even be dead."

"I am prepared for whatever the results may be."

'Should I dad, or should I not?' Sabastian asked in thought, as he looked at the picture of his father getting chewed out by his boss; it was still displayed on his computer screen.

He took a healthy sip of his sim-caf and then sunk back in his chair. Agreeing to help her out was what he believed he should do, even though there didn't seem to be enough clarity yet for him to feel completely comfortable. He thought about asking her a few more questions, hoping that it would help him to get rid of his reservations when his eyes wandered back over to his computer screen. It was then that his curiosity was urging him to focus on the image of his father's old partner. *'Joshua Brampton!'* Immediately, he put two and two together. And although it seemed utterly impossible, the newbie in his recent dream looked exactly like him. Did the long-ago deceased man somehow find a way to immerse himself in his thoughts as he slept? It was highly improbable. Notwithstanding that, the 'newbie' did say that his name was Joshua — and Sabastian clearly remembered what he had said to him.

"Adversity is always going to be a part of your life. It is up to you to find the best possible way to face it. You, Sabastian, are not only a highly trained soldier, but you were born to take on a task that very few are given. You are a special individual that has the same drive and determination as someone else that I once had known; someone whom I had the privilege of learning a lot from."

That memory produced a genuine smile — it also allowed him to make an unyielding decision. He was going to do what he was born to do. And it is exactly what his father would have done, even with the uncertainties that were there. "Ok. I will help you find your friend, Amy."

"Thank you very much, Sabastian. And to show you my gratitude, would you please accompany me to dinner tonight?"

If he didn't know any better, he'd have thought that Lizanne had just asked him out. But then he remembered that he was working and this was an occasional aspect of the business. Getting to know your client on a more personal level and believing in them as a person was also part of being a good detective — it was nothing more than that. He would just have to keep his libido in check and behave like an adult, not a starving teenager standing in front of an exotic buffet and trying to decide what to nibble on first. "What time shall I pick you up, Ms. Kinsworth?"

"Seven p.m. And please call me Lizanne."

2

Has it all been worth it? In his mind, he believed it to have been. Even upon moments of reflection, no real regrets have appeared. For that reason, he could do nothing but assume he made the right decision all those years ago to walk a path far more precarious than the average human being would.

Just a few short weeks ago, his daily ritual had come to a sudden stop. At first, Louie was unsure if he would be able to adjust to having a mundane existence. It didn't take him long though to realize that he could. Two days; that was all it had taken for the stress that had been a daily part of his life to nearly disappear — and it unexpectedly resulted in him no longer worrying about things that he should. However, Louie wasn't going to take his newfound autonomy for granted. Just because it could be assumed that no one knew where he was, didn't mean he couldn't be easily found. It's not like he was hiding out in some small, remote country in South America — he was in Chicago. For that reason, the belief he always had that a bullet was waiting for him around the next corner, could not be set aside. As always, he had to stay wary of that possibility because as they say, life has a way of catching up with you when you least expect it.

Shortly after Louie made the decision to return to the Windy City, he had made another one. Even though he had no way of knowing how long his hiatus was going to last, he was going to try his best to make his dream, one that he had always thought unattainable, come true.

Frequently, he wondered what it would be like to be a normal person, with normal responsibilities, or what it was like to be a recipient of the rewards that came along with being a father to Marco. It's not that he had never been willing to step into that role; it just wasn't at all possible. His chosen career made it impractical to have any set days off, let alone him having the weekends to do with as he pleased like the majority of others do. As it was, he was lucky to even get a few personal days every other month for himself.

Less than a week into his 'unscheduled vacation', Louie's mind inadvertently began to wander on down the road called, 'What If'. A desire to leave it all behind forever started to tempt him. He'd honestly have no problem whatsoever staying in Chicago, enjoying a daily pint of cold beer, or sipping on a glass of Walker's Club on the rocks and doing absolutely nothing for the remainder of his life. But as enticing a prospect as it was to start all over, it was just wishful thinking. He was married to the D.U.O. and 'divorce' was not at all an option. The only way out of his committed union was death. Yes, Antonio Marcone was no longer alive — but just because Louie was the heir apparent to the throne, it didn't mean that he had the power to magically dissolve the Detroit Underworld Organization. In some way shape or form, it would continue because there were several mid-ranking and junior members of the organization out there, domestically and in Asia and assuredly, one of them would have the balls to claim its leadership. And if that were to happen, it would only be a matter of time before Louie was hunted down and killed for turning his back on the 'family'.

Even though the percentages say otherwise, his back was essentially against the wall. There simply was no other option. It was up to him to ensure that an opportunity did not present itself for a hostile takeover to occur. Louie had to officially take the reins. Yes, he could ignore his responsibility and try to build a new life for himself, but he knew that he had long ago sealed his eternal fate. No matter what things he could try to do to change the error of his ways, it would never supersede everything else he has already done. He was destined for Hell no matter what.

Whether or not he wanted it, the leadership of the D.U.O. was his to embrace. So, after conceding to the inevitable, an understanding came to him. In order for everything to fall into place as he hoped, an enormous amount of sacrifices had to be made first. Most of them were of the personal kind. This meant that there was no possible way for Louie to have his cake and eat it too.

He was certain that he was going to continually chastise himself for leaving Chicago, but he could at least take solace in the fact that there would be some distance between him and Mirella. He honestly didn't want to harbor any animosity toward her, but she just refused to give even an inch.

He knew that it was a pathetic excuse, but he nevertheless decided to use her unwavering stance as the reason for his return to 'work' — even though the allegiance he long ago swore to was the culprit. Maybe, time was all that was needed. However, if things didn't soon change, she was going to get a taste of what Louie's life was really like. At that point, his retaliation would be hand-delivered. Then again, it might very well be carried out for him by proxy; by his son, if Marco was to ever learn the truth all on his own.

Until that day came though, Louie was going to focus on what was most important. He wasn't going to take it one cautious step at a time; he was going to push the envelope and work his ass off — not just so that his mind would not get distracted by the bullshit that existed within his personal life, but he hoped that by staying focused on his responsibilities as leader of the Detroit Underworld Organization, it would help to prevent any more unwanted visits from Maxwell Banks. *'Maybe I should track down a Chippewa Indian Shaman and have him place a protective ward around this office to keep Maxwell away.'* Louie crazily thought. A moment later, a possibility that was far worse than just being visited by his adversary, came to him. *"Knowing my luck, the next time Maxwell appears, he'll incessantly possess me."*

After that unnerving thought was over, Louie walked over to his wet bar, poured himself two fingers of Walker's Club, and then walked over to his office window. He didn't stare out across the cityscape; he stared down forty-some-odd floors to the ground and thought to himself, *"I've never before taken the easy way out of anything, but if Maxwell were to take over my body, I'd certainly have to consider this option."*

In just a few hours time, their initial face-to-face meeting with the United Arab League was scheduled to take place. Louie didn't want to get overly excited about this event, as there was no guarantee that the outcome he hoped for, would occur. However, if his men were to return afterward with an agreement in place, the D.U.O.'s foundation would then be stabilized and the first layers of new bricks would then be set into place. "Today, we have an opportunity to bring a new business partner into the fold. I'm sure that I don't have to tell you just how important this is... considering that right now, this is the only potential client that we currently have."

"We are aware of the significance of our meeting," Zhin replied. "What doesn't make any sense to me is why you have chosen to try and work out a business agreement with a group whose ideology is simply to bring better awareness to their culture and beliefs."

"To the naïve masses, that is what the U.A.L. appears to be. But in actuality, they are a latent terrorist group that is patiently waiting for the right moment to make their presence known. Since their inception, they have been very careful and cautious to not expose who they really are or their agenda.

"And you know this how?" Nicoli asked.

"We sold weapons to them once before. I have no doubt that they would have stayed on as clients of ours, but as a group, they were still in their infancy. After they got what they wanted they purposely distanced themselves from us, as they did not want to risk drawing any unnecessary attention. The timing just happened to be right when we called to inquire about them doing business with us again. Apparently, they are now very close to putting their objective into motion. It is why they are now interested in getting their hands on some of the newer kinds of weapons; weapons that we just happened to have access to." Louie then handed Zhin a piece of paper with the address on it. "I want you and Nicoli to go to this address and pick up the awaiting van. Casper has made arrangements for the vehicle to be pre-loaded with two bags of our sample merchandise. And Zhin.., I assume that you have conducted a business deal like this in the past?"

"Actually.., I haven't."

"I haven't either," Nicoli declared. "But I can't see it being too difficult of a task to complete."

This wasn't what Louie wanted to hear. Even so, he had faith in both men. "It's not. But it's something you should not take lightly either."

"We won't," Zhin said assuredly.

Before this meeting took place, Louie had already decided to accept the ex-Liberation member into the fold. Now though was not the right time to let him know of that. He knew better than anyone that complacency can contribute to a bad decision being made, and this assignment's completion was of the utmost of importance. "Once this deal is complete, Nicoli, I will review your overall performance. That though does not mean I will then render a decision as to whether or not an official position within our organization will be offered."

"I understand the need to be certain before committing to anything. If you do decide to accept me into the fold, rest assured that I will never give you a reason to question where my allegiance is."

"Good!"

After excusing his men, Louie went over to his wet bar and grabbed himself a beer. He wasn't stressed like he had been lately, so rye and a clove cigarette weren't needed to calm his nerves. Even so, now seemed like a good time to just relax and enjoy the peacefulness of his now-empty office. Nothing was scheduled nor did he have any tasks that needed to get completed. For the next few hours, all that he wanted to do was relax.

After turning on his computer so he could aimlessly surf the net, he took, then savored that first sip of his ice-cold beer. After it was about halfway gone, he decided to give Madelyn a call. He did this to not only selfishly see her personable smile, but he curiously wanted to learn what kind of progress she was making toward her objective of seducing the enemy.

At this stage of the game, he didn't expect much of a report — and that was exactly what was given. Nevertheless, his 'Kavorka' seems to have already laid down enough 'breadcrumbs' for Sabastian to take an interest. Now, it was only going to be a matter of time before the young man eagerly followed her right into his awaiting trap.

About an hour after she landed back home in Detroit, Jerrelle drove her classic car straight to Gino's Garage. It was located near the Southfield Freeway on West Eight Mile Road; a thoroughfare that bordered on the northern portion of the city and acted as a cultural boundary that divided the urban core from the upper class.

Before she was forced to choose between jail and the military, Gino Caravella was Jerrelle's last 'employer'. In hindsight, joining the service turned out to be the best thing that had ever happened to her, yet she still held a lot of animosity toward her ex-boss because of his actions and the reluctant choice that she was forced to make as a result. Now, after all these years, she decided that it was finally time to settle the score.

For just over two years, Jerrelle had worked as an, 'acquisition specialist' for Gino. His garage was consequently divided into two areas because of the nature of his business; a legal garage in the front and a cleverly hidden chop shop directly behind it inside an adjacent warehouse — that was where he actually made most of his money by taking in stolen cars and stripping them for parts.

Although she knew what she was doing was illegal, she just didn't care. Gino had paid her well; she had made more money during that time than she could have in five years of honest hard work. Of course, that could have had something to do with the fact that it had taken her less than four months to earn the complete trust and respect of her boss. The reason for this was because she would bring in more luxury vehicles than any of the other three 'specialists' that worked for Gino at the time. But then a day came in which all of that came to a sudden end, wherein her life subsequently changed forever.

She walked into work on Monday, as she had always done, not thinking for a minute that things were no longer the same. Immediately, her counterparts confronted her. They hated her, she knew that, and not just because she was a woman, but also because her acquisitions totaled more than double of theirs combined. It was embarrassing and ego-crushing to those boys. This, the three of them felt they could not allow to take place any longer. All of them were pissed off that this 'street trash' had wedged her way right to the front of the pecking order and had become Gino's pet. so they decided that this day was the day it all ended for Jerrelle. They intended to throw her far under the bus.

Over the previous weekend, the three of them had conspired to make it look like their fellow 'acquisitionist' had ripped off Gino's legitimate garage. That way, he would have no choice but to get rid of her. Jerrelle had stood there aghast when their false allegations were presented to her boss. She vehemently tried to deny it and defend herself, but with the continuous supporting lies of the other three, Gino became easily convinced that she was as guilty as what was being claimed.

Being the kind of person that he was; cold-hearted and generally unsympathetic, Gino could have actually had Jerrelle killed for stealing from him. But he didn't. He had taken a liking to her and honestly, didn't want to do such a thing, so he, uncharacteristically, just told her to get lost, to keep quiet, and to never return.

As pissed as she was, she knew just how lucky she had been to only be shown the door instead of being stripped down and recycled like a stolen car. So she reluctantly left. Of course, disappointment wasn't what she was feeling. It was anger, and she wanted nothing more than what she felt she deserved — revenge.

Yes, it had happened to her numerous times throughout her life; being accused of something that she was innocent of. Sometimes, she would just ignore it. Sometimes, she would make the individual regret their actions. Sometimes though, she knew she had no other choice but to concede to the will of the law.

This one oddly, hurt her on an emotional level — only because she had thought that she had found where she belonged. But as they say, paybacks are a bitch. Only Mother Nature had the ability to convey more fury and do more damage than what she intended on dishing out.

Later on that evening, she returned to the chop shop and waited outside for it to close — her now former associates were going to find out firsthand how a scorned woman retaliates. While she patiently sat in her car, she contemplated defying Gino's instructions by actually going to the police, but there were a few things that stopped her from doing that: she hated law enforcement, and they knew who she was and her history. Besides, she would be forced to implicate herself in order to shut down the illegal chop shop. She certainly wouldn't get a free pass for blowing the whistle, as her past record would be reason enough for the judicial system to put her back behind bars.

When that magical hour came and the shop closed, disappointment enveloped Jerrelle; Gino was nowhere to be found — only those three assholes were still there. That, however, she decided would be good enough for her. She really didn't wish to hurt her now ex-boss anyway. She had essentially thought of him as a father figure and was glad that he had left early — but the three who had been behind these false allegations, she had no qualms whatsoever about giving them a memory that would last a lifetime.

With a cast iron pipe in each hand, she got out of her car, snuck up behind them, and quickly attacked. Within a matter of moments, all three had broken bones: a leg; a collarbone, and an arm; it was enough damage done that each of them was going to be out of commission for a while. And although it had not been her intention, the streets of Detroit were now going to see a sharp decline in stolen vehicles for the next little while.

Satisfied that her revenge had been taken, she stood there and smiled. "You assholes fucked with the wrong woman. You are all very lucky that I took pity on you and only broke one bone each." Not thinking, Jerrelle then dropped the two cast iron pipes on the ground and left; the bar was the next place that she was going to go.

The following morning, a knock on her apartment door woke her up. Still somewhat asleep, she didn't bother looking out the peephole first to see who it was; she just casually opened up the door. Immediately, she chastised herself. She knew exactly why there were four police officers standing in the hallway — it was because she had made a stupid mistake. It wasn't just her day that was now ruined, but probably her life as well.

With both steel pipes recovered as evidence, the police arrested and charged Jerrelle with not only the theft of the garage, but with the assault on the three 'mechanics' who claimed they had tried to stop her from also stealing a Corvette that had been sitting outside the garage, waiting to be brought inside to be fixed.

Needless to say, those three assholes had screwed her over again. She was innocent, to a point, but it just didn't seem fair that the illegal chop shop was going to stay in business and Jerrelle was headed off to jail. Or so she thought.

Instead of expectedly facing one of the handfuls of judiciaries she previously had been in front of; each of whom would gladly throw the book at her because of her past, she was brought in front of the city's newest appointed circuit court judge. Initially, this had given her some hope. That was until she learned who it was that was sitting behind the bench — the Honorable S.J. Dole.

Jerrelle felt like she had gotten slapped hard in the face — by irony. That was because the judge just happened to be the older sister of B.J. Dole; the asshole from high school that incessantly would call Jerrelle every derogatory and racist name he could think of, including the one that pissed her off the most — the term 'Nigger Squaw' (because of her mixed ethnic heritage; half African American and half Native American).

By her junior year, she had had enough of his defamatory remarks. Jerrelle hated sports, but during homecoming, she showed up at her school's football game. After keeping a close eye on him from afar, the moment she had hoped for occurred. B.J. left the stands, alone, just before halftime, snuck around to the backside of them, and proceeded to light up a smoke. Four puffs into it, Jerrelle sharply whistled. He turned around and his face immediately met her fist. A series of rapid shots followed. When she ceased her assault, B.J. was on the ground, bloodied with a broken nose and both of his lips busted in four spots — he needed stitches to close two of them.

She felt no remorse for what she had done. In her mind, the asshole got what he deserved. Then, when B.J. returned to school two days later, everyone started calling him Frankenstein. She felt completely vindicated.

Needless to say, Jerrelle expected the worst when it came to her sentence. That though didn't happen. Instead, Judge Dole gave her an unexpected choice. It wasn't a great one, but it was one nevertheless that would eventually save and change her life forever. It was something that she could have never foreseen or even thought possible.

Anyway, shortly after Jerrelle was kicked out of the military, she unexpectedly crossed paths with Judge Dole at a pharmacy. When she asked her why she had given her the option to join the military, S.J. had said that it was her way of saying thank you. That declaration completely confused Jerrelle. When she asked for an explanation, she was told that B.J. got exactly what he deserved that day — and from that moment forward, he never ran his mouth or disrespected anyone ever again. He became a completely different person. Had that not

48

taken place, S.J. was certain that her brother would have gone down the wrong path and more than likely, would be either in jail or dead.

It had certainly been unintentional, but what Jerrelle had done that day to B.J. Dole, turned into being her first good deed ever done.

Supposedly, time heals all wounds — but not for Jerrelle. On her, they just stay covered up until she is ready to remove the 'bandage'. That was now, and it was why she had decided to return to Detroit. It was time for her to tie up those few loose ends she had, starting with those three bags of trash that needed to be permanently disposed of. She already knew that she was going to accept Sabastian's offer and move to San Antonio, but until she did what she came home to do, telling him was going to have to wait. It's not that there was a chance she was going to change her mind, she just wanted to have no reason to ever come back here to deal with something that could possibly rear its ugly head and ruin the fresh start she intended to make.

It was nearing closing time and quietly Jerrelle sat in her car, ironically in the exact same spot as before, watching the garage. In the five years since she had been there, the place had hardly changed and surprisingly, it was still in business. Patiently, she counted down the minutes. If their routine were the same, then at six o'clock, everyone inside would put their feet up and have a beer before going home. That would be the perfect time for her to strike.

After counting down the last few seconds, Jerrelle exited her car, calmly walked over to the building, used her vid-cell to bypass the digital lock on the front door, and then quietly entered. Just as she had hope, she made her way across the legitimate garage uncontested. At the far end of it, there sat a metal door; on it hung a sign that read 'Fire Exit'. That of course, did not lead to the outside. It instead, allowed access to a small hallway that in turn, lead straight to Gino's office. From there, you could enter the illegal chop shop. She could have entered it the same way the stolen vehicles were brought inside, via the back alley bay door, but that was highly secured with the latest of video surveillance and motion sensors.

Surprisingly, Jerrelle didn't need her vid-cell app to gain access to her old boss's office; the device on the door was an old-school, punch keypad and stupidly, Gino never changed the access code. She couldn't help but shake her head at his naivety.

Once inside, she crossed the room to the other end, took a quick look through the window right beside the door, and quietly said *'Bingo!'* They were all right where she had predicted they would be — and every one of them had their backs turned to her. *'I honestly didn't think I would be this lucky that all four of them would still be here after all these years.'*

As quietly as she could, she opened up the door, stepped into the chop shop, and was just about to announce herself when three other men that Jerrelle had never seen before, exited from the parts room over at the far side. *'Oh shit!'* The odds of four on one; she felt confident she could deal with. Seven on one; there was no way. If it was at all possible, she would have darted for the nearest exit — no longer was she young and stupid and believed that she was invincible. Unfortunately, her only way out was the same way she had come — and that path wasn't straight and unimpeded. She was pretty much fucked.

"Yo, Gino! Who's the bitch over by your office?"

He turned around and instantly froze. Never did he expect to see her again, as he had always thought that she was much smarter than that. Apparently, she wasn't. "You were told to never come back here, Jerrelle!"

"I... I figured that after five years, it was time for an apology."

"Ok.., let's hear it."

"I'm not here to apologize; I came to get one from you." Of course, that wasn't at all why Jerrelle had returned to Gino's garage — but it was all that she could think of at that moment to buy herself the necessary time she needed to possibly talk her way out of the mess that she had just foolishly walked herself into."

"You ripped me off, and you want an apology?"

"Do you want us to just get rid of this street skank?" asked the tallest of the three men that Jerrelle didn't know.

"No! She's not going anywhere!" said the oldest of the men that she did know; the one that she believed had influenced the others into setting her up. "We want an opportunity to pay back that gutter whore for what she did to us."

Even though the odds against her seemed rather astronomical, her confidence surprisingly did not waver. Maybe it had something to do with the fact that her anger was steadily growing because of the numerous derogatory terms spoken in reference to her.

Her rational thought process was slowly being pushed aside and ignored. The 'bitch switch', she could feel, was very close to being turned on. Allowing that to happen though, in this situation, wasn't a good idea. If she was going to have to fight, she had to be in control of her emotions.

After taking a moment to assess what was in front of her, she knew that this was not going to end well. Nevertheless, if she played her cards right, the injuries she believed she was about to sustain, would be acceptable in exchange for the revenge she had come here to get.

She could not show any fear. She had a reputation, and four of the seven in this garage knew it very well. For that reason alone, she looked in the direction of the three that did not know her and said, "I don't have any issues with any of you. So.., unless you want to experience firsthand what I did five years ago to Gino's three lackeys, I'd suggest that you just stay out of this. My issue is with them, not you."

"If our boss has an issue with someone, then so do we," stated the largest of the three men that Jerrelle did not know. He then stood there unyielding and boastfully puffed out his chest. The shortest one spoke next. He said, "Seems to me that a lesson needs to be learned. I don't have a problem making this Boudin regret her decision to wander onto our turf."

Boudin is French blood sausage — which is not at all a pleasant thing to eat. It is also a slang term that is used to label a woman as being ugly or a prostitute that is old. If Jerrelle only knew what she had just been referred to, then she would have probably exploded. As it was, she just stood there trying to figure out what order to attack the assholes so that she had the best chance of surviving what was about to be a monumental challenge. Leaving the garage on a stretcher, she could accept. In a body bag, she could not.

Slowly, she brought her hand down to her side and placed it over her sheathed honor blade. It's not that she wanted to do this, but for her to have any sort of chance of surviving, she more than likely was going to have to kill a few of them.

Just as she had begun to extract her knife, a loud crash resonated from directly behind her; it sounded as if a door was being kicked in. Promptly, Gino ordered someone to investigate — the one that had just offered to teach Jerrelle a lesson, volunteered. Not even three seconds after he had walked into the office, he flew right back into the chop shop through the adjacent window. Jerrelle's eyes couldn't help but follow the man's flight path. Unceremoniously, he landed right on top of a pool of engine oil that was lying underneath a hoisted, partially stripped Bentley Continental GTS.

Although she had no idea what had just happened, she could not help but laugh — it then morphed into a smile that metaphorically, stretched nearly as long as the Detroit River when the individual responsible for launching the human lawn dart, walked right on through the open office door.

"Who in the fuck are you? Gino demanded.

"That would be my always loving and endearing… I mean, ever-dangerous sister."

Bai Lin calmly walked over to Jerrelle, and without even exchanging a word, they both sprung into action. It had been a long time since she had fought alongside her, and a rush of pride and energy immediately consumed her.

With ease, she dispatched each attack that came her way and left some serious hurt on those she came to pay back. Likewise, Bai Lin had sent a clear message to the three men she took on, as they, one by one, dropped to the ground, cowering, and crying in serious pain. By the time the fight was over, only Jerrelle and Bai Lin were left standing — and both were relatively unscathed.

With contentment in her soul, and her right hand resting against her honor blade, just in case, Jerrelle got down on one knee so that she could look her one-time boss in the eye — Gino was sitting on the ground, leaning up against the skeleton of what was once a Mercedes-AMG GT coupe. "You know, you were as close to a father as I could get since mine had disappeared. But for some reason that I have never been able to fully understand, you closed off your mind and refused to see that I was completely innocent of ever stealing from you." Gino couldn't stand on his own for the broken leg he had. Jerrelle had no love lost for the man. However, some sympathy seemed to be there, so she picked him up off of the ground and gently sat him in the lone seat still left in the stripped vehicle. "Just so you know, those three assholes that work for you set me up because of their jealousy. But I don't care about that anymore. I have a good life now, and as far as I am concerned, we are even."

Feeling much better now that a not-too-proud chapter in her life had officially ended, Jerrelle and her sister exited the chop shop. On their way back to where she had parked her car, she took out her vid-cell and called Sabastian. Her old self would have just left Gino and his band of idiots there to fend for themselves, but her heart apparently had some kindness to give, so she decided to send them some help — just not from the EMT's.

Jerrelle preferred to avoid any contact with the police whenever possible, only because she had this fear that they would not listen or even believe her. For that reason, she asked Sabastian to contact the authorities on her behalf and let them know about the seven criminals that were now lying incapacitated inside of a long-running chop shop; a place that she no longer had any qualms about being responsible for it finally being shut down.

She thought that some guilt would appear, but surprisingly, none was there — she had to believe it was because she had done the right thing. It felt strange, but it also felt good. Not since she had been told of the transformation in B.J. Dole did she feel pride. Usually, that only came when she prevailed in what should have been an unwinnable situation. Sabastian was right. From the moment of their reunion, she had begun to change. She just wished that she had an idea as to what kind of an individual she was going to become.

After disconnecting her call, Jerrelle handed the keys over to her sister and then surprisingly, got into the passenger seat of her own car. This left Bai Lin a bit confused. Despite that, she was okay with driving her sister's most prized possession, so she got in and took a second to relive a cherished moment from her past. Only once before, had she ever sat behind the wheel of this Camero. It was on her fifteenth birthday. Her father had let her drive it, illegally, down the road to the Dairy Queen; it was only a few blocks from their apartment. And even though it seemed like an insignificant moment, it had been the first adult thing she had ever done. "Where shall I take you, sis?"

"Dearborn. I have one more piece of business to tend to there and then everything that I came back here to do will be accomplished."

Depending upon the traffic, the drive to their destination wasn't going to take more than ten/fifteen minutes. Throughout most of the short trip, both sisters stayed quiet — that was until Jerrelle asked the one probing question that Bai Lin had been patiently waiting to hear. "So.., how come your knee is not in a brace and that cut across your back is nearly healed?"

"Ancient Japanese techniques."

"You're going to have to teach me some of them one day."

"Maybe..." Bai Lin was laughing inside, as she knew that there was more than just the 'techniques' that were responsible for her quick healing — but she wasn't about to tell her what else she had done and used. Just because Jerrelle was her blood, didn't mean that she had to openly share with her a closely guarded secret — especially since Bai Lin has chosen a life that is supposed to stay buried deep in the shadows. As it was, her sister was pretty lucky that she'd been allowed to see and learn as much as she has about the Extremist Clandestine Liberation.

It was easy for Jerrelle to see that her sister was purposely holding something back — but that was all right because she couldn't have been more thankful that Bai Lin had shown up when she did. Looking back at what had just happened, she had no other choice but to acknowledge that her ego had encouraged her into making a foolhardy mistake. Had she thought back to her recent experiences with Sabastian, she would have realized just how stupid it was to think that nothing significant would be waiting for her on the other side of the front door. And because she failed to do that, she had unnecessarily placed herself in a situation that she should not have walked away from.

After making a promise to herself to never do something like that again, she said to her sister, "So.., I have to assume that you tracked me down again using the GPS that you had, without my permission, by the way, installed on my car?"

"That would be correct, sis."

"There was no way that you would have known ahead of time what I was going to be walking my ass into, or that you would have even had enough time to come all the way from Japan to back me up."

"Well duh.., that much is obvious."

"Then what is your reason for being here in my wretched city?"

"The Liberation is still investigating what happened to us. They thought it was best that I disappear somewhere, just in case there actually is someone out there who wants me dead."

"It's not you. I now think that somebody wants me dead?"

"You? What makes you say that?"

As they merged onto Michigan Ave. and headed west, Jerrelle told her sister who Jason Hernandez was and, when she and Sabastian were in Puerto Rico, an unmanned car had killed him. She then let her know what her suspicion was. "I know that it is only my mind looking for an answer, but it makes sense to me. The man, after all, accepted the bribe that I had offered to him in exchange for a black book and memory stick that he had stashed away that contained incriminating information about Antonio Marcone as well as a list of his personal clients."

"Hum..? Maybe you are right.., but then maybe you are completely wrong. We just need to be careful until we can find out what the truth really is."

"I agree. By the way... are you aware that Nicoli Nemchieve has left the Liberation?"

Bai Lin slammed on the brakes; she almost caused the car following behind to rear-end them. "What are you talking about, Jerrelle?"

"Sabastian's cousin, Sharice, told me about it while we were down in Puerto Rico."

"How would Sabastian's cousin know anything about a member of our European faction?"

"She is an agent with the B.I.A."

Jerrelle's sister didn't know what to think about this unsettling news — but instead of fretting over it, she got the car going forward again and allowed the street in front of her to become a focal point.

For the next few minutes, silence took over the interior of the vehicle as she thought. The quiet ended when Bai Lin said, "If Nicoli has indeed pissed on his allegiance, then it very well could have been him who tried to kill you?"

"I don't think so. He said in the restaurant that he didn't hold me responsible for Helfred's death."

"I'm just speculating, but maybe he just wanted you to get a false sense of security so that your guard would be down?"

"But then that wouldn't explain the driverless attack against Jason Hernandez."

"I know.., but I am betting that there is a connection between the two somehow. Once we figure out what that is, we should have a better idea as to what Nicoli might actually be up to.., and why."

This was a possibility that Jerrelle hadn't considered, nor wanted to contemplate. If Helfred's brother did have a personal grudge against her, then it meant that she had her own serious problem that she needed to promptly verify, as the last thing she wanted was to have to deal with an angry and highly dangerous German operative, while at the same time, trying to help Sabastian finish off what the two of them had started.

As Bai Lin had been instructed, she parked a full block down the street from their destination so that they would stay out of sight from any suspicious eyes. Unlike those associated with Gino's garage, Jerrelle's classic Camero was well known to everyone who worked at the place they were going to. And because there was an unresolved issue between her and the individual she had come to see, she did not want to lose the element of surprise before she had a chance to walk through the front door.

They exited the car, crossed the street, and made their way to an establishment called The Cough Inn. The owner had decided to name the club this by associating and honoring what the building's three former tenants had been. Originally, the structure was erected as a three-floor hotel in the early nineteen hundreds. When it closed down during the latter half of nineteen sixty-eight, it was converted into a medical clinic. Unfortunately, that place didn't stay in business too long because of the constant protests and firebombings that had happened, all due to it being the only legal abortion clinic in the state of Michigan at the time. After it was repaired following the last firebombing in late nineteen seventy-four, it was converted into a funeral home and crematory. The doors to that business stayed open for fifty years before closing in the middle of two thousand and twenty-five.

Up until five years ago, the place had remained vacant when it was subsequently bought and turned into a nightclub that initially catered to the Gothic and Emo communities. Surprisingly, after only a year of operation, its popularity had begun to attract just about anyone from every walk of life, thus becoming an amalgamated haven for everyone to enjoy.

Once they entered the club, minus a few regular customers, the place was empty and quiet — Jerrelle had expected it to be that way since it was still early in the evening. She hadn't come here today in search of one of the regulars; she had come looking for the club's owner, Cloe Churel.

The proprietor was a woman of Romanian and East Indian descent, whose last name, according to East Indian folklore, essentially means 'a woman who dies an unnatural death'. Jerrelle didn't know if there was any irony behind it or not, but she just assumed that may be the reason why Cloe had felt comfortable opening up a nightclub in an old funeral parlor.

She owed her ten thousand dollars; money that Jerrelle had earned while she had worked for Gino. And because The Cough Inn's owner was one of the few friends that she had at the time, as a favor, she had lent the money to Cloe in order to help ease the burden of the initial start-up costs that come with opening up a business like this.

Up until now, Jerrelle had been patient when it came to having the debt settled. But after five years, no longer was she willing to wait for what was rightfully hers to be returned.

This was why she had come here today. She wanted it back. Only then, would Jerrelle feel free to officially leave behind all those unwanted memories and lost hopes that had shaped her life in the Motor City. If she didn't get it back today, she would be left with no other choice but to renounce her friendship with Cloe, delay her move, and then do what she didn't really want to do — break some bones until her message was clearly understood.

After entering the establishment, she and her sister ambled straight up to the bar. Instead of ordering a drink, as one would normally do, Jerrelle simply asked the bartender, Inita, if Cloe was around. She didn't respond to her question or even acknowledge her presence. Instead, she promptly turned and darted right into the kitchen. Straight away, Jerrelle looked at Bai Lin and huffed in disgust.

"What's wrong?"

"The bartender knows who I am. She didn't leave to go and get the owner; she went to get some help in order to toss my ass out of here. I guess I should have just sent you in here alone to make the inquiry for me."

"Yeah.., you should have."

A rather large man with grease spots all over his whites came out of the kitchen, walked directly over to Jerrelle, stopped in front of her, and stood there quietly.

Bai Lin took one look at the massive man and thought, *'All that it would take is the right amount of force in the right spot and Goliath will fall.'*

There were times when Jerrelle felt a mental connection to her sister, and this was one of those instances, so she gently placed her right hand on her shoulder and hoped that simple gesture would be enough for her sister to get the message and stay put. It worked; the desire Bai Lin had to take matters into her own hands, disappeared.

As much as she was willing to hit the big oaf and take him out of commission, it was not her decision to make. Yes, she was the big sister and it was her job to be there, back Jerrelle up, and protect her, but for now, she just had to stay on the sidelines and wait until she was asked to get involved.

"I think you know why I am here, André?"

"I do.., and Cloe is not here right now. Nor does she have what you have come here for."

"I figured as much. Tell her my patience is now gone. She has had five years to save up the money and pay me back. I will not wait for it any longer. You tell her that I said she better have my

58

money when I come back here later on tonight. I have been nothing but accommodating up until now, and I no longer will tolerate being blown off."

"She won't have it for you, so don't bother coming back tonight. You'll just be wasting your time."

Bai Lin was actually impressed that her sister was staying as calm as she was. However, she could also tell that the Tasmanian devil that lurked within Jerrelle was eager to come out and play. Even a blind man could see that her tolerance was reaching its limit. Therefore, she decided to give the giant man a reason to persuade his boss to end her deliberate refusal of repayment. "You see this big ass tattoo that I have covering most of my body?" Bai Lin gracelessly spun around so that 'Goliath' could get the full perspective of it. And even though a good portion was covered up with her shirt, it was impossible not to see exactly how massive the artwork really was. "This tattoo means I am a well-respected member of a Japanese underground organization, the Extremist Clandestine Liberation. You need to let your boss know that if she doesn't have my sister's money when we come back here later on tonight, I will arrange to have a few of our members pay an unfriendly visit to your boss's family; either here in the Union or back in the old country."

That seemed to get André's attention. He took a good look at Bai Lin and determined that she more than likely was who she claimed to be. Although he appeared to only be a cook in a bar, his ambitions were much different. For the better part of his last four years, on a part-time basis, he has put himself through university. His goal was to one day become a criminologist. On top of that, André had a personal curiosity when it came to the world of the criminal underground — which meant that he was actually well aware of who the E.C.L. were and what they were all about. And even if Jerrelle's sister wasn't whom she claimed to be, he was still smart enough to assume that she was probably just as deadly. Therefore, he was forced to acknowledge right then and there that his boss's days of postponing the settling of her debt had come to an end. "Come back tonight after eleven. I will make sure to tell Cloe that you will be returning at that time. But I can't guarantee that she will give you back your money."

"She better.., because a night of drinking on her tab no longer will be enough for me to excuse her from returning what is mine."

André didn't say another word; he just headed back into the kitchen.

Satisfied that this visit had actually accomplished something, Jerrelle and Bai Lin turned and headed in the direction of the front door. However, the moment they took that first step outside, something directly across the street caught Bai Lin's attention. Immediately, she stopped, grabbed Jerrelle by the arm, and hastily dragged her sister back inside the club.

The front doors of it were beautiful; they appeared to be handcrafted out of oak. It also consisted of an etched and lightly smoked, decorative glass insert. Although she probably didn't have to, Bai Lin nevertheless stood back a few feet from the door and looked curiously through one of the few areas of the artwork that was clear. She then said, "Um, sis… Is that who I think it is across the street next to that bread van?"

Jerrelle took a closer look and instantly saw what had grabbed her sister's attention. She was right. The person who was standing near the back of the bread truck was exactly who Bai Lin had thought it was.

Why this place was chosen for today's showing and negotiation was beyond the understanding of Zhin. The United Arab League had asked that this initial meeting take place in a building that they had owned and used in the past when it came to private assemblies and discussions. It wasn't that it was unsuitable; Zhin was just annoyed with the fact that they had to park their van, a Mara's bread van, on the street. Ideally, he would have liked either a loading dock or bay door to drive into — but there wasn't one. Had the city not gone and blocked off both accesses to the back alleyway for an emergency sewer repair, they could have used it instead of being left with no other option but to unload their two rather large duffle bags full of the sample weapons, out in the open for everyone to see.

Cautiously, Nicoli exited the van. He then quickly performed a perimeter sweep. Other than the bar across the street, there was nothing in the surrounding neighborhood that grabbed his attention. A cold beer sounded good right about now, but that would have to wait. He and Zhin had a job to do; a task that he believed would all but solidify his position within the organization upon its completion.

Feeling satisfied that no one with curious eyes was watching them, Nicoli tapped twice on the back of the van; Zhin promptly exited it. By the time he had made it to the back doors, they were open and one of the two bags was already in his associate's hand. It was passed on to him; Nicoli grabbed the other one, shut the doors, and then followed Zhin right on through the front entrance of, what more than likely was at one time, a small retail store.

That was close. Although they had no way of knowing whether or not they had been seen, it did appear as if their presence on the other side of the glass door was not noticed. Nicoli had only looked in their direction for a few unnerving seconds and then went about his business. Still, it didn't mean that Jerrelle and Bai Lin had not been spotted, nor did it mean that they could curiously hang around and wait until something happened.

Questions immediately surfaced. What was Helfred's brother doing in Dearborn, Michigan? And who was the Asian man that he was with? Also, what in the hell was in those large bags? As interested as she was to learn those things, what seemed clear to Bai Lin was that Nicoli was involved with something that had nothing to do with the Liberation.

Although definitive proof had yet to be presented to her, she could no longer find a reason to dispute her sister's earlier claim — it appeared as if her old friend had chosen to ignore the oath he had long ago taken. For a brief moment, Bai Lin thought about walking right across the street and confronting Nicoli, but she was unsure that she would be able to satisfactorily explain her own reasons for being where she was? Instead, the only thing she could do was to accept what she was seeing with her own two eyes and act accordingly. Orochi was not going to be at all pleased when told of this.

After Nicoli and the Asian man disappeared into the old store, the sister's looked at each other — both had the same yearning to learn what was going on. But just as Jerrelle was about to open up the club doors, Bai Lin told her to wait. She then stood there for a moment and thought. The smartest thing for them to do at that moment was to just leave the area before they were spotted. Retreating wasn't normally what either of them liked to do. However, in this instance, that was the logical course of action for them to take — only because neither of them had anything, other than their honor blades, to defend themselves with, nor did they have anyone backing them up. Without having any Intel already in hand, it would be stupid of them to let their curiosity overrule their common sense. Besides, it was less than an hour ago that Jerrelle did that exact same thing — and she was lucky that her impetuousness did not result in the loss of her life. There was no reason for them to take such a chance and expect that the results would turn out differently.

When they were sure that the coast was clear, they both exited the bar and ran to where they had left their car parked. Once they had made it there and were safely on down the road, Jerrelle turned to her sister and said, "We're not going to ignore what we saw, are we?"

"No but... we need to be smart about this." Bai Lin then fell silent; she turned her head to the side and aimlessly watched as the scenery passed on by. About two blocks later, she said, "I wish that I had another G.P.S. tracker on me. I could have at least tagged the van. Then we could have..."

"Just like snooping in and around that building, doing that would have also been an unwise risk to take. And it probably wouldn't have given us any of the answers we want."

"I know, but... as a member of the E.C.L., it is my responsibility to find out why Nicoli has decided to turn his back on us." Again, the car fell silent. It wasn't until they turned onto the road that led to Jerrelle's apartment that Bai Lin spoke again, "When you return to The Cough Inn tonight to pick up your money, I am going to go to Mara's bread factory."

"Why? What will that accomplish?"

Bai Lin did not have an acceptable reply to give to her sister. She honestly didn't have a clue if her going there would achieve anything, but no other viable option seemed to be there for her to explore.

Jerrelle knew what it was like to desire some answers. She also knew that it could unexpectedly pull her sister deep into a

62

situation in which she may not be able to extract herself from. Like her, Bai Lin tended never to throw caution to the wind — only fuel on the fire. One of these days, that fervent and uncompromising nature of theirs was going to cost one of them dearly. "Promise me that you're not going to do something that will land your ass in jail. Like.., breaking into the factory?"

Bai Lin mockingly crossed her heart with her right hand and said, "I solemnly swear that I will only do a little recon and evidence gathering."

Jerrelle didn't believe her sister's declaration for one second.

"I'm hoping that the van will be returned to the factory tonight. And if it is, that will be the only thing I will break into."

"You better hope that there are no more than one or two of the bread vans in the lot."

"The number of vans there is irrelevant. My photographic memory has allowed me to retain the I.D. number that was on the back door of the vehicle."

Again, Jerrelle believed that her sister was lying. She didn't have a photographic memory. There were certainly times when they were young teens that she swore Bai Lin had an explicit, pornographic memory because of the way she used to talk about men as nothing but sexual objects and the outrageous things that she intended to one day do to them.

At that moment, Jerrelle decided it was best she not get into a trivial debate with her sister and attempt to squash her claim, as there were more important things that needed to be addressed before they even attempted to determine what Nicoli was up to. "Are you hungry, sis? My energy reserves are getting low and I need to build it back up in case I get into a fight later on tonight."

"Try not to do that, Jerrelle, because I won't be there to back you up."

"You know very well that it's extremely hard for me to refrain from pounding in some deserved asshole's head."

"I do. But since you plan on leaving Detroit for good, there really is no need to solidify your already well-known local reputation."

Jerrelle knew that her sister was right. She had always allowed those primal instincts within her to dictate her actions. Yes, it had gotten her into trouble more times than the age she was, but it also was what had earned her the standing she had on the street. Now, as she thought about her future, it became apparent that if she was ever going to become someone whose reverence was earned because of who she was as an individual and not because of her fists and feet, she had to change — starting with the acknowledgement that every single asshole she came across, did not need to be taught a lesson.

— ◯◯ —

As soon as Zhin and Nicoli stepped foot inside the place, they were told to set their bags of merchandise on the ground. Each was then boorishly patted down and their vid-cells taken — they supposedly would be returned upon their departure. Once that had been completed, they were informed of the procedure that they were expected to follow. For those who were a part of the United Arab League, this place was considered to be a religious sanctuary, even though it was clearly obvious as to what this building was/had been before. Nevertheless, it was expected that any guests that were welcomed inside, would respect their customs and refrain from any colorful language, gestures, or words that could be deemed insulting.

These rules seemed rather annoying and a bit imperious to Nicoli; Zhin however, understood their purpose and intended to abide by their rules. Though he himself was not at all religious, he came from a society that very much was. And because of this, his upbringing had taught him to show respect toward everyone's customs and beliefs, even if he thought that they were utterly preposterous or unfounded.

Once the initial formality was completed, Zhin and Nicoli were escorted down a short hallway, down a flight of stairs, and to a somewhat small-sized room. Inside it, two long tables had been provided for them on which to display their merchandise. They were then instructed to stay as quiet as possible while preparing the merchandise for presentation because the day's sun was nearing its end and League's members would be in the middle of their early evening prayer session in the room directly above them. Right before their escort had left, he informed them that the head of the local chapter of the U.A.L. would be the one who was going to review the merchandise they had brought, but not until after their worshipping was over.

The lighting inside the room was not that great, but there was still enough of it to serve the needed purpose. The air within it felt thick and had a pungent bite to it; it seemed to leave a thin layer of something unpleasant behind in your mouth and nose each time you took a breath.

Although the room wasn't a disgusting mess, Zhin could tell that the place had been previously used to either 'encourage' an individual to give up some information that was wanted, or was used to quietly eliminate someone. That was probably why he was feeling a cold presence within the small space. It wasn't a 'dead of winter' kind of cold, it was more like an eerie kind of chill that would slowly invade and then burrow deep into your bones.

For Nicoli, this place was giving him the creeps. He wasn't feeling what Zhin was, it was because of the claimed pious nonsense that was taking place right above them. This building wasn't a holy temple. What it was instead was a poorly disguised place of hell. Like his associate, he knew exactly what this basement was used for when deals weren't being struck. The U.A.L. was a terrorist group. Like any underground organization, trust was something never given. At any point, this arms showing could become something far more than what it is supposed to be. For that reason, Nicoli had to stay diligent, but not suspicious either. He had to hope their given word would be kept; otherwise, he and Zhin could end up leaving this place in a completely different manner instead of via their own two feet.

Neither one of them had expected this and neither had thought it necessary to have a plan 'B' already in place. Now, they realized that they needed one; they had to have a readied out clause if they found themselves with their backs up against the wall. In all, Nicoli estimated that there were probably thirty members of the U.A.L. currently praying above them. Fifteen to one odds were not at all favorable.

Zhin agreed with his associate — thankfully, he had felt it necessary to not follow the unwritten rules. Right before they had left to pick up the van, Louie had informed them that a longstanding agreement was in place with all clients wherein no accompanying ammunition was to be on-site during the showcasing of merchandise. He understood and agreed with that policy. However, his gut wouldn't dismiss the possibility that this might not be a straightforward viewing. The United Arab League was a terrorist organization on the verge of being revealed. Therefore, their trust could not be fully expected — even though Louie had assured them that the U.A.L. would not stab them in the back.

Shortly before they left the office, Zhin just happened to stumble upon a disconcerting bit of information. The League had actually been born out of the remaining handful of suspected American ISIS members that somehow were able to disappear underground after the official end of the terrorist organization.

Neither one wanted this showing to last any longer than was necessary, so they each took their large duffle bags and hoisted them up onto a table. Besides the featured merchandise inside the bags, Zhin's contained their insurance policy. He unzipped the side pouch on his bag and removed two Smith and Wesson handguns along with six spare clips of ammunition. "Don't ever let Louie find out that I brought these here." Nicoli did not verbally reply; he just nodded his head and accepted the gun and three clips from Zhin.

Once those items were concealed, they began to empty the contents of their bags onto the tables. Nicoli's contained the latest in modern technology — a Smith & Wesson 22 Match Heavy Barrel M-41-C series, a 38 Master Model 52-C Series Auto rifle — both of which fire compressed solid nitro tipped bullets, a Beretta Model 76-C Laser Pistol with an eight-inch muzzle which is used strictly for short, accurate and extremely quiet kills, a Winchester 70-D Magnum Laser-Sight Rifle, which not only fired conventional ammunition, but could be adjusted to fire those extremely hard to acquire S.M.A.R.T. programmable mini-missiles. And last, but certainly not least, Nicoli unpacked a Beretta CNML 86-B, compressed air mini-scud launcher.

Zhin's bag of toys was more hands-on. He laid them out across the table so that they would be easy to see. He had an assortment of small throwing knives, switch and butterfly knives, long and short fighting knives, retractable batons, and almost a Klingon-esq looking, half-moon, in-close combat style of weapon. He also displayed the latest in remote detonators, long-range radar detectors, jammers, and day and nighttime surveillance equipment.

The last thing that he unfolded out onto the table was a rather large display chart that showed what type of explosives were available, ranging from Micro-dyne (an explosive that is roughly the same size as an M-80 firecracker, but is just as powerful as a traditional stick of dynamite), Chemikill (a time-delayed release wet/dry chemical mix for those looking for a massive, intensive chemical fire), Digital grenades (which equals the destructive force of four traditional grenades in one), and the ever-popular Ex-Co patches. For obvious reasons, no physical samples of those items were on hand.

Once everything was in place, all that was left for them to do was wait; that was something Zhin was feeling oddly uncomfortable with doing. It's not that he wasn't a patient individual, but his mind was abnormally wandering. The reason for that, he suspected, was because of the lingering remnants of whoever had been killed in the room over the years. Or maybe, he just could not stay fully focused on the task at hand because this was his first time ever negotiating anything. Was it just a case of nerves, or was it a fear of failure? He could only assume the reason. What Zhin did know, was that he had to get his shit together before the head of the local chapter of the U.A.L. met with them.

Nicoli, on the other hand, was actually enjoying the wait. He scanned the room with his eyes, knowing that things took place here that only his imagination could hypothesize. A warped smile suddenly appeared on his face as he tried to picture some poor, defenseless, helpless soul being tortured and then beheaded. It was a twisted, demented thought — which Nicoli strangely found he was having more of lately, ever since his brother had been unnecessarily taken from him.

An ominous-looking shadow suddenly cascaded across the open threshold into the room; it caused Zhin's nerves to jump — but they promptly settled back down the moment he saw the two men responsible for casting it. One of them stood nearly six-foot-eight inches tall, had a full beard, and he wore the traditional clothes of his homeland of Libya. The other man was only an inch or so shorter, had a short and neatly trimmed beard, and was dressed in a similar fashion.

Surprisingly, a few calming, meditative breaths were all that it took for Zhin to feel ready to do what he had come to do. So, with unexpected confidence now there, he stepped forward, extended his hand in greeting, and introduced himself and Nicoli.

The offered greeting was not returned; it apparently was against the man's religion. "My name is Gohan Faaq Yusef. I am the leader of this regional chapter of the United Arab League." Although the unintentional humor in the man's name would be obvious to some people, one look at his daunting features and you immediately would keep that notion to yourself. "This is my trusted first, Ahmed," he said as he gestured with his right hand toward the man who stood to his left. "Where is Mr. Mazotti?"

"Negotiations are no longer his responsibility. That task has now been bestowed upon me and my associate."

"That is not acceptable!"

"My apologies.., but Mr. Mazotti…

"Pack up your merchandise and leave. We will not do business with the D.U.O. unless Louie is present."

That pronouncement caught Zhin completely off guard. He had not expected that kind of blunt refusal. It now left him at a loss. He wasn't sure what to do next. Immediately, those unfounded assumptions that had been present earlier, returned. His first instinct was to reach for his hidden Smith and Wesson, but he resisted. His weapon was only a last resort and in his mind, this meeting was far from over. He just needed to find the right words to say that would convince the head of the United Arab League to reconsider his stance. But before Zhin could say another word, Nicoli spoke up.

"May I ask you why it is that you only wish to negotiate with Mr. Mazotti?"

"Our previous deal was one that was, it's fair to say, rather insignificant. Nevertheless, he still went out of his way to make sure that we were satisfied customers. He even personally followed up with us a few days afterward and made sure that there were no lingering issues. Of all the other suppliers that we have dealt with since then, I found Mr. Mazotti to be the most respectful and trustworthy."

That was an admission that Zhin could work with. What Nicoli had asked, resulted in Gohan responding in a way that inadvertently revealed just enough information about him that in turn, allowed an assumption to be drawn as to what kind of an individual he was. The sudden doubts that consumed Zhin quickly vanished. He now felt confident that he had the right words in place to follow up Nicoli's question with. "Then I take it you haven't heard yet that Antonio Marcone was killed a few weeks ago."

"I... I have not. I am sorry for your loss."

"Thank you. Now.., with that being said, his passing has subsequently resulted in Louie Mazotti assuming the position of leader of the Detroit Underworld Organization. And since he is now the one in charge, making himself available for an undemanding task such as this, is unnecessary and also unwise. You have my word that even though he is not here, you will be treated in the exact same manner as before."

"What about Sal? Where is he?"

"He was killed in Germany not too long before Antonio was. Nicoli and I have stepped into his and Louie's previous roles, and that is why we are here now to do the negotiating."

A private huddle was promptly formed between both members of the League. Even though the conversation was in their native language, it was done so quietly that it was basically indiscernible. Roughly two minutes later, their short conference had concluded. Gohan then addressed their guests. "If Mr. Mazotti trusts you enough to negotiate this deal, then I don't see there being a problem."

"I'm glad you feel that way. Please take as much time as you need to look over the merchandise we have brought with us. And feel free to ask any questions."

About an hour was spent by them, meticulously scrutinizing everything that was on display, with Gohan asking only the occasional question about the capabilities of a few of the newer weapons. Once they were done, a satisfying smile could be seen on the U.A.L. leader's face. He thus agreed to purchase two dozen of every kind of gun on display, a handful of the fighting knives, and two dozen of every piece of electronic gadgets to start with — he didn't order any explosives as he already had all of the necessary chemicals that were needed to make whatever bomb they wanted.

Surprisingly, he then informed Zhin that he would need this same order filled again two more times over the next two months —

but that would only occur if the merchandise they have just ordered, produces the results they are looking for.

With an agreement now in place and a date and time set for their first official transaction, Zhin informed Gohan that it would take two or three days to compile his order. When that was complete, he assured him that Louie would be the one to make contact to let him know when everything would be delivered.

After bowing his head in a sign of respect, the head of the U.A.L. left the room while Ahmed stayed behind to observe as Zhin and Nicoli gathered up all their merchandise and repacked it back into the oversized bags. When that had been completed, he handed them back their vid-cells and promptly escorted the two of them out of the building.

Once outside, they quickly placed both of their bags back into the bread truck and hoped again that no nosy individuals were watching them. Not knowing if that was the case or not, they nevertheless got into the vehicle and immediately returned it to where they had picked it up earlier.

Yes, this negotiation had been successful — but it also could have ended in disaster. Thankfully, it did not. What each of them believed in the back of their minds as being a possibility, could have occurred because they had not been the one who controlled the environment. Therefore, while on the drive back to the organization's headquarters, Zhin and Nicoli came to a mutual agreement. From this moment forward, the location of any pending merchandise showing or transaction was going to be either agreed upon by both parties or determined solely by them and not the client. That way, they would either be on equal terms or they would have the upper hand, just in case some moron decides that they didn't want to play by the unwritten rules.

3

As a member of the S.N.A.F.U., Sabastian knew that at a moment's notice, he and his fellow soldiers could be sent on an assignment anywhere in the world. As such, the possibility was certainly there that a volatile situation might develop. Thankfully, not one of his previous missions had gotten to a point where he felt that his and the lives of his fellow brethren had been in any sort of real jeopardy. However, it didn't mean that when each assignment was over, someone hadn't been wounded. That was a likelihood that each member of the unit knew could happen to them — as was death. Luckily, since the unit's inception, not one member had been brought home in a flag-draped coffin — it was a statistic that Sabastian, even though he was no longer officially a member of the unit, hoped would never change.

To reduce such a possibility from ever happening, emotional and personal attachments were discouraged. The knowledge that their death could occur at any time already was a burden that everyone in their immediate family had to deal with. The last thing any soldier needed was another distraction that could unintentionally become the reason that they, or someone else in the unit, did not come home.

It's not that Sabastian wasn't interested in finding true love one day, but he felt that trying to balance a personal relationship with protecting his country from the most dangerous individuals or groups in the world wasn't impossible. That was why he, like the majority of those in his unit, practiced various forms of meditation in order to help keep their emotions in check. Self-hypnosis, variations of yoga, Tai Chi, and even some New Age relaxation techniques were implored to not only help them to stay focused when it was needed during a tense, unpredictable situation, but it also allowed them to control those sexual urges that would sometimes try to surface at the worst possible moment.

He wasn't expecting this would happen to him so soon after he had left the service, but it did. The first time, Sabastian had felt shame afterward. The two times after that, he had declared it to only be a bit of harmless admiration. This time though, it had easily broken through his erected barriers. Somehow, Lizanne had stimulated and then awoken those animalistic instincts he had for years, successfully kept secured under lock and key. No matter how hard he tried, he was finding it extremely difficult to resist nature. Admittedly, he could have at least tried one of those meditation techniques that he knew, but he honestly didn't want to use them. His excuse was simple — he had a lot of lost time to make up for and Ms. Kinsworth was unwittingly coercing him into wanting to do just that.

By far, Lizanne was the most beautiful woman who had ever crossed his path. And as he reflected upon his life and the subsequent events that brought him to where he now was, he realized the probability was unlikely that he would ever get another opportunity to get to know someone like her on a more personal level. For that reason, valid or not, he decided to grab a hold of the handle and open the door all the way. Once he stepped on through it though, he'd have to figure out a way to balance his work with those unfamiliar and untamed desires he had.

Sabastian met Lizanne at her hotel, the new Pershing Suites, and then they went to the one Michelin star restaurant that was located within it. As a gentleman should, he pulled out the chair for her and then slid it in as she sat down. Right before he claimed his seat directly across from her, he took a relaxing breath, and then reminded himself, '*I am not on a date; I am working. And as much as I would relish exploring every inch of her body, I have to behave.*' He took a sip from his glass of white wine and looked across the table at Lizanne. "Before our food gets here, I just thought I'd let you know that my staff was able to learn that there are at least six people in the Union by the name of Amy Amylia. To my knowledge though, they have yet to be able to verify any personal information on any of them. So as of now, all we can do is wait and see whether or not one of them turns out to be your long lost friend."

She nearly spit out her wine. She had just plucked that name out of thin air and assumed that it would be as fictional as Mickey Mouse. In hindsight, what she should have done first was taken some time and ran a general Internet search of the name to see if / or just how many there were out there. All she could hope for now was that those individuals that Sabastian's staff has found did not fit the criteria that she had given to him. "I… really didn't think it could be possible that there would be more than one person in the world with the same name as Amy. I had always thought her name to be unique."

"Apparently not.., and that is what is baffling me. You said that the others whom you asked to help you could not find her. Yet, those who work for me were easily able to find six people with that same name."

Madelyn knew that she was in a pickle. She had to quickly think of a convincing response to Sabastian's declaration otherwise, her lies would just continue to spiral out of control until they came completely unraveled. She couldn't fail. She owed a debt to Louie and she had to succeed at the task she was given. "Then I have to assume that those individuals were also discovered by the other PI's that I had hired. But I was never told by any of them of their existence. I was only told that my friend was nowhere to be found."

"Well… either they were right or they actually found her and were informed that she wished to be left alone."

"I honestly find that hard to believe."

"What one believes doesn't always end up being the case."

"So then.., does this mean that you are not going to help me track her down?"

"I am not someone who gives up easily. My associates and I will make sure that no stone is left unturned until we come to a wall that prevents us from going any further or in any other direction."

That affirmation was what Madelyn needed to hear. At least now she knew that Sabastian would continue to do what she had asked of him. If he hadn't decided to continue, then she had no idea how she was going to get him to follow her to where Louie wanted him to end up.

"Lizanne… I am also curious about one thing. Why is it that you are staying in a hotel? I thought you told me you were originally from here. Do you not have any family in the area?"

She stayed silent for a moment, realizing that she had again failed to completely cover all aspects of her story. "I do but… I grew up in San Marcos; it's a town about fifty miles from here. I suppose I could have probably stayed with one of them, but I did not feel comfortable asking."

"Why, may I ask?"

"Long before my parents decided to uproot us and move to Chicago, our relationship with them became somewhat strained. There is no real hate between us, but there was no real love either. It's probably been ten years since I spoke to them last, but... now didn't seem like a good time to try and reconnect." Happy that she had again recovered from a mistake, she took another sip of her wine, looked over at Sabastian, and tried her best to figure out what he was thinking. She wasn't sure if she had been able to sell any of her newly fabricated lies; she only hoped that he was not good at reading people — especially those who were blatantly being deceitful.

"Time heals all wounds. If I were you, Lizanne, I'd reach out to them. We only ever get one family. And I know what it's like to lose them forever."

"I don't know. We'll see."

A few moments later, the waiter came around with their dinner. Not much was discussed about the case as they ate. The only conversation that happened was the typical 'first date' kind of small talk. Little bits of personal information was traded, a bit of laughter was shared, smiles were exchanged, and after the bottle of wine was half gone, a few harmless moments of deliberate flirtation took place.

For Sabastian, this evening was falling into place just as he had hoped it would. Although his intention was to stay professional, the longer dinner went, the harder he found it to be. The detective that he knew was in him should have taken the opportunity to dig deeper into her past and extract as much pertinent information as possible — but he didn't. Lizanne had completely mesmerized him. So much so that he had completely disregarded the necessity that was there to fill in the holes that he believed were in her story.

By the conclusion of their meal, Sabastian's objective had not been attained. His focus instead, had been on one thing only — getting to know the woman sitting directly across from him on a more intimate level. Not only was she beautiful, but she was also captivating. She ticked off every single box there was when it came to his perfect woman.

At some point in the evening, Madelyn had forgotten why she was there. She found herself becoming personally intrigued by her mark. Somehow, Sabastian had turned the tables and gotten her to become fascinated with him. How had this happened? He checked off pretty much every box. Physically, he wasn't what she had envisioned her perfect man to look like, but those few traits could easily be forgotten. Had she just found her soul mate? It was certainly possible.

When the bill arrived, Sabastian immediately claimed it; he believed himself to be a gentleman and it just didn't seem right to expect Lizanne to pay for the dinner. Of course, she tried to convince him to at least let her pay for half of it because it was she who had invited him to dinner in the first place. But he refused — even though the cost of the meal was equal to that of a week's worth of groceries for a family of four.

After Sabastian paid for dinner, they left the restaurant and walked back toward the hotel elevators. When they arrived, Madelyn gently placed her hand on his left arm and said, "Thank you for accompanying me to dinner. I really enjoyed the evening."

"As did I. Would you..?"

"I would like to call it a day. I know it's still very early, but I should go up to my room and get some rest."

"Do you really have to? I mean.., I was kinda hoping that you would accompany me on an evening walk. It is, after all, supposed to be a beautiful night."

Just like she had hoped would happen, Sabastian was becoming very interested in her beyond that of her just being his client. She hesitated for a moment, trying to make it look like she was debating his offer — but what she really wanted to see was the eagerness in his eyes. And when it appeared to her as if he was not going to be disappointed if she turned him down, she decided to call it a night.

With an atypical smile on her face, she took a few steps in close to Sabastian, leaned forward, and gave him a kiss on the cheek. After saying goodnight, she turned around, pressed the 'up' button on the wall next to the elevator, and waited. In the mirror that hung in front of where she stood, she could see that Sabastian had graciously accepted her decision to end their 'date'. That was something she knew most men would have a hard time doing without showing some kind of disappointment. It also told her one very important thing about him — he was not a typical male. There was something very special about him and that was what had snagged her interest.

The last time her heart and mind felt conflicted like this was the day she left home; she just hoped that history didn't repeat itself as she didn't want to make a decision that would result in her never being able to take a completely different path than the one she was currently walking.

When she looked in the mirror again and subsequently realized that Sebastian was already halfway toward the hotel exit, her mind changed. Just as the elevator doors had opened up to let her in, she turned away from them and hastily made her way toward him. She wasn't doing this in order to help her complete her assigned task; she was doing this because she simply wanted to.

Just as Sebastian had stepped out onto the street, she caught up with him, slipped her left arm through his with ease, and looked into his eyes. "I think that I'd like to take that evening walk with you after all."

He was beyond thrilled. He felt like a kid in a candy store. With Lizanne suddenly changing her mind about going for that walk, it only confirmed what he suspected — she was as interested in him as he was in her. That little bit of arrogant cockiness that all men have, though seldom ever embraced by Sebastian, caused him to beam inside and out with pride. He was suddenly blessed with having the most beautiful looking woman in the entire city, walking by his side, and nestled in the crook of his right arm. Maybe there was a God after all, or maybe his long-ago decision to just be patient and fulfill his obligation first before he opened up his heart to someone, was the right one. It now appeared as if he was being rewarded for that decision.

He'd be a fool if he didn't take full advantage of the situation he now found himself in. So long as he didn't try to be someone who he normally wasn't or did something idiotic and embarrassed her, the evening should turn out to be one of the best in his young life.

From the outskirts of Historic Market Square, they walked aimlessly for almost two hours; sightseeing, window-shopping, and people watching. With having no particular destination in mind, they ended up at Woodlawn Lake Park, roughly two and a half miles from where they had started. As the early fall sun was setting, they made their way over to the water's edge. There, they watched the last of the daylight disappear.

Just like Lizanne, this ranked right up there as being one of the more beautiful things that Sabastian had ever remembered seeing — then again, having her there with him may have been what had allowed him to, for the first time ever, open up his eyes fully and appreciate something as simple and beautiful as a sunset.

Right after our galaxy's brightest star called it a day, Sabastian looked into Lizanne's eyes, and without hesitation, leaned forward and kissed her. From the moment their lips touched, it became apparent to him just how presumptuous he had been. Immediately, he felt as if he had just made the biggest mistake that he possibly ever could. Embarrassed, he pulled back and lowered his head in shame. He then apologetically said, "I'm so sorry. I should not have done that."

Lizanne lifted his head up, looked into his eyes, smiled, and returned her lips to his. This felt real to her. This wasn't an assignment that she was fulfilling or just another paid client. She simply had no other choice but to admit to herself that she felt a real attraction to Sabastian; an attraction that she had no inkling whatsoever would even develop. For some reason, she failed to completely shut the door to her heart. And because she had, her wants and desires had freely found their way to the surface. They had taken control and terminated the task she had been given. She was supposed to seduce Sabastian, but he had done that to her instead.

Admittedly, she wanted it as much as she believed he did; proven by the fact that she was unable to stop herself from tightly wrapping her arms around him in an embrace that could not be misinterpreted. And just because the sun had long since set, it didn't mean that the evening wasn't shining. Something had occurred between the both of them that neither could deny, resist, understand, nor even explain. Maybe it was fate that had drawn them together. Or maybe, it was purely happenstance. Whatever the reason, it simply didn't matter.

After they both released their lock, they looked at each other and neither one of them could speak. It could only be assumed, but each was fairly certain that the other felt the same. This special moment that they were sharing needed to be bottled up and preserved forever.

Had it not been someone across the way saying, "get a room", both of them probably would have been content to ignore the world around them and stay right where they were. The park, however, wasn't the ideal place to further explore what had just been initiated, so Sabastian took Lizanne by the hand and they walked to the Woodlawn Island House; luckily an unoccupied cab was sitting there in the front parking lot.

It was nearly impossible to behave in the back seat; a yearning in each was trying its damnedest to push aside common sense. Thankfully, the ride back to the Pershing Suites was short. Other than some kissing, not enough time had been there for them to do anything else.

After paying the cab driver, they promptly headed up to Madelyn's room. Once they crossed the threshold, even before the door had a chance to completely close, she started to rip away Sabastian's clothes. He thought about doing the same thing to her, but this was a once in a lifetime moment and he wanted to remember every second of it.

Meticulously, he removed what was hiding the treasure underneath. As it was being revealed, he suddenly felt unworthy. There, in a forest green trimmed, black lace bra and panties, was a dream come true. Had his jaw not been attached, it would have undoubtedly fallen right to the floor and shattered. In his eyes, she was the embodiment of perfection.

He didn't deserve this Goddess. Yet for some reason, he was being given this opportunity to experience a bit of heaven on earth. So he summoned up all the courage that he could find within himself and, even though he admittedly was still nervous, planted another kiss on her lips — and this time, it was filled with passion.

While he had her thoughts occupied with desire, Sabastian's hands began to explore the flawless surface of her body. Initially, his fingers gently traced the outside edges of her breasts, and then they made their way down to her washboard abs. From there, they spread out until each hand came to rest on her hips.

Sabastian had her hypnotized; his kiss had done its job by garnering her full attention. In fact, he was certain that Lizanne was unaware of what he was about to do — then again, he could only assume that she really didn't care at all. So expertly, he placed both of his thumbs and forefingers over each tiny plastic clip on both sides of her thong, and as easy as Houdini would escape from a pair of handcuffs, in one unseen move, unclasped them.

Madelyn broke the seal of their kiss and let out a gasp as the cool breeze of the room brushed up against her exposed womanhood. No longer was she herself, nor was she whom she was expected to be. She wanted Sabastian more than any other guy that she had ever been with before. Since the day she had lost her innocence at sixteen in a game of truth or dare, she had slept with hundreds of men. There had even been some with looks that qualified them to be on the cover of a romance novel, but none of them had been able to touch her wants and trigger her emotions as Sabastian had just done.

Willingly, she gave in to the needs and desires that she had long ago forgotten she had. It was a bit scary; it even felt somewhat foreign. Even so, she wanted this more than anything ever before. So, without a hint of objection or reservation trying to come forth in her mind, she allowed nature to take its course.

Jerrelle sat in her parked car in nearly the exact same spot as she had earlier in the day, just down the street from The Cough Inn, waiting for the top of the hour to arrive; and probably not the last hour in one of the longest days that she has had in a very long time. Being patience was a difficult thing for her; she continually checked the time on her vid-cell. It felt almost as if 'Gremlins' had somehow invaded the electronic world and were now causing the clock numbers to change slower. Then again, she knew that time seemed to be dragging only because she was anxious to get this last bit of business over with.

Although she had been told by André to be at the club at eleven, Jerrelle just couldn't wait any longer, so she exited her car and crossed the street to go and get her money. As she approached the club, she took the direct route to the front door, bypassing the long line of patrons that were still patiently waiting to get inside. As always when someone cuts to the head of the line, she heard the expected bitching and complaining from those who had an issue with what she was doing.

Deciding then that she wanted to have a little harmless fun before she went inside, Jerrelle stopped at the front of the line, and while looking directly at those who had protested the loudest, cracked a devilish smile. "Bitch all you want, but I have a special, one-of-a-kind V.I.P. pass." She then pulled back her spring jacket to clearly show to everyone the honor blade strapped to her hip. "Now, all you whiny little princesses need to shut the hell up and wait your turn. And while I'm in the club, none of you had better come anywhere near me and voice your displeasure or I'll make sure that you get a much more, up close and personal look at my pass." Jerrelle's face promptly became inscrutable. Almost immediately thereafter, four rather young, maybe even underage girls, all of whom were dressed as if their intention was to get laid, left the line and hurried off to where their car was parked.

Selfishly satisfied with the results she had achieved, Jerrelle allowed her jacket to again conceal her honor blade. Then, as if nothing had taken place, she continued toward the front door of the club. Right as she was about to step on through it, she received a piercing glare from the doorman; the identical twin brother of André. "Relax, Henré. I probably just saved you and this club from getting into trouble with the liquor board because I know that you would have let those underage girls inside."

Even after Jerrelle entered The Cough Inn, Henré's expression failed to change. He wasn't feeling the way he was because of hate, as he had none for her. It was because she was right. Part of his job was to make sure that the club had its proper ratio of good-looking women to horny guys. Therefore, he had no other choice on some nights but to break the law and let those who at least looked to be of age into the club in order to meet his expected quota.

Once inside, she headed directly to the bar. Oddly, Inita was still working behind it. What wasn't at all surprising was the woman's reaction to her arrival. Just like she had every single time Jerrelle would walk through the door, she turned and headed straight into the kitchen. A few seconds later, as expected, André opened the swinging

80

doors. He didn't come all the way into the bar though; he just stood there and motioned with his head.

Without a word or a nod of acknowledgment being given, she entered the kitchen. Once there, they walked together to the back corner and then past a break in the farside wall where the back alley emergency exit was also located. Directly behind that barrier was the access to a private staircase. From there, they ascended up two flights and then down the hall to the end where Cloe's office was. André knocked three times and waited a moment for a response. Once he got it, he opened the door so that Jerrelle could enter.

No words were exchanged the moment she walked into her 'friends' office — not until a good ten seconds had passed after she sat down in front of the old metal desk, was she spoken to.

"You do know that it has always been my intention to pay you back, but…"

"But what? I know for a fact that this club of yours is comfortably in the black. Why is it that you have chosen to not pay me back?"

"I was instructed not to."

"By whom?"

"Your ex-boss."

"Gino?"

"Yes!" Cloe paused for a moment and looked directly at Jerrelle. It killed her that she was not able to pay back her old friend, but she had been threatened and placed in a position that left her with no other option.

"What's Gino got to do with this?"

"Everything!" After a moment spent in order to make sure that her thoughts were organized, she said, "It all started right after he threw you out of his garage. He came by that same evening (which was why he was not at the garage when Jerrelle went back there to get her revenge) and told me never to give you back the money you lent me and never to allow you in here again. And so that I would comply with his demand, he took my Mustang Boss 302 and said that he would hold onto it for a while to make sure that I fully understood what he had said. Two weeks later, he gave me my car back — in a thousand pieces. He said that this is what would happen to me and my staff if I didn't do what he said. A few weeks after that, he showed up here again, gasoline in hand, and threatened to burn me down because he had heard that you had stopped by. That was right before you left to join the military. Every so often, from that day forward, the bastard would show up with his goon squad and would threaten bodily harm to either me, my employees, or their families. Twice last year, he even showed up here just before I was supposed to have a sold-out show take place and he trashed my entire club. It was his way to make sure that you were kept away. So.., now do you understand why I can never pay you back?" Cloe paused for a moment because her nerves were beginning to cause her hands to shake a little. "You do realize that if he ever finds out that you were here, he will…"

"He won't do a damn thing to you because…" That revelation really pissed of Jerrelle. The son-of-a-bitch not only had fucked her over, but he had gone out of his way to make her friend's life a living hell; a friend that she had honestly begun to hate because she had thought Cloe was purposely refusing to pay her back. But now that Jerrelle knew the truth, whatever regrets she may have had about what she and Bai Lin had just done to Gino and his boys, was no longer there. "…the asshole has been taken care of. My sister and I were at his garage earlier today. He and his lackeys were taught a lesson that was long overdue. He and his butt sniffers are now no longer in business."

This was music to Cloe's ears. If what Jerrelle had just said to her were indeed true, then the anxiety that constantly consumed her would be gone forever. "You know that I've always believed everything that you have ever said to me, but if you don't mind, I am going to call a friend of mine at the Detroit Police Department and see if she can corroborate your claim."

"Wait! If you have a friend who is a cop, then why didn't they do anything to help you with the threats and harassment?"

"My friend only graduated from the academy three months ago; I haven't heard from Gino in over six. He probably thought that you were still in the military and far away from here." Cloe took a moment and gathered her thoughts before she called her police friend. After a few minutes of waiting, they were able to confirm Jerrelle's story. "You don't know how much of a weight has just been lifted off my shoulders. Thank you."

"Well then.., once you pay me back my money, I can return the thanks."

Cloe laughed, got up from behind her desk, and walked over to her safe. A minute later, she returned with the money that Jerrelle had honestly thought she'd never see. "Here is what I owe you.., plus interest. Are we friends again?"

"It hadn't yet gotten to the point where we had become enemies." Jerrelle took a moment and quickly counted the money, surprised that there was twenty thousand there. "Why twenty thousand? I only lent you ten."

"Because I owe you and I feel bad about why I couldn't pay you back. Now don't argue.., just take it."

If she had only gotten her ten thousand back, Jerrelle would have been content. Some interest, she was hoping for. But a full ten thousand on top of it, she did not expect. This completely shocked her. In fact, she actually contemplated refusing the extra money, but Jerrelle did not want to drive an unnecessary wedge, even deeper into the middle of her apparently, just repaired friendship.

After placing the money into a small canvas bag that she had brought with her, then securely strapping it to her hip next to her honor blade, she stood up and followed Cloe back down the stairs to the bar, which now seemed to be beyond its capacity.

Crowds; Jerrelle did not like being in the middle of them. Thankfully, her old friend led her away from the sea of people toward a roped-off private area at the back corner of the establishment. Once they had made it there, Cloe had one of her waitresses bring them over each a pint of beer. It was time to celebrate a renewed friendship that both quickly declared they would never allow anything or anyone to ever ruin it again.

An hour later, Bai Lin showed up half expecting to see the bar destroyed. To her relief, it appeared not to be. However, several questions quickly formed in her mind. Had her sister been successful? Was she still inside trying to get what she came for? Jerrelle's car was still parked down the street, so it appeared as if she hadn't gotten herself kicked out of the place. Of course, the more likely of possibilities was that she had gotten herself arrested, for causing a bar fight. Thankfully, the bouncer at the front door had informed her that all was surprisingly well.

Once she weaved her way through the dense crowd and made it over to the owner's private seating area at the back of the club, the worry that she had, was completely gone. The only thing that she was uncertain of was the odd-looking young woman that her sister was joking and having beers with.

Unexpectedly, Jerrelle noticed that her sister was now standing only a few feet away; an authentic smile immediately grew on her face. After inviting her to join them at the table, she proceeded to introduce her to Cloe. But before that could even be completed, a pint of beer somehow mysteriously appeared and was placed right in front of Bai Lin.

To her, this was really odd. Nevertheless, she wasn't one to complain when free beer was given. So she thanked the waitress, took a sip of her ice-cold pint, and curiously scanned the room. The music was decent and not too loud, the crowd of people seemed very diverse, and the atmosphere seemed jovial. She was inside a strange, packed bar — yet for once, she surprisingly didn't feel like an outcast. She almost felt like she belonged; like she had been coming here for years. Now Bai Lin understood why her sister liked this place; it was a place that she could easily get used to coming to whenever she was in town. A place where every time she showed up, she would be respected and taken care of. A place that was just as welcoming as one's own home should be. "Oh, and by the way, sis.., I'm pretty sure that I have found what I went looking for."

Those words not only caused curiosity to develop within Jerrelle, but they also prompted a worry to appear — only because a feeling was now present that she and Bai Lin would soon be getting deeply involved in something that they should really just avoid.

It had been a while since Louie felt this good. Two things contributed to that: his first official deal as head of the Detroit Underworld Organization had been agreed upon, and during his brief vid-cell conversation with Madelyn earlier in the day, she informed him that she luckily hadn't had to work all that hard to draw

Sabastian's interest. By day's end tomorrow, she firmly believed that she would have a good grip on his heartstrings.

A desire to celebrate was there, so that's what he did. He knew full well that he should have stopped after only one drink, but he didn't. One beer had turned into three. Three glasses of Walker's Club on the rocks then followed that. Other than the night in Chicago when he had drunk that near full bottle of Krug, Clos du Mesnil by himself, it had been years since Louie had done that, just for the sake of drinking. Now, he had done it twice in just over a week. But he was in a good mood tonight and thought that he had earned a well-deserved night of indulging. Of course, he was getting up in age and he should have known that his alcohol tolerance wasn't anywhere near what it used to be — those beers and the ryes were all that it took for his night to be over, way before the midnight hour.

"Oh man, does my head hurt. What the hell happened to me?" Louie found himself feeling a bit disoriented. He wasn't sure where he was; it was just too dark for him to see. What he did know was that he was sitting. For some reason though, he could not move. "Where in the hell am I? And what the hell is going on?" Again, Louie tried to focus, but with the room as dark as it was, he just couldn't see anything in and around him that he could fixate on.

It took him a few uncertain moments before he finally realized the reason why he was unable to move — he was bound to a chair, a chair that seemed to be nailed to the floor. Whoever had done this to him; he was adamant they were going to pay. Whether it was today or not, they were going to pay.

He wasn't quite sure what to do, so he tried to call out for help, but the only response he got was the echo of his own voice bouncing all around him. 'Ok.., I'm all alone and tied to a chair in a dark room. Whatever idiot did this to me certainly has some balls.' Again, Louie cried out — and again, it was only his own words that he heard. Frustrated, he tried to pull his hands free of the restraints, but the moment he did that, they tightened. "What the hell is fuckin' going on here?"

Like before, no one answered. Now, Louie was pissed. He was about to issue a warning/promise to whoever had done this to him when his ears picked up on a faint, tapping sound; it was in a sequential pattern. After a few seconds, he determined that the noise was the result of some footsteps. Closely, he listened to them; they progressively got louder. It wasn't long thereafter that Louie realized whoever was responsible for making the cyclical sounds, was also directly behind and moving toward him.

He would have tried to turn his head around to see who it was, but he found that impossible to do. Notwithstanding the fact that, even if he were able to, there would have been no way for him to see anything because the room had not one ounce of light in it to begin with. "Who the hell is there?"

"I shouldn't have to tell you that, Louie. You should already know."

Those words, and the individual that spoke them, instantly caused his blood to boil. He indeed knew who that voice belonged to. And just like before, what should be impossible, was once again taking place. "Show me your damn face, Maxwell!"

A small circle of dim light suddenly appeared at Louie's feet. It slowly expanded and got brighter until a ten-foot area of illumination encased him. Surprisingly, nothing outside of that perimeter was visible — it was still as copiously dark as the room had previously been.

Other than himself, the only thing that Louie could see was a shadow off to his right that not only crept forward, but it was growing in size as it moved. By the time it had advanced beyond him and merged with the far outer rim of darkness, the owner of it was within his peripheral vision. Not long after that, his captor was officially revealed.

The smug look that was plastered on Maxwell's face needed to be slapped off. Unfortunately, Louie was not controlling this game and he had no other choice but to become an unwilling participant. He should be used to this by now because this was the third time his adversary had paid him an ethereal visit. Why he had appeared again, Louie had not a clue. The first time Maxwell had done this, was so that he could issue a warning; the second time was to issue a threat. Maybe this time, he had come back to actually kill him? "You know.., your gamesmanship could use some work. You'd have figured that *after being Antonio's pawn for twenty-five years, you would have learned how to control the board."*

Maxwell didn't say a word. He just stepped off to the side so that Louie would have an unobstructed view. Seconds later, another circle of light appeared directly ahead. Encased within it was an object; one that Louie did not need to guess what it represented. Almost immediately, he felt his heart rate jump. What he was seeing, hovering no more than twenty feet in front of him, was something that he had always feared — ever since his older brother thought it would be funny to lock him in one for an hour when he was eight years old. No, he didn't know for sure if it was Maxwell's intention to carry out what was obviously implied, but Louie was fairly certain that more than just another simple message was about to be delivered.

This wasn't just a case of déjà-vu with the roles now being reversed. This plainly was meant for Louie to experience what it was like to be in the shoes of someone whose existence was only a few moments away from coming to an end.

Knowing Maxwell as he did, he hoped that the man still abided by the same principles he had when he was alive. That was what he had to bank on — but his enemy was dead, and Louie had no idea if the 'rule book' still applied in the afterlife. "Is this your way of handing out a little poetic justice, Max?"

"In a manner of speaking... Yes."

Trying not to show the trepidation that consumed him, Louie pasted on a contrived smile, then looked right at his enemy and said, "I don't believe you for one second, nor do I believe that you are real. None of this is real. This is just a figment of my inestimable imagination, brought on by all of the stress I have been under."

"You are right... yet you are wrong. A mind is like a placebo. Given the right circumstances, it can make you believe that something is real."

"Your analogy is unfounded."

"Your heart is now racing is it not?" That just proves my point."

In an instant, Louie was no longer tied to the chair. He was now lying flat on his back and again submerged in total darkness. A momentary bit of uncertainty appeared as he again tried to get his bearings — at least, his hands were now free. He felt around and what he discovered were walls and a ceiling that was so close, it was like he was in a box. Of which he was.

The worst experience of his entire life was suddenly being relived. Panic consumed him; memories of his brother's hysterical laughter also promptly returned. Somehow, he had been transferred to that free-floating 'casket' that Maxwell had earlier revealed. "Let me out of this fuckin' thing, you sick bastard! Let me out!"

"Um... No! I want you to have a taste of what it was like for me inside that metal box. Just be thankful that I have no intention of beating your ass within an inch of your life and then encasing you in concrete."

Did Maxwell know about Louie's Feretrophobia, or was this just coincidental? Whatever the case may be, he needed to get the hell out of the damn thing before this 'dream' actually did kill him. "This isn't funny, Max! Only an insane person would do something like this."

"Well... if that's not calling the kettle black. I, unlike Antonio, am not insane. But you, my long-standing adversary, are cut from the same cloth as he."

"I am not at all like him. I only did what I did because I was following his orders. Now let me out of here!"

"And I am merely doing what must be done, as it is the only way for you to truly understand what lies ahead of you."

His panic was beginning to intensify. As a result, Louie's breathing was becoming labored and his thoughts were doing their best to convince him that he was actually going to die. Negotiating his way out of the coffer didn't appear to be an option. He was all but screwed.

As much as he still wanted to believe that this whole thing was not real, he no longer could dismiss the possibility that it was. After all, his enemy was in control of this entire scenario and it didn't appear to him that there were any options left on the table for him to explore — except for maybe one. That though, he knew was something his enemy would never in a million years, believe he would be sincere about. Nevertheless, he had no other choice but to try. "If I tell you that I'm truly sorry for everything, will you release me from this box?"

Maxwell let out a laugh that was reminiscent of Louie's brother's; it sent an unwanted chill straight down his spine and again caused his childhood memory to return. The fear that had already been present promptly intensified. He was quickly nearing the point of no return. Desperately, he wanted to be set free. "Dammit, Max!" Louie yelled as he frantically banged on the walls of his worst nightmare. "Stop this madness and fuckin' let me out of here!"

"No, I will not! I need for you to fully comprehend what awaits you. Soon, your existence on earth will be coming to an end... and there will be nothing that you can do to avoid or prevent it. The ability to deviate from the path that you are on is no longer there. The end is in sight. And when it is reached, your physical existence will cease and your soul will cross over the threshold of a realm in the afterlife in which judgment has not only already been passed, but comes with a sentence that is well-earned."

"Fuck you, Banks! You are just a bad dream. I am not soon fated to die. I will, in fact, live long after I have taken the life of your misguided son."

Maxwell stood at the head of the 'casket' and rested his elbows on top of it. He then leaned in closer and whispered in a deep tone, just loud enough for Louie to still hear him. "Ashes to ashes, dust to dust. The lord won't take you, so the devil must." Maxwell then stood back as a large black blanket appeared out of thin air into his hands — he then draped it equally over the floating box. Embroidered in the center of it was a large, inverted, blood-red pentagram. And in the same red-color, written right underneath the bottom, single point of the devil's symbol, was the Italian words 'Dannato per l'eternità' (Damned for all eternity). "When you see a hearse go by, you WILL be the next to die." Before Louie could respond, Maxwell yanked the blanket off of the 'casket' in the same manner that a magician would reveal the success of his illusion. The floating box was gone, right along with Louie.

Maxwell stood there alone for a brief moment, displaying a satisfactory smile; it stayed with him as the room that he and his old adversary had been in was transformed back to the representation of

89

his apartment. "Had I had access to this 'holodeck' when I was still a police officer, I have no doubt that things would have turned out much differently."

Both he and his bed were drenched in sweat; Louie was also completely underneath the sheets and tucked in the fetal position. He couldn't stop shaking. If he didn't find a way to end these unwanted visits from Maxwell, he was surely going to lose his mind.

Even after realizing that he had returned to reality, it took Louie nearly a half an hour before he was able to get on with his day. Upon finally leaving his room, he walked straight to his kitchen, opened up his fridge, and poured himself a glass of V8 Plus. From there, he walked over to his balcony and then leaned up against its railing. After a few moments of watching the morning come to life, and those who were already out and about, Louie felt ready to dispel the chaos that had invaded his mind last night. That was until his eyes caught sight of a black vehicle that passed right in front of his place. It wasn't just any ordinary black vehicle. It was a hearse.

It was right then and there that he had to concede. Whether or not Maxwell's declaration was going to come to fruition, Louie had no choice but to accept the possibility of it. These visits: the warning, the threat, and the promise; he had to take them seriously. He needed to prepare himself for whatever future may or may not lie ahead for him. No longer could he procrastinate. He needed to ensure that his affairs were in order.

With his nearly empty juice glass in hand, he went back into his apartment and headed directly to the desk in his study. Once there, he turned on the lamp, plopped his butt into his synth-leather chair, and fired up his computer. This was something that Louie knew he should have done a long time ago, but the arrogant part of him always assumed that he'd live a very long life. Now, he wasn't so sure how much of it was left.

The remainder of his morning was spent taking care of several very important things. First, Louie updated his will and then printed out a physical copy of it. Then he wrote two letters: one for Mirella, and one for his son, Marco. Once those were completed and signed, he placed all three items into separate envelopes and placed them in his briefcase so that he could take them with him to the office. There, he would lock them in his safe, only to be removed if and when it appeared that Maxwell's declaration was about to come true.

She sat on the edge of the couch, uncertain how she should be feeling. On one hand, what she had witnessed seemed like it was well deserved. Her conscience, however, was telling her the line that should never be crossed, had been. Apparently, the afterlife had its own set of rules that took precedence over those any sentient being was expected to abide by. To her, that just didn't seem right. But despite how she felt, she had to keep reminding herself that Louie Mazotti, although not completely responsible for her, her husband's death, and their son's disappearance, did play a significant role in all of it. Therefore, she had to accept the fact that, in this instance, what had just been done to him was justified. Even so, the pure heart and soul that Sylvia had, could not help but feel pity for the man. She didn't know him, nor had she ever met him before, yet she sensed that somewhere within him, there existed a good person who just took a wrong turn and could not find his way back onto the right path. "Did you have to do what you did in order to get your point across?"

Maxwell looked at his wife, baffled that she had even asked that question. "Yes!" As far as he was concerned, a small sample of what he went through seemed appropriate. "If it had been at all possible for me to physically harm the bastard, then I would have."

Sylvia stood there with a look on her face that was impossible to read; she honestly didn't know how she felt about her husband's declaration.

"What? He deserves a good ass-kicking."

She did not think Maxwell had the right to make that sort of determination. Clearly, her husband had an innate desire to punish Louie instead of doing what he was supposed to do and let the man's death occur when it was scheduled to. Never before had she witnessed that sort of mindset from him. His entire being was genuine and caring; that was why she had fallen in love with Maxwell. Now, he was starting to show a completely different side of himself that she never knew he had. And it scared her.

At that moment, she started to believe that her husband was going to somehow find a way to achieve what is supposed to be unattainable. And if he were to somehow succeed, the man she loved would undoubtedly be reprimanded in a manner that would result in Maxwell spending the rest of eternity in a place completely different than she. She did not want that to happen. "You know very well that revenge cannot come at your hands. The torch has been passed on to our son. Only he can settle the score and restore our family's honor. The only thing you are allowed to do is manipulate and influence Louie Mazotti so that his fated destiny is fulfilled."

"I am aware of that, Sylvia. But..."

"There are no buts! And your wife is right, so quit trying to find a way to change the game in order to get what you want."

Both Maxwell and his wife turned their attention away from each other and focused it on the other voice that had joined them in their manifested apartment. Today, the angel was dressed very casually. He was wearing denim jeans with holes in each knee, and a bold Hawaiian shirt. His long hair was freely hanging; not tied or braided in a ponytail as usual, and he wore on his head a Detroit Tiger's baseball hat. If Maxwell didn't know any better, he'd swear that Nefieti had been binge-watching old Magnum P.I. episodes; the original, not the reboot. "I know that this is your realm, but this..." with a slight hand gesture, he referenced the room they were all currently occupying, "...is our private space. At least, that is what I was under the impression it was to be."

"What my husband is trying to say is that we would appreciate it if you would first knock before you grace us with your presence."

"When your husband can be completely trusted to do what is asked of him, then this space will be respected. But until I know for certain that he will, I will come and go as I please."

"I am doing everything that I am supposed to. Louie is now solidly on his fated path."

"Yes.., he is. But you are also turning out to be a bigger pain in my ass than what I am willing to tolerate."

"How so?"

92

Nefieti walked over to the lazy boy recliner that was opposite of the couch that Maxwell had been sitting on. He then took up a seat in it and said, "You were told not to visit your son."

"I have not!"

"Ok.., technically you haven't. But in a roundabout way, you have. When the aperture opened up the other day, you summoned your old partner, Joshua, and then sent him to your son to do what you were told not to. His path did not need to be altered."

"Joshua did not alter it. He only prevented him from stepping off of it."

Nefieti could not argue that point — he was just annoyed that Maxwell was pushing the envelope when it came to what he was allowed to do. He now understood all of the frustrations that Christopher White had to suffer through during the man's time as a police officer. "I, and the Sister's of Fate, all agree that what is supposed to occur, now will. What we are afraid of though, is that you will do something stupid at some point that will end up causing more damage than what can actually be repaired."

"I'm insulted and I'm hurt you would even think that. Not once have I ever done anything without first thinking of the possible consequences. I don't do things that are stupid, only things that may seem illogical. You can't dispute my track record. It speaks for itself."

A near millennium has gone by since Nefieti had gotten angry. He found it extremely difficult to understand why Maxwell Banks chose to do things in an unconventional manner, then sit there and justify his irrational behavior as being necessary instead of just simply doing what he was told? If his hair could at all turn grey, the angel was certain that this ex-cop would be the reason for that taking place. "Now you listen very closely to me, Max!"

He didn't wish to be rude toward Nefieti, but he didn't want to get his ego ripped to shreds while his wife sat there and watched. So with the utmost of sincerity, he said, "Nevertheless, I promise to stay right where I am and just observe. If I happen to notice that Louie has found a way to step off of his path, I will do only what I feel is necessary in order to ensure that the bastard's soul ends up in your boss's possession."

A wave of needed relief washed over the angel. Although his trust in Maxwell was far from absolute, for some unknown reason, he actually believed that the ex-cop was only going to do what he had just stated — and nothing more. "Good." Nefieti looked over at Sylvia and produced a genuine smile. And as a sign of good faith, I will now allow you both to visit your son. However…"

Immediately, many different emotions consumed both of them. That was the only thing each had wanted since they first saw what their son now looked like via the Apollo's Stone.

"…so that there is a nominal possibility that his destined path will become altered, you will only get one very brief visit each. Therefore, I highly recommend that you wait until Sabastian really needs you. A social visit on your part, though I'm sure you would be content with making, would be a waste of my generosity. Use your one visit wisely."

Maxwell reached over and took a hold of his wife's hand. As much as he had wanted to go to his son in that very moment, the joining of his hand with his wife's was what had helped to keep his emotions in check. Soon, the love they both had for their son would be shared with him. And when the time came that they could let Sabastian know of this, the burden of not ever having their constant love be present in his life would finally be set free in each.

"Thank you for that gesture. I don't know if you realize just how much that means to us."

"As I am not a parent, I can only guess." Nefieti then stood up and said, "The next time I come for a visit, I will knock. Unless…"

"I know. There's no need to remind me."

Before another word was said, the angel disappeared; Maxwell and his wife just sat there, gobsmacked. Never in a million years did either think that their one and only wish would be granted. Now, they had to each determine when the best time would be to visit Sabastian. Like the angel had said, they needed to make sure that their appearance wasn't determined by their emotions. It needed to be done with an intended purpose that in turn, would have the most profound and positive effect.

Maxwell took the Apollo's Stone, set it down on the coffee table in front of both he and his wife, placed his arm around her, and held her tight. Collectively, the love for their son brought the stone to life. All that they wanted to do was watch their son for a while. What they saw, however, caused immediate embarrassment in each. Sabastian wasn't doing something he should not. Instead, he was right in the middle of something that should be kept private and behind a locked door.

The moment he returned to his office, he claimed his chair, closed his eyes, placed his feet up onto his desk, and allowed his thoughts to take him far away from his current existence — to a possible life he hoped to one day live.

Like every morning, he had a schedule to follow — and in about a half-hour, he had to be at his post. Yes, Beezel could easily cover for him, but the minion was far from a welcoming, personable individual. Besides, Nefieti was never someone to pass off his responsibilities because he simply wasn't in the mood.

Time was what was needed; patience was all that it was going to take. It wasn't until about a half a century ago that a crazy thought had come to him — only then, it seemed not just unlikely, but impossible. Now though, it didn't. However, in order for it to become a reality, he first had to put his faith in someone who could be just as unpredictable as life itself. It was a given that things weren't going to simply fall into place for him. It was going to take a lot of work — and some luck. Even so, he now believed it was actually achievable.

Like most individuals, whose potential paths had been made known to him throughout his time as keeper of the Netherworld, the angel initially didn't pay any attention to Maxwell's. It wasn't until Lachesis, one of the Three Sisters of Fate had mentioned to him what the man's actual destiny was to be, that Nefieti started to think his dream could become a reality. It wasn't until years later though, once he was able to see just how significant of an individual Maxwell was going to become, that he knew the ex-private eye was the ideal candidate. The only thing that sucked was that no timetable could be given as to when the stars would finally align. It could be a year, a decade, a century, or even more before Nefieti was able to begin his day with having to only make one decision. What to do with his free time?

At a quarter to the hour of what would be nine a.m. on earth, EST, he stood behind his welcoming podium and patiently waited for the first of the day's arrivals to appear. During that time, he started to ponder over whether or not he should come clean. There were pros and cons to each. So far, the need to know had not been necessary — and the angel hoped that it would stay that way for a long time. Still, Maxwell Banks was an honorable man and out of respect, he should be told the whole truth. Yes, Louie's soul was damned for all eternity, but it wasn't actually sought after by the Lord of Darkness. The angel wanted it for himself instead because the mobster's essence was unlike the majority that would arrive at Hell's Lounge.

Due to what he had always felt was a needless burden placed upon him by his boss, Nefieti occasionally required sustenance in order for his immortal existence to continue in the same manner that it was — and Louie's soul had the ability to provide that for him. However, a deal would first have to be struck. That was no big deal except, he would then have to pay much closer attention to his Netherworld guest. The reason for that was, if Maxwell was to ever find out that his enemy's eternal home wasn't where he believed it to be, that it was going to be in the same neighborhood as his instead, not only would some serious animosity develop, but the angel's hopes and dreams would also be seriously in jeopardy of ever being realized.

The sun had nearly broken free of the horizon. Sabastian though just did not want to acknowledge that the day had already started. The bed was where he wanted to stay. Last night, he had experienced something that he never thought he would. His mind, because it was not yet fully awake, wrongly thought that by delaying the inevitable, the magical evening he and Lizanne shared, could continue. That of course, was untrue because reality was knocking on the door — and on the other side of it was waiting a bunch of questions that were going to take quite some time before they got answered.

Conceding to the certainty of life, Sabastian grudgingly rolled out of bed, walked around to the other side, and then stopped. He could not help it. Even as Lizanne continued to sleep, his 'Goddess' looked just as beautiful to him as she had the previous evening.

96

Gently, he placed his right hand on the lower portion of her bareback, leaned over, and softly kissed the side of her head. He really didn't want to leave, but he had to. Responsibilities awaited him and he had people who would expect him to be at the office. By now, he should be sitting at his desk, an English tea in hand, looking at his family photo, and either wondering what if or contemplating his future.

He was going to be late today, but he really didn't care. Ideally, he should take a shower before he left, as trace evidence of last night's amazing experience could very well be present. But time wasn't on his side. Therefore, he would just have to wait until later on in the day, right after he had finished his workout at the gym, to clean up.

Quietly, he gathered up his personal effects, snuck out of the room, and left for the agency. Normally, a gentleman would have at least left a note, but he knew that he would be seeing Lizanne again in only a few short hours.

When Sabastian entered the agency, all that he got from those that were there was a 'Good morning', and not a 'Why are you late' or a 'What the hell did you do last night'. *'I wonder if anyone suspects anything?'* he thought.

Unsure if no comments were a good thing or not, he went about his morning ritual: stop at the kitchen nook and grab a sim-caf, and then tap Baylor on his shoulder as he passed him on the way to his office. Unbeknownst to Sabastian, his friend vacated his computer chair and promptly followed him. Once both of them were inside the room, he said, "I've never known you to be late for anything before."

"There is always a first time for everything?"

"That's a standard answer. It's also not an acceptable one. Why were you late, Sab?"

"I overslept. I am no longer in the military, so I don't have to be up by five in the morning."

"Well.., because you were late, I was forced to answer an important call for you."

"Who was it?"

"Why were you late?"

"That's none of your business!"

"When it comes to you, everything is my business. Besides.., I'm not your personal secretary."

"If doing a simple favor for me bothered you that much then you should have just let Savanna answer my call."

"She was busy doing your research."

"There's no reason for you to intentionally be a pain in the ass, Baylor," Savanna said from across the lobby.

"Sure there is! Secrets can end up ruining a friendship."

"We are all allowed to have a certain amount of privacy. Just because we know that Sabastian went out to dinner last night with Ms. Kinsworth, doesn't mean he is obligated to give us a full report."

"I know.., I just wanted him to be honest, because…" Baylor took a very obvious inhalation of air through his nose as he leaned in close to his friend, "…we all have a pretty good idea that dinner wasn't the only thing that took place."

"You are assuming way too much, old friend. Just because I spent a nice evening at a restaurant with a beautiful woman, doesn't mean that any extracurricular activity took place afterward." Sabastian found it very hard to keep an authentic smile from generating on his face. Just because he had gotten lucky last night, and it had ranked as being the greatest evening in his relatively short life, it didn't mean that he was obligated to share all the details of his conquest with everyone in the room. "And for the record, I did oversleep."

"Well, I can all but guarantee that it was not because you ate or drank too much at dinner!"

Deciding it was best to not respond to his friend's implication; Sabastian took a moment, closed his eyes, and enjoyed that long-awaited first sip of his morning tea. He then asked, "So.., do I have to wait here all day or are you going to tell me who was on the other end of that call you answered for me?"

With his fun now seemingly gone, Baylor informed his friend that Jerrelle had called and wanted to know if a favor could be done for her. She had a fingerprint of someone and wanted to know whom it belonged to. Unfortunately, he had to let her know that he did not have access to the necessary equipment or the clearance that was needed in order to run a print through the AFIS database. Thankfully, before Baylor even contemplated breaking any laws in order to acquire what

Jerrelle was asking for, Savanna stepped in and made an inquiry with Captain Lutherage at the San Antonio Police Department. Surprisingly, he agreed to do what was being asked of him.

"I wonder why she wanted to know who owned that print."

"I don't know, but she said that the identity of the individual would probably confirm a suspicion."

"Suspicion? What suspicion?"

"I don't know. She didn't say."

The unknown now had Sabastian worried. Jerrelle did tell him after all that she had a few loose ends that she needed to tie up — he just hoped that it didn't involve her doing something that would either get her arrested or killed. "Thanks for taking that call for me, Baylor. I probably would have just handed her request over to you anyway."

"Yes.., but then you would have pestered her after that until she came clean and told you exactly why she wanted to know this person's identity. And knowing you as I do, you would have jumped on the next available flight to Detroit in order to back her up with whatever it is that she is doing."

Sabastian took another sip of his morning tea, while at the same time acknowledging that Baylor was one hundred percent correct in his assessment. In fact, there was a part of him that wanted to do just that. But Jerrelle was a big girl who was very capable of taking care of her own self. If she were in any kind of trouble, she would ask for help. He just had to trust that whatever she needed the information for; it would allow her to tie up those last few loose ends.

Once Baylor had left his office, Sabastian turned his attention to his computer so that he could work on the task at hand. Before Lizanne arrived, he wanted to have some news to give her — though he honestly was unsure if that would be possible

By the time he was done his morning tea, he was surprisingly able to eliminate one potential person from that list his team had compiled the night before. This Amy Amylia had hailed from New Jersey. Not only was the woman ninety-two years old, too old to be Lizanne's friend, but she just recently got married for the fifth time.

Deciding that he wanted to take a short break before he continued on with his research, Sabastian left his office and headed over to the kitchen nook to prepare another English tea. In the midst of him doing that, Savanna was able to eliminate another person from that list. Though this individual was only a year younger than Lizanne, this Amy Amylia had moved to Boston from New Zealand, two years ago in order to attend the Berkley College of Music. *'Maybe,'* Sabastian thought, *'we might actually be able to find the correct Amy before Lizanne arrives.'*

About fifteen minutes later, Savanna was able to eliminate a third person. Without a shadow of a doubt, this individual could not be the one that Lizanne was looking for, as she had formerly been known as Amile Amylia, just four years earlier before the completion of his/her reassignment surgery.

About halfway through his second cup of tea, Sabastian was able to cross off one more potential candidate. This person was in her mid-thirties and was ten years into a twenty-year prison sentence at Central California Woman's Correctional Facility for a string of armed bank robberies.

About ten minutes after that, Savanna was able to eliminate the fifth Amy. Although this one had family ties to the Chicago area, there was no way that she was the one that Lizanne had been searching for as this young girl had just celebrated her second birthday the other day.

That left one potential Amy Amylia to look into. Without jumping to any conclusions, Sabastian needed to be certain that this was the woman that Lizanne was searching for, so he joined Savanna at her desk and together they began their extensive research. What they found twenty minutes later, was all the proof that they needed. It was also heartbreaking.

He was all but certain that this person was Lizanne's friend, as she was the correct age and at one time, had lived in Chicago. Unfortunately, during their research, they stumble across a news article on the New York Times website. Written was the revelation that, just two weeks ago, a drunk driver had killed Amy. This was subsequently confirmed when they found her posted obituary.

Though there was no reason for it, Sabastian still felt like a failure. They had been a mere fourteen days too late. If Lizanne had only come to him earlier instead of going to those other private detectives, then they might have been able to find her in time. She would have then reached out to her old friend, and the events that had lead to Amy's death might not have occurred at all. But then again, who is to say that she would still be alive today. Lizanne's friend had died because she was supposed to die. And even if Sabastian had somehow found her long before now, fate probably would have intervened and her death would have occurred in some other manner.

Death is a part of life. It's also usually the hardest part to deal with. And although Sabastian barely knew Lizanne, he honestly didn't want the burden of being the bearer of bad news. But he knew that it was his responsibility to tell her what he had found; that her best friend from high school had died. "I'll be in my office, Savanna. Please let me know when Ms. Kinsworth gets here."

"Of course."

About ten minutes after Sabastian had sequestered himself, Madelyn arrived at the agency. Upon the moment she entered, she could sense that the aura was much different than it had been yesterday. Yes, Savanna had smiled and warmly greeted her, but it also felt as if Sabastian's secretary's words and mannerisms were somewhat contrived.

A few seconds after her arrival, Sabastian opened his office door and invited her to join him inside. Once she had, he asked her to take a seat in the chair that was directly in front of his desk. Instead of walking around to the other side, as she expected him to do, he claimed the seat that was right beside hers. He then said, "I have some news for you. I believe that I found Amy, but..."

As he had been since he first learned of Amy's fate, Sabastian's mind was searching for the right words to use. Unfortunately, he just could not find them; it meant that the news he was about to give her, more than likely was going to cause Lizanne's world to come crashing down. There simply was no easy way of doing this. Sabastian just had to get it over with and then be there for her afterward. "I've got some bad news pertaining to your friend. According to the information that we found, Amy died in a car accident two weeks ago."

'Is he kidding?' she thought. 'Did he actually find an Amy Amylia that was as old as I am and had lived in Chicago?' Madelyn was stunned — not by the news of this poor woman's unfortunate death, but that she had chosen a name out of thin air and there had actually been someone who had met the criteria that she had devised. *'This wasn't what I expected.'* Madelyn thought. *'Even so, I could still use this tragedy to my advantage. All that I have to do is make a slight adjustment to my original plan.'* After a few seconds of making it look as if she was trying to hold in her emotions, Madelyn said, "Can I please see the information that you found on Amy?"

Sabastian brought Lizanne around to the other side of his desk and showed her the New York Times online obituary. He then navigated to the article about Amy's death so that she could read it.

Though Madelyn had no idea who this woman was, she actually felt sorrow. Amy was the same age as her and it just didn't seem fair. Her life could have become memorable or it could have affected someone else's in an unimaginable way. Unfortunately, it had been cut short by an individual's own stupidity.

What she was doing wasn't right either. Although she wasn't yet as guilty as that drunk driver was, Madelyn had hastily accepted an unethical task. Upon its completion, it was probably going to haunt her for the rest of her life. Yes, there was still time to change her mind, but never before had she gone back on her word. Oddly enough, she was aware that she was now standing at a fork in the road. If she really wanted to, she could make a course correction before it was too late. She didn't know what she should do. She liked Sabastian — a lot.

After a few seconds of thought, Madelyn made her decision. She was certainly going to hurt inside because of it, but it was what she had to do — her word was her word and she knew that she had to keep it. So she reached out with her right hand toward Sabastian's computer screen, and in a symbolic-like false gesture, touched the accompanying image of Amy Amylia. Her former line of work, prostitution, called for her to be whoever her client wanted her to be. And because of that, Madelyn had become well adapted at role-playing.

She considered herself to be a pretty good actress, so she summoned up some fake tears. Sabastian saw this and immediately shifted himself closer to her for support. Right after he did this, Madelyn added another bit to her act by placing a pair of trembling hands over her face. A few seconds later, she laid her head and 'crying eyes' against the side of Sabastian's chest.

This is exactly what he had expected. Nevertheless, it hurt him to see her suffering through such emotional pain. Yet, he knew that for it to be dealt with, it first had to be released before he could step in and offer up his support and advice.

He didn't wish to come off as being rude or insensitive, but after the passing of a few minutes, Sabastian gently removed her head from his chest and then spoke softly in her ear; words that let her know he was going to leave her alone in his office for a while.

Roughly ten minutes later, and after assuming that Lizanne was probably all cried out, he returned with a fresh cup of sim-caf for her. "I'm so sorry, Lizanne, but you knew that this was a possibility."

"I know, but… I was hoping for better news."

"I know you were. I'm sorry."

"Thanks for the sim-caf, Sabastian, but I think that I am just going to go back to my hotel. I would like to be alone for a while." The real reason for this was because, while she was left alone in Sabastian's office, a pit started to grow in her stomach; it felt like she had somehow swallowed a bowling ball. Her conscience had awoken and had caused her to begin to hate herself because of what she agreed to do to Sabastian. She knew that it was wrong, but she just could not see there being any other viable option to take.

"Of course. Let me walk you out."

Lizanne got up out of his chair and headed into the lobby; Sabastian was right behind her. From there, he walked her out of the agency, accompanied her down the elevator, and then escorted her outside to an awaiting cab that Savanna had graciously called. Once Madelyn was inside the vehicle and on her way back to her hotel, Sabastian went back up to his agency.

When he re-entered his office, he sat down in his chair and was about to unknowingly drink Lizanne's untouched sim-caf when he heard a vid-cell ring. He knew that it wasn't his, because his ring tone wasn't the same song that was playing, 'A debt in my heart', by Boo Boo Magoo. *'That's a strange song for a ring tone,'* Sabastian thought. It then took him a moment to clue into the fact that the ringing vid-cell was inside of Lizanne's purse. She had forgotten it in his office.

Sabastian walked over to where it was, on the floor beside where she had first taken up a seat, picked it up, and contemplated. *'I shouldn't look in it. I mean.., doing so would essentially be the same as sneaking a peek in her lingerie drawer.'* But the phone kept on ringing and his curiosity was getting the better of him, so he opened it up and removed her vid-cell. Of course, as soon as he picked it up, it stopped ringing. His intent was to immediately place the device right back into her purse, but his eyes chose to stay locked onto the ID screen. *'Why in the hell does that number look familiar to me?'*

───────────── ◯◯ ─────────────

"It is the obvious which is so difficult to see most of the time. People say 'It's as plain as the nose on your face.' But how much of the nose on your face can you see, unless someone holds a mirror up to you?" (Quote from Isaac Asimov – I, Robot)

Sabastian took out a pen from his top desk drawer and copied down the number. After placing Lizanne's phone back into her purse and closing it up, he spent a few minutes trying to figure out whether or not he knew it. Easily, he could have just sat there and racked his brain over this mystery for the remainder of the day but instead, with the number in hand, left his office and went straight over to Baylor's desk. "Hey, um… Any chance you can spare a few minutes and confirm whom this belongs to?"

"I suppose."

Baylor took one look at the number and immediately knew whose it was; he then gazed up at his friend with an 'are you serious' look on his face. "I may come across as being, or even acting like an idiot sometimes, but intentionally trying to get me to waste my time by looking up a number that I already did, isn't at all funny."

Sabastian stood there, stunned at Baylor's response. Only after a few moments of awkward silence had passed did he then realize whom that number belonged to. He felt like a complete moron. "I… I meant… can you confirm which one it is?"

"That is his office number."

"Oh, ok. Thanks for your help."

"Uh-huh…" Baylor slightly shook his head and then went back to whatever it was that he had been working on.

While en route back to his office, Sabastian was literally kicking himself. Certain things should never be forgotten, especially things that were associated with the enemy. *'Does Lizanne know Louie Mazotti? Why did he just call her?'*

While sitting behind his desk, Sabastian let every possible scenario there was run through his mind: he was a business associate of hers, he was just a family friend, they were related, or she was working for him? Any of those was a distinct possibility.

Of course, the more he thought about it, the more confusion grew within his mind. This was probably why Sabastian was unable to come up with an acceptable explanation as to how she knew him. He certainly didn't want to believe it, but the only conclusion he could draw at the moment was that Lizanne was in cahoots with the enemy, even though not one ounce of proof was there to support that supposition.

Hoping to find some clarity, he reached across his desk and picked up his family portrait. For various reasons, anger was consuming him: his own stupidity, the freely giving of his inherent trust, being far more gullible than he ever thought he was. He almost felt like a brand new Fender Stratocaster that he willingly handed over to her, for which she then played with proficiency.

That was something that had never happened to Sabastian before — and it was something that he was adamant was never going to let happen to him again. So after a few minutes spent staring at his framed family photo and not miraculously finding any of the answers he'd hoped for, Sabastian set it back in its place and made a decision. He was going to approach his job, a private detective, the same way he did during his tenure in the military. From this moment forward, his male urges were going to be controlled and suppressed. He was going to be professional and never allow himself to become easily infatuated with another female client again — ever. No matter how smoking hot she was.

He spent a few minutes and gathered his thoughts. While doing this, he took what was Lizanne's untouched sim-caf and drank the entire thing in two gulps, hoping that it would help him to relax and think clearly. It didn't. In fact, an urge kept growing to just go straight on over to her hotel and confront her. However, he was smart enough not to submit to it, as the last thing he wanted to do was accuse her of something she might not be guilty of. The logical course of action for him to take was to just be patient and let this whole thing play itself out. In time, he would learn whether or not his initial thoughts were correct.

After diligently weighing all of his options and concluding that he still wasn't exactly sure what he should do next, Sabastian determined that it was best to just ignore everything for the moment and go do the one thing that usually alleviates his stress. He hadn't planned on going to the gym until later in the afternoon, but now seemed as good a time as any to work out. By doing this now, not only would he be able to take that much-needed shower afterward, some time spent focusing on something other than the confusion residing within his mind might be all that it takes for that to start sorting itself out.

He left his office with his intent to not speak with anyone as he exited, but Baylor ended up stopping him right as he got to Savanna's desk. "Hey, Sab! I just got the results back from Captain Lutherage on the digital fingerprint that Jerrelle sent. Should I call her or do you want to?"

Sabastian paused, turned, faced his old friend, and tried his best to focus on the moment. He was curious as to why she wanted to put a name to the print, so he told Baylor that he would call her back.

After taking the results from his friend, he went back into his office. Before he made his call though, Sabastian took a moment and looked them over. He had never before heard of the name that was associated with the print — but after reviewing all of the other information that Captain Lutherage had kindly provided, he now understood why Jerrelle had wanted an answer.

After reclaiming his chair, he picked up his vid-phone and called his friend; now even more interested as to what she was up to. "Hey, Jerrelle! I've got what you asked Baylor for."

"Great! Who does the print belong to?"

"It belongs to a man named Zhin Wi."

"I've never heard of him." Jerrelle took a moment and asked her sister if she knew of him; Bai Lin shook her head. "And my sister has never heard of him either."

"Your sister? Is she with you in Detroit?"

"Yup!"

This revelation was a welcome bit of relief; it also gave Sabastian one less thing to worry about. With Bai Lin being close by, he knew that Jerrelle's back would be covered when it came to whatever it was that she was doing — it also meant that there was no need for him to get to the Motor City any sooner than he had originally planned. "Well.., I'm surprised that she has never heard of this Zhin Wi before because, according to the information that Captain Lutherage has provided, the man is a confirmed member of the Detroit Underworld Organization."

"The D.U.O.? Why would my sister know that?"

"He is a Chinese citizen. I would have thought that the Liberation would be aware of any of the D.U.C.'s associates with overseas ties."

"Normally, yes," Bai Lin said, who had been listening in on her sister's conversation, "but I've never heard that name before." Jerrelle then said, "Anyway.., thanks for the info there, Sab."

Sabastian wasn't about to let his old friend hang up on him without an explanation as to why it appeared to him that she was investigating the D.U.O., so he blatantly asked. "Why are you pursuing the enemy without me?"

"I'm not! Bai Lin and I just happened to coincidently see Helfred's brother, Nicoli, here in Michigan. We thought it was strange. He was with that Zhin Wi guy, bringing two large bags of something into an old abandoned store. But um…"

"But what?"

Jerrelle paused for a moment, as she finally understood the connection. "It all makes sense now; Jason Hernandez, his death, and the attempt on my life. Seeing Nicoli with a member of the D.U.O. must mean that he has officially renounced his affiliation to the Liberation and joined up with them."

"So much for thinking the Detroit Underworld Organization was now weak and vulnerable. With Zhin Wi and Helfred's brother now in the mix, and the S.M.A.R.T. technology undoubtedly at their disposal, this now makes them even more dangerous than they were before."

107

"I hate to admit it, but I think you are right," Bai Lin said.

Sabastian paused for a moment to gather his thoughts. *'What is Louie up to? Is he after both Jerrelle and I, or is there more to this than what it appears to be?'* Apparently, he now had two problems that he had to deal with.

Satisfying his suspicions pertaining to Lizanne and her connection to Louie Mazotti no longer seemed to be that important — though that didn't mean he was going to ignore it either. If she was associated with him, she was probably only a small part of whatever plan the man had devised. What that was though, Sabastian could only guess. If he were a betting man, there would be no doubt in his mind that his elimination was the endgame. He also had to agree with Jerrelle's assumption. Nicoli was probably convinced that she was responsible for his brother's death. And somehow, Louie had learned about this and used the man's animosity in order to recruit him into the fold. Whether or not that was the case, Sabastian's objective wasn't going to change. "Now that we know all of this, I can only assume that the enemy is up to something big. I have a small issue here that I have to make sure does not become a bigger problem than what I fear it may be. Once I do that, I am going to fly to Detroit and meet up with you. Promise me that you will not do anything until I get there on Friday."

"Are you serious? You expect me to sit on the sidelines for the next two days, knowing that Nicoli is here and is looking to kill me?"

"Yes! I don't care if you watch and observe him, but don't engage the enemy until I get there."

As much as this was going to gnaw away at Jerrelle to basically do nothing for the next forty-eight hours, she knew that she had to comply with Sabastian's request. This was still his mission and he had to call the shots. "Ok. I'll see you on Friday."

After returning his empty coffee cup to the kitchen nook, Sabastian left the agency for the gym. Although he surprisingly wasn't as aggravated as he had been only a few moments ago, there was still enough within him that needed to be divested. Besides, he was finally beginning to notice the lingering smell of his previous night's escapade and he now desperately wanted to remove any evidence of it before anyone, especially Baylor, decided to question what that was.

4

*~ Sometimes there are things that can never be explained;
things that even the greatest minds of ours, and of past generations,
have unsuccessfully tried to answer and thus are forced to concede
defeat. Likewise, there are moments in life when something
unexpected occurs and unfortunately, we are obliged to accept the
ramifications that come as a result. When this takes place, we at least
hope to be able to understand some of what has happened.
Subsequently, we can either brush it off as being something of little
consequence, or we can mentally beat ourselves up over it until we end
up paying an unnecessary price. Of course, trying to figure out how
we let all of this happen in the first place is simply a waste of time
because logic dictates that anything unforeseen can never be predicted
or even prevented ~*

It's a given that at some point in your life you will find
yourself in a position in which the best course of action to take is to
just walk away: from a job, a relationship, a temptation, or an
unwanted situation. Yet there are times when, as much as you want to
distance yourself from whatever it is that you are immersed in, you just
have no choice but to suck it up and stay.

Since his return to Detroit, Louie has had to deal with
restarting the organization that he loves being a part of, accepting the
wishes of the mother of his uninformed son, and dealing with a
reoccurring nightmare from his past. The stresses of those first two
issues were something that Louie knew he could deal with, but those
damn unwanted appearances by Maxwell have seriously begun to mess
with his sanity.

Seeking out the demon doctor wasn't a mistake. What was,
was Louie's refusal to accept the man's denying of his request. He
was very lucky to have walked away after issuing his threat. Had it not
been for Nicoli, Cain's wolf would probably still be gnawing away on
his bones.

Experiencing what he had might have deterred anyone else from ever trying anything like that again, but not Louie. He was bound and determined to find a way to prevent his nemesis from making another appearance. There had to be some way to stop his nemesis from ever visiting him again.

The one thing Louie was certain of was that his mind was not causing his 'problem'. It was stable and strong. However, if the madness didn't soon come to an end, his near future more than likely consisted of death by his own hands, or three meals a day and a padded room.

Unfortunately, he did not have any free time on his hands to explore any other unconventional option. Business came first and right now, his two associates were patiently sitting on the opposite side of his desk and waiting for him to begin. Before he addressed them though, Louie decided to let the room stay quiet for a few more minutes. Sometimes, that is all it takes for uncertainty to build. And when that occurs, those under one's command tend to find themselves unsuspectingly walking on eggshells. His men hadn't done anything to deserve the silent treatment, but Louie just wasn't in any hurry this morning to get his meeting started. What he wanted to do instead was enjoy his vices, so he just sat there deadpanned and took a few puffs of his clove cigarette. In between that, he savored every sip of his sim-caf.

Right after taking the last possible puff, Louie said, "Well, I hope you two didn't have any plans for today because there is a lot of work to be done. Our 'shipping clerk' has informed me that we will be able to deliver the League's order on Friday. This now gives us two whole days to find ourselves another client."

"Would it not make sense to wait and make sure that this transaction goes down smoothly first? I mean.., there were some unexpected developments shortly after the last two orders of weapons were delivered."

Before he addressed Zhin's concerns, Louie finished off the remainder of his sim-caf. "It would. But to thrive in business, you can't let a few bumps in the road become the reason why forward progress is halted. As the old saying goes, he who hesitates gets left behind."

"True. But I would suggest that we not sail out any farther than the distance we can swim back."

"We are nowhere close to being stranded on a sinking ship with no land in sight, Nicoli. Therefore, I would like for you and Zhin to do as I have asked. We have an ample supply of street and hunting weapons that are taking up space in our storage facilities; I'd like to get rid of them as soon as possible. If there is indeed a leak along the chain somewhere that is allowing the government to find and confiscate our weapon shipments, then I want to at least try and get rid of all of the other merchandise that Antonio had stockpiled."

That, Zhin and Nicoli could understand. This was Louie's organization now, and getting rid of any residual ties to the previous regime certainly made sense.

"Take that prospective client list we made the other day and try again to get them to agree to do business with us. Or at least, try and get them to agree to not shut the door completely."

"Ok, but... I honestly don't think that any of them will reconsider their decision."

"Sometimes, people just need to sleep on it. Besides, we now have another card to play. The fact that the League has agreed to do business with us, might be all the incentive someone needs in order to change their mind."

"Ok," Zhin said. "Should we not try and contact the C.R.A.P.? Are they not a longstanding client of ours?"

"They were. But after what had happened in Germany, I think that it's best to just leave that sleeping giant alone."

"Fair enough. Nicoli and I will go back to my office and..." An unexpected knock on Louie's door caused Zhin to pause his words; he got up from his chair and went to answer it.

Standing on the other side of the threshold was the hotel courier; he had a small package in his hand — and he looked nervous. "I'm sorry for the interruption, Mr. Mazotti. I know that I'm not supposed to be up here, but Ms. Yale gave me access because she thought that what I have here might be important. I know that our policy is for all your mail to be left at the front desk, but this small package just arrived and it was marked 'URGENT'."

"Thank you... Um? I'm sorry... I don't know your name?"

"It's Lance Lathrup, sir."

"Thank you, Lance. And you don't have to apologize for doing your job. I'm not Mr. Marcone, nor am I a suspicious fool like he was. So long as Ms. Yale first deems whatever arrives here as being important, you will be welcomed to deliver it up here to me."

"Thank you, sir." After allowing a wave of calmness to wash away the nerves he had, he walked into the office and handed the package to Louie. Lance then smiled and left. Zhin and Nicoli did the same so that they could commence with their assignment.

Now alone with his thoughts, he took an inquisitive look at the unexpected delivery. No postmark or return address was on the box — which only enhanced his curiosity. Strangely, no reservations were there. Neither was the thought that any sort of danger might lie within. Louie just opened it up, looked inside, and then stared blankly at the package's contents.

Lying there, rolled up in tissue paper, was a small item. When he removed the wrapped up trinket he noticed that it had been laying on top of a Tarot card, the Dark Lord of Hades. from the mystic deck — otherwise known as the card of death. Curiosity immediately enveloped him, as he was unsure if this was a joke or not.

For a moment, Louie thought that maybe Maxwell had now found another way to fuck with him, but common sense was what had allowed him to look at this disconcerting thing in a more pragmatic way. The D.U.O. had admittedly made many enemies over the years and quite possibly, one of them decided that now was a good time to 'poke the bear' because the organization was clearly nowhere near solidly back on its foundation.

Deciding it was best to see what else was in the package before he drew his conclusion, Louie unwrapped the item sitting in his hand. Upon its revelation, he knew immediately what it was — a miniature statuette of 'Eternal Silence', otherwise known as the 'Statue of Death'. No more clues were needed. He now unreservedly believed that someone had just issued him a threat.

He was about to pick up his vid-phone and call Zhin and Nicoli back into his office in order to have them investigate the source of this unsettling package when he noticed that there was one more item still inside. There, lying flat on the bottom of the box was a piece of old parchment. He removed it, opened it, and handwritten in Italian was a brief letter.

"Abbiamo emesso un avviso, ma è stato ignorato. Pertanto, una punizione deve essere emessa in risposta ai peccati commessi. Tuttavia, ciò non sarà fatto da chi attende pazientemente di accogliere quelli come noi nel suo dominio.

Fino al momento in cui ciò accada, custodire ciò che resta. Quando alla fine viene portato via, capisci che la storia scritta non diventerà un'eredità, ma solo un ricordo che merita di essere dimenticato.

Il Partito Comunista Rivoluzionario"

Which when translated to English, it said.

"We issued a warning, yet it was ignored. Therefore, a punishment must be handed out in response to the committed sins. It, however, will not be done so by the one who is patiently waiting to welcome those like us into his domain.

Until the time comes for that to take place, cherish what is left. When it is finally taken away, understand that the written history will not become a legacy, but instead, only a memory worth forgetting.

The Communist Revolutionary Assembly Party"

This is not what Louie needed right now. He had enough things to deal with, let alone an apparent proclamation from the most feared underground organization in the world. No way in hell was he ready to go to war with a radical political group as large as them.

Though he had no way of knowing, Louie had to assume the worst. The C.R.A.P. was known to issue a death warrant on anyone who screwed them over. His only hope, he feared, was to get on his knees, eat a whole lot of crow, and try his damndest to smooth things over — which would be impossible if they were aware that he was the one responsible for ending the life of Vladi Chemzot.

Though it hadn't even passed the hour he normally reserved for breakfast, Louie needed a drink before he did what he really didn't want to do. After pouring himself two fingers of Walker's Club, straight up, he pounded it back, wiped his mouth, and turned to head back to his desk. Before he could take that first step though, he changed his mind, turned back around and poured some more. This time, he emptied what had been left in the bottle.

He didn't slam the three-plus ounces of it down there; he took it back with him to his desk. After claiming his chair, he took five minutes, polished off his drink, gathered himself as best as he could, turned on his vid-phone, and hoped for results that probably weren't going to come.

———————————————————— ◯◯ ————————————————————

Sabastian found it hard to stay focused on his reason for being at the gym. Thirty minutes into his workout, he quit. He just couldn't seem to find a way to dismiss the uncertainty that followed him from his agency. For some reason, his mind decided to create a bunch of unsubstantiated facts that in turn, caused undeserved animosity to appear.

What he felt certain of was that his emotions had been intentionally played with. And even though the temptation to go to Lizanne's hotel and confront her, still lingered, Sabastian resisted. He wasn't a heartless prick. In order for him to figure out what was what, he had to be patient and take things one step at a time. In no way shape or form could he give any indication that his opinion of her had changed.

At first, he was just going to leave the gym and go straight back to work, but doing so now would be counterproductive. Before he did anything else, he had to be clearheaded. For that to happen, Sabastian had to find a way to free his thoughts, so he decided to go and sit in the sauna for a while. Doing this, he hoped would in turn, bring forth the results he had sought by coming to the gym in the first place.

Was he being played? Was the Detroit Underworld Organization actually responsible for the perpetual thefts of the Union Military's weapons? Is Louie actually trying to eliminate both he and Jerrelle? What other illegal things was the man up to that needed to be stopped before it was too late? With all of those unknowns existing somewhere within his cluttered brain, Sabastian was honestly surprised that he didn't have a permanent migraine.

Thankful that no one else was inside the sauna, he tucked himself into the far corner and closed his eyes. After choosing what meditation technique he wanted to use, he began the process of clearing his mind. In a matter of minutes, he was able to find that tranquil space within his own psyche. Serenity; it had been a long time since Sabastian had been able to find some. Once he was able to sort through it all, he'd push all the amalgamated bullshit to the side so that he would then be able to separate what was important from his wants.

"Hello, my son."

Keeping his eyes closed, Sabastian chose to ignore the voice that had disturbed his psychosomatic Eden. He was immersed in a peaceful state and that was where he wanted to stay. Unfortunately, this person that had decided to join him in the sauna chose not to respect his wishes.

"Are you sleeping?"

Somewhat perturbed, Sabastian opened up his eyes and looked at the man sitting kitty-corner from him. Strangely, the man wasn't in a towel. In fact, he was still fully clothed. "Can I help...? Dad?"

"Yes, son.., it's me. I must say that you have grown into a fine young man."

This could not be possible. There was no way that his father, his deceased father, was now in the same room as he. "This can't be real! You're..."

"Dead! I know."

"How?   This is impossible!"

"Said who?"

"I don't know? It just is!"

"I see. So then.., am I to assume that you have all of the answers to everything?"

"Trust me.., I do not."

"And that is why I am here."

Sabastian has always had an open mind — and that is what had allowed him to accept the possibility that he was the long lost son of Maxwell Banks. Now, he had to open it up again and believe that the man sitting right across from him is his birth father. Somehow, someway, the man had come back from the dead.

Maxwell left his spot in the sauna and made his way across to the other side where he then took up a seat next to his son. What he wanted to do at that moment was hug Sabastian, but this appearance was taking place while his son was in a state of respite. If he were to embrace him now, it just wouldn't be the same as a real one. Besides, Maxwell had yet to figure out if the Apollo's Stone would even allow that sort of thing to occur.

He had been content to hold off his visit until a much later date, but he felt that his son needed him now. In his mind, this didn't technically count against his allotted visit because he hadn't actually made an appearance in the land of the living. Chances were though that Nefieti wouldn't see it that way. So, in case his pending argument fell on deaf ears, Maxwell needed to be certain that his appearance left an everlasting and profound impression on his son.

This was a little strange for Sabastian. He was never very religious or believed in ghosts or spirits, but when he was on his journey to find out who he truly was, he had to admit to himself that something unknown had been there by his side, a mysterious co-pilot perhaps, guiding him to where his destined path was to begin. It was impossible for him to know for sure without asking, but he now wanted to believe that it had been his father. "I... I don't know what to say?"

"You don't have to say anything." Maxwell wasn't sure if everything should be explained or not. It wasn't that he didn't believe that his son could handle the truth, he was just afraid that divulging too much might result in the privilege that he and his wife had been given to be able to keep watch over Sabastian, being taken away. Therefore, for maybe the first time ever, Maxwell chose his words carefully. "I am aware of what now lies ahead of you. And it is going to be a challenge that I am certain you will be able to confidently face and conquer. However, if you continue to allow unimportant and irrelevant things to worry you, then what is to come is going to result in you not fulfilling your destiny.

"And what is my destiny?"

"You found out all on your own who you were. That is what placed you firmly onto the path you were born to walk. Everything that you have been doing since then is exactly what you should have done. Your friends, those who love and care for you, and even your heart, will help guide you along the way.., so long as you don't allow your thoughts to get distracted by things that can cause you to lose your focus."

"I thought I knew what I was supposed to do, but... now I am not so sure. Everything has changed within the last twenty-four hours."

"You were thrown a hundred-mile-an-hour fastball instead of a changeup. It's understandable that you missed it."

Sabastian was a bit unsure if he understood the meaning behind that analogy. Even so, he was fairly certain that his dead father was already aware of Lizanne. "What exactly do you mean?"

"You know what I mean... the beautiful woman who will not escape your thoughts; the one that has unexpectedly taken possession of your heart."

"She... Lizanne doesn't have my heart. She just played me."

"You don't know that for sure. Don't judge her so quickly, as there is still a lot to be revealed. In time, it will be." Maxwell had to stop himself at that point, as he almost started to divulge some information that Sabastian needed to find out all on his own. So after a moment taken in order to gather his thoughts, he continued. "Like the old saying goes... You can't see the forest for the trees."

Sabastian hated idioms. "Can I trust her?"

"You'll have to figure that out for yourself."

"What about Louie Mazotti? Is he gonna kill me?"

"Only if you let him, he will. Trust your gut, listen to your friends, allow them to help, and you will succeed."

Sabastian sat there quiet for a moment. Every single possible emotion that there was, was consuming him. This was the first time that he had seen his father in the flesh. Well, not actually, but it was the closest he knew at that moment that he would ever get to that actually happening — and he so desperately wanted to reach around and give him a hug, just like Sydney would do to him. But Sabastian sensed that that would not be possible. Not just because his father was dead and had come to him in spirit, but because he would have done so already if he could.

It wasn't much of a consolation. Nevertheless Sabastian looked into his father's loving eyes and asked a question for which the answer he hoped to hear would then provide him with almost as much emotional fulfillment as any hug would, "Is Mom with you?"

"Yes, she is, my son. You are the apple of her eye. She is so proud of you. She and I both love you very, very much. We always have and we always will. And we will always keep watch over you." It was a promise he was unsure he could keep, but unless he was going to be allowed to hang onto the Apollo's Stone for all eternity, the belief that he forever was going to keep watch over his boy would have to be enough.

All that he had ever wanted to hear was that his parents loved him. And now that he knew it, his emotions let loose. Tears began to stream down his face. He had never in his wildest dreams thought that he would see any of his parents. And now, there was so much of his life that he wanted to share. But at least, he could take solace in the fact that both of them will forever be keeping tabs on his life. "I love you, dad. I just... I..."

"I know, son. But I must go now so that you can finish what I long ago, started."

"Am I ever going to get to see Mom?"

"If a time ever comes when you are in need of her, she will appear."

Before Sabastian could say anything else, his father lovingly smiled then evaporated into the mist that filled the sauna.

When he opened up his eyes, Sabastian realized that he was still alone — for that, he was glad because his face was flush and there were still a few residual tears. And although what had just happened to him was probably not real, anything was possible. Case in point, the dream he recently had where he had seen all of his military brethren dead, definitely had a real message in it. For that reason alone, Sabastian could not dismiss what he had just experienced. It could have simply been a result of his mind's imagination, influenced by his own desire to see his father — but then again, it could have just been created because of all the stress and uncertainty that he was going through.

From the first moment Sabastian had found out whom he was, he wished for this day to happen. And now, it essentially had. Though proof that his father had actually just visited him in the sauna was highly unlikely, he at least now felt a bit of sureness that he had not been alone since he embarked on this crazy journey.

Before he exited the sauna, Sabastian made sure that the remnants of his tears were completely gone and that his towel was securely around his waist. Straight to the showers he went — finally. Afterward, he got dressed and left the gym.

Since he was now in a much better frame of mind, Sabastian concluded that it would be okay for him to head on over to Lizanne's hotel — but not before he first made a quick stop at his agency to pick up her purse. He could just wait and give it to her tomorrow, but bringing it to her now would help him when it came to portraying the image of a concerned and thoughtful friend.

Less than a block away from the gym, his father's words of wisdom repeated in his head. Too many trees indeed were in the way for him to know exactly what was beyond them. Therefore, he was going to keep to himself what he so far knew, along with what conclusions he had already drawn, and give her the benefit of the doubt. If he did not do that, then he might end up unintentionally saying or doing something unbecoming of a gentleman — or something that will all but ruin what chance there may still be for Sabastian to move beyond being just mere acquaintances with Lizanne.

If he hadn't shown up at her hotel when he had, he would have missed her because as he was entering the building, he saw Lizanne standing at the reception desk and checking out. Casually, he walked over to her and said her name; that caused her to become slightly startled.

The instant their eyes met, Sabastian thought that he had seen some dishonesty within them. At the same time, he also saw some confliction. It's a good thing that his better judgment stepped in long before he walked on through the front door of the Pershing Suites, as he more than likely would have unfairly confronted her. "Are you okay, Lizanne?" Sabastian hoped his question sounded sincere. "I didn't think that you would be leaving already. I assumed that you would be here 'till at least tomorrow morning."

Madelyn looked at Sabastian and smiled. Inside, she was really happy to see him — but her thoughts were so confusing. Leaving San Antonio was what she was supposed to do, hoping that he would follow her. That was why she had left her purse behind at his agency so that he would come to her hotel to return it. But when he didn't show up with it right away, she didn't know what to do — she hadn't worked that possibility into her plan.

After an hour had gone by, she decided to just check out of her hotel. She was then going to go back to the agency and apologize for leaving her purse behind. At that point, she was going to feign an emotional breakdown and hope that Sabastian would be a gentleman and at least bring her to the airport. Once there, she was going to do her best to convince him to go back to Chicago with her. Thankfully, she didn't have to do that now.

Sabastian handed Lizanne her purse and conjured up a smiled. "You left this in my office. I would have brought it by earlier, but I couldn't get away until now."

When her hand touched his, her emotions took over — and they were doing their best to make her ignore her obligation. More than anything, what she wanted to do was take him right back up to her hotel room and make love to him again. Never before had she met anyone like Sabastian — and it killed her that she was obligated to mess with his heart. "Oh my god!" she said with as much authenticity in her words as she could. "How stupid am I? I almost left San Antonio without it."

"I'm sure you would have realized that you didn't have it with you when you went to pay for your hotel room."

"No, I wouldn't have. I gave them my credit card number when I checked in because I didn't know exactly how long I was going to be here."

"Sabastian walked up closer to her and gently placed his hand on her back. Instantly, the emotions that consumed him last night had returned; emotions that trumped over those other unsure thoughts that he had about her. His father was right. He needed to wait until he had all the facts. And that was what he was going to do; find out the truth before she left. "Are you renting a car or taking the bus to Corpus Christi?"

"What?"

"You said that you have a photo shoot there this weekend."

Madelyn felt so stupid. She completely forgot that that was part of her lie. She hoped that her 'blonde moment' didn't give Sabastian any reason to suspect that he was being played. "I, uh... I canceled it. After learning about what happened to Amy, I just couldn't see myself working this weekend."

"I can understand that. Are you going home then?"

"Yes."

"When is your flight?"

"I don't have one yet. I was just going to go to the airport and hope to get on the standby list. If that wasn't possible, I was going to just wait around there until I could get on the next available flight to Chicago."

Sabastian looked over at the hotel clerk and asked her if it was possible to pay for another night on Lizanne's room. After the woman confirmed that the room was still available, he pulled out the agency's credit card and paid for another night. "Let me take your bags back up to your room. When I return, we'll go for another walk and then I will take you out to dinner. I will also call Savanna and have her book us both on the first available flight tomorrow."

Madelyn didn't know if she should be happy or not. She admittedly was overjoyed that she was going to get to spend some more time with Sabastian. His volunteering to go with her to Chicago however was unexpected. She honestly thought that it was going to take a lot of coaxing on her part to get him to go with her. Oddly, his revelation caused her to start questioning whether or not what she was supposed to do, was what she should still do. She felt almost as conflicted as she did just before she left home at eighteen to take on the real world. "You don't have to come with me. I am fine. I knew there might be a chance that Amy could be dead. I've accepted it now and I will survive." Madelyn really hated having to continue on with her lies, but she had made an agreement. Never before had she, nor was she ever going to go back on her word — even though her conscience was telling her to.

"I know… but I still want to make sure that you will be all right. Besides, I have a close friend in Detroit that I haven't seen in forever. Chicago is not that far away from there, so I can go and visit them afterward." That wasn't exactly a lie; it was more so an exaggeration of the truth.

Though not always, most difficult decisions do come with some sort of consequence. Usually, a price is paid without having any second thoughts because the cost ends up being rather nominal. For Madelyn, the deal that she had struck with Louie was now one that she had wished she had first taken the time to think through instead of allowing her desire for retribution to be the foundation for her decision. The agreement, she now unequivocally believed, was going to end up costing her way more than just a broken heart.

Patiently, she waited in the lobby as Sabastian had asked. He then did what any gentleman would do; he took her bags back up to her hotel room. However, his reason for doing this wasn't so genuine. In order for any of his doubts to be satisfied, he had to act like a private investigator. And as luck would have it, an opportunity had presented itself that he just had to take advantage of.

Honestly, he did not want to do this, but he felt there was no other alternative. If he were a cold-hearted bastard like Louie, he'd simply accuse her of siding with the enemy. Instead, he decided to use a technology that has been around since the mid-twentieth century and hoped that it would provide him with some more insight or pertinent information before they left San Antonio.

After setting Lizanne's bags down on the bed, Sabastian took a moment and looked around the room — it didn't take him long to find the perfect place to plant a bug. Once he was sure it was concealed well enough that even the maid wouldn't discover it, Sabastian went back down to the lobby.

As he expected, upon his exit from the elevator, Lizanne greeted him with a smile. The pessimistic part of him did not for one minute believe that it was genuine. Nevertheless, he had to keep playing along and act as if it was real, so he produced one of his own, offered her the crook of his elbow, and the two of them headed out the front entrance of the hotel.

Throughout the evening, Sabastian did everything that he could to get to know who Lizanne was as an individual. He didn't pry too much; even though some of the questions he asked were rather personal — he hoped that she didn't feel as if he was being overly intrusive. Patience; it was what he had to continuously remind himself to have. Unfortunately, as the end of their evening neared, no clarity whatsoever was obtained, as Lizanne had been very careful with every single reply she gave and every bit of information she divulged.

Just over two hours after they had left the hotel, they returned. Outside of the threshold to her room, they spent a few minutes kissing each other. It's true that resistance can sometimes be futile. Sabastian just wanted to pick her up, carry her inside, and continue on where they left off last night — but logic did what it was supposed to do; it took over and allowed him to realize that sleeping with Lizanne again would not be the smartest thing for him to do. So he reluctantly said, "As much as I would love to be in your company for the remainder of this day, I can't. I've spent too much time already out of the office and I have a lot of things to catch up on," he lied, "and too many things to just ignore if I am going to be away for a few days."

"I understand." Madelyn leaned in closer, wrapped her arms around him, and just laid her head upon his chest. Even though she hated what she soon would have to do, she spent a few minutes absorbing his warmth, feeling his tenderness, bonding to his heart, and connecting to his soul. Sabastian was a special man and she had to find a way out of her predicament. She didn't want to lose any chance that she might still have left to find a permanent way into his life, even if it killed her in the process.

They both looked at each other, content to just stay in that moment. It was difficult for them, but they both knew that tonight had to come to an end. So reluctantly, they released each other and stood there in a manner that felt, and probably looked awkward.

Before she had a chance to convince him to stay, Sabastian looked deep into Lizanne's beautiful eyes and said, "I have to go. As soon as I know what time our flight is tomorrow I will call you. If Savanna has been unable to book us one, I will let you know first thing in the morning. We'll then figure out some other way to get to Chicago."

"Ok." Madelyn leaned forward and again kissed Sabastian, not passionately, but she gently touched his lips with hers. After producing a genuine smile, she opened up her hotel room door and stepped in. She fully expected for him to stay standing right where he was; conflicted about leaving. But that wasn't the case, as his back was quickly turned to her wherein he then headed toward the elevator.

She stood there for a moment, baffled. Men just don't usually give up that easily. She thought about calling out to him, but her womanly desires did not outweigh what was a necessity. Tonight, she had to be alone: with her own thoughts, her knowledge of what was to come, and her wishes that she all but believed were never going to come true.

Right after Sabastian disappeared into the elevator, she closed the door to her room. From there, she headed straight to the bathroom. She needed to relax and the only way she knew how to do that was to soak in a bubble bath. *'Why did you have to walk into my life? I never thought that I would ever find true love. And now, because of you, I know that even someone like me deserves to live happily ever after.'* Madelyn sunk down as far as she could into the bubbles and stared up into the plain white hotel ceiling. A tear trickled down her cheek, as she knew that by the end of tomorrow, she was going to have to give up what her heart was telling her she wanted more than anything else. *'I don't want to hurt you, but I really don't have any other choice. I just don't know what to do?'*

Aimlessly, she looked at the surrounding bare walls, trying to find an anomaly that would be interesting enough to focus her thoughts on. The last thing she wanted to do today was sit, wait, and do absolutely nothing all day long in her apartment. To have the knowledge that Nicoli was in her city, apparently working for the enemy, and had intentions to kill her, was all the motivation that Jerrelle needed to go out and do something about it. But Sabastian was her friend and he had asked her to do nothing until he got to Detroit. It wasn't that unreasonable of a request on his part, even though she had contemplated ignoring it. Then again, Nicoli wasn't some regular asshole that just needed to be taught a lesson; he was a dangerous man who was easily capable of killing her. Jumping out of a plane without a parachute would be knowingly allowing your death to occur. Going after Helfred's brother without the right amount of trusted back-up was in essence, the same thing. For that reason, Jerrelle just had to hold off on getting her revenge against Nicoli for the attempt on her life until sometime after Friday.

Bai Lin, however, was free to explore the city — her indisputable argument was that no one else associated with the D.U.O. knew who she was, so there was very little risk of any attention being brought to her. If she just happened to accidentally bump into Nicoli, she would simply act oblivious to the facts she now knew and pretend that her relationship with the man had not changed. It's not like the two of them had never crossed paths before in another country. If she were to sense any sort of hostility in him, she would promptly take the necessary steps in order to carefully remove herself from the situation. However, if Nicoli didn't believe in mere coincidences and decided to follow Bai Lin back to Jerrelle's apartment, he would then find out firsthand just how stupid of a mistake he made by choosing to become an enemy of theirs.

Just after breakfast and after repeatedly playing the same card 'she-knew-every-nuance-of-the-city-and-that-she-might-need-backup' until her sister finally gave in, they headed toward the same area that the New Book Cadillac Hotel and Casino was located. Bai Lin had no intention whatsoever of going anywhere near the place. What she planned on doing instead, was just hang out a few doors down and outside on the patio at the District Bar & Grill; a place that was on the same side of the street and two buildings south of the Old World Café & Restaurant. Nicoli and Zhin Wi were their main targets. That didn't mean though that those who worked for the hotel or casino would be left alone. Anyone who just happened to be in their uniform and walked into the 'Café' or the 'District' was fair game. After all, there wasn't a better place in the world to discuss work or complain about it than in a bar or restaurant.

Usually, Jerrelle would be ok with gathering Intel from unwitting sources. Not today though. For some unknown reason, she left what little patience she sometimes had at home. Had she been the one to come up with their plan of action, she would have suggested that they do something that was clearly unwise — like walk right on through the front door of the hotel. She knew that in all likelihood, she was barred from ever stepping foot anywhere near the place because of her successful night of gambling from not so long ago at the adjoining casino. But unlike her ability to count cards, she couldn't count on the chances of her simply being asked to leave the premises. The pessimistic side of her all but believed she would be confronted by a posse, either on or off the property and then sent a message in retaliation for her 'dishonest' card playing.

Her sister could have joined her on the patio of the restaurant, but Bai Lin felt it was best that Jerrelle act as her lookout. That way, a heads-up could be given if either Zhin or Nicoli made an appearance in the area.

This part of the city, at this time of the day, it wasn't all that easy to find a parking spot close to wherever it was that you wanted to go. Luckily, Jerrelle was able to park her Camero right across the street from the District Bar & Grill. The only thing that sucked was that the mid-afternoon sun was piercing through her windshield.

Sitting in her car alone wasn't at all foreign to her. Many times in the past, Jerrelle had to do this while waiting for her mark to show up. For some strange reason though, today she was experiencing some anxiety. Usually, that only happened when she had to appear in court. Why that was happening now, she had not a clue. After all, her only real responsibility was to keep an eye on her sister and back her up if necessary.

Maybe, her fretfulness was being caused by something else — like her foolishly leaving her honor blade at home. At least, if she needed a weapon, the Camero's glove box contained a retractable staff. Then again, it could be the fact that there were a lot of people who frequented this area who also had issues with her. Yes, this part of the city was considered to be one of the safest, but the thought of being ambushed just wouldn't leave her — after all, she and Bai Lin did just beat the living shit out of Gino and his boys.

She took a comprehensive look at her entire surroundings. Feeling content that there was currently no potential danger nearby, and knowing that she had to pull herself together, Jerrelle closed her eyes and tried to focus her thoughts on something positive. Unexpectedly, a curiosity was able to find its way to the forefront of her thoughts. *'What exactly was it that Nicoli and that Zhin Wi guy were doing across from The Cough Inn yesterday? And what in the hell was each of them carrying in those large bags as they entered the building?'*

She thought about her promise to Sabastian. No, she wasn't going to break it, but she also wanted to satisfy her sudden suspicion, so she made a somewhat imprudent decision. In her mind, what she now wanted to do would actually be considered 'recon' and would fall into the category of 'observation' — which was exactly what her friend had told her was the only thing that she could do until he got there. So Jerrelle called her sister and informed her of her intentions.

Fully expecting that Bai Lin was going to object to what she wanted to do, Jerrelle was surprised when her sister not only thought that it was a good idea but did not insist on going with her. Her reason was simple — the mission parameter for this day was to just gather Intel, not kidnap someone and interrogate them. There was no reason for her to leave her spot. It was perfect and she would be fine all on her own. She also trusted that Jerrelle would do what she said she was going to do; gather information only and not stick her nose where it didn't belong.

Fifteen minutes later, Jerrelle was in Dearborn, parked in front of Cloe's place. Instead of going straight to the old boarded-up store, as she had initially intended, she decided to go inside The Cough Inn. Once again, Inita was behind the bar — and she disappeared faster than the balance on a stolen credit card. Moments later, just like always, André came out of the kitchen. "You got your money. What do you want now?"

"I would like to speak to my friend."

"Why don't you just go away? We don't need any more of our customers being afraid to come in here because of you."

"It's too early for me to scare off your underage drinkers. I only have a few questions about the boarded-up building across the street."

André wiped the residual meat juice off his hands onto his apron and then motioned for Jerrelle to take a seat at the bar. He

128

pulled up a stool next to her and looked her in the eye. Now it was he that was curious as to what it was that she wanted to know. "Why are you interested in that place?"

"Because I saw someone yesterday I know go into it with someone that I don't."

"That is not a good reason, Jerrelle."

"I know, but… I really can't tell you why I want to know about that place."

"Then don't expect me to tell you anything." André was about to go back into the kitchen when Jerrelle stopped him.

"Listen! All that I can say is that the man I don't know, whom I saw with the one I do, is associated with the Detroit Underworld Organization. I don't know what's going on over there, but my sister and I saw them each carrying two rather large bags into the place."

Although Jerrelle had never been one of his most favorite people in the world, André was aware from talking with Cloe over the years that she had always been a straight shooter — she had never fed anyone any bullshit. If she wanted something, she came right at you for it. She wasn't the kind of person who would lay down a bed of glass and then expect someone else to walk across it barefoot in her place.

He thought for a moment and then he looked at her very seriously. "That place has been closed down, per se, for about three years. Someone who is known to be associated with the political group, the United Arab League, owns the building. Usually, every afternoon, a group of them, around thirty or so, go inside for about an hour. They don't often stay any longer than that. However, Henré has told me that, on occasion, usually just before the bar closes he will see a handful of people bringing either an oversized bag or long box inside with them. Time will vary as to how long they stay, but when they leave, it's always empty-handed."

"There could be any number of reasons for that."

"I know but.., I've heard through the grapevine that the U.A.L. is actually a local, budding terrorist group."

After listening to what André had to say, Jerrelle tried to put two and two together. If this building was indeed owned by a terrorist organization, then it was probably just used as a showcase for Louie to sell the U.A.L. some weapons. This was something that needed to be looked into further. "Thanks for the info, André. What we just talked about will be handled with the utmost of discretion… You have my word."

"I know."

"By the way, how would you feel if I told you that there may be a way to shut that place down and get them out of your neighborhood for good?"

André didn't answer her, he just smiled; it had actually been the first time he had ever authentically done that. Usually, a smile would only occur when he and his twin brother had to throw her out of the club.

That honest gesture of his was all that she needed to see. Content, she left The Cough Inn and returned to her car. Her initial objective for coming here no longer needed to be completed, as André had given her all the information she sought — albeit, secondhand.

Promptly, Jerrelle drove straight back to where she had been earlier. Once she got there, she was able to luckily park her car in the exact same spot it had been in some forty-five minutes ago. Happily, she saw that her sister had not moved from her patio seat, so she grabbed her vid-cell and called Bai Lin.

Surprised, but understanding that plans do tend to change, she finished off the remainder of the sim-caf she had been drinking, left the District Bar & Grill, headed across the street, got inside her sister's car and without a word being said, buckled up as Jerrelle drove off. Once they had completely left that section of Woodward Ave., she said to Bai Lin, "We don't need to worry about Nicoli right now. I found out something really important that Sabastian is going to want to hear. So.., until he gets here on Friday, let's just spend the rest of the time getting shitfaced."

"I can go out and have a few drinks with you tonight, but I can't get drunk."

Jerrelle looked at her sister and asked, "Why not?"

"While I was waiting for you to return, I called Orochi and filled him in on everything that we have found out. Now that we know my life is no longer in danger, and there is no direct threat to the Liberation anymore, I've been ordered to return home to Japan."

Jerrelle's look went from being serious to utter disappointment. She didn't want her sister to leave — she was so ready to get used to Bai Lin being around her. But deep down, she understood that her sister had a life and a commitment that she had to go back to. At least, she was happy with the fact that she had had the opportunity to fight beside her one more time — and they certainly had kicked some serious ass.

Five minutes later, Jerrelle had parked her car and brought her sister into the 'Hole'n D'Wall nightclub'. This was where she wanted to spend whatever time she had left with her sister — and this was a place where she knew they could easily find a fight. One more time; that is all she wanted to do with Bai Lin.

This was something that Louie wasn't looking forward to doing. Not too long ago, he had found himself in the unenviable position for which he had to beg — only because it had been his job then to try and get the Communist Revolutionary Assembly Party to change their minds and agree to meet with the D.U.O. in order to discuss the possibility of making a deal. This time though, his pending call was strictly for the purpose of trying to prevent the removal of his manhood.

Out of all of the organizations they had ever dealt with over the years, the C.R.A.P. was the only one that he knew you didn't screw over. Yes, he was the one that pulled the trigger, but Antonio had given the order. Even so, Louie was now responsible for every action and decision his predecessor made, because the moment he claimed leadership of the Detroit Underworld Organization, he inherited them.

In his mind, trying to convince the C.R.A.P. that they were not responsible for what had happened in Germany would be similar to that of a group of conspiracy theorists successfully being able to prove that the United States Government were the ones who were actually responsible for the 911 terrorist attacks.

As much as he was dreading this, there was simply no way to avoid the inevitable, so Louie picked up his vid-phone. Honestly, he hoped that his call would go unanswered, but it was after only one ring. Staring right back at him on the vid-screen was a man whom he surprisingly recognized — considering that he had only met the man

131

briefly once before, some twenty-five years ago. The moment they were introduced, Louie sensed that this individual had an indisputable arrogance about him; one that gave off the impression he honestly believed he was going to be a man of importance within the Revolution one day. His name was Uri Drakonna and he had tagged along with Vladi during that initial meeting they had, long before the C.R.A.P. had become the feared entity they now were.

From what Louie had remembered, there were several men who ranked well above where Uri had stood within the organization at the time. Now, with it being him who answered his call, he had to assume that, just like he had within the D.U.O., this Serb had somehow found a way to vault right up to the head of the class. He definitely could not take the man lightly. "I remember you. Your name is Uri, is it not?"

"That would be correct, Mr. Mazotti. And I am to assume that you have called to let us know that you have received our little care package?"

"I would have preferred touching base with you for reasons pertaining to business instead of feeling obligated to respond to the representation that I have to believe your gift is implying."

"You know as well as anyone else who is in the industry that you and I are in, that a knife is always in someone's hand. But just so you know, I never stab anyone in the back. Instead, I prefer to let them know that their throat is about to be cut."

It was clear that a cheap shot had just been taken. Louie also knew, even without it having to be stated, that his assumption had been correct. Even so, he wanted to hear the admission himself, so he came right out and bluntly asked, "Just exactly what have we done to warrant your organization sending us a threat like this?" Louie then held up the statue and the tarot card.

"Our boss, my mentor, was killed while in the middle of finalizing a deal with the D.U.O. Although we still don't know all of the details as of yet, we feel that your organization should be held responsible."

This could work in Louie's favor. If he could plant the seed of doubt into Uri's mind that they were not to blame for Vladi's death, and that it had been Sabastian Banks that had done the deed instead, then they would be off the hook and Maxwell's son would thus become their target. "We were not responsible for what happened to your predecessor. And I can prove it."

"How is it that you are not?"

"If you'll humor me for a moment, I'll try to explain to you, to the best of my knowledge, what actually happened." It was time to manipulate the truth — Louie just needed to make sure that his soon-to-be composed story didn't have any glaring holes in it.

He began by telling Uri that, while they were right in the middle of the exchange, a young man, hell-bent on vengeance, drove a pickup truck right on through the front window of the building, ran over his associate, Sal, killing him instantly, and then began to spray bullets through the truck's open window. Louie then, with as much sincerity as he could convey, made it known that he was unsure as to what had actually happened during the chaos because both he and Antonio had high-tailed it out of there. He then made sure to emphasize the fact that they both had been very lucky to escape out through the back of the building. "I can only assume that your predecessor's death happened as a result of a stray bullet being fired from that young man's gun."

Uri stayed quiet; his body language also did not give Louie any indication as to what the man was currently thinking. It caused him to fill with nervousness. If both men had been in the same room, even a Scottish Claymore Sword couldn't cut the tension. His mind promptly concluded the worst. He had absolutely no idea whatsoever whether or not his given explanation was being accepted.

"Your elucidation is plausible. However.., even if what you have just told me is the truth, it will be impossible for us to ever trust your organization again. The circumstances surrounding my predecessor's death cannot be taken into consideration, as Vladi's safety was yours to ensure."

"Yes, we failed to provide that. I would apologize, but that would be as worthless as a treasure chest full of wooden nickels."

Although Uri had not ever heard that specific analogy before, it was easy for him to comprehend the meaning behind it. Louie was correct.

"I hope this doesn't mean that we are now mortal enemies?"

133

"As of now, we are not. But heed this warning. If you get in our way or do anything that prevents us from accomplishing our goals, then we will not hesitate to eliminate everyone who is associated with the Detroit Underworld Organization."

"I promise that we will keep our business practices out of eastern and central Europe."

"That would be wise of you."

"Well then, goodbye, Uri."

"Goodbye, Louie. Oh, and please accept my condolences on the loss of Antonio." Uri then disconnected the call.

Louie sat back in his synth-leather chair and exhaled a sigh of relief. A few seconds later, he opened up his top desk drawer and removed his stainless steel cigarette container, opened it up, removed a clove cigarette, and lit it. As he did this, He began reviewing in his head what had just taken place. Somehow, he had successfully bullshitted his way out of a situation that by all accounts, should not have gone in his favor. Inside, he celebrated, as this was technically his first victory as leader of the Detroit Underworld Organization. But as he puffed away on his cigarette, something disconcerting popped into his head. *'How exactly was Uri made aware of the fact that Antonio had died? His death was not made public?'* Louie pondered that question for a moment; there didn't seem to be a plausible answer for it. *'Well.., I guess that it doesn't really matter. I have more important things to worry about.'*

Louie took a few more puffs of his cigarette, walked over to his wet bar, grabbed a cold beer out of the fridge (since there was no more Walker's Club), returned to his desk, and turned his vid-phone back on. After taking a well-deserved sip of his brew, he called Madelyn — not just because he missed her, he also wanted to get an update on her progress when it came to luring Sabastian into his well thought out trap.

An hour after Sabastian returned to the office and a cup of English tea later, the bug he planted in Lizanne's room had sent a signal to his vid-cell. This was the first time Sabastian had used the new app that Jerrelle had uploaded to his phone. Not only did this program sweep for bugs and explosives, but the latest version of it could also receive a signal from any bug in which its frequency had previously been programmed into the app.

Sabastian took his vid-cell, set it on speaker mode, sat it on top of his desk, leaned back in his office chair, and anxiously awaited the conversation that was about to take place. After only a handful of words were exchanged, it became apparent whom Lizanne was talking to. Anger, among other emotions, ran through his body each and every time Louie spoke.

His fears seemed all but validated. The woman who had caused his hormones to come alive did, in fact, know Louie Mazotti. What was the hardest thing for Sabastian at that moment, was keeping his fury at bay. If he didn't do that, he would not be able to keep an open mind. With clear objectivity, he had to closely listen to what was being said, digest all of the information learned, and then come to a rational decision.

"Have you been successful in convincing Sabastian to follow you to Chicago?"

"I never had to convince him. He volunteered to come back with me."

"That's not surprising, Madelyn. You are an enchanting individual."

'Did he just say, Madelyn?' Sabastian was a bit taken aback. He knew once he had seen Louie's number on her vid-cell that there was a good possibility Lizanne wasn't who she said she was. And now he knew that for sure.

It wasn't intentional, but for some reason, she could not put together a response to Louie's words, as they were somewhat unbecoming of the kind, caring individual she thought he was when they had first met. It certainly appeared to her that layers of his true personality were slowly being peeled away and revealed.

"When will you be returning?"

"I'm not exactly sure yet? Although I do believe that it will be sometime tomorrow. When I know for certain, I will send you a message."

"Tomorrow's cutting it close. That won't give me too much time to get prepared. Nevertheless, I'll just have to find a way to make it work."

"If there is nothing else, Louie, I'm going to let you go. It's been a stressful few days and I want to turn in early."

"That is it for now. Have a good night's sleep, Madelyn."

Sabastian shut off the bug app on his vid-cell and turned his chair to the side so that he could look out the window of his office. He was both hurt and confused. Not only had this woman, whom he had quickly developed feelings for, lied to him about who she was, he now knew for sure that she was working with the enemy.

Inside, he was mad — but his father's words just would not escape him. *"Don't be so quick to judge her. There is a lot yet that you don't understand."*

His father was right. There was still a lot that he didn't understand. Going with her to Chicago, he believed, was still what he needed to do. But now, he had a completely different reason for doing it — and he was certain that once he got there, he would find out a hell of a lot more than what he already knew.

After tapping on the doorframe, Savanna stood at the threshold of Sabastian's office with her spring jacket draped over her arm. "I was able to book you and Ms. Kinsworth a direct flight to Chicago. Unfortunately, it's at seven in the morning. Check your e-mail for the details."

"Thanks a lot, Savanna. I couldn't do this job without you."

"That's what your father used to say. See you when you get back, Sabastian."

He would have produced a genuine smile, but his mood this evening simply would not allow it. Even so, he meaningfully said, "You have a good night."

After Savanna left, Sabastian fired up his computer, checked his e-mail for the flight information, and then called Lizanne / Madelyn to let her know what time he was going to pick her up. He purposely kept his conversation with her brief for fear that he may say something inappropriate or accidentally reveal what he now knew.

When those uneasy few moments were over, he closed his office door, locked up the agency, and went straight home. He had a long day ahead of him tomorrow and he wanted his mind to be focused. If it wasn't, he had no doubt whatsoever that he would make a costly mistake. Clearly, something was planned for him. He had a pretty good idea as to what that might be, but Sabastian didn't think that it would take place shortly after his arrival in Chicago. After all, like the man's predecessor, Louie enjoyed playing games.

5

Normally, Louie would have called it a night hours ago, but Zhin and Nicoli had walked into his office shortly after seven in the evening with some last-minute good news. At first, they feared that they were going to have to report that they had again failed to convince any potential weapon buyers to do business with them, but just before Zhin dialed the number for the last organization on their list, they unexpectedly called.

A rather small group known as The Muskegon Militia, a faction that rose from the ashes of the previously thought to be extinct Michigan Militia of the late twentieth century, wanted to meet within the coming days in order to view the types of weapons the D.U.O could provide that would also fit their specific needs. The reason behind their sudden change of heart was simple. As it had been explained to Zhin, they realized that if and when they ever needed weapons, their order could be filled and then delivered to them in a relatively short period of time, due to the fact that both organizations were located in the same state.

Louie was happy, as he now had a buyer in place for the entire stockpile of street weapons that he desperately wanted to get rid of. His day had suddenly gone from bad to good, then to great. To end his day on such a high note was what he needed before tomorrow's all-important event took place — the final curtain call for Sabastian Banks.

His intention was to brief his men the next morning about his plans, but with Madelyn informing him only a few minutes earlier that she was leaving San Antonio for Chicago first thing in the morning, their own sleep would have to wait. He could theoretically postpone everything until morning, but he'd rather not risk an issue coming up beforehand that would cause them to not be ready when their guest arrived. Therefore, Louie felt that it was best they just leave for Chicago now, get a decent amount of sleep upon their arrival, and then at the crack of dawn, get themselves ready for the planned events to unfold.

In less than an hour's time, he and his men had gone home, packed a light bag, and returned to the office where they all got into the organization's new jet black Cadillac Escalade IV. Once they were on the Interstate, Louie briefed his men on what his intentions were. After subsequently listening to the suggestions that followed from his two associates, and making a few proposed adjustments to his plans, a reassurance came to him. Not only did he now feel more relaxed than he had since his brief sabbatical following Antonio's death, but by the end of tomorrow, he was reasonably sure that the one last major obstacle in the path of the D.U.O. would finally be removed.

Sometimes, it can be easy. For the most part, though, life is hard. If it was nothing but straightforward, then what purpose would there be to live? Every once in a while, we will come across an unexpected roadblock wherein our first instinct is to stop, turn around, walk away, and pretend that it wasn't even there. For some people, the first thing they think to do is to barrel right on through. Others will choose instead to simply just go all the way around. Whichever of those options are taken, it doesn't necessarily mean that they have forever left that roadblock behind. If not properly dealt with, it may end up getting in their way again at some point   Stopping, analyzing the situation, and then determining the best course of action to take is the only way to completely clear it out of your path so that life can then continue on as it was, and as uncomplicated as possible.

'This is going to be a long flight,' Sabastian thought. *'Sitting next to Madelyn on the plane is going to be like being locked in a Baskin Robbins; hungrily, you look at all the delicious flavors that are there and you want to sample each and every one of them, even though you know that too much of that good stuff not only wouldn't sit well in your stomach, it would result in serious regret afterward.'*

He had never felt like this before. Inside, Sabastian was kicking himself for succumbing to temptation and allowing his better judgment to be overruled. It just wasn't fair that women were given the innate ability to make any engrossed man become weak at the knees. And even though he knew he had been deceived, he was still finding it very difficult to resist wanting to again reexamine every inch of 'Lizanne's' perfect body.

The worst part of the three-hour flight was trying to act as if he knew nothing. He was never a good liar; his grandmother was proof of that, as Edith Burelli always could tell when Sabastian wasn't being truthful. That inability of his was why he was finding it difficult to treat Madelyn as if she was still the same person he had just met only a few days ago.

Every time she asked him a question, most of which were trivial, he kept his replies as brief as possible. Everything seemed to be going okay; that was until she implied that he was being intentionally standoffish with her. His reply was lame and far from creative; telling her simply that he just didn't get much sleep and the altitude was causing him to get a migraine.

Sabastian knew that she wasn't at all a stupid person, but he hoped that his words would be enough for Madelyn to just leave him alone until they arrived at their destination. Eventually, he was going to have to engage in a normal conversation with her. Before that commenced though, he wanted to make sure he was in the best possible frame of mind so that he did not end up making a mistake that could not be rectified.

The last hour of their flight took place in relative silence. It was not until they had landed that Sabastian said, "Once I am sure you are home safe and you will be ok, I'll call a cab to take me to the nearest hotel."

"That isn't necessary. You are welcome to stay at my place. It's the least I can do to repay you for accompanying me home."

As happy as that suggestion should make him, it was also a very bad idea. Sabastian was only a few days removed from tasting a bit of heaven on earth and animal magnetism would surely draw the two of them back together for another night of unambiguous sex. At this stage in their brief relationship, and with it being as uncertain as it was, giving in to those desires could result in Sabastian accidentally stepping off of his path. Until things started to get a little clearer, he could not let anything cause him to forget about, or ignore what his objective was.

Upon claiming their luggage, they exited the airport, hailed a cab, and then went directly to Madelyn's place. Inside the vehicle, Sabastian was once again being quiet; she just could not understand, nor would he even explain to her why he was being this way. She was worried and concerned. Something was eating away at him, bombarding his thoughts, and causing him to shut her out. Desperately, Madelyn wanted to know what that was, yet she hardly knew the man at all and it wasn't her place to pry.

'Does he know the truth?' she wondered. *'He is a private detective, after all.'* Until she knew for certain though, she had to continue on with her charade. If she were not to give her full attention to the task at hand, she more than likely would slip up. At that point, she'd have to do what she was nowhere near ready to do — confess, and then pray that the special connection she knew the two of them had, would not be forever broken.

After exiting the cab at their destination, and right as their ride was driving away, Madelyn reached over and attempted to take Sabastian's hand; it was a gesture she had hoped would allow him to realize she cared about him. But he did not accept it. Frustrated, her emotions caused her to do what she knew she should not — only because she could not stand being shunned anymore. "Come on, Sabastian. You have barely spoken to me since we left San Antonio. What in the hell is wrong?"

"Nothing!"

"Have I done something wrong?"

In Sabastian eyes, she had. He knew he should not be profiling her, but he was having a very difficult time looking beyond the fact that she knew the enemy. "No, Lizanne.., you have not."

She stopped in the lobby of the building, set her bags down, and then grabbed a hold of his arm. Pulling him to a stop, she looked at Sabastian and said, "I know that we have only known each other for three days, but I've never felt more connected to anyone in my entire life. You have awakened things inside of me that I never knew existed. And I have to believe that the same thing is true when it comes to how you feel about me."

141

If she only knew how accurate that assessment was — but there was no way that Sabastian could let her know that. Not now, at least. Not until he knew why she was aligned with Louie. "To be honest, I'm not sure how I feel."

His answer hurt her — and she knew that he was lying. There was something much deeper inside of him that was preventing him from admitting his true feelings. She was determined to bring them out. Again, she reached for his hand. This time, she made sure that she got a hold of it. The instant they touched, she knew she was right. She could feel how much he cared about her; feel the energy transfer the moment their palms clasped together.

Before he could voice any sort of objection, she led him toward the awaiting elevator. When they got to the twentieth floor, they exited, walked down the hall, and then stopped at their destination. After Madelyn opened up the door, pulled Sabastian inside by the hand, shut the door, and unceremoniously dropped her bags to the ground, she threw herself at him. As tight as a boa constrictor would, she literally locked her body around his — there was no way that she was going to let him escape. She then looked into his befuddled eyes and gently placed a kiss on his lips. It was at that moment she knew she had him under her spell — she also knew that the connection she believed they had, was indeed there.

The sexual energy that instantly transferred between them had reignited those emotions, which Sabastian had earlier declared to himself he was going to ignore. He attempted his best to resist, but it was impossible. Easily, he submitted. He now belonged to her.

After placing his arms underneath her butt, he carried her into the direction that he assumed the bedroom was. And once he found it, he laid her gently across the bed, kissed her, broke the body lock that had temporarily made them one, and stood back. Hungrily, he gazed at the treat that lay spread across the top comforter.

With more zeal than that of an anticipating teenage virgin removing his tuxedo on prom night, Sabastian promptly got naked. Madelyn had stripped herself just as fast, all except for her purple and black laced undergarments — because she knew that the sight of her wearing them would only enhance the desire that she could see radiating from him.

She was stunning. Nothing about this woman's physical appearance was disappointing. Yes, Sabastian could clearly hear the angel on his shoulder telling him not to be tempted, but his hormones were calling the shots. She knew exactly how to use what she had been gifted with to lure him in. Was any of this real? He did not know. Was this, right here right now, the culmination of a well-crafted plan that placed him within reach of the enemy's clutches? He had not a clue. For some reason, his mind just could not find a way to sufficiently separate his desire from his ability to think rationally.

Even now, it was still hard for him to fathom why someone, who was as physically perfect as Madelyn, would be interested in someone like him. In no way shape or form did Sabastian think that he was good-looking enough to rank high up on the stud-o-meter. Yet, she apparently saw something that was very appealing to her. It must be true then — beauty is in the eye of the beholder.

Whether or not their paths crossing had been planned, Sabastian could not dismiss that that event had changed his life — and hopefully, Madelyn's had changed because of it as well. But there was only one way for Sabastian to find that out for sure. He had to let this whole thing play itself out and then hope that it didn't get to the point where he totally fucked himself.

Madelyn pulled back all the covers and stretched out across the bed, positioning herself, intentionally, in a very inviting manner. Essentially, she had just issued an open invitation to sample the buffet that was now spread out before him. It's safe to say that not one single straight man on the face of the earth would refuse what was now being offered to him.

Eagerly, he crawled onto the bed; he looked like a hungry, drooling wolf. However, Madelyn stopped him right before he was about to place his paws on her. She raised herself up into a sitting position, gave him a gentle peck on the lips, and with an unwavering look on her face, said, "When we make love, I don't want to see you touch me. I only want to feel you and your body against mine. Could you please shut off the lights?"

Making love to a woman wasn't supposed to be done in the dark. Madelyn had nothing about her body to be ashamed of. Even so, there was no legitimate reason for him to pose an objection to what was being asked of him, so Sabastian got up off the bed, shut off the lights, and then used the tiny ray of sunshine that had snuck past the drawn curtains as a guide to find his way back. Once there, he sat on the front corner of the mattress and placed his right hand on her leg. He then began to trace every inch of her soft body with his fingertips, taking his time until he had worked his way up to her lips.

He had only been partially leaning over Madelyn's body, but that had been enough of an opening for her to wrap her legs around his torso. Then, in one fluid motion, she rolled him over. She was now sitting right on top of him. At the same time, her legs stayed hooked together around and under his upper thighs. "I know that you can't see me, but I want you to close your eyes anyway and feel me exploring every inch of you. I want you to trust me to make you feel like you never have before."

At first, Sabastian was a little leery about giving Madelyn complete control, but it had been he who had assumed that the first time they made love, so it was only fair that he give in to her request this time. "Ok, this is your home and you can do what you want to me." Sabastian stayed on his back as instructed and then felt the tips of Madelyn's hair tickle his bare chest as she slowly worked her way up toward his face. Unexpectedly, she took one of his arms and placed it up over his head; she then did the same with the other one.

Unsure as to what exactly it was that she was doing, he questioned her, but she quickly silenced him with a long, passionate kiss. Once she released their liplock, she handcuffed his hands together to the headboard.

"I honestly never thought that you were the kind of person who would be into this sort of thing."

"I'm not, but..." Madelyn slid herself down to the end of the bed, stepped off of it, and then quickly tied both of Sabastian's feet to each post. Once she had done that, she walked away from the bed and said, "...I'm sorry, Sabastian. I simply have no other choice."

Now completely immobile, Sabastian's mind should have wondered what was going on — but it was easy for him to figure out. Suspicion had been with him throughout this whole scenario that this wasn't what it was being presented as; an evening of pure, hot, passionate, kinky sex. Nevertheless, he had to go with the flow in order to see where this may lead him. What was clear now, was Madelyn's allegiance — and obviously, it wasn't with him, even though she literally did end up fucking him.

A surprising look should have appeared on Sabastian's face when the lights in the room finally came back on, but there wasn't one. He was disappointed when he noticed that Madelyn was nowhere to be found. She was responsible for the predicament that he now found himself in and she should have had the balls to be there so that he could ask her why she had done what she did. Instead, it was Louie, along with two other men, who were now standing at the foot of the bed. "You are much easier to lead into a trap than your father ever was."

"Where's the two-faced bitch?"

"If you are referring to Madelyn, she is no longer needed and has now left the building. However, from where I'm standing, the bitch is still in the room... and that would be you."

Sabastian wasn't that, but he was certainly an idiot for not thinking that the trap he fully expected to be waiting for him, would be sprung only moments after he arrived in Chicago. He felt confident that whatever Louie had planned, he would be able to handle it and then walk away as the victor. Now, it appears as if his assuredness was going to cost him. If he had only ignored his father's advice, he would not be bound to this bed right now. Then again, that thought was only him looking for an excuse. Sabastian's dilemma was nobody's fault but his own. "With it being obvious that I can't defend myself, I have to assume then that you do intend on beating the shit out of me like you did my father?"

"No. Unlike my predecessor, I'd prefer not to use any unnecessary violence against someone who I need to eliminate. Instead.., I have decided to make your death a slow and painful one."

Sabastian watched as Louie's men went over to the closet where they removed a large metal barrel and a small box. Though he was unsure as to what those things were, it was easy for him to determine that they had something to do with his pending elimination. There was no need for him to have that verified as he was sure that everything would be explained to him in the next few minutes. Therefore, he decided to engage in some irrelevant conversation and try in the process to plant a seed of doubt. "So.., you must be Zhin Wi.., and you must be Nicoli Nemchieve?"

Neither one of them took the time to reply to Sabastian's query.

"You do know that your brother, Helfred, died because of Louie's bum buddy, Sal, and two crooked German cops; one of whom was actually responsible for killing him."

Nicoli placed the barrel in its position on the floor, looked at a naked, vulnerable, prone Sabastian, and said, "It is because of that skank friend of yours that my brother is dead. And once we are finished with your execution, I will hunt her down and do to her exactly what your forefather's used to do to her kind."

"You will get your revenge in time," Louie stated, "but we have more important things to worry about right now than satisfying a desire."

Nicoli nodded in understanding; he then went back to finish the task that he was assigned.

He could not help but sympathize with his new associate's longing. For twenty-five years, Louie had wanted to kill Sal. Had he done that, the D.U.O.'s significant advancement probably would not have taken place. Publically, he would never admit this, but Salvadore Osiris Batiste had been just as important an individual to the organization as he and Antonio. So in hindsight, he was glad that he had not acted on his impulses.

In only a few short moments, the last of the past will forever be put to rest. Louie could not help but feel haughty because he was just about to do something that neither of his former associates even came close to doing — eliminate the last of a serious threat. "Look at me, Sabastian. I need your undivided attention here. This steel barrel at the foot of your bed contains a biochemical liquid gas known as 'Decomp-agent 6'. It was discovered by accident in Columbia when a Cocaine purification lab mistakenly mixed the wrong chemicals during the process of making the drug."

Sabastian could only imagine what Louie's intentions were. During his time in the military, on a few occasions, the possibility had been there where the enemy had been known to use chemical warfare.

Now it appeared as if he was going to experience that kind of hellish demise firsthand.

"You see.., once what's inside the barrel becomes airborne, a chemical reaction with the oxygen in the room will take place. Almost immediately, your exposed skin will begin to absorb the mixture. Roughly ten minutes later, the infestation will be throughout your entire body and any chance of survival will be gone. About an hour after that, you will have completely disintegrated. The only way that they will be able to identify your remains is if the forensics lab just luckily happens to find an intact portion of you that they can extract DNA from."

Before Sabastian could put together a response to Louie's horrifying revelation, he noticed that Zhin Wi now had two Ex-Co patches in his possession.

"Considering that you will still be alive and able to feel the sensation of your body being slowly eaten away, I'd say that your pending death is going to be even more heinous than what your father's demise was. But that's okay… your bloodline needs to be cauterized anyway."

"You're just as sick and twisted as Antonio was."

"I have my moments. I am only like this when I need to be." Louie then requested that Zhin hand him the Ex-Co patches, as he wanted the honor of 'lighting the fuse'. In a sanctimonious manner, he then displayed them not far from Sabastian's face. "With you having been in the military, I'm sure you are familiar with these?"

There was no reason for him to give Louie the satisfaction of a reply; the man knew very well that he knew exactly what those items were.

With a pleasing smile pasted to his face, Louie turned and looked at Nicoli. With no words needing to be exchanged, his newest associate moved up to the head of the bed and placed duct tape across Sabastian's mouth.

"Goodbye, young Mr. Banks. And say hello to your father for me, will ya?" His plan had happened exactly as it had been drawn up. Madelyn had done what he had asked her to do and conveniently served the enemy up to him on a silver platter. Only one thing was now left to do.

As he lay there helpless, Sabastian tried his best not to allow his thoughts to stray, as doing so would be wasting what precious little time he had left. He understood exactly what was going to happen next, and there was nothing that he could do about it. He couldn't curse, he couldn't scream, and he couldn't get out of his restraints to try and stop this before it got past the point of no return. All that he could do was watch Louie slap those two Ex-Co patches onto the barrel and pray that his fate hadn't yet already been sealed.

Right after the enemy left the room and locked him in it, Sabastian heard them doing something else that seemed rather odd. To him, it sounded as if they were using a drill to screw the door shut, essentially barricading him in so that there was no way of escaping.

Sabastian was fucked, and he knew it. Even if he were able to get out of his restraints, his body would probably be half-eaten by then. But as futile as things now seemed, he wasn't about to give up. Unfortunately, he could not think of a clear answer to his dilemma.

Never before had he found it this difficult to concentrate. Even during those times when he was in a somewhat precarious situation during one of his past military assignments, he was able to focus. But Madelyn, for some reason, would not leave his thoughts. Something was interfering with his mind and wouldn't allow it to clear away her memory. If he was going to die today, the image of his parents was the last thing that he wanted to remember and not the one who had played with his emotions.

Once they were all inside the Escalade, the three of them celebrated their victory with smiles, laughter, and a few inappropriate remarks in reference to Sabastian's predicament. Shortly after they departed from the complex, Nicoli turned to Louie and said, "You do realize that the Decomp-agent 6 is going to also destroy your apartment?"

"I am aware of that and I really don't care. It's not like I have any reason to ever come back to Chicago."

Madelyn sat in the back seat and kept to herself. Her debt was now paid, but the anguish within her own self could never be removed. She had led a good man, whom she had quickly developed deep feelings for, to the butcher to be slaughtered. She didn't feel like celebrating; she felt like slicing her own wrists. She wasn't even sure what she was going to do now. She only knew that she could not work for Louie. She couldn't even fathom accepting the offered job of a bartender at his casino. All that she wanted to do instead was get away from any reminder of what she had just done.

She didn't know what was going to happen next. She only hoped that Louie, the kind-hearted version of the man she had first met, was still there and would agree to let her walk away. Chicago wasn't where she wanted to be, but it seemed like the better option instead of being brought all the way back to Detroit.

Lying shackled to a bed naked while waiting for your life to end isn't something that Sabastian had ever imagined would happen to him. He had always just assumed that if his life had ended untimely, it would be in some war-torn country while he was in the service. Knowing firsthand what those Ex-Co patches were all about, he figured that it would only be a matter of minutes before they ate right through the thick-lined steel container that held the Decomp-agent 6. And when that happened, his life was going to be over: a life that he had only just recently embraced, a life and a destiny that he now was ready to fulfill, and a life that he had felt honored to live.

Was it too early for him to concede defeat? Yes, even though the reality of his situation gave very little, if any hope for survival. Still, he could not give up. It was not in his nature to quit. So he closed his eyes; it was the only thing that he could think of doing.

To anyone else, what he was doing was simply wasting valuable time. But in order for him to find a solution to his problem, he concluded that he first needed to clear his thoughts.

By using one of his many meditation techniques, Sabastian was able to go straight to that quiet place in the back corner of his mind. Once there, he began to search for the answers he needed. First, he replayed all of his past situations that initially had seemed bleak — his reason for doing this was to try and find inspiration from one of them. Unfortunately, there wasn't a single scenario that Sabastian had lived through which he could now use again to help him to escape. He then took his thoughts away from his past and tried to recall some of his unforgettable dreams; dreams that at the time did not make much sense — that included the recent one he had where he was standing right in the midst of a room full of his dead military brethren.

"This is not where you need to be looking for the answers, my son."

Sabastian quickly abandoned the dream he was reliving and was promptly pulled back to reality. His father; that was who had just spoken to him. "Dad? Where are you?" Sabastian quickly scanned the bedroom, but he did not see him. "Dad! Are you here?"

"Let your heart speak to you. It will help you find the solution to your problem."

"What? What are you talking about?"

There was no reply. The room fell silent, only to be disturbed when Sabastian suddenly realized that the Ex-Co patches had done their job and eaten right through the metal container. Ten minutes max was all that he now had to find a way out.

Desperately, he looked about the room to see if there was something that he could use to help himself escape. He could not find anything — it wasn't as if he could leave the bed anyway. The only thing that he did see was that Madelyn had left her bra draped over the center finial on top of the headboard. It was then that his senses honed in on why he hadn't earlier been able to expunge her from his thoughts.

'Vanilla!' Not only was Madelyn the most beautiful woman he had ever met, but that scent she wore when they had made love admittedly was what had intensified Sabastian's desire for her — and it was that same scent that now led him to hone in on what he needed to escape. There it was. Something was in the bra that should not be there. Yes, she had used him, but Madelyn had not betrayed him.

He wasn't as angry as he should be. Maybe it was now clear to him what side she wanted to be on. Strangely, it all made sense to him as to why she did what she had. Just like the predicament he now found himself in, she too was trapped.

Sabastian pressed the side of his face against the pillow and then rolled it. The duct tape began to peel off. Because he hadn't shaved in three days, it hurt like hell — but he did it over and over again until all of it was completely off of his mouth. Then, using every available inch of slack there was in his bindings, he lifted his head up and grabbed Madelyn's bra with his teeth. When he yanked it down, it landed with one of her C-sized cups nearly covering his entire face. The residual scent of vanilla went straight up his nose.

It certainly wasn't the ideal circumstances for him to be doing this, but the feeling of her empty bra cup resting against his skin, caused him to have a harmless, brief fantasy of Madelyn's beautiful, perfect bare breasts. Mere seconds later, reality slapped him clear of his ill-timed thought. Even so, he smiled; not because of what his mind had just conjured up, but because the key to escaping his predicament was within his reach. All that he needed to do now was extract it from the bra.

He had a pretty good idea what that odd-looking, small bulge tucked inside the lace-trimmed cup was, but trying to remove it with only his teeth was going to take some time — and some luck. Three minutes later, and with some careful finagling of the hidden item, success had been achieved. What was now clenched between his teeth was the key to his freedom.

Sabastian let go of the micro-remote; it gently fell onto the pillow. With his nose, he then pressed the release button and his hands were freed from the electro-magnetic handcuffs. He then sat up, shifted toward the front of the bed, and untied his feet. Once that was complete, Sabastian hastily got dressed.

Just because he was no longer immobile, didn't mean that he was safe; the room was secured and it was beginning to fill with the deadly gas. He needed to quickly find a way out.

As he expected, when he tried the bedroom door, it didn't budge because it had been screwed shut from the other side. That left him with only one other option — leaving via the balcony. Promptly, he made his way over to it but he quickly realized that the sliding glass doors had also been micro-welded shut. *'You've got to be fuckin' kidding me?'*

Without getting discouraged, Sabastian took a second to re-evaluate his situation. As hopeless as it still seemed, there had to be a way for him to get those glass doors open. But the problem he saw was that there didn't appear to be anything heavy enough in the room for him to use to break the tempered glass. Yes, the steel barrel would do the job except, with the outer shell of it already compromised, the leaking gas would still end up doing harm to anyone both close by and

151

within the vicinity if he was to throw it too hard and it was to somehow land beyond the balcony railing.

Sabastian took a few seconds and logically tried to think of a way to open up the door, but he was beginning to find it difficult to concentrate. That was when it dawned on him that he was now starting to feel the early effects of the Decomp-agent 6 working its way into his system. Panic could have easily overtaken his mind at that moment, but he stayed calm, cleared the rapidly developing cobwebs from his thoughts, and allowed an idea to unexpectedly appear.

He walked over to the bed, yanked the sheets off of it, and the removed the mattress and box spring from the frame. Thankful that it wasn't all bolted together, only press-fit, he quickly disassembled the bed. He then used what strength he still had and picked up the headboard. After taking two steps with it toward the patio door, he launched it. It worked. The glass shattered upon impact and as a result, a sudden wave of fresh air slammed up against his face.

He inhaled a few deep breaths and walked toward the open balcony. Unfortunately, Sabastian now had another problem to solve. Time was certainly not on his side; he quickly needed to make a decision. Ideally, he would like to be able to weigh all of his options, but he clearly only had two — and neither was appealing. His first one was to just stay outside on the balcony away from the Decomp-agent 6 and wait to be rescued, but by the time that happened, the gas inside the room would have made its way outside, subjecting Sabastian to the effects of it anyway. Option number two also came with an immense risk as he was twenty stories up with nothing but a concrete slab below to catch his fall. Heights were no issue for him, but scaling over the edge without the proper safety equipment is something that only a thrill-seeker would do — which Sabastian wasn't. Nevertheless, it was what he had to do so he covered his mouth and nose as best as he could with his shirt and went back inside the room to grab the bed sheets. Once he had them, he went back outside to the balcony, tied them together as an escaping convict would, and secured his makeshift rope to the balcony railing. *'This is going to be fun!'*

Though this wasn't the same thing as abseiling from a helicopter or over a mountainside, Sabastian used his military training, stepped over the balcony railing, and then lowered himself to the apartment balcony below. Once he got there, he stepped over the railing and then calmly knocked on the glass door — it was pure luck that the person in the apartment on the other side was a retired Chicago police officer.

This man must have heard a lot of wild stories during his thirty-plus-year career. Surprisingly, the one that Sabastian had just sprung on him did not cause any doubt to appear — probably because the smell of the Decomp-agent 6 was now starting to make its way down into his apartment.

As he had long ago been trained to do, the retired officer took control of the situation. Immediately, he grabbed his vid-cell, called 911, and then the building superintendent. If it had been any other resident of the apartment complex making this type of crazy call, the insistence that the entire building needed to be evacuated would have probably fallen on deaf ears.

Moments after the man's second call was completed, a building-wide alarm sounded and the abandonment of it had begun. The mass evacuation became what Sabastian had hoped for — a sea of humanity that could easily camouflage his exit. As he walked through the front door of the building, what he did not want to see in the parking lot, he did — the entire circus was already pulling into town.

Drawing on his military training, Sabastian stayed well hidden behind a family of five — but only long enough until he reached the outside corner of the building. From there, he took a hard right and hastily made his way straight to the back. Once he got to the end of the property, he climbed over the six-foot fence that segregated the parking lot from the ravine that ran parallel to it.

For about three minutes, Sabastian followed the ditch until he came upon a short pedestrian bridge that went across it. It was there, he surmised, that he was now far enough away from the apartment complex to return to the main streets.

As he continued walking, he meticulously looked himself over, wanting to be sure that there was no missing skin or parts of his body. Once he was certain that he was still whole, he flipped open his vid-cell and tried to call Madelyn. She didn't answer. Honestly, he never thought that she would. With her more than likely still being in the presence of the enemy, it would be extremely stupid for her to do so.

Not wanting to unnecessarily place her in any sort of compromising position, he decided that he would wait an hour or so before he tried to make contact with her again. As he walked, he kept his vid-cell in his hand — not in case Madelyn decided to call him back, but because he was using it to keep tabs on his surroundings. Courtesy of Jerrelle's app wizard friend, his cell now allowed him to monitor a perimeter of one hundred feet as he walked. Anyone within that area, he could keep tabs on every move they made.

At four blocks away from the apartment building, he felt confident that no one was following him, so he turned off the app and stopped right in front of a nice looking café. He hadn't done this intentionally, but after what he had just been through, a craving for a fresh sim-tea was there. After grabbing one to go, he called a cab and asked the driver to take him to the train station so that he could make his way to Detroit as he had originally planned.

As the train was pulling away from the station, Sabastian tried calling Madelyn again — like before, she did not answer. An hour later, he tried one more time and got the same result. Because his call had gone unanswered for the third straight time, negative and unhealthy thoughts started to appear — even though he knew better than to allow that to occur. *'That piece of shit must have had something on Madelyn to force her into doing his dirty work for him. And now, he probably has no further use for her. If he has harmed her in any way shape or form, I won't hesitate to gut the bastard. Then again, I may do it just so that one less asshole walks the earth.'*

Although it can seem somewhat unclear at times, you should always listen to, and trust the voice that exists within you, as it is there to guide you, encourage you, and to help you to make the right decisions. Sabastian chose to ignore his; all because of the animosity he harbored toward his family's enemy. That hatred resulted in him unfairly characterizing Madelyn. And because he had done that, his mind became all but convinced of something that wasn't even close to being true. What a complete idiot he had been.

By the time his train had reached the Detroit city limits, Sabastian had again tried two more times to call Madelyn — and like before, she had failed to answer. Though grounds were there, he wasn't going to allow the worry he had to get in the way of why he had come to the Motor City. He needed to stay positive and believe that she was all right, even though Louie's reputation would suggest otherwise. Patience — it is what he knew he now had to have. This time, he was going to trust his gut. Soon enough, be believed that Madelyn's path was again going to intersect with his. And when that happened, he was either going to keep going forward in the same direction he had been or make a slight course correction that would alter his life, one more time.

Other than his failed attempts to make contact with her, the only other call that Sabastian had made while on the train was to Jerrelle. During their conversation, he informed his friend of everything that had happened to him over the last three days. If there was one thing that he had learned recently, it was to not keep your true feelings to yourself, as they could end up doing more damage to you than what they could if they had become known. That was what had happened to Jerrelle, and Sabastian was certain that she was scolding herself for keeping quiet about the love she had for Helfred. It was why he decided to come clean and tell his friend everything that had taken place between him and Madelyn.

When she met Sabastian at the train station, there was no denying the uncertainty that surrounded him. A window was also open for Jerrelle to bust his balls concerning this woman who had walked into his life and used him. But she resisted. She knew exactly how he was feeling and remembered how he was there for her, not too long ago, during her worst hour. She was going to do the same for him, as that is what friends were for. "Don't worry, Sab. We will find her, and we will make Louie pay for his sins."

"Oh, I know we will. And… when did you get that cut on your forehead?"

"Oh that.., um… It happened last night. My sister and I went out for a few drinks because it was her last night here."

"Did she go home?"

"Yes!"

He could tell that his old friend was both happy and sad; sad that her sister went back to Japan, but also happy that they had done what was easy for Sabastian to assume — the sisters had purposely gotten themselves into a bar fight. "Ok, so.., where should we look first?"

"Actually.., I was thinking about bringing you to a place that a friend of mine owns."

"Why?"

"I'll explain once we get there."

"Ok. This is your city. You are in charge."

It didn't take them long before they arrived at The Cough Inn. The moment they did, an uncertainty became evident in Sabastian. Promptly, Jerrelle assured him that this place wasn't one of those dives that she liked to frequent and insisted that he wouldn't feel uncomfortable once inside.

As soon as both of them stepped through the front doors, Jerrelle realized that something was different. Cloe was tending bar. "Is Inita sick?"

"No, she is not working here any longer. I fired that lying, two-faced bitch this morning."

"Why? I liked her."

Cloe knew that was far from the truth. "She showed up late for work the other day. Normally, that's no big deal however; I ended up finding out that she has been lying to me since day one."

"Lying how? You mean to tell me she's not a paranoid schizophrenic."

"No, Jerrelle. I was talking to my police friend again yesterday and she told me that Nino's niece had shown up with his lawyer in an attempt to get him released."

"What's that got to do with Inita?"

"Everything! She is the scumbag's niece. She is the reason the bastard was able to keep constant tabs on this place and know whether or not I had made any sort of contact with you over the years."

"Ah... That explains why she acted the way she did whenever she saw me." Now that she knew what was going on, Jerrelle encouraged Sabastian to take a seat at the bar. She then introduced him to Cloe; moments later, two pints of ice-cold Budweiser was set down in front of them. As they each took their first sip, Cloe left the bar and went into the kitchen.

After taking another healthy sip of her beer, Jerrelle began to fill her friend in on everything that had happened to her since she had returned home to Detroit. By the time she was finished, Cloe had returned from the kitchen with a plate of nachos to share. Sabastian thanked her for the kind gesture and then removed his vid-cell from his pocket — but before he made the call he intended to, he looked over at Cloe, then to Jerrelle. His friend returned a simple nod, letting him know that her friend was someone who could be trusted — after all, his call had to do with the continued security of the Union. A moment later, he was engaged in conversation with Captain Swilling.

Once Sabastian finished passing along the information that Jerrelle had given to him about the possibility of the D.U.O. selling stolen Union military weapons to the United Arab League, the wheels in the military man's brain began to spin. Normally, when information such as this is acquired, it is immediately passed along to the Union Bureau of Investigation so that they could then verify it. However, since the U.B.I. was solely responsible for sending the S.N.A.F.U. to Tijuana on an unsanctioned mission without actually having any concrete evidence to support the assignment, which luckily did lead to the confirmation of what was suspected, Captain Swilling felt that this was the perfect opportunity for him to send a friendly F.U. back to those in charge of the bureau. Yes, he could get into some serious trouble for keeping this information to himself, but he felt that proper procedure could be ignored in this instance. His reasoning for this was simple. Even though the rumor was second-hand and quite possibly inaccurate, the nature of it could not be foolishly dismissed. Therefore, he deemed it necessary to investigate this further before bringing it to their attention. He knew that he was taking a chance that could result in some serious backlash, but he trusted Sabastian's word. In his mind, what he intended to do was exactly what the U.B.I. had previously asked of his unit. If this were to turn out to be something significant, Captain Swilling would then promptly put an end to his investigation and hand the reins over to the Bureau.

It wasn't what Sabastian expected; he only really needed some support. Instead of obliging his request of 'borrowing a few good men' to back him up, his now-former commanding officer surprisingly informed him that he was going to send the entire platoon to Dearborn,

Michigan, to assist. Yes, it was agreed that there might be a potential threat to their country; it was why it made sense for them to come here. Sabastian's conscience, however, was telling him to object to that decision. It just didn't feel right to him to take advantage of his association. Having all of his former brethren at his disposal would certainly increase the odds of him achieving his goal, but it would also be a gross misuse of a national institution.

After graciously thanking Captain Swilling for his willingness to send him the entire platoon, Sabastian respectfully requested that he instead, send only half. Like before, he asked that Richard Atwater be a part of this 'operation' and he asked that his friend is given the responsibility of assembling a team of thirteen.

Upon the completion of his conversation, he exhaled, set his vid-cell onto the bar, and finished off the remainder of his rapidly warming beer. During that time, Sabastian's mind started to construct a potential plan. It made sense to him, but once Richard got here, he was going to sit down with his friend and Jerrelle and hear what they collectively thought before making any final decisions.

He didn't ask for it, but Cloe set another glass of beer down in front of him. Normally, Sabastian wasn't much of a drinker, but he didn't wish to be rude to his cordial host. Besides, he had a favor to ask of her that would throw a monkey wrench into the tentative plan he had so far come up with if she said no. "Would it be possible to use the top floor of this place as a command post?"

"If that is what it will take to get those fuckin' Abba-Dabba's out of my neighborhood, then be my guest."

Sabastian looked over at Jerrelle, stunned at her friend's words. Although not an actual racial slur, it undoubtedly was said in that context. Normally, he wasn't someone who turned a blind eye when it came to any sort of intolerance, but he could understand the motivation behind something like that being said. He didn't know Cloe at all, but he had a feeling that she had been treated negatively and disrespectfully on numerous occasions because of the way she looked or simply because of her gender. It was unfortunate, but people could be just as cruel and merciless as Mother Nature. Besides, she had been strong-armed for years into complying with a set of rules that had been laid out for her by a scumbag body shop owner, all because she was friends with Jerrelle. Over time, an accumulative amount of insufferable things directed toward someone can cause a good person to do or say things that would never be expected of them. For those reasons, and for this time only, Sabastian was willing to let what was said slide by without a response from him.

"Um... Let's hope that we get lucky and kill two birds with one stone."

"I wouldn't bet on that happening, Jerrelle. Louie isn't anywhere near as careless as his predecessor was."

"That may be so, Sab, but now that you are supposedly dead, he may rest on his laurels and think that he and his organization are now untouchable. Antonio Marcone is proof that that kind of arrogance can evolve into a superiority complex."

"I can't imagine the D.U.O. becoming lackadaisical due to it now appearing as if no one can stand in their way. They've been in business for generations. That alone tells me that they won't ever take anything for granted."

Jerrelle oddly didn't agree with her friend's supposition.

After taking the first sip of his second beer, Sabastian then continued, "Based upon their reputation alone, it's safe to say that what you and your sister saw, is what you and I both believe it to be. That being said, our eyes don't always allow us to identify what the entire story is. So until we see exactly what lies beyond the walls of that boarded-up old store, we can't allow our supposition to become the reason that we make an egregious mistake."

"Well... I can guarantee you that it's not a private, social club," Cloe interjected.

"Unfortunately, we have to wait until my old platoon gets here before our curiosity is satisfied." Sabastian took another sip and then said to Jerrelle, "I'd like to use the free time that we now have on our hands and visit with Governor White. I feel obligated to inform him of what we have planned."

"You could just call him."

"I know, Jerrelle, but I'd also like to visit with him for a bit while I'm in Michigan."

"What about Madelyn?"

159

Sabastian was certainly worried about her wellbeing, but his country came first. And even though he technically no longer was a permanent member of its military, that sense of duty would never leave him. "Once we are done visiting with the governor, then we can return to the city to try and find her."

Jerrelle pounded back her beer and proceeded to leave the bar. "You better hurry up and finish your pint because if you're not in the car by the time I put it in gear, I'm leaving you behind."

Sabastian looked over at Cloe. "She wouldn't do that, would she?"

Cloe just smiled and waited for Sabastian to hand her back his glass of beer. In all honesty, he was glad that Jerrelle had chosen to leave right away, as he really didn't want to consume two full pints. Until everything was known: what was across the street and where Madelyn was, Sabastian preferred to keep his mind as clear as possible. Yes, it wouldn't have been that much alcohol in his system, but beer had a tendency to make his ass drag once the effects of it began to wear off.

He took one last giant gulp, set the pint down on the bar, thanked Cloe for her hospitality and for agreeing to his request, and then headed toward the front door. Just as he was about to open it up, an unwanted thought appeared — the moment he stepped out onto the street, he was going to see nothing but the cloud Jerrelle left behind after she smoked the tires and took off on down Michigan Avenue without him. Thankfully, that had not been the case.

The drive to Lansing had a whole different feeling for Sabastian than it did just over a month ago. The last time, he was still getting used to his newly discovered identity and he was unsure what kind of reaction he would get from Governor White. Even though the two of them have since formed a friendship, he could not even begin to guess what Christopher's reaction was going to be once he informed him of everything he knew and suspected concerning the Detroit Underworld Organization and the United Arab league.

Upon their arrival, Sabastian first made sure that Jerrelle left her weapons in the car — including her honor blade. He wasn't worried about her using them, but her hard-edge look and unyielding personality were more than likely going to give someone at one of the various seen and unseen security checkpoints throughout the government building a reason to label her as being a suspicious individual.

After walking past the two main security desks: at the front doors and at the entrance to the governor's wing of the building, Sabastian and Jerrelle arrived at their destination without once being stopped and questioned. That seemed to be just a little bit strange to both of them. It was as if everyone who worked there had known them for years.

The governor's secretary was sitting behind her desk, organizing some paperwork, and enjoying an afternoon cup of sim-caf. Sylvia had never liked the addictive drink before, but after being surprised with unsuspected visits from Maxwell, Savanna, Sydney, and Sabastian in less than a month's time she had decided to try it. Quickly, she realized it was the only thing that seemed to keep her nerves calm whenever she felt any stress starting. "Well, hello there, Sabastian. The governor is expecting you."

Sylvia's revelation came as more of a surprise than did the lack of any questioning he received from those they passed by on their way to see the governor. It caused him to pause and think. It was assumed that Christopher expected him to one day return in order to finish off what his father had started. Still, Sabastian was nobody of any importance; he should not have been able to walk right up to this office uncontested — nor should Sylvia have been forewarned of his pending arrival.

Unexpectedly, one of those mysteries was solved when he was informed that, on the day he left San Antonio, Savanna had sent a quick V-mail to the governor. Apparently, she felt obligated to let him know that Sabastian was going to be in the area on Friday. "Ok, but... how did you know that I was in the building?"

"Did you forget that Detroit is hooked up to a C-4 network? Once the governor was told that you were on your way here, he had your name and image attached to the 'persons of interest' list. The moment that you stepped off of the train, the governor was alerted to your arrival."

"Ah… and with his learning of this, he subsequently alerted this building's security to keep an eye out for me and to just let me walk in here unopposed."

"Correct! Nice piece of detective work," Sylvia lightheartedly said.

After sharing a private smile with the governor's secretary, Sabastian remembered something very important. Though it was boorish of him, his forgetting was clearly unintentional. "Oh, I'm sorry. This is my best friend, Jerrelle Robinson."

Sylvia extended her hand in greeting.

Jerrelle reciprocated and immediately confirmed her initial suspicions that this young woman was everything in a female that she wasn't, nor ever wanted to be. The governor's secretary was as feminine as they came. Her hands were overly soft, her grip was too gentle, her perfume was too strong, and her personality bordered on being too passive. Jerrelle had always believed that a woman needed to be strong; both mentally and physically. That way, no one would be able to assume that they could overpower them and make them submit to their demands or be controlled by somebody else's will. But that was the way Jerrelle was, and most women were not like her. She wasn't normally one to judge the way a person was when she would first meet them, but Sylvia appeared to be the universal template for the majority of her gender. Of course, that didn't mean that Jerrelle could not like her — eventually. "It's nice to meet you."

"Will you both please take a seat in the lobby and I'll see if the governor is finished with his conference call." Sylvia then walked down the hall to Christopher's office. She could have just called him from her desk, but she hated to do that when she knew he was in the middle of something important. About five minutes later, from at the end of the hall, she motioned for Sabastian and Jerrelle to come. Upon their arrival, she courteously held open the door for them.

"It's good to see you again, Sabastian," the governor said, as he shook his hand. "And I take it that you must be Jerrelle?" The governor then offered his hand and shook her firm grip. "Please take a seat. So then.., I have to assume that you are here because you have found out something important that you feel I should be made aware of?"

162

Jerrelle looked at Sabastian, surprised at how vigilant the governor was — but then she remembered that the man had spent twenty-five years as a police officer before tossing his name in the political ring. Both occupations required the possession of an astute, unwavering skill set. For a man not too far away from enjoying his golden years, Christopher White still seemed to be a very sharp-witted individual.

"My uncle told me that my father had always hated, yet quietly envied your ability to read people and know when they are bullshitting you or when they are keeping something from you that they should not."

"It's a talent that I was forced to acquire early on." Christopher produced a wry smile; so did Sabastian — only because he knew that the governor's words were in direct reference to the intentional difficulties that his father used to cause him.

After that shared personal moment was over, he encouraged Jerrelle to tell his father's old boss what it was that she knew since she was the one who had brought the information to his attention in the first place.

As her story unfolded, the governor listened intently; he learned long ago to never dismiss something because it sounded too preposterous to have any sort of merit. Once her briefing was completed, Christopher turned his attention to Sabastian and then listened to his account of the recent events that had taken place in Tijuana and Puerto Rico.

If all of that wasn't enough for him to absorb, what came next was something that Christopher White could not have predicted. The Union's elite military platoon was now on their way to his state to confirm the possibility of terrorist activity. He was well aware of the rumors that the U.A.L. might be a front for a terrorist network, but now with this new information that he had just been given about the possibility of that group buying stolen weaponry from the Detroit Underworld Organization, as far as he was concerned, this just became priority number one.

The governor suddenly found himself standing at a crossroad. Even though the information he had just been given was a collection of hearsay, he had an obligation to pass it along to the Union Bureau of

Investigation. However, Sabastian unexpectedly made a request that suddenly placed him in a difficult position; he was unsure that he could comply with what was being asked. Ironically, it was somewhat similar to those same kinds of requests that his father would, back in the day, occasionally ask of him.

After taking a few moments to remember the consequences that would follow after agreeing to do what Maxwell would ask of him, Christopher's reservations began to disappear. No significant damage had ever been done to the police department, his reputation, or to any of those who had been under his command. In fact, each and every time he granted such a request, a stagnant investigation ended up taking a significant leap forward.

What Sabastian had asked of him, was that he temporarily refrain from informing the Bureau about the S.N.A.F.U.'s intentions. The reason for this request was because he believed the League, if they were to somehow learn that their group was being observed or investigated, would probably end up doing one of two things: disappear deeper underground, or prematurely unleash whatever plans they may have in the works.

Christopher took a moment and pondered; he certainly could not dismiss Sabastian's supposition. What made things more difficult for him though, was that his responsibilities could not be blindly ignored either. When he was a police captain, the worst thing he feared concerning his career, was a decision that in turn, cost him a suspension. As the governor, a foolhardy decision could cost him not only public embarrassment but his job as well. So after weighing all of the pros and cons, he decided to walk a fine line and play the old 'one card at a time' game. "I'm sorry, Sabastian, but I'm obligated to call the U.B.I.'s Northern District Director. I have to at least make him aware of the fact that the S.N.A.F.U. is going to be in Michigan. I'm sure that he (Mark Quills) will push me for a reason as to why, but I promise you that I will not privy him to that information. For now, he will only be told what I feel he needs to be told... nothing more. That is until you can provide me with more concrete evidence. At that point, I will then let him know exactly what is going on. I'm sure he'll be pissed off afterward that I neglected to tell him everything up front, but this is my state, and when it comes to protecting it, I'd rather leave that in the hands of you and your military brethren instead of him and a bunch of overpaid suit jockeys who are more concerned about their own images than the actual Union itself."

Sabastian smiled inside. This was what he had hoped for when he came here to Lansing to inform the governor of his and the S.N.A.F.U.'s intentions. In retrospect, this visit should not have been necessary, as his lone objective had only been to finish off what his father had started. For years, the D.U.O. had somehow been able to steal weapons from the military and sell them to whomever they wanted. And as has happened before, more weapons appeared as if they were about to end up in the hands of a suspected terrorist organization. It's somewhat ironic that Sabastian is connected to both problems. It also gave him even more motivation than ever to put a stop to not only Louie's madness and to the D.U.O.'s existence, but the potential threat that was now out there to his beloved country.

After the obligatory goodbyes were exchanged, Sabastian and Jerrelle left the governor's office and headed back to Detroit. Once they got there, the only thing that he wanted to do was to try and locate Madelyn. It wasn't going to be easy, but if and when he did, he hoped that it wasn't too late.

The largest city that sits on the eastern side of Lake Michigan is Muskegon. Surprisingly, just beyond its northern boundary, still sits quite a lot of untapped nature. Roughly five miles from the outskirts of the conurbation, nestled right in the middle of a thousand plus acres of private land, is where the militia has their base of operation.

It took Zhin and Nicoli just over half a day's travel to arrive there with the sample merchandise for the militia to view. It wasn't an easy trip for two people from two different worlds, China and Germany, but they both managed to make it there without any issues and close to their projected time.

"I hope this deal gets done quickly. I need some serious sleep before we head back to Detroit."

"As do I, Nicoli. I don't want to be at all tired, and then have that turn into a liability if for some reason the delivery we will be making to the U.A.L. in two days becomes something other than straightforward."

As they had hoped, the showing of the merchandise went smoothly and relatively quick. Within twenty minutes, they had reached a deal with Mr. Collins, the head of the militia, to take the weapons that Antonio had stockpiled off of their hands. It was a deal that would see the D.U.O. deliver twenty Smith & Wesson 22 Match Heavy Barrel M-41-C series rifles, twenty 38 Master Model 52-C Series Auto rifles, two dozen Beretta series M9A1 handguns, two dozen laser-guided Glock .45 GAP, and a dozen police issue tasers to the Muskegon Militia.

Judging by what they had ordered, it was obvious to Nicoli that this group wasn't just a shooting club. They had an obvious agenda. And although he was curious as to what that could be, he knew that it was none of his concern. What mattered was that he and Zhin had accomplished what they had set out to do.

For Nicoli, he felt that there was no way Louie could question where his allegiance now lied. He had not only helped to broker two agreements with two different organizations, but he had saved him from a situation in which his life could have prematurely ended. In the past, he would have balked at a task as menial as negotiating something for their superior because there was no glory attached to it, but after having been a part of that process twice now, a sense of accomplishment like none he had ever experienced before was there — and he actually liked that feeling. He was surprisingly proud of himself and finally realized that being an important part of the machine didn't necessarily mean that you had to limit yourself to only one specific function. Before, he was just the muscle. Now, he wanted to become someone that Louie could rely on for anything.

Zhin was also thrilled that things had gone smoothly — but he honestly didn't care for the isolation of the woods. He was a city person and didn't want to be where he was; he wanted to be back in Detroit, a place that he was quickly growing fond of.

He knew that it was stupid, but for some unknown reason, he had allowed a concern to grow. Undoubtedly, it was brought on by the importance of the upcoming transaction with the United Arab League. Zhin knew that his worry had nothing to do with the deal itself; it had to do with the importance of it to Louie. The last thing he wanted was to fail the man whom he had long respected and admired from afar.

Undoubtedly, the completion of the deal would then give him the reassurance he sought; that the decision to bring him to the Union to become the organization's new number one associate had been the right one. He knew that Louie had faith in him — he just had to find within himself to accept the given, unwavering belief.

Just as Jerrelle and Sabastian returned to Detroit, the sun had called it a day. This recurring event was going to both hurt and help them. Under the cover of night, the possibility of any curious eyes being drawn to them was greatly reduced. Conversely, being able to keep tabs on their surroundings was going to be somewhat of a challenge. Notwithstanding that, they were going to be only a stone's throw away from the enemy's front door. Therefore, their instincts and their better judgment were going to have to be relied upon even more than usual.

Each on their own, they walked up and down the streets, checking out all the known establishments that the D.U.O. owned, hoping to catch a break and either find a clue as to where Madelyn would be or learn something that they could use in their quest to shut Louie's organization down.

After two hours, they yielded to a lack of success — though that didn't mean they were ready to call it a day. As had been planned earlier, they both met up at the District Bar & Grill. There, they could have just stayed for a while and observed as Bai Lin had previously done, but Sabastian was leery about being out in the open for all to see. Knowing his luck, word would somehow find its way back to Louie that he was in the neighborhood. The last thing he wanted was to give up the advantage he had of being 'dead', so they crossed the street and went back to where Jerrelle had parked her Camero; in almost the exact same spot that her car had been in yesterday.

Of all the legitimate businesses that the enemy owned, the Old World Café & Restaurant was the nearest one to the New Book Cadillac Hotel. Its proximity to it, however, didn't mean that someone associated with the D.U.O. would make an appearance tonight. Sometimes, you just have to get lucky. The night sky was clear and the stars were shining rather bright. With that being so, it was quite possible that a few of them were also aligned.

They didn't go anywhere; Sabastian told Jerrelle that he wanted to sit in the car for a while and observe, just like his father used to do when he was a Detroit police officer. He wasn't sure if anything would come from his decision to do this but apparently, luck was on their side this evening.

Shortly after nine p.m., one block down and headed in the direction of the restaurant, Jerrelle's radar just happened to lock onto what she determined as being an odd-looking couple. The man was clearly much older in age than the woman — and in her opinion, was not nearly handsome enough to deserve to even be seen with someone who was as beautiful as his date.

Sabastian caught on to what his friend had been looking at and soon realized that she had unknowingly spotted what he had hoped to see. A rather large weight was instantly lifted off of his shoulders. Madelyn was alive and appeared to be all right. Unfortunately, she was still with Louie.

For a brief moment, thoughts of betrayal returned. Only seconds though had passed before he was able to read between the lines — even from as far away as he was. No longer were any of those unwarranted fears there that had consumed him during his train ride to Detroit. Instead, Sabastian began to feel a sense of urgency. Yet, he knew that he had to be patient and wait for the right moment to rescue Madelyn. And as hard as it was for him to believe, it didn't appear that Louie had any malicious intentions toward her. Freely, she was walking with him.

Unexpectedly, Sabastian got out of Jerrelle's car. She almost called out to him, wanting to know what he was doing, but she didn't — her curiosity and her gut seemed to be at odds. Therefore, she decided to just let things play out and see what her friend was up to. Barring any unusual heavy traffic this evening on Woodward, she should be able to catch up to Sabastian within only a few seconds if he needed her help.

Without actually crossing the street, he got as close as he could to Louie and Madelyn; he then snapped a few discrete pictures with his vid-cell. The camera on it was exceptional, but not one phone currently on the market was advanced enough to take crystal clear photos of anything at night. Nevertheless, what he wanted the photos for they would be good enough.

After placing his vid-cell back into his jacket pocket, he returned to Jerrelle's car, got into the passenger seat, looked over at his old friend, and smiled. Although she was curious as to why Sabastian had just done what he did, there was no reason for her to inquire, so she just started the car and drove off. It wasn't until they were a few blocks down the road that she asked him why they didn't follow Louie and Madelyn into the restaurant. The answer she was given was one that she somewhat expected. Sabastian felt it would not be wise to confront the enemy at this time and reveal his surprising return from the grave. He had the advantage; it made sense to hold onto it for as long as possible. Hopefully, he'd be able to do that until he was ready to finish off the war between the Detroit Underworld Organization and his family.

Had he not come to the conclusion that Madelyn was safe, he probably would have made a different decision. Because he believed she was, Sabastian could in good conscience, put aside his personal mission for now and focus his attention fully on what else was important — what he and the S.N.A.F.U. were planning on doing tomorrow.

Sabastian was exhausted; it had been a long and stressful day. Thankfully, Jerrelle's apartment was less than a five-minute drive away from the downtown core. When he crossed the threshold into her place, he noticed that it was nearly empty except for the stack of boxes piled up neatly in the spare bedroom — other than her bed, the only piece of furniture left was an old tattered couch. People have the right to live their lives the way they choose. Still, Sabastian was curious as to why Jerrelle had chosen to live like this. So he asked her.

She just shook her head. Only after a moment taken to enjoy a private laugh did she then tell her friend she had spent nearly the entire day yesterday packing up her place because she intended to move.

Joy consumed Sabastian; he also felt pretty stupid. He knew in his heart that Jerrelle was going to accept his offer and move down to San Antonio. The moment he saw her apartment the way it was, he should have put two and two together. But apparently, his slowly developing detective skills completely disappear once fatigue begins to set in.

The next morning, they both got up early and headed to Selfridge Air Force Base to meet up with Sabastian's platoon. Their timing could not have been any better, as they had arrived just as the S.N.A.F.U.'s transport plane was touching down — and it was a good thing that he still possessed his military credentials, because there would not have been any way whatsoever that he and Jerrelle would have been granted access to the highly secured airport grounds without them.

Ten minutes later, Sabastian was welcoming his brethren to Michigan. He smiled warmly as his friend, the recently promoted Richard Atwater, exited the aircraft. Right afterward, in a moment of unexpected surprise, Captain E.J. Swilling stuck his head out through the open door of the plane. Sabastian's instincts immediately kicked in; he promptly stood at full attention and saluted the man who he held in high regard.

"At ease, soldier. Or should I say, First Lieutenant!"

That caught Sabastian off guard, as he had no idea that a promotion could be handed out after someone had officially been placed on reserve status. "Sir.., may I ask why you are here?"

"Since I am the one who agreed to provide you with the services of the unit, it only makes sense that I accompany them as well. I know that this is your operation, but if for some reason it becomes something other than what we are here for, I am going to step in and take over."

This was the first time that Sabastian ever remembered disagreeing with a superior officer's decree. The S.N.A.F.U.'s only purpose for being in Michigan was to back him up, not to step on his toes and take over. Therefore, he needed to make sure that he and Captain Swilling were on the same page and it was understood that he was going to call the shots. If this evolved to a point in which a crucial decision needed to be made, then Sabastian was going to be responsible for that as well. "Sir.., can we talk privately for a moment?"

"Absolutely!"

They took a walk down the tarmac, stopping once they reached the tail end of the plane. It was there they felt they were far enough away so that their conversation could not be overheard by anyone else. Five minutes; that was all it had taken for them to come to an understanding.

Upon their return to the group, they made their way over to Jerrelle where she was then introduced. Captain Swilling promptly shook her hand and thanked her on behalf of the Union Government for the significant role she played in the success of the mission in Puerto Rico. Once that was done, E.J. asked that everyone follow him into a building that had been set aside for them to use; it was there that he reminded everyone in the unit that this was unsanctioned and what their role was going to be. Sabastian then took over and made sure that everyone understood what their objective was — confirm whether or not stolen military weapons were being sold, and whether or not the supposed recipient was a terrorist group. Following that, he assigned everyone their tasks, and then let them know what his plan was.

If things unfolded as he hoped, in a similar manner to those other recent missions, then Sabastian would get what he wanted — another implicit dagger stuck in the back of the Detroit Underworld Organization. If luck was on their side and they were able to obtain definitive proof that stolen military weapons were being sold to a terrorist organization, he would then step aside and willingly hand over the reins to Captain Swilling.

Previously, Cloe had made it known that she was willing to help them out in any way she could; it was why Henré had met up with them at Selfridge Air Force Base with the Cough Inn's courtesy shuttle. There, they loaded it up with all of the S.N.A.F.U.'s supplies (uniforms, observation equipment, gear, and weapons). The reason for this was so that no one would suspect that something, other than a daily task related to the club, was actually taking place.

Henré didn't return to the Cough Inn alone; Jerrelle had ridden back with him — this was done so that he would have help to unload the van as quickly as possible so that the chances would be greatly reduced of any curious eyes wondering if something strange was going on.

Once Sabastian received word that this task was completed, he and four others, at staggered intervals, would then show up at the bar in normal street clothes in order to pass themselves off as everyday patrons who were just going inside for some food or a drink. Once that was complete, they would then make their way up to the third floor, change into their uniforms, set up their temporary command post, and become part of the main observation team.

Of the remaining nine members of the unit, eight of them had it relatively easy. They were to be split up into two groups of four, with each group being positioned at either end of the block, parked and waiting in one of their two windowless vans. The lone remaining soldier, the platoon's sniper specialist, Stanley 'Zeik' Zeikulliamon; it would be his responsibility to obtain a stealth position on top of one of the buildings that sat directly across the alleyway behind the old store. There, with a sniper rifle, grenade launcher, and digital day/night vision camera, he would monitor all activity and keep in constant contact with the team inside The Cough Inn.

Now, they just had to hope that something was going to happen that would confirm what is suspected. It would certainly be a waste of their time if they ended up staking out the old boarded-up store for more than a few days and nothing remotely suspicious happened. Sabastian believed that what Jerrelle and her sister saw, was indeed a weapons showing taking place between the Detroit Underworld Organization and the United Arab League. But if definitive proof could not be obtained in an acceptable amount of time, there would be no other choice but to cancel their operation and conclude that the place in question was nothing more than what it appeared to be on the outside.

By one o'clock in the afternoon, Sabastian, Jerrelle, Captain Swilling, Richard Atwater, Ben Fraisure, and Jeff Trantor were in two adjoining empty rooms above the nightclub; rooms that gave them a perfect view of their target. Zeik was hunkered down in his rooftop position and the other eight soldiers — well, since they were not needed at that moment, they had been temporarily stationed at a nearby hotel. It didn't make sense to leave them stuck in a vehicle, waiting and wondering. However, if this 'mission' did change from one where only Intel was to be gathered to one where their assistance was needed, they would then be dispatched to their assigned positions. Which Sabastian honestly hoped, did not need to take place.

6

~ If it ever gets to the point where it is believed that you have all the answers, an accurate portrayal of you can then be drawn in which no argument could be had that you are nothing other than someone who is usually full of shit ~

Because she had failed to take into account any potential consequences, the hole she had already been in, got a little deeper. All that she had wanted was a semblance of revenge. Achieving a want though doesn't usually happen without first having to make some sort of sacrifice or pay some sort of price. At the time, she was more than willing to do so. What she didn't expect, was that one very special individual would end up turning the world she knew, completely upside.

Ever since she has been on her own, she found it difficult to take a chance on something. Admittedly, it was because she was afraid of making another huge mistake like she did when she abruptly left home at eighteen. That impulsive decision certainly did not turn out how she had expected it to. And as a result of that misguided belief, guilt continually existed within her.

Occasionally, the thought of self-termination would appear — but she was always able to dismiss that crazy notion. After what she had done to Sabastian though, it returned more domineering than ever before. Thankfully, she had found the strength to ignore that urge.

There, mixed in with all of her chaotic thoughts and emotions, was hope; hope that the one and only person who ever found a way into her heart, would rescue her, become a part of her life, and then allow her for the first time, to not be ashamed of her past decisions and who she currently was as a result of them.

On the sofa in her hotel suite, Madelyn sat there counting down the minutes before she had to go to work. Although she didn't want to, she had to. She was stuck right where she was and she could not let it be known that she wanted to be somewhere else. So until she found a way to leave the hotel on her own accord, she had to pretend that she was the same person Louie believed her to be.

Today was to be her first day bartending at the Cadillac Club Room inside Louie's Casino. It had been a very difficult decision for her to come back to Detroit afterward. If it weren't for the fact that a bit of optimism had found its way into her wounded soul, she probably would have done something stupid before the Escalade she was in, got beyond the Chicago city limits.

"Pull over!"

Nicoli turned around and gave her a 'are you serious' look. Before he could say what he was thinking, Louie asked, "Why?"

"I just don't feel so well."

"I'm sorry, but we can't stop the vehicle right now."

"Then stop it as soon as you can, please. My stomach is churning and I think that I just might throw up back here."

The last thing Louie wanted was for Madelyn to toss her cookies in the back seat of the organization's brand new SUV, so he promised her that he would try to find a place for her to get sick at as soon as he felt that they had distanced themselves far enough away from where the execution of Sabastian Banks had just taken place.

In reality, Madelyn wasn't sick. She instead, was deeply regretting the decision she had made. Because she had found herself in an unfamiliar situation, the only course of action she believed she could take was to follow through with what she had been asked to do. What she should have done in hindsight was what she had never done before — follow her instincts. By the time she realized it, it was too late — Louie and his henchmen were waiting on the other side of the bedroom door. It was why her only option was to improvise and hope that the few trifling clues she left behind would be noticed before it was too late.

Lifelong happiness just never seemed to be in the cards for her. Somehow, she had convinced herself to simply accept the shitty hand she had long ago been dealt. For seven years, she willingly sold herself and ignored her morals. It wasn't until she unexpectedly experienced a small taste of what things could be like, that change actually appeared to be possible. Not at all was Madelyn a gambler, but unless she took a chance, there'd be no way for her to remove herself from the situation she was in.

No longer did she wish to be associated with Louie Mazotti. Unfortunately, she had not a clue how to cut her ties. What she did know though, was that she could not do it alone. She needed help. Her best chance of success was with Sabastian's assistance, but she had no way of knowing if he was even still alive — or willing.

While sitting alone at the very back of the SUV, she thought of bailing out the door of the vehicle. What was stopping her from doing this was that she didn't think she had the courage to jump. And even if she was successful, she doubted very much that she would be able to outrun any of her three accomplices.

Uncertainty continued to flood her thoughts. With each stop the SUV made, the opportunity was there for her to escape — but she kept chickening out. She didn't know what to do. As they were approaching the next red light, Madelyn noticed that there was a police vehicle, three cars behind them. If she was ever going to find her backbone and bail, this coming stop had to be the one. However, just as she was about to reach for the door handle, she felt a series of low vibrations. Her senses immediately directed her where that was taking place — inside her purse. It was then that she realized someone was trying to call her. Her heart immediately skipped a beat in anticipation.

As anxious as she was to know if it was Sabastian or not, she knew that she had to resist the temptation to look at her vid-cell screen. As low risk as it might appear to be, she just didn't want to take a chance that someone inside the vehicle would see what she was doing.

Quickly, she weighed her options. She was going to take a chance — but not what she had been contemplating. Instead, she decided to stay right where she was and do what she had done throughout her escorting career. She was going to slip into actress mode.

Because Louie was already aware of her warning that she was feeling somewhat sick it made perfect sense to pretend that she really was now. So, for a good thirty seconds, Madelyn feigned a cough. She then followed that by making it seem as if she was actually about to

176

throw up in the car. This caused Louie to order Zhin to quickly find a place to pull over. Hastily, his associate drove the Cadillac into the closest parking lot he found and then stopped the vehicle just a few feet away from the side alleyway of a restaurant.

After saying thank you, Madelyn got out of the vehicle and hastily walked about twenty feet away from it, right toward a garbage dumpster — it was where she decided would be the best place to not only seclude herself behind and away from any inquisitive eyes, but where she would learn whether or not her prayers had been answered.

Once she was as concealed as she could be, she opened up her purse and removed her vid-cell. While doing that, she continued to act as sick as she could be by making several, very disgusting noises — thankfully, Louie, Zhin, and Nicoli chose not to pay any attention to her 'throwing up'.

The moment she looked at the missed call screen, elation overwhelmed her — some of her guilt disappeared as well. She owed Sabastian a rather large apology the next time that she saw him — she just hoped that he was willing to listen to it.

Just because he had apparently survived though, didn't mean that the threat against him was over. Madelyn's wellbeing was also not assured. Easily, she could take the opportunity she now had and make a run for it, just like she had earlier contemplated, as no one appeared to be paying any attention to her. But she had run away from her life twice now, and she wasn't going to run anymore. And who's to say that, if she did take off, Louie wouldn't hunt her down and kill her, just like he tried to do to Sabastian.

Even a blind man could see the position Madelyn was in. She was on the inside and she had Louie's trust. She needed to use that to her advantage. Turning the tables on him was the logical thing for her to do. And if she were to succeed, it would be something that Sabastian could surely use against him. It also might help to make up for what she had just put him through.

To make certain that there was no chance that neither of her three 'guard dogs' would ever discover who had actually called her, she took out a small handkerchief from her purse and wrapped her vid-cell in it — her intent was to make it look as if she had gotten sick into the cloth and not onto the ground. She then put it in the dumpster in *the middle of a bunch of rotting table scraps at the bottom. That deception, she hoped, would eliminate any possible chance of one of them getting out of the Cadillac to verify that she had indeed gotten sick. Checking the ground was one thing; dumpster diving for proof was a task that very few would volunteer to do.*

After Madelyn returned to the vehicle and stepped inside, she again thanked Louie for pulling over, informed him that she was feeling much better, and then stated that she did not believe there would be any more episodes of sickness. For her, the time between now and their arrival in Detroit, four hours, was going to be filled with both hope and resentment — at least, the remorse that had earlier consumed her, no longer seemed to be there.

With her now knowing that Sabastian had survived, her abhorrence for Louie Mazotti started to grow. Madelyn would have never thought this to be possible, but apparently, a tiger can change its stripes. How could she have been so naïve? Never before had she been used like this. She had always been the one to call the shots. When you let your emotions dictate the decisions you make, something like this is bound to happen. And because that is what had taken place, she now felt like an idiot, a fool — even worthless. But those were things that she wasn't. She was a strong and independent woman. Now, she needed to become fearless.

She looked at the clock and saw that she had ten minutes left before she had to report to her new job, a job that in actuality would be her first real one. And even though she knew that her days working as a bartender at the New Book Cadillac Casino were going to be numbered, she was admittedly curious as to what it was like to have a normal job — she just despised the fact that Louie was technically her boss.

The offspring of the organization's enemy was no more. By tomorrow, the deal that Louie's men had procured would be complete. He didn't want to jump the gun and celebrate, but he finally felt like he had accomplished something noteworthy. This pending deal wasn't some smalltime back alley agreement with a local gang of gutter punks, this was a high-profile transaction that not only would do a lot for Louie's confidence but solidify him as a legitimate leader in the world's Mafioso society.

After completing his necessary vid-phone conversation with Casper, Louie called both of his trusted associates into his office. Upon their arrival, he briefed them on their assignment and then followed that with a bit of gratuitous endorsement. And although it wasn't at all necessary, Louie felt the need to remind his men of just how important this delivery was — only because he firmly believed that the organization's continued existence depended upon its completion.

After accepting from their boss a small piece of paper with an address on it, Zhin and Nicoli left to go and pick up the preloaded truck of merchandise. Neither felt that their assignment was going to be nothing other than straightforward, but both were also markedly aware that in the profession they chose to work, anything at any time could happen. Therefore, each had to remember to stay on their toes and make sure that nothing unexpected and unwanted took place.

Once his associates had left, Louie again felt the urge to celebrate — after all, he had proven Maxwell's prophecy to be nothing but pure rhetoric. However, just as he was about to head toward his wet bar, he remembered that Madelyn had to work her first shift tonight at the Cadillac Club Room. Nothing could stop him from going there to visit, but his admitted admiration of her was not for the general public to become privy to. So instead, he just thought it best to leave her alone and let her work without any more unnecessary stress than what she already had to deal with.

After a few moments of contemplation, he determined what his evening was going to consist of. As anyone else would, he should have just called the hotel's amenities service directly, but they did not have access to the top floor. Therefore, he picked up his vid-phone and called Connie Yale. After first apologizing for again asking her to be his liaison, he requested to have two of the hotel's best masseuses sent up to his office. He hoped that a relaxing massage would ease the weeks of tension that still caused his muscles to ache. What he prayed did not occur, was that it sent him straight into dreamland, as the last thing he wanted right now was another unwanted visit from his, certainly going to be pissed off, ethereal adversary.

The traffic in front of The Cough Inn seemed to be a bit scarcer than what it should be for a Friday night. In fact, there was an abundance of open parking spots on both sides of the street. It's commonly known that most young club-goers don't usually start showing up until later in the evening, but it was only an hour before midnight and there was not yet a line of people waiting to come into the club. That wasn't ideal. Preferably, they would like to have that so as not to give anyone any reason to suspect that anything else out of the ordinary might be going on.

Just off to the side of a third-floor window, Jerrelle stood, staying out of sight as she kept an eye on the streets below. Sabastian was sitting in the back corner of the room watching the live video feed of the alley from the remote night vision camera that Zeik had set up. Richard, E.J., Ben, and Jeff were all sitting at a table playing euchre and eating the complimentary burgers and fries that Cloe had sent up to them.

Although she was admittedly nervous about the military being inside her place, she was actually happy at the prospect of the U.A.L. being removed from her neighborhood. Feeding the soldiers was the least she could do. Unfortunately, it was nowhere near equal to the gratitude she felt. Yes, they hadn't yet done anything, but them simply being there was enough to strangely put her at ease. Time and patience were all it was going to take now for the uneasiness she had about her neighbors, to finally go away — she hoped. "Jerrelle.., Sabastian.., is there anything that I can get for you?"

"Not at the moment, but when this is over, a few cold beers would be nice."

"There will always be a cold beer here for you, Jerrelle." Cloe then smiled and left everyone alone.

The room stayed quiet for several minutes before Richard asked Jerrelle a rather presumptuous question, "Are you helping us with this because you still feel that you haven't yet made up for your past inability to live up to the expectations of being a Union soldier?"

Her integrity suddenly being questioned would normally have gotten that person severely beaten up, but Richard was one hundred percent correct. She had failed in life at a lot of things, and her recent reunification with Sabastian not only showed her that old wounds could be healed, but her life could actually have meaning.

That event had caused her to look far into her checkered past. She admittedly made a lot of mistakes, but the one she regretted the most was throwing away the golden opportunity she had been given to be a member of the Union military. Her recent experiences with Sabastian in Japan, Germany, England, and more recently in Puerto Rico, had awoken a sense of pride in her and had helped to erase all of the self-pity she wallowed in her entire life. "Up until now, I had an I-really-don't-give-two-shits, fuck-the-world attitude; especially when I was a part of the military. But a lot of things have happened to me since then that have made me change my entire view on life."

"Did you have an epiphany?"

"No, Sab. I just decided that it was time I try acting like a normal adult instead of a rebellious teenager convinced that the cruel and unfair world was the lone cause of all of my frustrations."

Sabastian listened intently as his longtime friend spoke; a bit of vanity enveloped him afterward. Jerrelle was indeed changing — and he was happy to have been a small part of her transformation. She was still as lethal as ever, but it now looked as if she finally realized that she hadn't been cursed with having the world's shittiest life.

Unexpectedly, Sabastian's attention was drawn to an alert from Zeik. Immediately, he looked at the monitor in front of him and spoke directly to his brethren through the headset he wore. On the screen, he could see that a city-owned vehicle was pulling up in the back alley behind the abandoned store. It was already known that some emergency repair work had just been completed in that same alley, so Sabastian wasn't too concerned about it — that was until Jerrelle spoke up and alerted everyone in the room that eight men were now entering the front door of that same boarded-up store.

This sudden coinciding occurrence was all that it took for Captain Swilling to leave his half-eaten delicious burger and card game behind. Quickly, he moved to the front window, confirmed Jerrelle's report, and then made his way over to where the monitor was to verify what Sabastian had seen. Following a few moments spent reviewing what he had just learned, he pondered over what their next move should be. Unfortunately, it wasn't his to make.

He was sure that what Sabastian was thinking, wasn't the same thing he was — even though he knew that it was far too early to even be contemplating tossing aside their game plan.

He went back over to the table and took another healthy bite of his burger. For some strange reason, food always seemed to help him to stay focused. Once he washed it down, he returned to Sabastian's side. Yes, it was agreed upon that this was only supposed to be a recon mission, but Captain Swilling just didn't want to lose what might be the best opportunity they'll ever get to shut down an unsuspecting terrorist cell — especially one before they became active. Therefore, he decided that another conversation needed to take place. But before he could initiate that, Sabastian surprised him.

He knew that his former commanding officer was itching to do something that he clearly should not — and he also understood why. If he were the one in charge of the S.N.A.F.U., then he would probably consider taking the same, ill-advised course of action that Captain Swilling was mulling over.

There was no reason for this, but he strangely felt as if his back was up against the wall. No pressure was being put on him, but his conscience was telling him to do what, by all accounts, should not be done. Sometimes though, what appears to be the wrong decision is in fact, the right one. Therefore, after assuring himself he would allow no regret to appear afterward, Sabastian looked directly at his ex-commanding officer and asked E.J. to join him in a private conversation — so they stepped out into the hall.

"I know that we made an agreement, and even though we don't yet know exactly what is going on here, my gut is telling me that if we continue on with this in the manner in which we had agreed, we very well might miss a golden opportunity. I don't honestly want to place this burden into your lap, but you know as well as I do, sir, that one's own regret can be just as bad as the result incurred by any form of physical interrogation."

Captain Swilling had never heard that idiom before. Even so, it was easy for him to know exactly what Sabastian was referring to. For a few moments, he stood there inert and looking almost lost. Before accepting the offered torch and issuing a directive that could end up costing him everything, he needed to not only find validation but be comfortable with making such a crucial decision.

"If my fath… Captain Burelli was still alive he would have done what was necessary to ensure the safety of this great amalgamated nation of ours. The S.N.A.F.U. was subsequently bestowed upon you because there was no one else more suited to lead it. Your decision should be the same as what his would have been."

There was simply no denying that his former subordinate was right, so E.J. shook his head in acknowledgment. He then opened up the door to the room everyone else was in, entered, grabbed his radio off of the table, and called their two awaiting units, ordering them both to leave their hotel at once and to take up their assigned positions, just off to the side of each access point of the back alleyway.

By now, all of the men that had gathered out in front of the abandoned store had disappeared into it. Oddly, nothing out of the ordinary had yet to take place in the back alley since the city vehicle's arrival. It just sat there. This caused everyone in the room to fill with anxiousness; only because each of them knew that they were soon going to be called upon.

After a handful of unnerving seconds of nothing had passed, Sabastian's instincts nudged him to satisfy a curiosity. "Hey, Zeik! Is there any way that you can change the angle of your camera and get me a better shot of the driver of that city vehicle?"

"Sure. Give me a moment."

A minute later, Zeik had found the perfect angle. As hoped, it now clearly showed who the individual was sitting in the vehicle's driver's seat. It was none other than Zhin Wi. "Captain! I have just confirmed that the man behind the wheel is a member of the Detroit Underworld Organization."

That put a smile on the E.J.'s face. "Good! At least we now know that there is a connection between both organizations. What would be even better though is if we were able to get us some proof."

"Since I am not a member of the S.N.A.F.U., I can try and sneak up to the back of the truck and take a few photos of what's inside with my vid-cell," Jerrelle suggested.

"I appreciate the offer, but… If there are weapons in there, I'd rather have them offloaded and delivered to the League. That way, the evidence will be indisputable, and we will then be able to do what we are all trained to do."

"With all due respect, sir, what we now know should be enough for the U.B.I. to have grounds to conduct their own investigation. This should be passed along to them," Jeff Trantor said.

"All we have is the conclusion we have drawn. We have yet to get the definitive proof that the D.U.O. is here to sell stolen military weapons to a suspected terrorist group. If you are uncomfortable with what we soon intend to do, Sergeant, you are more than welcome to stay right where you are and twiddle your thumbs."

Right before Jeff had a chance to turn down Captain Swilling's debasing offer, Sabastian received another transmission from Zeik; he immediately called Captain Swilling to his side. There, on the monitor, it showed that six men had exited through the back door of the old store and were now offloading steel boxes from the city vehicle; the same exact kind of containers that are used when military weapons are shipped overseas. This pleased Sabastian. This was what they were hoping to see, and this just strengthened the belief that the United Arab League was more than what they portray themselves as being.

An opportunity was now in his hands, one that even his father probably never had, to slip a noose around the D.U.O.'s neck and then tighten it. This pending raid, he assuredly felt, was going to hurt them far worse than any of the others. In fact, Sabastian was all but certain that Louie Mazotti would be left with no other choice but to speculate that there was still someone out there fucking with his operations. Of course, this was untrue. Even so, this lone conjecture could be the catalyst that nudges the man right to the edge of the proverbial cliff. On top of that, it would all but eliminate any lingering thought the man might still have that Sabastian had somehow survived his execution.

A small part of his conscience suddenly caused him to pause and think. As much as he wanted to put a stop to what he and everyone else believed was going on inside the old abandoned store, the possibility could not be ignored that what they were now mere moments away from doing, might result in an unwanted consequence. Even if their actions ended in the outcome expected, the fact that this entire operation is unauthorized to begin with could be the only reason needed to have not only the leadership abilities of Captain Swilling come into question, but the need for the existence of the Special North American Freedom Unit as well. It seemed as if they were stuck between a rock and a hard place.

Five minutes was all that it had taken for every one of the metal boxes to be unloaded from the back of the city truck and the alley to empty of people — including Nicoli and Zhin, as they had followed right behind the last of the six members of the U.A.L. into the building.

This was it. He only had a few seconds to make up his mind. Either he volunteered and became a part of what Captain Swilling intended to do, or he stayed right where he was and washed his hands of any involvement. Unsurprisingly, the decision was easy for him to make.

No official recall had been given, but Sabastian was still technically a Union soldier. It was the love he had for his country, and the respect he had for anyone who donned a uniform to defend it, that gave him all the reason he needed to not sit this one out. So Sabastian picked up his gear, looked over at Captain Swilling, and said, "I suggest that we don't wait any longer, sir. Now would be the best time for us to raid the store and deal with the potential threat."

E.J. agreed. Without having to be told, everyone else in the room quickly gathered up their gear, including Jerrelle, and they all promptly headed to the stairs that would lead them down to the back alley exit of the bar. Before they completely left the building though, Captain Swilling made a courtesy call to the Dearborn Police Department. Their inclusion in this was something that Governor White had previously arranged, shortly after the S.N.A.F.U. had arrived in Detroit. They weren't going to be needed for backup; their only job was to ensure that no innocent bystanders were nearby in case Michigan Avenue turned into an impromptu warzone.

Within two minutes, police cruisers were positioned at each end of the block. As barricades were being set up, officers on foot had dispersed throughout the area and had begun to usher away as many of the pedestrians as they could. While this was going on, Captain Swilling issued his orders to those who had been patiently waiting in the vans. Each group promptly exited the vehicle, precisely fanned out, and then walked in a parallel line down the somewhat darkened corridor toward the old store and their advancing brethren.

Earlier, Jerrelle had briefed Cloe on every possible scenario that may occur — and once she saw the six of them leave her club, she knew what was about to happen. Quickly, she went over to the brothers, André & Henré, and had them make sure that the front of the club had no one left waiting to come inside. She didn't care that by letting them in it might actually put her over the bar's legal capacity, but her customer's safety was her main priority. Once everyone was safe, Cloe had Henré lock the front doors. Per her instructions, no one was going to be allowed to leave The Cough Inn until it was verified that the military's operation was all over.

Following in line behind Captain Swilling, the six of them marched down the west side of the club. Instead of continuing on across the street, the order was unexpectedly given to halt their forward progress at the nearside curb. Just because the building in question had every one of its windows boarded up and no visible outside security cameras didn't mean that an attempt to breach it was going to go unnoticed. Modern-day technology allowed other ways to monitor activity in and around a place. Of course, the S.N.A.F.U. always had the newest gadgets at their disposal — and it would be stupid of them not to use it, so before they went any further, Sergeant Ben Fraisure removed the E.D^2 (Electronic Device Detector) from his pack. Although the device was designed to detect every single electronic item that is in use within a one-block radius, it did not have the ability to determine exactly what those devices were.

Ten constant signals were detected in all. Based upon their strength, it was believed two vid-cells, a palm-top, two home computers, four televisions, and a heart monitor were generating them. There was an intermittent one as well; Ben thought that a ham radio operator was causing one.

Satisfied that not one of the detected signals were the result of an electronic monitoring or motion detection system in use, he gave Captain Swilling the all-clear; E.J then promptly gave the order to continue forward toward their target. The moment they got to the front door, two Ex-Co patches were applied to the lock. Nearly at the same time, the decimation of the back door took place, courtesy of Zeik and his laser-guided grenade launcher.

As they had been trained to do, they immediately tossed a few sonic microbursts through both open doorways. Unless an individual was familiar with these items, whoever was in range when they went off would not have a clue as to what to do to protect themselves from the effects. Their neutralization was essentially guaranteed.

When the correct amount of time had passed, the soldiers cautiously moved forward into the building. They knew that this unplanned raid had the potential to turn into a blood bath, but their years of intense training had prepared each of them to conduct an assault such as this as effectively and efficiently as possible: find the first target and eliminate them, move aside, and then let your brethren do their assigned job. A trained S.N.A.F.U. soldier was not to get trigger-happy and take it upon himself to eliminate as many targets as he could. That would only put himself and everyone else in an unfavorable position. Just like a game of tag, one at a time, each member of the unit took their turn and did their job; moving, confusing, and picking off the suspected terrorists.

Less than two minutes was all it had taken before the situation was fully under control. Through the lingering haze, a combined byproduct of the back exit being blasted open and the old building's dust being stirred up, Sabastian took a quick survey and counted eight suspected terrorists down. Elation consumed him. This unplanned raid happened as near to perfect as it possibly could have — or so he thought. "No!" he whispered under his breath. One of the downed men was not a terrorist after all.

When Richard noticed the look of disbelief on Sabastian's face, his eyes quickly followed over to where his friend was looking. Immediately, he saw his mortally wounded brethren. Ben Fraisure was dead. With a heavy heart, he walked over to him, knelt down, and noticed that his fallen comrade had been shot five times: three in his vest and one in his shoulder. Had the fifth bullet struck him anywhere other than it did, right through his jugular, he would have lived to fight another day.

They had counted eight suspected terrorists entering this building along with two known members of the Detroit Underworld

Organization. The body count didn't add up. Three individuals were still unaccounted for, so until they knew for sure where they were, everyone in the unit had to stay on their toes and forget about their sorrow.

A quick search of the building was ordered by Captain Swilling; a search that produced the discovery of a private and secure room off to the east end of the structure. At first glance, the space appeared to Sabastian to be a place where people of faith would spend time and pray. Right now though, it clearly was being used as a makeshift office. There, scattered all across a table at the back of the room was a lot of money. When he took a closer look at it all, he noticed that a few of the bills were moving slightly — this was due to a light breeze. To his right, Sabastian then noticed the open window; it was facing the back alley. No hypothesis was needed to be drawn, as he knew that those who had been in this room had escaped through it.

Assuming that their backs had been covered, he radioed Zeik and asked him if he had seen anyone escaping through the window. He said that he did; he then apologized right afterward because he was only able to take out one of the three men attempting to flee. The other two got away.

Disappointment, frustration, anger, and sadness jumped between his thoughts. Trying to attain any sort of focus at that moment was impossible. What he did believe though, was that this mission had ended up becoming what was feared — a failure. Yes, a growing terrorist group had been stopped before they had a chance to unleash any plans they had and another shipment of military arms had been recovered. Unfortunately, a good man had lost his life in the process. What next? He honestly did not know. He just hoped that the collective support they gave to Captain Swilling didn't end up costing everyone their hopes, dreams, and livelihood.

Zhin and Nicoli knew that they had been extremely lucky as they both should be dead. Right after the sniper on the rooftop shot and killed the escaping member of the U.A.L., his weapon appeared to jam. That was what had given them the time they needed to get back inside the city vehicle and leave the alleyway. Each has had their fair share of injuries and wounds, but never had either of them had such a close call before — but that didn't mean when they returned to the D.U.O. headquarters and gave their report, they would leave there unscathed. Chances were that Louie was going to lose his mind. The only solace that seemed to be present was that their boss was nothing like his predecessor when it came to dealing with incompetence.

They say that you should always look on the bright side of things. Sabastian found that rather difficult to do, even though some positives had come as a result of what had just taken place. Ideally, the arrests or even the deaths of Zhin Wi and Nicoli Nemchieve would have been preferred. Instead, he had to settle for the stolen weapons being recovered, and the confiscation of nearly six figures in Union dollars that had been hastily left on the table.

As Sabastian reflected upon what had just taken place, it dawned on him that his loyalty to the Union military, specifically the S.N.A.F.U., could have ended up costing him the advantage he had. The smart thing for him to have done was to stay inside the Cough Inn in order to assure that his assumed death continued. Thankfully, the revelation of his still being alive and well had not taken place during the raid.

Captain Swilling came over to where Sabastian had been standing; the look he saw on the young man's face was exactly how he was feeling. Both of them knew that it wasn't going to be too long before the shit hit the fan. His ability to lead this platoon was certainly going to come into question — and it really didn't matter that the results of the raid, all but confirmed what was suspected.

They both understood the magnitude of what was to come; it was unavoidable. So that there was little chance their decision to engage would come into question, they needed to find some more hard evidence, so Sabastian and Captain Swilling began a thorough search of the makeshift office. As they were doing this. Jeff Tranter and Richard Atwater searched the other three rooms on the main floor. Jerrelle surprisingly volunteered to search the basement.

After about twenty minutes of finding nothing significant, E.J.'s anxiety suddenly lowered to a more manageable level — only because he had come across something that he hoped was exactly what they were looking for. Unfortunately, he just had no way of knowing, as it wasn't written in English.

He really wasn't all that religious, but he silently prayed that this was the irrefutable proof that the United Arab League was indeed a terrorist organization. However, for that to be confirmed, he needed some help. "Sabastian! Could you go and find Sergeant Dhanali and have him come in here, please."

"Yes, sir!"

A minute later, Sabastian returned with Aryo Dhanali, a man of Muslim faith whose family, ten years ago, immigrated to the Union from Syria. "Could you please look at this and interpret it for me, Sergeant?" He then handed him the piece of paper that he had found stuck in the back of the Qur'an.

Aryo quietly read it to himself, taking his time to make sure he understood it, as it was written in a different dialect than the one he spoke. After handing it back to the Captain, he said, "Two days from now, an attack was scheduled to take place at nineteen hundred hours at Comerica Park during the middle of the baseball All-Star game. The plan was to use half a dozen drones to fly over the stadium, drop impact scatter bombs on the field, and then when the park started to empty from the mass hysteria, every local member of U.A.L. would be lying in wait to open fire on the exiting crowd."

That information appalled Captain Swilling; it made Sabastian sick to his stomach as well. Had Bai Lin not noticed Nicoli as she exited The Cough Inn, had Jerrelle not told Sabastian of what she suspected, had he not contacted his former commanding officer, no one would have had any inkling whatsoever that another horrifying day would have ended up having to be added to the history books.

"Did you find anything?" Jerrelle asked as she entered the prayer room.

"We did." Sabastian then told her about the piece of paper they found inside the Qur'an. Jerrelle was beyond shocked to learn of what had been planned.

"Did you find anything?" Captain Swilling asked.

"Um.., yes but… Don't go down in the basement."

"Why not?"

"Let's just say that whatever forensic team draws that assignment, they are going to be down there just as long as any archeological team would be inside a newly discovered Egyptian tomb."

Five minutes later, the building had all but been vacated and Ben's body had been removed. As it was being placed in the back of one of their vans, and as the last of the recovered stolen weapons were being loaded into the other one, Sabastian crossed the street and took up a seat on the same stool Henré would normally use during the evening when checking IDs.

His night wasn't yet over; he still had one more important thing he had to do — inform Governor White of everything that had just taken place. He hoped that his father's old friend was all right with the fact that an actual military assault had just taken place in one of his communities, considering that he had been told earlier that it was only supposed to be a recon mission. Sighting national security as a reason, Sabastian could refuse to give him a report of any kind and just tell him that there was no other choice but to do what was done, but he had the utmost respect for the governor and the man deserved to know every single detail — including the fact that an attack on his hometown had been a mere few days away.

Upon learning what he had, anger promptly consumed the governor — but not toward the S.N.A.F.U. He applauded their efforts and the result that came from it. As much as he would have liked to never have a military incursion take place anywhere in his state, he told Sabastian that he fully supported their decision. Nevertheless, it was now his responsibility to contact Mark Quills and give him that full report.

Just as he disconnected his call to Governor White, Captain Swilling walked up beside him. As they made their way inside The Cough Inn together, he informed him of the conversation he just had. It was fully expected that the U.B.I. would show up; E.J. just wasn't looking forward to what was more than likely going to turn into a rather large pissing contest instead of a typical inquiry. So long as he was given an opportunity to fully explain himself and then present the evidence they now had, it should end with everyone being satisfied. If the Bureau's usual unwillingness to listen takes place, then Captain

191

Swilling's worst fears could become a reality. He would be more than ready to accept the unwelcomed ending of his military career, but the dissolution of the Special North American Freedom Unit could end up being the penalty that is paid instead.

Within only a few hours, the U.B.I.'s investigative team was on scene and combing through every single nook and cranny of the old store. Captain Swilling, as he foresaw, had been promptly ushered upstairs to one of the rooms above The Cough Inn by the northern district director.

Normally, during the early hours of the morning, no one other than the cleaning staff would be in the bar, but Cloe had invited all of the members of the S.N.A.F.U. to stay inside, relax, and have a few well-deserved drinks; drinks that would have been thoroughly enjoyed in celebration of their achievement had an unwanted asterisk not been attached. André had volunteered to cook up a huge breakfast and his brother had made sure that the local media stayed far away from the club. It wasn't a time to accept praise and it wasn't time to tell the world what had happened; it was a time to stay isolated with one's own thoughts and reflect upon what had become for everybody, a life-changing experience.

By eleven a.m., Captain Swilling had finally finished his debriefing and interrogation. Without saying a word, nor was one directed his way, he walked over to Sabastian and sat next to him. He kept his thoughts private as he stared at the back of the bar — it looked as if he was trying to determine which one in the line of liquor bottles would become the one to drink in order to numb his mental anguish. But before he could make that choice, Cloe brought over a sim-caf, set it down in front of him, and after producing a smile of appreciation, left him alone with his thoughts.

After he took that much needed first sip, he thanked Sabastian, and then Jerrelle. That was all he said. He then took another sip of his sim-caf and continued his forward stare — the captain was either all talked out from his inquiry, or he was deeply regretting his decision and was now contemplating what the future held for him. Whatever it was that was going through his mind, Sabastian and Jerrelle both knew that his thoughts were not theirs to learn and dismissed any notion to satisfy their curiosity.

About a half an hour later, the platoon left The Cough Inn, got into a bus that Mark Quills had arranged for them, and they returned to Selfridge Air Force Base to fly back to Houston. To show their gratitude, Sabastian and Jerrelle remained behind at The Cough Inn to help clean up the remnants of the S.N.A.F.U. having been there.

An hour earlier, Sabastian had pulled Richard aside in order to make sure that his old friend was all right. Before everything that had taken place, he had intended to ask him to stay behind and do him a small favor. But after a few minutes spent in an in-depth conversation, he knew that would not be possible. By no means was he responsible for what had happened to Ben Fraisure, but some undeserved guilt had seeped its way into Richard's soul.

It was understandable; time was all that he needed. And knowing him as well as Sabastian did, he knew that his friend would use this experience in a way that would make him a better, stronger person. In fact, he could already see some leadership qualities in Richard that his friend probably never thought he had. And whether or not he wanted it, by default, he had become the unofficial leader of the platoon since Sabastian's 'retirement'.

As the time neared for The Cough Inn to open up for business, Cloe decided to do something that she had never done before — close the doors for an entire Saturday. After staying there for twenty-four hours straight, she, along with her dedicated staff, needed to go home and get some much-deserved rest. Before she sent everyone on their way though, she went over to Sabastian and Jerrelle and personally thanked them both for everything they had done, extended an open invitation to visit anytime, and promised to help them in any way she could, if it ever was needed.

As they walked out of the club, Henré smiled and locked the doors behind them. The cab they had called was already waiting out front to take them to Jerrelle's apartment. While on the way there, Sabastian took out his vid-cell and sent off a brief text.

"Who are you messaging, Sab?"

"Someone I need a favor from. Other than you and Richard, there is only one other person I know of that I can wholeheartedly trust."

Minus a few cuts and scrapes on their arms and legs from escaping through a rather small alley window that was never designed for use as an emergency exit, Zhin and Nicoli were fine. Although both of them were well aware of the events that took place shortly after the completion of the recent weapons deliveries, neither of them honestly expected the building to be raided while they were in the midst of one, let alone it being as well organized and precise as it was. They were both very lucky to have escaped with their lives.

It wasn't the first time during their careers that they had been surprised like that. Even so, with the importance of the task given, it was an inexcusable mistake for them to make. They were delivering weapons to a terrorist organization; they should have paid far closer attention to their surroundings. Instead, they arrogantly believed that if the U.A.L. was to be raided, they would be long gone before it happened.

For almost twenty years Nicoli had been a member of the E.C.L. and his past experiences were what should have allowed him to see this coming from a mile away. The unexpected; he should have expected. But he had wanted to solidify that Louie had not made an error in judgment by accepting him into the fold, so instead of dividing his attention equally, his focus had been linear. The completion of the weapons exchange had wrongly taken precedence over all of the potential what-ifs.

Zhin was just as angry as his associate. Not because they had been attacked, but because the responsibility of this failure rested solely upon his shoulders. At least, that is how he felt. He was a man of honor, and what had been asked of him had not been completed. No longer did they have possession of the weapons; which would have been all right except, none of the agreed money had left the building with him. For that error alone, Zhin expected to be relieved of the position that he had been given. Not only that, he fully expected to be severely reprimanded. In his mind, he honestly believed that he was going to be sent right back to China and then dropped down to the lower rungs of the positional ladder; all the way to where it would then become his job to wipe the asses of all those who were now above him.

Hesitantly, they both walked into their boss's office the next morning, each fully expecting to get reamed out. As they made their way to the two seats in front of Louie's desk, a word was not said, nor did their boss even look at them. He just sat there quietly enjoying his morning sim-caf.

The reception they got; Zhin hoped was an indication that their boss had not yet heard about last night through the proverbial grapevine. He did try to call him right afterward but got no answer. Yes, it had been late, but he should have at least tried one more time instead of choosing to wait until morning to let the cat out of the bag.

He would never let this be known but his stress levels were nearly maxed out. In a matter of only a few weeks, Louie not only had taken over complete control of the Detroit Underworld Organization, but he was also tasked with the responsibility of figuring out what exactly needed to be done so that it could run as efficiently and effectively as before. On top of that, he had to find a way to deal with the adamancy of his son's mother — it continually aggravated him. And if that wasn't enough, he also had to endure untimely and unwanted visits from his old adversary. All of that was why Louie had decided to shut off his vid-cell last night. He hoped that by doing that, he might actually get a full, undisturbed night of sleep.

Before he could inquire about the previous evening's assignment, his astuteness directed him to the visible injuries that each of his men sported: cuts and scrapes to the arms, legs, necks, and foreheads. At that moment, he didn't need any verbal confirmation. Something clearly had happened. Oddly, not an ounce of annoyance resided within him. "Am I to assume that the transaction did not go smoothly?"

"That is correct, I'm afraid." Zhin and Nicoli looked at each other, believing that they were only a few moments away from experiencing a fate similar to that of a traitor. There was just no way to avoid what was to come, so after a few seconds of unnerving silence, Zhin gave his report. By the time he was done explaining what had taken place, the expected response had not come — and it was probably the reason why the little tension that previously had been in the room, did not increase.

Louie sunk back in his chair, taken aback by what he had just been told. A precise S.W.A.T. team strike by the U.B.I. usually meant that surrender was the only option for survival. Yet somehow, his men had escaped apprehension. What had happened was not good. This was now the third time he had delivered weapons, only to have the recipient of them be raided shortly afterward. This didn't make any sense to him. Clearly, it wasn't happenstance. The only persons who were aware of these transactions were he, the two men sitting in front of him, and Casper. If this had been an isolated incident, then Louie would have probably placed all of the blame for this failure on both of his men. After all, they had left behind the merchandise and neglected to bring back the money for it. But he couldn't. This left him with no other alternative but to assume that there was someone out there tipping off the feds. Louie knew that it could not have been Zhin and Nicoli, as they both had yet to be handpicked by him to be his number one and two when the first raid had taken place in Tijuana. Therefore, logic dictated that it had to be someone else along the food chain. But who?

It didn't matter to Louie that it was just past nine in the morning. He wanted a drink, so he went over to his wet bar and poured a healthy glass of Walker's Club. Upon his return, he took a sip, sat down in his desk chair, and drew the only assumption he could.

Casper has been the D.U.O.'s shipping clerk for the past twenty-five years. Since the day the military man became a subcontracted 'employee', he had stayed anonymous, been discrete, and had been well compensated for his services. It just didn't make any sense, yet the finger seemed to be pointed directly at him.

Louie took a moment and placed himself in Casper's shoes; he wanted to see if he could find a reason for him to turn his back on them. The only thing that made any sort of sense was that the man had decided that time was nearing for him to call it a career.

He honestly hoped that this was just his mind trying to search for an answer to what was certainly a rather large problem. If it wasn't for the fact that he knew Sabastian was no longer alive, then his suspicions would be directed toward him instead. It really wasn't what Louie wanted to believe, but he could not think of anyone else that could be the culprit.

He took a moment, pounded back the remainder of his rye, and then made a decision. Whether or not Casper had stabbed them in the back; today was as good a time as any for the D.U.O. to take that first step into a new direction. Therefore, with regret, Louie said, "With this now being the third time that a raid has taken place, it is clear that the feds are being tipped off. As much as I..."

"It's not the feds," Zhin declared. "That raid last night was a concise, surgical military strike."

Nicoli then said, "Because we were delivering to a terrorist group, I'd be willing to bet that it was the S.N.A.F.U. that stormed the place."

Louie took a moment and considered his associate's affirmations. If the Special North American Freedom Unit was indeed responsible for the raid last night, then there was definitely a leak. And although there was no guarantee, because the stolen military weaponry was hastily left behind, and now confiscated as evidence, Louie had to acknowledge that the possibility was now there that the same elite military unit just might soon kick in their front door and take them down as well.

There was no doubt in his mind. What Louie had been contemplating, now needed to be implemented. Clearly, it was time for all ties to the organization's past to be cut. "For decades, we have been supplying clients with stolen military weapons; weapons that have been provided by a man who himself, is also a part of our Union's military. And although there are no facts whatsoever to support it, to me, it does appear as if those raids, and Casper's affiliation to those who have conducted them, are not merely coincidental. Therefore, I have no choice but to label him as being a liability to us. Whether or not it is he who has been tipping off his fellow brethren, I feel that the time has come for us to begin cleaning house. However, we do have a small problem. I don't even know what the man's real name is."

"Why not?" Nicoli asked.

"It had been agreed upon a long time ago that no one would ever know Casper's true identity so that he could continue on with his military career in anonymity while he supplied us with arms."

"The not knowing has essentially fucked us."

"That it has, Zhin. Nevertheless, I would like for him to be found."

"Ok!" Nicoli and Zhin both said in unison.

There had been many times that Louie hadn't always agreed with Antonio's decisions. Nor was he always able to find a logical reason as to why he had made them. But now, he finally understood why his ex-boss had decided, all those years ago, to temporarily change the D.U.O's business practices while he was in jail to a more 'safe' kind of venture. He had to give the authorities a reason to leave him alone and forget about him so that whatever heat was on him would have time to go away. That tactic, Louie now had to implement. "Once we locate Casper and deal with him, we will then sit down and collectively figure out what the best direction would be for us to take this organization in."

Both Zhin and Nicoli agreed and were happy with that declaration. As society changes and advances, so should a business. The D.U.O. has basically stuck with the same formula since its inception in the mid-twentieth century. Now, it was time to move forward and get out of the arms business for good. "What if we can't find him?"

"No loose ends. Until we find and deal with him, no matter how long it takes, the D.U.O. will be in a holding pattern." Louie got up from behind his desk, went over to his wet bar, poured himself a cup of nearly two-hour-old sim-caf, and returned to his desk. Before he took that first sip though, he looked at his men and said, "I know this is going to be a difficult task, but it is one that I firmly believe you will complete. Use whatever means you deem necessary to find out who Casper is, and then terminate his employment with us."

With a nod of their heads and a sense of relief that they were now seemingly off the hook for the clusterfuck that took place the previous evening, they both got up and exited the office, leaving their boss alone with his thoughts.

Was Louie doing the right thing? He did not know. Was he using Casper as a scapegoat because of a series of unlucky circumstances, or was the man actually the one responsible for all three raids? Those were questions that Louie quite honestly, didn't think he would ever get an answer to. Little did he know that those incursions were the result of a domino effect; one that had first been started by a governmental agency's speculation and suspicion. Had the truth come to light that Sabastian Banks and his military brethren were the ones that conducted those raids; Louie may very well have ended up doing something far more illogical than what his predecessor had ever done. And whatever that may have been, it would be all but guaranteed that the dissolution of the Detroit Underworld Organization would follow as a result.

It was early evening and a knock resonated on Jerrelle's front door. She had been up for about twenty minutes; Sabastian was still soundly asleep. There were only a few people who knew where she lived and were welcomed to visit. And because she resided in an apartment building, very rarely did a random stranger stop on by.

Admittedly, she was feeling a bit cranky. More than likely, this was due to her being up for more than a full day and then only getting six hours of sleep once she got home. On top of that, the death of a man she did not know at all seemed to be lingering within her thoughts. Just like Helfred, what had happened Ben Fraisure was something that should have been avoidable.

In her mind, whoever was waiting in the hall had better have a good excuse because Jerrelle was not in the mood for any sort of bullshit. So, with her honor blade in her right hand, she took a look through the peephole and — she instantly relaxed. If it had been anyone else who was waiting on the other side, she might have just reenacted her favorite horror film scene and rammed her blade right on through her front door. Instead, she slipped her weapon back into its sheath, undid the security chain, and turned the knob. Out of everyone she knew, this was the last person Jerrelle would ever expect to show up at her apartment. Then again, Sharice had a tendency to do that when it was least expected — and usually just in time to save their asses from some sort of mess that they had gotten themselves into.

After inviting her inside, she bluntly apologized for the lack of décor and then encouraged her to head over to the couch so that she could have the honor of waking up her cousin. Jerrelle left them alone and went into the kitchen to get a bottle of water from her fridge; now she knew who it had been that Sabastian had texted in the cab on the way back to her place. But the question was, what was the favor that he needed from his cousin?

"You're wasting away what's left of this beautiful day!"

"Um… Good morning, Sharice. I'm glad you could come."

"Like I said before… Anytime you need me, I will be there. And.., it's early evening, not morning."

"Right… Here, I have something to show you." Sabastian then grabbed his vid-cell and scanned through his photos until he got to the one he wanted, entered a command on the screen, and tapped his phone against his cousin's in order to wirelessly transfer the image to her device.

Even though it was really none of her business, Jerrelle curiously wanted to know what it was that Sabastian needed his cousin's help with. While drinking her water, she headed back into the living room. However, after only taking two steps beyond the kitchen, she stopped. There she stood completely dumbfounded. She wasn't dreaming. She knew that she had just let Sharice into her apartment only a few moments ago, but the woman was now nowhere to be found. "Um.., where is your cousin?"

"She only stopped by because I needed to show and give her something."

"Ah… What was it?"

"It's nothing really that important. I just want her to make a delivery to someone whom I can't get close to at the moment."

Jerrelle walked over to her old sofa and then leaned up against the front end of the arm. She wished that Sabastian would stop doing this to her; keeping her in the dark. The last time he had done that, he had withheld the information that he had reached out to his 'adopted father', Terrance Burelli; a man she had hated since the day he had, in her mind, stabbed her in the back. In the end, the holding back of important information did not cost her in any way. That day, it had actually resulted in Sabastian's life being saved. Had she known ahead of time that he was going to be there, she would have blatantly refused to be anywhere near the man. Or worse, the actions she might have taken could have inadvertently changed fate and her friend might be the one dead instead of Antonio Marcone.

It's impossible to predict what might have happened. Upon reflection, Jerrelle was glad that she had not been told. In fact, she now acknowledged that certain situations sometimes call for things to stay a secret until such time that it becomes necessary to reveal it.

Then upon that taking place, she had to trust that the reasons given would be valid.

When her water was finished, Jerrelle left the living room and returned to the kitchen. She took the empty bottle, crushed it, and tossed it in the garbage underneath the sink. After she did this, she aimlessly gazed through the tiny window in front of her. It was then that she realized Sabastian had not withheld anything from her; he just chose to not make it so obvious. Privately, she smiled knowing that her friend's desire to get a message to Madelyn was now going to happen. Jerrelle just hoped that this woman, who had taken possession of his heart, felt the same way about him.

Together, she and Sabastian spent the rest of the day doing almost nothing, other than loading up the eighteen boxes that contained her personal belongings into a small cargo van. She was going to sell some of her larger pieces of furniture and replace it all with new ones once she got to San Antonio, but a young immigrant family that had recently moved into her apartment building, really didn't have much, so she decided to do a good deed and give it all to them: A small kitchen table and chair set, a recliner, a three-piece coffee table set, a couple of old lamps, and a large curio — which had already been in her apartment when she first moved in, so it was fitting that it stayed behind.

Jerrelle had not rented the van. Sydney had. She was surprised that he had done this. That small, but also greatly appreciated gesture from him only reaffirmed that her decision to leave Detroit for good, was indeed the right one. Not only would she soon be living closer to her best friend, but a new extended family would also be waiting there with open arms to include her in their inner circle. Finally, after all this time, not only had she found direction in her life, a sense of actually belonging was also now there.

Day one had come and gone and Madelyn had actually felt good about herself. She never made any really big mistakes, nor did she embarrass herself behind the bar. In fact, the two waitresses who had worked with her had thanked her for a job well done. Actually, they were just pandering her because they both knew that it was her looks and not her bartending skills that had drawn in more business than usual in the overly expensive Cadillac Club Room — which subsequently had allowed them to earn more tips than they were normally accustomed to.

She walked into work the following day a few minutes before five p.m. and could see that the place was nearly empty. There was an older looking couple sitting in front of the wall of hundred dollar slot machines, a young, geeky-looking man sitting by himself at a virtual strip poker machine, and a young woman sitting at the bar whose blessed beauty was admittedly comparable to her own.

This woman was a well-tanned, stunning blonde who appeared to be in her mid to late twenties. If Madelyn had to guess, just from the few seconds she had observed her; she was probably either a model or someone's trophy wife.

When it came to her sexual preference, Madelyn's first choice had always been a man. Because she had dabbled in the world of bi-sexuality on numerous occasions, a choice not freely made by her, but was a part of her old job requirements; she came to discover that she was actually attracted to both sexes. Not equally, but enough where she does considers herself to be pansexual.

Madelyn found it difficult to keep her eyes off of this woman's alluring beauty. Nevertheless, she had to stay professional. She wasn't here to have a drink and pick someone up for the night. She was here to work.

There were still a few minutes left before her shift started, so she walked into the small staff room and did her best to clear her thoughts. When the time came for her to begin, she walked behind the bar and, just like she had been taught, checked on the woman to see if her drink was getting close to being finished. Again, Madelyn was finding it hard to not stare at her. There was something magnetic about this woman that she found very hard to resist. Nevertheless, she took a few composing breaths and then asked her the appropriate question, "Are you ready for another drink, Miss?"

The customer looked at her curiously for a moment; it was almost as if she was trying to determine whether or not she knew her. "No, I'm good. You though might want to consider leaving."

Madelyn stood there, speechless. She had no idea how she should respond to this woman's suggestion. "I'm… sorry. Did I just hear you right?"

The customer took a moment and looked around the room, making sure that the four other people that were there; the three customers, and the one waitress who was also just starting her shift, were not paying any attention to her. She then finished off the rest of her martini, leaned forward a bit, and said, "Your name tag reads, 'Madelyn.'"

"Yes. That is my name."

"And your last name is…"

Madelyn stood there quiet. She didn't want to be rude and tell this woman that her last name was none of her business.

"…Kinsworth, is it not?"

Dumbfounded wasn't even the word to describe the state she was now in. She had only just started her shift and now this woman had shocked her twice. "How do you know my last name?"

"Because you know somebody that I know."

"And that person would be?"

The woman took something out of her purse that was wrapped in tissue and handed it to Madelyn. "I was given this by our mutual friend and was asked to return it to you."

When she opened up the wrapped object, her eyes could not believe what she had in her hands. It was the same micro-remote that she had left with Sabastian so he could escape the handcuffs that she was forced to put him in. "You are a friend of Sabas. ."

The woman held up a finger to her lips and stopped Madelyn from finishing her query. She then stood up, slid a folded twenty-dollar bill across to her to pay for the drink she had, and said, "You're a friend of my friend, which means that you are now one of mine as well. Just like my friend, I will be there if and when I am needed. Goodbye, Madelyn."

"Wait! You could at least tell me your name?"

"It's Sharice… your friend's cousin." She then turned and left the Cadillac Club Room.

Madelyn wasn't sure what she should do next. She believed that the window to her complete freedom would eventually open up, but she never expected that it would be so soon. However, she was also smart enough to realize that it had only been slightly cracked open — it wasn't yet wide enough for her to escape through.

She took the money for Sharice's drink and went to ring it in the till; it was then she realized that hiding in between the fold of the money was a note. Knowing that the bar had an impressive security system keeping watch over every transaction made, Madelyn palmed the note and then discretely put it in her pocket. Two hours later, during her first break, she read it.

"Please meet me across the river in Windsor at the Oldé Towne Tap & Grill in the Chrysler building on the riverfront at noon tomorrow.

Sabastian."

Not wanting to accidentally be caught with this in her possession, Madelyn took out a lighter from her purse and burned the note. But as she watched the piece of paper become nothing but ash, a probing thought crossed her mind. *'How did Sabastian's cousin know who I was? He only knows me as Lizanne, not Madelyn. He must have discovered the truth while he was searching for my fake friend. Maybe that was why he was as quiet as he was on the plane ride to Chicago. But then again, why would he follow me all the way back there instead of just confronting me in San Antonio? And why did he voluntarily follow me up to Louie's apartment?'*

Madelyn stood there again taken aback and trying to find a way to validate her uncertainty — but she just couldn't find any sort of confirmation. She was left with only one option. She had to trust her instincts and hope that she would make the correct decisions from this point forward; decisions that she hoped would eventually give her the opportunity to talk to Sabastian and put all of those 'whys' she had to rest. *'I certainly hope that woman was telling me the truth about being Sabastian's cousin. I mean, she had a British accent. For all I know, she actually works for Louie and he just sent her here to test me to see where my allegiance lies.'*

What her heart was telling her was that Sabastian wanted to see her. How he felt about her though, was impossible for her to predict. He did try to call her. That simple act was what had allowed Madelyn to believe that he did care about her and wanted to let her know that he was all right.

She put her right hand in her pocket and removed the micro-remote. She then took a moment and looked at it. To most people, this would just be a useless object, but to her, it was a symbol of hope; hope that the emotional connection she truly believed was between her and Sabastian was real, hope that he would help to liberate her from the mess she was in, and hope that the man she had unexpectedly fallen in love with, would forever be a part of her life.

Before any of that could ever take place though, she had one rather large problem that first had to be solved. Somehow, Madelyn had to find a way to leave the hotel tomorrow morning, unnoticed. That was going to be difficult for her to do, as she was certain that Louie would want to know where she intended to go. If he then agreed to let her leave, like every single time before, either he or an assigned escort would have to accompany her. That taking place would all but end the hope she now chose to hang onto.

As she was just about to return to work, her mind suddenly posed an unsettling question. Was it possible that she was not eliminated after 'Sabastian's' execution because Louie was actually obsessed with her? Madelyn hoped that was not the case. What she wanted to believe instead, was that the completion of her task had earned her some trust and that was why she was here now. Whatever the case may be, she had to ignore her ambiguity for the time being and concentrate solely on trying to figure out a way to get her hands on a 'day pass' so that she could go alone to where Sabastian had asked her to. Only then, she felt, would some sort of clarity begin.

7

This was going to be by far the toughest assignment that either Zhin or Nicoli have ever been given. In the past, each had been asked to locate someone — but at least that person had an actual name that they could work with. Even so, they accepted the challenge — notwithstanding the likelihood that the reprimand they had somehow earlier avoided, would then be implemented in an even more severe fashion if they ended up failing again.

Although it hadn't been declared, both could easily assume that they were standing on thin ice. In order for them to be back firmly on solid ground, they had to find Casper — and somewhat quick. Unfortunately, the only thing that they knew about the man was that he was a part of the Union military. They could reach out to the same former FBI computer geek who was able to hijack the C-4 network for Antonio and ask him to do the same thing to the N.R.C.S.P. (National Records Center for Service Personnel), but doing so would pose too much of a risk. By now, it was a given that the D.U.O. was on the military's radar; it didn't make sense to give them another reason to show up on their doorstep. Besides, the best hackers in the world generally refrained from trying to access governmental agency databases. Not just because it was extremely difficult to penetrate the security measures that protected their systems, but the possibility of being locked away in the same 'non-existent' Union prison as a suspected terrorist would be, forgotten forever, was enough of a deterrent. This meant that Zhin and Nicoli had to think outside the box in order to accomplish what was being asked of them.

With it known that Louie's predecessor had kept extensive records locked in a safe at the D.U.O.'s safehouse in Ann Arbor, they had hope that they might be able to learn something that could at least point them in the right direction — so that was where they went first. Why anyone would want to meticulously document their criminal activity was something that Zhin just did not understand. Maybe, Antonio had been planning on writing a book, confessing to everything that he had done, and then releasing it as he was nearing the end of his natural life. What made more sense, was that he probably kept it, just in case he had to use whatever information he had gathered over the years as leverage against someone or some other organization. Whatever the reason, the deceased ex-leader of the D.U.O. was known to have been a very unconventional man.

Once the sought after information was in their hands, they needed to then carefully sift through all of it. Although it wasn't expected, hope was there that Antonio had actually known Casper's real identity — or at least, knew where the man resided, as that would make the task they were assigned, so much easier to complete.

No reminder needed to be given by Louie beforehand, as both Zhin and Nicoli had been in the game long enough to already know what was expected of them. Upon gaining access to the collective records, they had to stay conscious of the fact that everything they will learn will be information that is to be kept in complete confidence and then brought with them to their graves.

Only so much can be done to protect one's secrets. To help limit the possibility of any sensitive information accidentally ending up in the wrong hands: a sworn enemy, another underground organization, an unscrupulous individual looking only to make a buck, or the authorities, they had been instructed to assuredly destroy all hard copies after they were digitized. The main reason for converting them was so that if for some reason it ever became necessary, the records could easily be erased from existence by the simple stroke of a computer key.

Upon their arrival at the organization's safehouse, Zhin and Nicoli made themselves at home. The structure itself didn't look any different than the surrounding homes on the block. In fact, it was actually right in the middle of an eight-square-block area of rentals that were full of college students from the University of Michigan.

This location didn't make any sense to Zhin; he just could not fathom as to why the organization chose to have a safehouse, right smack dab in the middle of a university community. Nicoli, on the other hand, understood exactly why it was where it was. The best way to hide something was to do so in plain sight, and with the consistent parade of university students and weekend partiers throughout the neighborhood, it was the perfect 'camouflage'. No one would ever suspect that the house was what it was; they would just assume that it was another student rental.

Once inside, it didn't take long for Nicoli to locate the safe. Unfortunately, there was one rather large obstacle that first had to be overcome before they could proceed with their assigned task. Antonio was the only one who knew what the combination was. This problem seriously annoyed Zhin. Nicoli though felt confident that it wasn't going to be that difficult of a hurdle to get past. Other than being the 'muscle', the one thing he got good at during his time as a member of the Extremist Clandestine Liberation, was gaining access to anything that was locked. Very rarely had he come across a lock that he could not open or a security network that he could not disable or bypass. When such a rarity did happen though, he simply blew it up.

The moment that Nicoli laid his eyes on the hybrid digital, tumbler lock system, he knew that cracking it open was going to be a significant challenge. Thankfully, he had brought with him the latest in safe cracking tools: infra-red scanners, digital ears, a frequency shuffler, and an electronic invader — also known as 'Gremlin'. If a locking mechanism just happens to also come with an X-slot (there for maintenance purposes only), then the Gremlin can be connected to it, wherein an 'invading' program will then be installed. Upon completion and its execution, the locking sequence will become overridden. Unfortunately, as dependable as that device was, it was the incorrect one in this case. This particular digital locking mechanism ran in a parallel sequence. If the specific codes for each weren't entered in an alternating manner within a few seconds of each other, then the locks went into failsafe mode. Once that took place, the only way to gain access was by brute force. For Nicoli, it wouldn't be the first time he had to break into a safe that way. The only problem with his doing this was that items such as a good old-fashioned torch, Ex-Co patches, or unidirectional explosives, tended to either cause damage to, or the complete destruction of the contents. That was the last thing he wanted to do in this case.

After taking a few moments to review what his options were, Nicoli determined that he was going to have to crack open the safe, one patient step at a time. Mostly, he was going to have to rely on the frequency shuffler. It, which normally is used by law enforcement to gain entry into a residence, apartment building, or a car without the use of force, was designed to make any electronic code on any lock think that it had been factory reset to the original default codes (that being 0000). However, just like the shortcomings of the 'Gremlin', the dual digital lock was going to cause problems for the shuffler — though not many that Nicoli thought would prevent him from successfully gaining access to the safe.

From what he could see, the locks on the safe appeared to either be first or second-generation devices. That assessment was what allowed some of his uncertainty to dissipate. Still, it didn't mean that the task ahead of him was now going to be a piece of cake. In order for Nicoli to be able to learn the combination, absolute quiet was what he needed. Hearing the pin fall inside the tumbler was not the easiest thing to do — even with the assistance of the digital ears.

While his associate was busy trying to gain access to the safe, Zhin began to go over the information that Louie had given to him pertaining to their last three shipments. There was no obvious link between them; the only thing similar he noticed was that these military weapons were all brand new. That revelation was what allowed Zhin to assuredly assume that they must have been taken either directly from the factory or from one of the storage facilities.

After coming to the conclusion that it would be easier to steal the weapons from a warehouse instead of from where they were manufactured, Zhin started to compile a list of places throughout the Union where military weapons were stored. There were eight in total: Nevada, Colorado, Texas, Alaska, South Carolina, New Jersey, California, and Alberta. The four that were located north and south on each coast also happened to be distribution hubs. Logic dictated that they were probably the facilities in which the stolen weapons had originated from.

Forty minutes later...

"Bingo!" Nicoli yelled; he had successfully gained access to the safe.

"Hold on a minute, don't open it up yet. Is there any way to tell if the safe is booby-trapped? I wouldn't put it past Antonio to do that."

"Unfortunately, I don't have a bomb-sniffing device with me. The only thing we could do is to crack open the door and use the infra-red scanner I have. It won't tell us if there are security measures in place, but we will be able to speculate about any unusual object that we can see on its monitor. Hopefully, there won't be anything inside the safe that looks as if it doesn't belong there."

"Okay, go ahead and use the infra-red scanner. Let me know what you see."

"I'm not doing that. I unlocked it, so it's only fair that you open it. I am gonna go outside and take cover."

Though a little perturbed that Nicoli was passing the buck, Zhin nevertheless walked over to the safe and cautiously cracked it open a few millimeters wide; just enough so that the infra-red scanner could do its thing. He then carefully scrutinized what he saw on the monitor. After a few seconds of deduction, Zhin came to a grateful conclusion. The safe appeared to be safe. Upon opening it, and to his surprise, there were no physical documents inside like Louie had believed. It appeared as if Antonio had stayed with the times and had already documented everything electronically. It's a good thing that Nicoli didn't have to resort to breaking into the safe the hard way, as that would have probably destroyed the personal palmtop Zhin was now looking at.

He removed it from the safe, brought it to the small kitchen table, and noticed that the battery life was sitting at just under fifty percent. Unfortunately, the charger for the unit hadn't been in the safe. Logic, however, stated that it had to be somewhere in the house — Zhin hoped. If he couldn't locate it, then five hours was about all he had before the unit went completely dead.

Luck must be on his side; he didn't have to waste time or any of the palmtop's battery life trying to log onto it. For some reason, no password was needed, retinal scan required, or encryption of any kind used. Relief washed over him — then a trifling thought came. He didn't know if it had been cockiness or just confidence, but Zhin could only assume that Antonio must have wholeheartedly believed that no one but him would ever be able to gain access to the safe. What other reason would there be for the palmtop to be this easily accessible?

It had only taken him about an hour of looking at the device's contents for him to construct a plausible theory. Although he hadn't been able to learn what Casper's real name was, he was able to postulate as to where within the Union their target resided. However, before the two of them left the safehouse and hit the road in search of him, one more thing needed to be done.

Because of where they intended to go was in the complete opposite direction of the 'home office', Zhin felt it best not to take any sort of unnecessary risk — even though it only was a nominal one to just take the palm-top with them. So he created a zip file of all of the device's contents, uploaded it to the organization's Cy-space account, texted Louie the coordinates, and then did what he had originally been instructed to do to all hard copies.

Although he understood why it had to be done, Zhin suddenly felt unsure about destroying the palmtop — only because anything can happen to the contents he just transferred. If it was to somehow get corrupted or intercepted or stolen, then all of the collected incriminating information: about other crime organizations the D.U.O. had a trusted working relationship with, payoffs to specific city officials, bribes of local businessmen, a list of unscrupulous lawyers, an extensive list of shell companies, a list of established businesses that the organization had forced themselves into a partnership with, then eliminated said partner shortly afterward, and even a detailed account of the events that led to the elimination of Maxwell Banks, would be gone forever. With no backup, all the leverage they might one day need would not be there for them to ever use.

Zhin sat there for a handful of minutes, contemplating whether or not to ignore Louie's directive and copy the files to the microSD card from his vid-cell — but making a duplicate wasn't something that he was told to do, so he reluctantly handed the palmtop over to Nicoli.

"We need to tell Louie about her."

During his research, Zhin had stumbled across a bit of information about a woman named Cecelia. What he had learned about her was enough for him to draw a conclusion wherein he believed that a day might come where she would show up out of the blue and do more damage to the D.U.O. then any group or individual ever could. "I'm sure that Louie is aware of who she is, Nicoli."

"Do you think he is aware of the fact that she, the disowned daughter of Vance Palmalino, got married and had a child three years after his 'disappearance'?"

"That, I do not know. People are allowed to get on with their lives. She chose to leave and renounce her ties to her family, right along with any association to the organization. I'm sure that she did not weep when Antonio had her father killed. The way he died, more than likely solidified her decision to leave behind everything she knew and everyone she ever loved."

"Still, we need to do some research on her and her child and make sure that neither of them ever contemplates trying to claim what is rightfully theirs."

"As much as that makes sense, we cannot do that. Once Louie has time to review all of the information that I uploaded, he will learn of this all on his own and then whatever preventative measures he chooses to take, I'm sure we'll be asked to implement them. Until then, we just need to keep this information to ourselves."

This was the first time that Nicoli didn't agree with Zhin, but he was no longer a part of the E.C.L. where it was expected that every member immediately passes along any and all pertinent information to those in a position of leadership. He instead, was now part of an organization where you accepted your position and did only what was asked of you — even if you had acquired information that you suspect might turn into something very important one day.

"I completely understand why it is that you think we need to take it upon ourselves to ensure that the D.U.O. is not one day blindsided, but you know very well that our assignment takes precedence. Once it is completed, and once Louie has decided that the organization is ready to take that first step into a new direction, if he has not yet educated himself to the potential threat that Cecelia or her daughter poses, we will bring it to his attention then."

"Ok."

"Here! This palmtop needs to be destroyed. Take some of those Ex-Co patches you brought and go outside and have some fun."

Destroying the device wasn't going to allow Nicoli to overlook the fact that they were intentionally ignoring a potential danger to the D.U.O., but it would certainly give him a few minutes of gratuitous fulfillment — almost the same kind of satisfaction that a young boy would get using a magnifying glass to harness the sun in order to fry some ants.

Just because they felt that they had assembled enough information to start their search, it didn't mean that it could begin. They still had a lot of planning to do, so Zhin got up from the kitchen table, grabbed himself a glass of water, and then walked into the living room where he plopped his butt in the recliner. After taking a sip of his water, he began to go over the notes he had made. He could have stayed right where he was, but the kitchen chair he had been sitting nearly two hours on, had gotten rather uncomfortable.

A few minutes later, Nicoli came back into the house and walked right on through it to the front door.

"Where in the hell are you going?"

"Judging from what I see, I have to assume that we will not be leaving here anytime soon. Therefore, I'm going to go out and score us some beer and pizza. This is a university community after all, so finding those items should be relatively easy."

Zhin had to smile at that. Maybe Nicoli's view had some merit to it after all. Hiding the safehouse in the middle of a university community may not seem all that logical, but its location made for certain amenities to be accessed rather easily.

By the end of the day, Jerrelle had everything loaded into the van except for her bed and that old couch; she was planning on leaving that piece of crap behind anyway. Originally, she had wanted to be on the road to San Antonio at the crack of dawn, but Sabastian had thrown her an unexpected curveball when he informed her that their departure would have to be delayed — but he didn't say why or until when.

Plans changing, especially when they were out of her control, were another one of those things that typically annoyed her. Today though, it strangely didn't. Ideally, she would have preferred a rough estimate be given as to how long Sabastian was going to be gone today. But since he had failed to tell her anything, she could only make an assumption as to when he might return. Therefore, she decided that she would use her free time and go back to The Cough Inn and say goodbye to her friend. And if Sabastian just happened to return to her place before she did, she wouldn't feel bad about him wondering where she was since he had already done the same to her.

For the first time since she could remember, André produced a welcoming smile as she entered the club; Cloe promptly came out from behind the bar, walked around her cook, the 'human roadblock', went right up to Jerrelle and gave her the biggest, warmest hug ever.

Though words had yet to be exchanged, her friend had somehow seemed to know that this visit was probably going to be the last one for a while. A sudden and unfamiliar mixture of feelings ran through her body. It wasn't too long ago that Jerrelle mended the rift that had existed between her and Sabastian. Then, a few days ago, she had done the same thing with Cloe. She honestly never thought that such a thing would happen, but the world she had forever known had somehow been transformed, literally overnight, from being one where she had always felt segregated and forced to be self-sufficient, to one that was now amalgamated, giving, and extremely rewarding. After all these years, she was finally beginning to understand what it could be like to have a real family and a close-knit circle of friends. Openly, she was embracing these changes. The only thing that bothered her about this was saying goodbye to her friend. She never imagined just how hard that was going to be.

Right after their embrace ended, Cloe took her friend by the hand and led her into the kitchen. There, sitting on a stainless steel prep table was a cake with ten candles on it. Jerrelle looked at her friend and wondered what she was up to. Only seconds had to passed then it dawned on her that today was her birthday, a day that was usually no different for her than any other day. Still, what she was seeing was unclear as she was obviously much older than what the ten candles appeared to represent.

As she stood there blankly and searched her mind for an answer, the memory of the day hers and Cloe's paths crossed, suddenly returned.

She stood across the street from Sombreado Casa de Empeño (Shady Pawn Shop), leaning up against the corner of a recently closed down store. Jerrelle really didn't care that she could easily be seen. Unlike a predator that patiently would wait in the weeds and then attack when the moment was right, she preferred her target to be aware of the nearby threat. That way, if they ran, she would have an excuse to break an appendage. If they stayed right where they were but were unable to satisfy her reasons for hunting them down, she might end up just issuing an ultimatum. If she feared that her message wasn't being clearly heard, she would then give them a reason to think twice about defying her. There's nothing like a black eye and a swollen face to remind you to not fuck over Jerrelle Dakota Robinson.

Ten minutes was all that it had so far been. Usually, she had no qualms about waiting for as long as was necessary. She was owed only twenty bucks. Still, it was her money. It irked her that she had to hunt him down. Never again was she going to make a bet with another punk like Chorister 'Cory' Black. After six months, it was clear that the man had no intention of paying off his debt.

She could count on one hand the number of times she felt pity for someone. Right now, that was what was trying to penetrate her stone-cold heart. For as long as she had known Cory, not once had he held a respectable job. He made his living as a thief — and this pawn shop was the only one in the entire metropolitan area that accepted his stolen goods with no questions ever asked.

Not too often would she listen to the little voice inside her head. Today, it was telling her that she was wasting her time and that she wasn't going to get what she came for. As regularly as the man frequented the pawnshop, it could just be one of those few days where Cory simply had no reason to show up. Then again, it was entirely possible that the piece of shit finally got busted.

She had nowhere else to be, even though this day should be an important one to her, so she decided to stay where she was for a little bit longer. Five minutes later, and after receiving a suspicious look by a cop as he passed her by in his cruiser, she decided to give up and try another day. Just to be sure though that she hadn't somehow missed his arrival, Jerrelle headed across the street to the pawnshop; her intention was to take a quick look through the front window and verify whether or not her target was actually inside.

Halfway there, she saw this odd-looking young girl, close to her age she believed, leaving the same pawn shop. Without a care in the world, this teen turned west and then headed on down the sidewalk. After Jerrelle had finished crossing the street, she stood curbside and curiously watched the gothic teen. Because she had lived in this area of the city her whole life, she knew pretty much ever face that called it their home or at least, frequented it. This young girl was either new to the neighborhood or just visiting someone. Her story was really none of Jerrelle's concern. Nevertheless, she decided to follow her. She didn't know why, nor did her gut urge her to. She just did.

Two blocks later, the teen turned the corner and headed where no one in their right mind, let alone a female, should walk alone — into the 'Dead Zone'. This wasn't her responsibility; she had never been anointed someone's guardian angel, yet Jerrelle promptly hurried her pace.

The moment she entered the ingress to this dangerous part of the city, she noticed that the young girl seemed to be unfazed with her surroundings. That surprised her. Even so, Jerrelle knew that the chances of something happening to the young teen would increase the further she went. Therefore, she augmented her own gait. She didn't want to accidentally frighten the girl as that could cause her to run — then again, frightening her might be the best thing to do to get her to stop her forward progress.

There, on the ground right in front of her, Jerrelle saw an empty wine bottle. As she came upon it, she bent over and picked it up while in stride, then launched it as far forward and across the street as she could; it smashed up against a building about fifty feet ahead of the gothic teen. That stopped her dead in her tracks. Curiously, she stood there and looked at her surroundings. She saw nothing out of the ordinary. But then she turned around and trepidation, which she almost never experienced, appeared.

She was unsure what she should do; run or fight. Other than when she was mad at one of her three brothers, she had never been in a physical confrontation before. She was also in an unfamiliar city; a place that she and her family had only moved to a week ago, so

running would probably result in her getting very lost or turning the
wrong corner. Therefore, she decided to remove the item she had just
purchased from the pawnshop, a Royal Romanian World War II Eagle-
Head knife, and stand her ground.

"Relax! I'm not going to hurt you. I only came to warn you."

"Well... I'm warning you. I have a knife and I will use it."

"It'd be a shame to get blood on that beautiful piece of
European history."

That declaration stunned the teen.

"My name is Jerrelle, and you and I need to leave here. This
area of the city is not a very safe place to be walking alone."

Her linear bloodline, strangely allowed her to sense things she
knew very few others could. What she first felt wash over her when she
turned the corner was quite alluring. She had thought that she had
stumbled upon a part of Detroit where she could come to and be
amongst others like her. But now, as the presence she felt continued to
intensify and move toward her, a realization came forth — it had
malicious intentions. This stranger was right. They needed to leave.
"My name is Cloe." She placed her knife back in the bag it had been
in, walked up to Jerrelle, then both of them turned about-face and left
the Dead Zone, side by side.

That memory, and the cake with the ten candles had done it.
Ten years to the day, on her birthday, their path's had crossed. She
was never one to wear her emotions on her sleeve. Today though,
Jerrelle did nothing to stop them from being displayed. Freely, she
allowed a few tears of happiness to trickle down her cheek. She
couldn't remember when the last time was that she had ever gotten a
cake on her birthday, let alone someone even remembering it. That
thoughtful gesture was all it had taken for her to now know for certain
that one more of her thought-to-be, long lost and tattered friendships
had been completely repaired.

After accepting a huge hug of appreciation and a kiss on the
cheek from her friend, Cloe sliced the cake, put three rather large
pieces of it on plates, and led Jerrelle back out to the bar where André
had three pints of beer waiting for them. There was a lot to celebrate

this day, and Jerrelle's birthday just happened to be one of those things.

———————————————— ଚ —————————————————

Madelyn woke up around nine a.m. to the sound of her room's vid-phone ringing. A bit of trepidation suddenly appeared. This was the one morning that she hoped to be left alone, even though she knew the chances of that was relatively slim. Every day since the day she had 'moved' into the New Book Cadillac Hotel's presidential suite, Louie would call and request that she accompany him to either breakfast or dinner at his favorite restaurant. Today, she really didn't want to go. Yes, she could survive the hour or so being with him, but she knew there was a good chance that she just might slip up and do or say something that she should not. The last thing she wanted was to give Louie any sort of indication that their relationship had changed.

After saying hello, to her surprise and to her relief, he let her know that his reason for calling this morning was only to inform her that his schedule for today was full and that he wasn't going to be able to see her. What shocked her more than that though was when he informed her that he no longer felt it was necessary to send an escort or a security detail with her whenever she wanted to go out somewhere. She was now free to come and go as she pleased.

It was as if the praying she had done last night had been answered. What Louie had just told her was music to her ears. No longer did Madelyn have to try and figure out a way to sneak away from the hotel today to go and see Sabastian — but that still didn't mean discretion did not need to be used. Zhin and Nicoli were usually nearby, and just because an unequivocal trust was now being given to her, it didn't mean that they would do the same as well.

By eleven a.m., Madelyn was in a cab and heading toward the border. This was it. She was going to have to explain why she had done what she had to Sabastian. And even if he accepted her reasons, it didn't mean that he would forgive her. So long as he kept an open mind and allowed her to pour out her heart, there was a chance for her to repair the damage she had done.

Then what? There were more skeletons in her closet and those could become the reason why she does not get what she now wants more than anything. She could keep that to herself, but it's a certainty that they will one day come to light. And when that happened, the damage will be far worse than what her past could do now. If there was any chance of her desire coming to fruition, Madelyn had to come clean.

As soon as the cab crossed into Canada, a useless thought entered into her head. *'Too bad this country wasn't still an independent nation instead of being part of the Union. If it was, then I could actually keep on going and get as far away from Louie as I possibly could.'* But that would be the same as what her thoughts had been back in Chicago — she would be running away from her problems instead of addressing them. In order for her to gain back complete control of her life, her slate had to be wiped clean.

Her cab arrived at its destination; she wasn't at all looking forward to what awaited her. Essentially, what she was about to walk into was an inquisition in which the adjudicator already had a preconceived notion about her — and she was nowhere near prepared to present her case.

Nervously, she got out of the vehicle and entered the Old Towne Tap & Grill. Graciously, she was met at the door by the hostess, welcomed, and then informed that her 'lunch date' was already waiting inside.

Madelyn was led to the far side of the bar area where Sabastian was sitting alone in a booth. When she got closer, he didn't smile or even acknowledge her. That caused some anxiety to appear; her thoughts immediately brought forth every single negative possibility she had pondered since she had left her suite. This wasn't off to a good start. She had a lot of work ahead of her if she was going to break down the massive wall that Sabastian had apparently erected.

As she took her seat directly opposite from him, she asked the hostess for a tall glass of water. Once the woman had left, Madelyn took a look across the table and knew that she was in the presence of an individual who was not at all happy. She honestly could not blame him. She too would be pissed off if the man she loved had intentionally led her to an awaiting death. "Sabastian... I..."

He held up his hand and silenced her. He didn't want to be this way: cold, rude, insensitive, but some anger still lingered within him because of what she had done. For now, he decided not to dismiss it — not until after she explained herself. Only then would he know whether or not his father was correct.

After allowing Madelyn to take a few sips of her ice water, the tension between them had gotten to where Sabastian had wanted it. He was now ready to get his 'interrogation' underway. However, instead of asking her the obvious question, the one he posed could have never been anticipated. "Do you love me?"

Madelyn was not at all ready for that one; it left her speechless. What did this mean? What reason would there be for him to ask that question first? In her mind, there had to be a million other ones that should be asked before that one. "Do I love you? Is it not obvious, Sabastian? If I did not love you, then I would not have left you the key to escape."

"I'm assuming that there is an incredible story as to why you led me into the clutches of that bastard, Louie Mazotti?"

"Yes, there is... and I don't even know where to begin."

"Why don't you begin by admitting to me who you really are?"

Sadness enveloped Madelyn as she could hear the spite in his voice. "My name is not Lizanne. Well, it is in a sense. It's my middle name. My real name is Madelyn, but... you already knew that. I was born and raised in Chicago. And as you probably figured out, I never actually had a friend named Amy Amylia. It was just pure coincidence that you found someone with that name who happened to be the same age as I." She paused for a moment and took another sip of her water, knowing that what she had to say to Sabastian next would be the dealbreaker when it came to whether or not there would be any chance of them one day ever being together. "Sabastian, I... I used to be a high-class escort.., which is how I met Louie. Although, I do want to make it perfectly clear that I never, ever slept with him." Madelyn then took a moment, took another sip of her water, and continued. "Shortly after I met him, something terrible happened to me. I didn't know what to do afterward, but he had told me that if I ever needed anything, to look him up. So I did."

Though her story was incomplete, it was easy for Sabastian to speculate as to the direction it was taking. So he said, "You asked him to help you get a measure of revenge, didn't you?"

"Yes. And that is why I had to do what I did to you. I owed him."

Sabastian couldn't fault Madelyn for wanting revenge, as that same desire consumed not only his father, but it also existed within him as well. Her only mistake was allowing that yearning to be the sole reason for her accepting the first offer made instead of taking into consideration what other options might have been there. "What exactly happened to you that caused you to ask Louie for his help?"

She wasn't at all sure if she wanted to relive that horrible evening again, but Sabastian needed and deserved to know everything about her; even the darkest parts of her past. Otherwise, there would not be a chance in hell of a real relationship ever developing between them.

Before she went into the details of what had happened, Madelyn first made certain that Sabastian fully understood why she had chosen to do what she had for a career. It was difficult for her to open up about her family and everything she had to endure while she grew up. However, it was nowhere near as difficult for her to explain as it was when it came time to tell him about the worst night of her life when those eight frat boys from the University of Chicago, gang-raped her.

Sabastian listened intently to her. He could not help but feel the emotions that resonated within her words, nor could he even begin to fathom the horrific experience that she had somehow survived. On the outside, you would never know what had happened; on the inside, he was sure that she was deeply scarred. His heart broke for her.

Oddly, there was a small part of him that did not wish to extend any sympathy. Revealing that though would be hypocritical of him. Case in point, his adopted father had made one rather large mistake that he regretted his whole life, and Sabastian chose to forgive him for it. It's nearly impossible to go through life without wanting a do-over for something.

Everyone deserves a second chance. For that reason, he chose to absolve her of her past decisions. What mattered was the here and now. "I'm really sorry for what happened to you, Madelyn. Believe me when I say that I can understand your motivation for doing what you did, but… I have to know. Do you really love me, or was your tugging on my heartstrings just part of your assignment?"

His questioning her love for him a second time only upset her — but it was also easy for her to see why he didn't have any faith in it. However, she wasn't about to kill herself in order to prove how she truly felt. "You know, Sabastian. I never intended to get close to you. My task was simply to get you to like me and then follow me back to Chicago, but..." Madelyn took another moment to gather her thoughts because she could slowly feel her emotions taking over. "But there is something about you that has awakened inside of me that one thing I never knew I even possessed. You made me feel like I was finally worth something; that I too deserve to find happiness… and even find true love. All it took was that first night together for me to realize that you were what I had always longed for."

Sabastian was about to dispute that statement, as once again that pessimistic side of him was looking for a reason to not believe her. However, the genuine, kindhearted man he was simply would not allow himself to unfairly dismiss someone who was baring their soul. Besides, he could see that she still had a lot to say — and needed to say. Soon enough, he knew, everything would be revealed. Then, and only then, would he know whether or not to allow a new path to run parallel to the one he was already on.

"I fully intended to live up to my end of the agreement with Louie, but you ended up causing me to doubt that I could even go through with what I had been asked to do. You have no idea how torn up I was. I know that you may not be able to fully understand just how I felt at the time, but the more I thought about it, the more I started to believe that I had no other choice but to do what I did. I didn't think that there would be any other way out of the deal I made with Louie other than to complete what he had asked me to do. I'm so sorry that I put you through what I did." She couldn't hold it together any longer; Madelyn immediately broke down and cried.

This was what Sabastian was hoping to see. Yes, it was cruel of him to make her open up like that, especially out in public for everyone to see, but he had to know for sure where her heart was.

He got up from his seat and went over to the other side of the booth. There, he nestled right up to her, put his hand on hers, and looked caringly in her flooded eyes. "I too am sorry. But in order for me to see who you truly are, I felt that it was necessary to get you to bare your soul." Sabastian picked up the napkin that was on the table and gently wiped away the trail of tears on Madelyn's cheeks. "I wish that you had been able to trust me enough to ask me to help you get out of your predicament instead of thinking that you had to complete what you committed yourself to."

"Up until now, I never felt a reason to trust myself." She looked into Sabastian's eyes through her own glossy ones and the contempt that was there when she had first arrived, had vanished.

"Do you love me, Madelyn?"

Without any hesitation, she responded, "Yes, I do love you, Sabastian."

"And I love you."

Their lips touched with a tenderness that was reserved only for moments like these; moments where two hearts become one — moments when the past becomes forgotten and forgiven forever.

They would have probably stayed this way if it hadn't been for the waitress finally coming over to their table to take their order. After asking only for drinks and appetizers, Sabastian looked at Madelyn and said, "I don't care about your past. We all have things in our life that we are not proud of. The only thing I care about is what you want your life to be from this moment forward."

"What I want to do right now is get away from Louie, but... I know that there is an issue between the two of you, and I don't know what that is. If you tell me why he hates you so much, maybe I can help you?"

"I doubt that you can, Madelyn."

"Are you forgetting that you are presumed dead and that Louie adores me? That is why I am living in the presidential suite of his hotel. I am on the inside, I can freely come and go as I please, and I can help you with whatever you need me to do."

Sabastian thought about what she had just said to him. It actually made perfect sense for Madelyn to stay right where she was at the moment. However, the one problem that he had with that suggestion was that she would constantly be in harm's way. He took a moment, sipped on his newly delivered beer, and then contemplated what he felt were the available options. There were several, but all of them were selfish in nature. Madelyn was right. Her help was needed if he was ever going to put the Detroit Underworld Organization out of business. So reluctantly, he agreed with her offer to stay right where she was, behind enemy lines.

The next hour was spent with Sabastian telling her everything about his life: from his father's history with the D.U.O. to his discovery of who he actually was, to his promised retribution for what had been done to his family.

Never in her wildest dreams did Madelyn have a clue as to what Louie Mazotti was really capable of. But when she had found out what his two men had done to those who had sexually assaulted her, her suspicions began to develop. What she was finding difficult to comprehend, however, was how someone could portray himself as being two completely different people. His personality appeared to be split right down the middle. When he was around her, he was the perfect gentleman. When he was in business mode, he could be an evil bastard.

Yes, she had volunteered to walk right back into Louie's world, but she knew that this had to be done as it was the only way that both she and Sabastian would be able to completely free themselves of the individual history they both had. While there, if she happened to find herself in an unenviable position where she had to do something far beyond what her principles would normally allow in order to get what was needed to help Sabastian accomplish his goals, then she would. She only hoped that it didn't come down to once again having to practice the oldest trade known to mankind.

Right before Zhin and Nicoli headed to the organization's safe house to gather the information they needed to help them locate Casper, Louie had made them aware that, in three days time, the Muskegon Militia's weapons order was to be delivered. In hindsight, they were lucky that their 'shipping clerk' wasn't needed for this, as the firearms the group wanted were stored in one of the riverfront warehouses that the organization owned. Had Casper's services been required, Louie would have regrettably found himself with no other option but to back out of the agreement.

Seventy-two hours didn't leave them a whole lot of time to figure out who and where their target was. Nevertheless, it was a mystery that Zhin and Nicoli were confident they could solve without having to postpone the other task that awaited them. The sooner they got this done, the sooner the organization could move forward into its much needed, new direction.

Because the safe house was located in a university community, at least one of them should have recognized that sleep was something you didn't get much of — especially on the weekends. Not even for an hour did the streets quiet down. The neighborhood was an all-day all-night party. And because of this, Zhin and Nicoli had no choice but to stay up.

Not being able to sleep turned out to be a blessing — sort of. It had given them the extra time they needed to continue with their research and planning. By six a.m., the uncertainty that had been there yesterday was gone. Every single stolen weapon that had been sold by the D.U.O., no matter what storage facility it had originated from, ended up being transferred first to the Monmouth County shipping yards in New Jersey before it was subsequently delivered to a client. This information is what allowed Zhin to draw, what he believed, was a reasonable conclusion — this distribution hub had to be the same one that Casper worked out of.

Maybe it was because he was beyond tired and would right now, welcome an injection of sim-caf directly into his veins, but an annoyance overtook what should be utter satisfaction. He had blatantly missed the obvious. It wasn't until after he had come to his conclusion that he realized he had already possessed a significant clue. The contact number Louie had for the man, suggested that he also lived somewhere in the vicinity of that very same city. Had Zhin not been so focused on his research, they very well could be in Casper's backyard right now.

After first apologizing to his boss for calling him at the crack of dawn, Zhin informed Louie of everything they now knew. Following that, he let him know that a complete digital copy of Antonio's files was now accessible to him via the D.U.O.'s Cy-space account. He then added, "We'll be on the road within the hour. I'll call you when we get to New Jersey."

He was happy that his associates were able to make significant progress in such a short amount of time. And although the temptation was there, Louie felt there was no need for him to give any more instructions or even suggestions. Instead, he took a moment and organized his thoughts; he didn't want to call Zhin back because he had forgotten something that might have actually been important. Once he was sure there was nothing, he disconnected his call.

Zhin sat there in reflective thought. Although he still felt as if he was in the proverbial doghouse, he had to think that the good news he just passed along to his boss had at least lengthened his leash. Still, a lot of uneasiness existed; he just could not banish the negative thoughts that lingered. It was unfounded, but he just could not stop thinking that, had the D.U.O. been rooted in his homeland and not the Union, his manhood would have already been removed and then quietly served as a battered entrée in a Chinese restaurant as punishment for their recent failures.

As much as a good twelve hours of uninterrupted sleep would do his body and mind some good right now, they had a deadline to meet. And although time was still on their side, Zhin didn't want to risk not having enough of it, so he looked at his associate and said, "Let's lock up and get out of here."

The moment they hit the road, Nicoli's first thought was to acquire a GPS tracking program for his vid-cell; a specific program that would display the location of where an answered call took place from. Thankfully, he knew of an individual within his old faction of the E.C.L. who could provide him with that bit of technology — he just hoped it had not yet been learned that he had renounced his allegiance and joined a rival organization.

After carefully testing the waters with his contact, there seemed to be no indication that they were yet aware he had turned his back on them. He was glad for this; otherwise, his continued existence would be far less certain. It was inevitable that he was going to be tracked down and made to pay for his decision. However, until that day came, he wasn't going to allow worry to become the reason he constantly looked over his shoulder.

Ten minutes later, and after installing the sent app onto his vid-cell, an unforeseen possibility came to Nicoli — this same app could also be used against him. What if it had actually been known that he had 'quit' and his contact had simply acted as if his defection was not yet known? That way, the moment that he turned on the app to use it, the Liberation could, themselves, backtrace it in order to learn where he was.

Nicoli had been in the game long enough to know that death could be waiting around the next corner. He had never fretted over that possibility before, and he wasn't about to do it now. Doing so could end up interfering with the mission at hand. He and Zhin were already on shaky ground; a reason need not be given to Louie to bury them both beneath it. Besides, Nicoli had already earned his place within the D.U.O. and he was going to do everything in his power to keep it. Yes, using the app was a very big risk to take, but he honestly felt that locating their target without the help of it would be almost the same as discovering that your own back yard contained a huge deposit of crude oil.

When they arrived in New Jersey early that evening, Casper's vid-cell number was called; it only took two rings for his location to be learned. There was no need to speak to him, so Nicoli promptly disconnected his vid-cell. If the man were to call them back, an apology would simply be given for mistakenly dialing a wrong number.

An hour later, they arrived at the very location where the call had been answered — and it did not take them long to realize that luck had been on their side. Although there was no way for them to confirm it, both were fairly certain that they were now sitting right across the street from the off base residence of their mark.

Since the raid on the U.A.L. building, neither of them had gotten any amount of sleep. After being awake for nearly two whole days, it was understandable that both of them were exhausted. Zhin was glad that they had left Ann Arbor when they did. Now, time was on their side. With their search now seemingly over, and the sun close to setting, they found a discrete place to park their SUV — each would take their turn watching their target's residence while the other slept. They both doubted that Casper was going to go anywhere this evening, but if he did, it was highly unlikely that he would be gone for long.

Tomorrow was Monday, and unless he was on vacation, he'd have to go to work in the morning.

Twenty-six hours after they left Michigan, they had their first visual confirmation; their target was headed out his front door, dressed in his military clerk's outfit, and on his way to work. He looked to be a man of seasoned years, roughly five-and-a-half feet tall and severely out of shape. Even so, both of them knew that they should not judge a book by its cover. Just because Casper looked as if he was use to only handling a bucket of chicken or an extra-large pizza, didn't mean he did not have the ability to defend himself from a would-be threat to his life.

With their target now in sight, it would only take one bullet to kill the obese man, but a public execution was something that neither Zhin nor Nicoli preferred. And even though they had been given the freedom to get the job done any way they wanted, they mutually agreed that this was not the right time. Yes, the man was going to die, but he at least deserved a little dignity and respect because of the years of service he gave to the Detroit Underworld Organization.

As they had assumed, his destination this morning had been the Monmouth County shipping yard. Again, they could have just shot him as he exited his vehicle, but they were now on a military base and, even though only a few guards could be seen patrolling the grounds, it would be an unwise risk for them to take. Besides, they had devised a plan on their way there that both agreed would achieve the desired results.

They allowed their target to walk into his work unopposed. Instead of following him right afterward, they waited for about five minutes, just in case Casper had become aware that he had been followed. None of the guards had moved from their post during that time, nor had any other military men appeared in the area. Although that didn't mean anything, both felt that it was safe to take the next step.

After activating the GPS tracking program on his vid-cell, Nicoli called Casper. Just like yesterday, the moment he answered, the call was disconnected; they only needed to know what his approximate location was within the facility.

With that now known, they discretely made their way onto the grounds. From there, they entered through an open bay door of a storage warehouse that looked to be more than a football field in size and packed from floor to ceiling with every single sort of munitions imaginable. Like two sugar-deprived kids in a candy store, Zhin and Nicoli marveled at the massive supply of weaponry; some of it, at one time or another, they fantasized about holding in their hands and firing. The others they never even knew existed but were now curious as to what their capabilities were.

The temptation was certainly there for them to just forget about Casper, take what they could grab in their hands, and then just leave. But stealing weapons was not their objective this day, so they dispatched their wayward thoughts and headed toward a room located off to the far right of the bay door they had just entered through. Once they got there, they didn't knock; they just walked right on in.

There was no need for them to announce their presence. Instead, Zhin and Nicoli just patiently stood there, side-by-side, arms crossed, and waited for Casper to notice them. When he did, his face became deadpanned. It wasn't until a handful of ticks on the clock had gone by that he said, "It's over, isn't it?"

Casper was a fictional character, a ghost, and that was what he was supposed to be. He hoped that by using this alias, it would allow him to never be found. But he knew very well that a day was going to come in which his long-ago decision was going to end up costing him everything. Today appeared to be that day.

He hadn't the faintest idea as to who these two men were, but it was clear to him what their purpose was for being in his office. Casper had been far luckier than he ever thought. He had no regrets about associating himself with a criminal organization. After all, his family was now financially set, and at the same time, he had stuck it to his imperious father.

During a few seconds of idiotic thought, he contemplated opening up the top drawer of his desk and removing his military-issued sidearm. He never claimed to be the smartest man alive, but common sense oddly took over and made him realize that if he did do what he was thinking, any hope he had for survival would all but be eliminated. Besides, Casper knew what his level of expertise was with a sidearm

— it was all but guaranteed that these two rather intimidating individuals were much more proficient and experienced than he. "I take it that you would like for me to go with you... somewhere?"

Zhin unfolded his arms; he then encouraged Nicoli to do the same, as there was no longer a need to demonstrate who was in charge. After that, he politely said, "That is correct."

"Why?"

"The D.U.O. has decided that some restructuring is in order. This is due in part to the belief that somewhere along the line, a rather large leak exists that needs to get plugged."

Casper stood there, taken aback. It was easy for him to conclude what was being implied — after all, he was fully aware of the seizures of those last few shipments of weapons he had arranged. However, in no way shape or form was he going to accept the fate of a traitor when he knew that he wasn't one. Therefore, to Zhin, he said with the utmost of conviction, "Although I knew that a day would come in which the D.U.O. would find me and want to have an official face to face meeting, I never expected it to be because of an assumption of guilt. I, Casper, have done nothing to warrant what I now fear you intend to do to me."

"You made your bed..."

"But without proof, there is no reason to expect me to have to lie in it!"

"Even so, the contract you verbally agreed to isn't unique. It is like any other one wherein your employment can be terminated without just cause."

Yes, it hadn't yet been officially declared that his services were no longer required, but it was clear that he was perilously being dangled over the edge of the cliff, and soon to be let go. Casper had lasted just over twenty-five years living in anonymity, in a world that he had been much happier existing in than the real one. He loathed being an active member of the service; especially early on in his career. Several times, he had tried to get himself discharged. But instead of that happening, his father, a four-star general, had stepped in each time and used his clout to keep his son right where he was. The last time he tried to get thrown out for something that should have ended with him being court-martialed, the result was instead, just a

transfer and a job that his father believed he could not screw up —
being a shipping clerk at the New Jersey munitions depot; a position
for which he gladly exploited. "I wish that you both would just go
away and forget that you ever found me... But that isn't going to
happen, is it?"

"Nope!"

"If I let you boys walk the warehouse and do some early
Christmas shopping, would you do it then?"

As tempting as that offer was, Nicoli looked at Casper and
said, "We don't have any more time to waste. Let's go!"

Again, another idiotic thought invaded his mind. He could try
and fight his way past these two men, then hope that he could get
outside the warehouse where the patrolling guards would be able to
protect him — but he was admittedly out of shape and probably
wouldn't get five feet past his office door before he got a bullet in his
back. Dying on military soil oddly bothered him more than the fate
that apparently awaited him. Therefore, appeasing their request
seemed like the only option he really had — he just had to hold onto
whatever thread of hope there was that before they did to him what he
suspected, he would be able to find a way out of this mess.

With both men flanking him, he walked out of his office,
through the warehouse, and then out the open bay doors. As they
made their way toward the parking lot, his eyes did not wander in
search of someone to help him — even though he knew all the guards
and where they were posted. Strangely, he felt calm. The anxiety that
usually consumed him whenever he got even a little stressed wasn't
there. It was almost as if he had found peace, even though he honestly
wasn't ready for his time on this earth to come to an end.

When they arrived at the parked Cadillac, he got into the back
seat and then quietly confessed his sins — just in case the Almighty
Lord was watching what was going on. From the moment they drove
away, and for the next ten minutes, not a word had been spoken; not
until Nicoli surprisingly said, "Louie wishes to speak with you." The
German man then turned in his seat. "You are to only listen to what he
has to say. Do not interrupt him and do not grovel."

"I don't deserve to die."

"No one gets to chose when that happens. You agreed to walk a path, side by side with ours. And because you did, you don't get the luxury of determining when and where you step off."

"You are aware that Louie has never seen my face before, nor have I ever seen his."

"That's about to change." Nicoli hit the send button on his vid-cell and then handed it to Casper. "Now keep it short and don't deviate from your instructions."

He had a lot of respect for Louie Mazotti and he didn't want to go to his grave with any hate in his heart. Therefore, he decided to just do what he was told. When his now apparent ex-employer's face appeared on the vid-screen, a sense of failure suddenly consumed him. This was the very first time he had ever seen what Louie Mazotti looked like. And now that that had taken place, even if he were to somehow earn a reprieve from his pending death sentence, it was highly unlikely that things would stay as they were.

Casper kept quiet and listened, only speaking when asked a question — and he kept his reply as brief as he could. He didn't plead for his life like his conscience was prodding him to, nor did he even ask for a second chance. Instead, he just thanked Louie for the opportunity that he had been given and said that he understood the D.U.O.'s decision.

Louie returned the thanks to Casper for his loyal service, apologized for having to make this difficult decision, and then promised him that a small 'pension' would end up in his family's hands. No other words were exchanged after that. He didn't even say goodbye, nor did he even ask him to reveal what his real name was. He just coldly disconnected the call.

After taking back his vid-cell from Casper, Nicoli looked into his eyes and sincerely said to him, "You don't have much time left. Since you have been a valued employee for the organization, I have been instructed to allow you to send a message to your loved ones." He then handed Casper an e-tablet. "Take this and write them a letter, apologizing for the secret life you chose to live and explain to them why you won't be coming home from work today."

"Thank you, but... before I write this, I want to again, for the record, state my innocence. I am not responsible for this supposed leak. Without proof of my guilt, I honestly don't understand how judgment can be passed."

"Just because something still has value and use, does not mean it should still be kept."

No matter what reason or argument he gave, nothing could save his life. Soon, that final nail will be hammered into his coffin. The only thing that Casper could do at that moment was what had been suggested to him; pen a heartfelt letter to his family. So that is what he did.

As he wrote, he made sure not to divulge any specifics or details; his loved ones did not need to know anything that one day, could be used against them. Besides, he had sworn an oath of non-disclosure when he became a silent associate with the Detroit Underworld Organization — and it was an oath that he decided he was going to uphold.

After Nicoli had proofread the letter, he allowed Casper the privilege of sending it off to his loved ones. Once that was done, he sat quietly in the back seat of the Cadillac and nervously waited for the end to come. If his totalitarian father were still alive, what was about to happen to him would be worth all of the years of deep-rooted bitterness he harbored. His one final wish would then be for General Donald Sperron to bear witness to his execution because it would immediately become a symbolic F.U. to the man for forcing his hand into choosing a dishonorable life; one that was going to forever leave a black mark on his family's military legacy.

Both wanted desperately to spend the rest of the day together, even though they knew it to be impossible — life and its expectations awaited them. But until it came time to concede to that, they were going to cherish the few moments they had left.

Upon their cab's arrival at Campus Martius Park, Sabastian gave Madelyn a hug and a kiss goodbye. Reluctantly, he then got out of the vehicle and watched it leave in the direction of the New Book Cadillac Hotel. An urge quickly enveloped him to grab another cab and follow her — only because fear still existed within him that he had made a huge mistake in permitting her to walk right back into the enemy's lair. But he could not let his worry ruin the advantage he now had. His father never had one as significant as this. With a mole on the inside, Sabastian knew that the chances of the D.U.O. finally being shut down would exponentially increase. For that reason alone, he had to believe that Madelyn not only was going to be all right, but that she would come through for him.

For a moment, he thought about taking a walk around and seeing what the downtown core of Detroit was all about, but the enemy's headquarters wasn't all that far away from where he now was and he'd probably end up within its shadow — and being tempted to invite himself inside. Besides, this day wasn't his to do with as he pleased, as Jerrelle was patiently waiting for him to return to her apartment so that they could leave for San Antonio.

When he had arrived at his friend's place, her car was nowhere to be found. Sabastian's first thought was that she had already left, as she would have no qualms whatsoever about heading down south without him. It was a known fact that Jerrelle had very little patience if any — especially if someone didn't give her the exact time of their return. And since he had not done that, Sabastian could only hope that she had just gone out to tie up a few loose ends or something like that.

Casually, he approached the front door of the six-floor apartment building. Just as he was about to pass under the front awning, it dawned on him that she hadn't given him the access code to get in. Like anyone else would who wanted access, he could just hang around and wait for someone to leave or enter the building and then grab the open door afterward. But that would only get him inside. Then what? Sabastian really didn't want to loiter in the hallway outside her place and give off the impression that he was up to no good.

Undeterred, he took a moment to think — it was then that he noticed the fully loaded rental van parked in the lot. Briefly, he contemplated waiting inside the vehicle, as he did possess the key. But again, sitting in the driver's seat for what could be hours upon end, waiting for her return, could also cause an unfounded conclusion to be drawn by someone passing by who possessed overly suspicious, speculative tendencies.

Logic dictated that he just call her and find out where she was, then ask how long she was going to be — but he didn't want to be an impatient friend either. The fault for this inconvenience clearly was his for not keeping her in the loop to begin with.

After a few moments spent brainstorming, he walked to the back of the apartment building. There, right at the corner of it, was an oak tree. Oddly, he had never climbed one during his entire youth, but he had scaled a climbing wall hundreds of time throughout his military tenure, so up he went. Once he was even with Jerrelle's second-floor balcony, he shimmied across a large branch that ran nearly parallel to it and roughly two feet away. Once he stepped off it and went over the railing, he walked over and casually grabbed the handle to the sliding glass door. To his surprise, it didn't budge. *'Why would she lock the balcony door when her place is now all but empty?'* he wondered.

Now what? It didn't make any sense for him to take another risk and climb back down to the ground. Knowing his luck, he'd slip and fall and break more than just his neck. Again, he contemplated calling Jerrelle, but knowing her as well as he did, she'd probably take her sweet old time getting back to her apartment, just to get a laugh out of Sabastian's own stupidity.

Like the hallway or the van, right where he now was might draw someone's unwanted attention. Unfortunately, there was nothing that he could do about it. Besides, it was actually cooler on this side of the building: the concrete balcony, the shade from the tree, and the lack of visible sun made the early afternoon relatively enjoyable to be outside. So if he had to wait anywhere, where he was seemed like the best place to do that.

There wasn't any furniture for Sabastian to sit on and he wasn't about to stay standing until Jerrelle returned; it left him with only one other option. With nothing else to do, he decided to take advantage of his alone time and take a power nap, so he sat down on the concrete and wedged his self up against the wall in one corner of the balcony.

The shade was a natural blanket; it draped over his body and allowed him to get comfortable. In fact, it had only taken him a few minutes after he had closed his eyes before he was able to slip into a welcomed state of respite.

"Hello, my son!"

Sabastian opened his eyes and saw this beautiful young woman, no older than he was, sitting cross-legged directly in front of him and leaning up against the balcony railing. At first, he thought that someone had climbed the tree and joined him up on his perch — but then he sensed that this woman should be familiar to him. He stood up and inquisitively looked at her.

She stood up as well and stepped toward him. She honestly thought that fear would exist inside Sabastian and it would urge him to keep his distance — but he did not move. Taking this as a good sign, she reached out with her left hand; the closest that she could get to her touching his arm was about an inch away. It was disappointing, but it would have to suffice, as she knew it to be impossible for her to make actual physical contact.

From her hand came a gentle static-like charge that seemed to connect the two of them. The immediate sensation was one that Sabastian could not describe. It was otherworldly, but it also strangely felt natural — notwithstanding the fact that the anomalous tether had caused the hairs on his uncovered arms and legs to stand up.

Without any doubt, he should be feeling apprehensive with what was going on, but he wasn't. Maybe it was because there was a calming, gentle, and comforting sensation running through him that could be compared to that of a loving, maternal caress. It was then that Sabastian's one and only desire became realized. He should have known who this was the moment she appeared, as he had looked at her image every day and longed for her to be in his life. Just like he had thought when it came to his father, he assumed his own death would be the only way they would ever see each other. "Mom?"

"Yes, my son."

In that instant, he wanted to spring forward and hug her, but his unassuredness kept him in place. His heart was racing and his mind was full of confusion. He was so young when she was taken from him, he doesn't even remember being held by her. If that one thing could happen, Sabastian would surely welcome it. Time though, he feared, was not on their side. This visit, he was fairly certain, was for an intended purpose only. It wasn't to simply have that long-awaited reunion.

236

"You have grown into such a handsome young man; one that any mother would be proud of. And I'm so sorry that I was unable to be there for you when you needed me the most."

"It's not your fault. None of us had any control over what had taken place. Things were meant to be this way for a reason."

"You are right about that. Without me, your life has taken on a whole new purpose. Believe it or not, you are now destined to achieve great things; things that would not have happened had I not died when I did. So please do not allow yourself to feel cheated because we were not a part of each other's life. You must accept the path that you were born to walk and go out and create a legacy that will forever be praised and admired."

"I have. And I promise that I will."

"I also want to make sure that you listen to what your heart is telling you."

"My heart?"

"Yes. Do you really love Madelyn as unconditionally as you claim?"

"I have never felt this way about anyone. I mean.., I've never known what it is like to fall in love with someone, but I'm..."

"You are unsure if you can wholeheartedly accept her past or find a way to forgive her because of the way that she came into your life."

"I can look beyond her life choices, but. ."

"But what? Had she not been associated with Louie Mazotti, the two of you would have never met. You must be able to completely forgive her for having that affiliation with him before you can openly welcome her into your life as she has you."

Sabastian sat there in silence looking at his mother. He knew that she was right. He had to completely forgive Madelyn before the love he claimed he had for her became unequivocal. He thought he had expunged the doubt that had earlier been there, but he now realized that it was still lingering. "I guess I have a lot of soul-searching to do."

"Yes my son, you do." Sylvia took a moment and looked into her son's eyes, happy that he had turned out exactly like she had hoped he would. From the first moment she had held him in her arms as an *infant at the hospital, she knew that her son was a special boy, but never could she have imagined at the time just how important his life would become.*

It killed her inside that appearing to her son as an apparition was all that the Apollo's Stone would allow. If it was at all possible for her to actually embrace Sabastian, she had hoped that Maxwell would have figured it out before now. Nevertheless, she was thankful that she was being allowed to have this mother/son moment because parents who have ever been taken away from their children prematurely don't get the opportunity to do what she now was.

Sylvia raised her right hand up, brought it up to her son's cheek, and made contact with it in the same exact manner as she had with his arm. After only a few seconds, she produced a loving smile; it came as a result of her now knowing for sure just how much love he had for her.

Sabastian's body was consumed with emotion; he knew that his mother was about to leave him again. It was certainly not what he wanted. He wanted her to stay. He wanted her to be there whenever he needed her. He wanted to make up for all of those lost years. But none of that was going to happen.

What was taking place was rare, special, and he was certainly fortunate to experience what he was. For that, he too was thankful. This was what Sabastian had always wanted — a moment where time stood still and he could finally experience the love that his mother had always had for him.

Sylvia lowered her hand; the amorous gaze that radiated from her did not waver. This private moment they were sharing, she did not want it to ever end — but it had to. And she had to let it. Her allotted time was almost up. "Although we must now part ways, rest assured that your father and I will always be there to guide you and help you."

"I know.., mom."

Sylvia stepped forward and gave her son the closest thing that she could to a kiss on the cheek. "I love you, my son. I always will." She then dissolved into the early afternoon shade that covered the balcony.

Sabastian stood there for a moment and reflected upon what had just taken place. Although his mother had come to him to ensure

238

that his heart and head were where they were supposed to be, her visit was also meant to make sure he knew that she loved him. He assumed that she always had, but to experience that first hand, just meant the world to him. Now, he could move on with his life without any uncertainties being the reason that he did not fulfill his destiny.

Sabastian woke up to an unknown noise. It was then that he realized he was no longer sitting down on the balcony. He was standing in the middle of it. Just like the visit from his father, this one with his mother had seemed all too real. Maybe it wasn't, but this time, Sabastian's heart was telling him that it was. Yes, his father and mother were no longer alive, but now he knew for certain they were never going to leave him. One day, the three of them would be reunited. Until then, he was going to continue following the path that fate had placed him on — and when the time was right, invite Madelyn Kinsworth to walk it with him.

Again, he heard the noise. This time, he recognized that it was coming from inside of Jerrelle's apartment. Cautiously, he looked through the sliding glass door and saw that it was his old friend. Where she had been, he didn't know — he was just happy that she did not leave town without him.

Not thinking anything of it, Sabastian knocked harder than he should have on the glass door. That was a big mistake, as the usually perceptive Jerrelle had been caught off guard.

Startled, her instincts kicked in. Without taking a moment to see who was there, she drew the gun that had been tucked in the back of her pants and fired it at her balcony door. Luckily, Sabastian was able to recognize what his friend was blindly doing. Right as he hit the ground, he endured a shower of broken glass all over his back. "It's me, dammit! Don't shoot!"

"Sab?"

He pulled himself up to his knees, shook off the shards of glass, rose to his feet, and carefully walked through the shattered balcony door into Jerrelle's apartment. Almost immediately, Sabastian could smell the booze on her breath. "You've been partying again, haven't you?"

"Yeah.., but it wasn't my intention to. It's all Cloe's fault. I went to say goodbye to her and... she had a birthday cake for me. I don't even remember the last time anyone baked a cake for me, Sab? Anyway.., one beer led to... I don't know how many I've had since I got there but... this is the best damn birthday I have ever had."

"I'm glad you had a good time today, and I'm thankful that you are buzzed just enough so that your aim is off."

Jerrelle cracked a devilish grin as if to suggest that she missed intentionally, even though she felt relieved that she had luckily missed killing her best friend.

If I may make a suggestion.., I think that it would be best that you grab a few hours of rest so that the alcohol can have time to work its way out of your system. The last thing you need to be is half in the bag and behind the wheel on the freeway."

"You know, for once in your life, I think that you are right." Jerrelle then staggered off toward her bedroom.

Sabastian just stood there laughing inside. "Oh, and by the way... Happy Birthday!"

Jerrelle just kept on walking, raised her left hand in the air, and then jokingly shot him the finger. "As if you even remembered that it was my birthday today!"

Two hours later, she woke up to the smell of Kentucky Fried Chicken. Although she hadn't gotten anywhere near as drunk as she normally would have whenever that was her intention, Jerrelle still felt a little sluggish. Two pieces of birthday cake were all that she had eaten since she had first woken up, so the chicken was technically her lunch — and although she generally never ate that, or pizza, or burgers without beer, she decided that she had had enough already.

"You're not pissed or anything about me giving you the finger earlier?"

"No. Only one time was I ever hurt when you gave me the finger, and that was right after what had happened between you and my 'adopted' father."

"Yeah... I guess I owe you an apology for that one also."

"Don't worry, it's long forgotten."

They basically remained in silence while they polished off the ten pieces of chicken and the large box of fries. Once that was done, Sabastian took the containers they came in and tossed them outside on the balcony on top of the shards of glass; he had no intention of cleaning that up for Jerrelle. "By the way.., why did you fire on me when I knocked on your balcony door?"

"You scared the shit out of me. Besides.., no one in their right mind would try to enter into someone's apartment through the second-floor balcony without expecting to get shot. I honestly thought that you were Nicoli. I guess I owe you an apology for that one also?"

"Just promise me that you'll lay off of alcohol until we officially put an end to the Detroit Underworld Organization."

"You know very well that I can't do that. Besides, you can't guarantee how long it's going to take to accomplish this mission of yours."

Sabastian stayed quiet; he knew that she was right.

"Just out of curiosity... How do you plan on putting them out of business?"

"I'm not exactly sure yet."

Sarcastically, Jerrelle then said, "Why don't you just waltz right up to Louie's office door and ask him for a face to face meeting so that the two of you can negotiate the terms of his surrender."

Sabastian expunged a halfhearted laugh. "I had actually thought about doing something similar to that, but the get-together I had this morning ended up turning out much better than I had first anticipated."

"Care to fill me in on the details?"

"Let's just say that I now have someone on the inside that I am hoping will be able to get us some useful information."

That not-so-subtle revelation had all but confirmed Jerrelle's previous suspicions. The favor that Sabastian had wanted from his cousin had something to do with his 'girlfriend'. Without needing any confirmation, she now knew that sometime yesterday, Sharice went to Louie's Casino to see Madelyn. Then this morning, he didn't want to leave for San Antonio as they had earlier planned because he had something important that he wanted to do. "You met up with your girlfriend this morning, didn't you?"

241

Sabastian rolled his eyes at Jerrelle's premature insinuation. "Yes. And she volunteered to go back inside the enemy's lair and be my mole. I'm gonna give her a few days to find something useful for us to use against Louie Mazotti. Whether or not she does, it makes sense to use the man's trust in her to our advantage."

"That's what a good agent, soldier, or police officer does. They maximize whatever advantage may come their way. If it had been me, I would have done the same thing as she."

"I know, it's just... what Madelyn is doing is very risky. And she's far from trained to handle something like this like you or me."

That much was a given. It was also easy for Jerrelle to see just how uncomfortable Sabastian was letting his 'girlfriend' do this even though he knew that it made perfect sense. "I can tell that you selfishly hate the fact she willingly went back, but I also know that you are smart enough to realize that she is in the perfect position to help us. You know that you had no other choice but to allow her to do this. If you were to insist that she not go back there, it would completely change Madelyn's whole perception of who she believed you to be as a person."

"I know, it's just... she is in there all alone with no way of protecting herself."

Jerrelle went over to her friend and placed a hand upon his shoulder. "She'll be fine." She then left the living room area and went into her bathroom to take a shower. While she was doing that, Sabastian changed his mind. Not about Madelyn, but about the dangerous mess that was lying outside, so he walked out to the balcony, bent over and grabbed the empty KFC containers, and then he carefully began to pick up the glass from the shattered balcony door. The smart thing to do would be to use a broom and a dustpan or a vacuum, but Jerrelle had packed those up with everything else and loaded them into the van parked out front of her soon-to-be old apartment. It left Sabastian with nothing else to use except for his shoe as a makeshift broom and the box that the fries came in as a dustpan.

Once he had finished 'sweeping' up as much of the broken glass as he could, he stood up against the railing and looked out across the back parking lot, directly through the absolution of the bright afternoon sun that had finally made its way to that side of the building.

He then spoke softly; just loud enough for only his own ears to hear. "I don't know if you can hear me or not, mom.., but you were right. I am still somewhat conflicted. But I also now know what I want. I want to get Madelyn away from that asshole as soon as I can because I'm afraid to lose any possibility of ever being with her. I don't think that I will be able to stay on my destined path if I lose the best thing that has ever happened to me."

Sabastian stood there quiet for the next few minutes as a previously non-existent breeze began; it thus caused a few of the leaves from the tree that he had earlier climbed, to break away from its branches. Seemingly, they all fell in Sabastian's direction. Moments later, something grabbed his attention. His gut may not have been responsible, but he felt compelled nevertheless to look at the row of identical apartments that sat back across the way on the other side of the fence that divided the properties.

Since he did not have a pair of sunglasses with him, he shaded his eyes from the overhead sun as best as he could with his right hand and tried to focus on what was directly ahead. There, something was enveloped in the conduit of rays that filled the area between two buildings. After he spent a few seconds trying to determine what it was that he was seeing, he came to the conclusion that it was a person — and they were looking right back at him. Unfortunately, he just could not distinctly make out their features.

As if his own thoughts had been heard, the breeze unexpectedly stopped, just as a single cloud in an otherwise wide-open sky, blocked the sun — it gave Sabastian a much clearer view of that person. It was then that he realized who was looking right back at him. "Mom!"

Sylvia smiled, turned around, and then walked between the two apartments in the opposite direction of her son. *'Look past what you see with your own eyes and learn to trust your feelings. They will lead you to the happiness that you seek, desire, and deserve.'* Those words didn't just pop into his head; Sabastian had actually heard his mother speaking them. Joy overwhelmed him. He now knew that whenever a time came in which his mother was needed, she would be there in a way that only no one else could ever understand.

8

Upon making it back to Detroit in record time, the only thing that Zhin and Nicoli wanted to do was go straight to bed — even though it was only nearing six in the evening. The rotation of power naps had helped, but complete exhaustion was creeping up on them fast. Neither wanted to do anything else but sleep.

Feeling obliged to at least stop by the office before going home; they walked in and were surprised at what they saw. As expected, Louie was sitting behind his desk and looking at his computer. What was unusual was that their boss was way overdressed for work — there was also a noticeable hint of musk in the air. Each immediately looked at the other. Apparently, big plans had been made for the evening. And if that were indeed the case, then it would mean neither of them was going to be needed for anything else today. They literally crossed their fingers and hoped that their assumption was correct.

After Louie invited his men in, he asked them to take a seat. As they were doing this, he shut down his computer. Although he still had some work to do, he decided to put the remainder of it off until tomorrow — not just because none of it was of any real importance, but he had a dinner date scheduled less than an hour from now and he wanted his mind free and clear of any unwanted distractions.

Roughly fifteen minutes after his associates arrived, their brief summary of what had happened was completed. Louie simply could not help but give his praise for a job well done. With nothing to work with, they had found out who Casper was, where he was located, drugged him, snuck into a meat recycling facility (The same place where all of the state's meat product waste was sent to and then either processed into animal feed or fertilizer), and deposited his lifeless body into a boiling vat.

Normally, he would not have had a problem sitting there all night, having a few drinks, and conversing with his two associates, but he could tell that they were both mentally and physically exhausted.

244

Also, the clock on his office wall was nearing the time he intended to pick up Madelyn, so after making sure there was nothing else either he or his associates needed to discuss, he excused them.

Happy that things finally seemed to be going his way, he walked into his private bathroom so that he could check in the mirror and make sure that he was looking as sharp as he felt. After applying a bit more cologne, Louie left his office and headed over to the elevator — the hotel's presidential suite was his destination.

It had been a few days since Madelyn had been in his company, so tonight Louie decided that he'd break from the norm and take her someplace other than one of the establishments that the D.U.O. owned. Shortly after their arrival at Calabrese's Restauranté, he presented her with a small gift. To his surprise, it had been relatively easy for him to find a place in Detroit that made chocolate flowers; the same item that had been directly responsible for connecting them in a way he would have never thought.

Under normal circumstances, Madelyn would have been tickled pink over receiving some more chocolate flowers, but now that she knew the truth about Louie, she only humored him, slipped on her best pair of acting shoes, and amiably thanked him for being so thoughtful.

This evening was undoubtedly going to be a tough one for her, having to be as close as she was to the person who not only had tried himself but had been a part of several other attempts to kill the man whom she had fallen in love with. But she had volunteered to do this, and tonight seemed like the perfect opportunity for her to try and extract some information from Louie. Hopefully, something that would be of use to Sabastian.

An hour later, they left the restaurant and made their way directly back to the New Book Cadillac Hotel. Dinner and her company were the only things that Louie had wanted from Madelyn tonight. Admittedly, it was getting harder and harder for him to resist the temptation that was there. Still, he intended to stick to his guns and not break the vow he had made to himself to never cheat on his soul mate — even though he was fairly certain that he and Mirella were never going to work things out and get back together. Besides, that disturbing dream he had from not too long ago in which Madelyn had morphed into Maxwell was enough of a deterrent to prevent him from taking a chance. It's not like what had happened to him in that dream would ever occur in real life, but until he knew for certain that his ethereal problem was gone forever, he was going to abstain from pursuing any sort of intimate activity.

As the old saying goes, a woman always gets what she wants — and that is because they are born with what all straight men crave. Madelyn was counting on that very thing once they arrived back at the hotel. Surprisingly though, it took a lot of coaxing before Louie finally gave in and agreed to get out of the limousine with her instead of staying behind and taking it to his home.

Had it been any other woman, he would have been unapologetically rude in order to officially end their 'date' instead of accompanying her up to her suite for a nightcap. But Madelyn; he just could not deliberately step on her like a doormat and wipe his feet clean. So, as a gentleman should, the moment they entered the suite, Louie started to make his way over to the wet bar in order to pour them each a nightcap — but he got stopped. Madelyn quickly pointed out that this was not his apartment or office; this was her suite. Tonight, he was her guest. It was he who should be getting comfortable, not her.

Louie was an old school kind of man. He could be a heartless bastard sometimes, but when it came to a woman, he still believed in chivalry. However, just like the intent he had with the D.U.O., he too had to change with the times. And there seemed like no better time than tonight for that to begin, so he claimed a seat on the extra-long synth-suede sofa and respectfully watched Madelyn make her way over to the wet bar.

Knowing that he liked Walker's Club, she prepared him a double on the rocks. Because she had planned on this nightcap taking place, and because there was a clear line of sight from the living area to the bar, she had placed in the bottom of his glass beforehand a couple of crushed 'chill pills'; it was a drug that some escorts began to use a few years ago. It had been created for the purpose of being an alternative medical treatment for individuals with severe anger issues. The pill, as advertised, did not come with the same potential, harmful side effects other similar medications did. However, it inadvertently ended up serving another purpose.

Those in the escort service soon realized that this pill helped to mellow out an overly aggressive client. Conversely, because of how effective it was, some escorts began to use it in an unscrupulous manner — hence the reason for it being dubbed the 'chill pill'. If more than one of the recommended doses was taken, the client would end up losing the capability to differentiate between what was right and what was wrong. They would become overly co-operative. At that point, and with the inability to fully understand what was going on, the client could be, and most often would be, taken advantage of. Usually monetarily, but in some instances, it was physically.

Once word of this practice made its way throughout the industry, the legal escort services promptly banned the drug's usage by their workers for fear that a client might take legal action against them — or worse, a client might end up having a fatal reaction to it.

Since the day of the drug's availability, Madelyn had always kept a few of those pills in her possession — even after her employer prohibited it. Now, seemed like the perfect time to utilize them.

After making herself a gin and tonic, she made her way over to the sofa, handed Louie his drink, and took up a seat next to him. Now, she just needed to stay calm and not give him any indication that this evening was actually something other than what it was supposed to be.

Ten minutes; that was all it had taken before his disposition began to change. Louie was starting to over relax — and he was also beginning to babble. The window was now open for her to get what she wanted, but she had to be quick because it wasn't going to stay that way for very long.

Beginning with the ones that Sabastian had written down for her earlier in the day, Madelyn asked a series of questions; ones that would not seem to Louie as if she was prying. After the last one, she could tell that he was no longer in control of his better judgment. He essentially was putty in her hands.

A part of her was feeling guilty. Another part of her though, promptly reminded herself that he had no qualms whatsoever about taking advantage of someone. So she quickly dispatched those growing, penitent feelings and continued on with her agenda by posing questions specifically pertaining to any future business transactions that the D.U.O. had planned. Freely, Louie admitted to her that there was one scheduled for tomorrow. That revelation unexpectedly caught her off guard — but she embraced this information all the same.

This 'interrogation' had worked out exactly as she had hoped. Throughout her old career, she had to spend time with individuals that essentially made her skin crawl. That, of course, had not been the case with Louie. With that being said, she now found it to be very difficult to be in his presence because of the abhorrence that now existed within her. In fact, she loathed him equally as much as she did those eight who had each taken a turn raping her.

Five minutes after she had acquired exactly what she stayed behind for Louie was beyond comprehension. He had begun to slouch, slur his words, and even drool. Madelyn could tell that he was almost to the point of passing out. She had to move quickly or he would end up being nothing but dead weight.

A terrible thought suddenly popped into her head. The crazy thing was that she was actually contemplating it. She was alone and in her suite with a defenseless man. How easy it would be for Madelyn to end this madness in the name of the Banks family. Certainly, there was something within these quarters that she could use to kill Louie where he now sat. But engaging in such an act would make her no different than him. She was not an evil, cold-hearted bitch. Being degraded, violated, deceived, manipulated, exploited; those things had unfortunately been a consistent part of her adult life — the latter three, Louie had also done to her. But in no way shape or form was that grounds for her to cross over to the other side. The right to be judge, jury, and executioner, wasn't hers. Things had to happen the way fate intended them to.

With a bit of effort exuded, she lifted Louie upright and then began the daunting task of walking him to the elevator, and from there, once it opened up at the top floor, to the other side of the hotel to where his office was. Her struggle lasted almost ten minutes.

After fishing through his suit jacket pockets for a key, she opened up the door, dragged his nearly lifeless body over to his extra-long, synth-suede couch, laid him across it, and then left him alone to sleep. Madelyn had made it there just in time; Louie was as useless as a lump of coal in a Christmas stocking. The next morning, she was sure that he would question how he had ended up in his office, but she knew that she would be able to easily convince him that he had begun to doze off from the excessive amount of alcohol that he had consumed at dinner and in her suite. Yes, that was a lie, but even if he had checked his surveillance cameras, he'd see that Madelyn had kindly helped him to get to his office for the night.

After returning to her suite, she locked her door and then — she swore. She was anxious to tell Sabastian everything that she had just learned, but couldn't — all because she had screwed up. Stupidly, she had forgotten to get his vid-cell number before he had left her alone in the cab. It had slipped her mind completely that she no longer had it.

If her thoughts had been clear back in Chicago when she was faking being sick, she would have thought to remove the SIM card from her vid-cell before depositing it in the dumpster. But because she hadn't, Sabastian's number was now long gone. It's not like she could call him now anyway, as she had yet to get herself a new vid-cell.

Her options now seemed limited. Since she no longer needed to be escorted if she wanted to leave the hotel, she could walk throughout the downtown core of Detroit and hope that she'd luckily bump into him — doing that though, would be far less successful than searching through a hundred haystacks, trying to find one single needle. She could just wait around until Sabastian made contact with her again, but the information she had would probably be useless by then. There had to be a way for her to get a hold of him.

After racking her brain for over a half-hour, an idea finally came to her. Her suite had its own palmtop. No, she wasn't going to use the device, look up Sabastian's agency's number, and then contact him that way. She couldn't risk that a snooping or tracking program of some kind was already installed on it. The last thing she wanted was for her Internet activity to be looked at and then used against her. However, she was going to use the palmtop for a different task. For her to learn what Sabastian's number was, she had to first go to www.track-u.onion. It was a site that existed on the dark web.

Once Madelyn logged into her account, she expunged a sigh of relief. It had been a few years since she had used this site and was beyond thrilled that it was still up and running, considering that what it helped you to do, was very illegal.

She had first learned about this site from a 'streetwalker' that she was familiar with, but not at all close to. Apparently, this girl would use the site so that she could keep tabs on her pimp's whereabouts. That way, she could turn tricks on the side and make some extra cash without him knowing.

Track-U was a site that hacked every telephone company, vid-cell provider, Internet provider, e-mail and vid-mail service, credit service, and social media platform throughout the world. They then steal and compile every bit of electronic information available on everyone. For a small fee, the site will then provide everything they have on whatever individual you inquire about. In addition to that, it could also be used to anonymously send any kind of electronic file: text, images, video, or even cryptocurrency, without any worries of your activity, ever being traced.

It took her a few minutes to navigate to where on the site she wanted to go. Once she was there, she requisitioned her own phone records so that she could find Sabastian's number. Once she had it, she submitted a request to unsubscribe to the site and to have her profile be scrubbed from existence as she had no plans, nor did she think that there would ever be a need for her to log onto it again.

Restlessness then consumed her. She immediately wanted to leave the world she was currently immersed in — but then she realized just how late in the evening it actually was. What she now knew, and what Sabastian needed to know, was going to have to wait until morning. She just hoped that when that came, Louie wasn't already outside her suite, knocking on her door, and wanting an explanation of what had happened to him last night.

For some unknown reason, he found himself walking across a rather large field that appeared to have been burned away not all that long ago — and there even seemed to be a hint of the charred landscape that still lingered in the air. With each step he took, some of the thin layer of soot that lay on the ground clung like a magnet to his alligator shoes. He wanted to stop, but he just couldn't. Something was coercing him to continue on forward.

Off in the distance, he saw a lone figure appear just over the horizon. It looked to be miles away, yet it had only taken him a few seconds to realize that the individual was in fact, moving rapidly in his direction. Strangely, this person didn't seem to be walking as a normal human being would; it almost looked as if with each step taken, several yards were being covered at once. He wasn't sure if he wanted to know who/what this figure was, but his innate curiosity seemed to be preventing his mind from making sense of this strange occurrence and figuring out what was really going on.

It was almost as if he was being mesmerized by the approaching figure. It was not until the individual got to be just about a stone's throw away that he finally realized it was another man. But who was it? His features were still indiscernible.

Although it wasn't a certainty, it appeared to Louie that he, yet again, had involuntarily become immersed in what was probably going to be an inescapable nightmare. That was his guess, only because he had already been an unwilling participant in a few of them. If he could run away in order to avoid what might come, he'd consider it. But his body just didn't want to move. Even if it could, where would he go? The ominous terrain encompassing him stretched out as far as the eye could see.

Once the approaching individual reached a point of being only a handful of yards away, their identity finally became clear. Anger promptly consumed Louie. He hoped that he would never cross this individual's path again. When the man was alive, he had made his life a living hell. It should have been impossible, yet somehow after death he had found a way to make it even worse.

His body seemed disconnected from his mind; it wanted him to retreat, but he just kept on moving forward. There appeared to be nothing that he could do to avoid the inevitable. One more time, he was going to be subjected to another round of torment.

"Welcome to Louie-ville," Maxwell said, and then produced a cheeky grin.

Louie's forward progress abruptly halted — had his feet not been 'glued' to the ground, he probably would have fallen flat on his face. "I am getting fuckin' sick and tired of you appearing in my dreams, Banks!"

"Well, you'll be happy to know that this will be the last time."

"Good! Now get lost and leave me alone!"

"Not yet, as I am here out of the goodness of my heart to let you know that your corporeal existence is rapidly nearing its conclusion."

Louie could not help but laugh. "Sal must have hit you in the face one too many times before he knocked you out cold. You have absolutely no idea what you are talking about."

"Oh, I do... You see, this right here," Maxwell encircled the landscape with his outstretched arms, "is a rather accurate representation of your entire life."

"My life is not like this burnt field."

"As usual, you have failed to see far beyond the obvious. You, Louie Mazotti, have contentedly destroyed those in your way to make a wide-open and clear path to whatever it is that you have wanted. You purposely stepped on the toes of many in order to become Antonio's righthand man, and you have had no qualms about eliminating those who have the potential to ruin you."

Louie just stood there and arrogantly smiled; he could not deny those stated facts.

"But the end is near. You, my old adversary, are exactly like this charred field. There is very little to no life left in it."

"You, Max, can take your goddamn metaphors and go fuck yourself. I no longer have anything in my way... and there is nothing in the world that can stop me from planting seeds in every corner of it. I, Louie Mazotti, am destined to achieve greatness."

"If that is what you believe, then your arrogance will end up shortening what remains of your existence even more."

Louie was not at all impressed that he had been brought here against his will, nor was he happy that Maxwell Banks had invaded his dreams again — and it thoroughly pissed him off that he was being preached to. "Your steadfast prophecy did not come true. Your son failed to finish what you had started. So instead of haunting me, you should go to him and tend to his wounded pride."

There was no reason for Maxwell to reveal the truth, as Louie's ego was soon to be his undoing. Of course, he had no problem using the opportunity he now had and nudging the inevitable to take place just a bit sooner. *"Whether or not you agree, you are cut from the same cloth as Antonio was. Like he, your obsessions will be the cause of your demise."*

"I am not obsessed!"

"You are! And you will die because of it."

"Like hell, I will!"

Maxwell walked right up to Louie and placed his hand upon his shoulder. He hadn't invaded the man's dreams, nor had gone to visit him on earth in corporeal form. Louie's entire essence had again been conveniently in a state where he could be summoned to the same realm that Maxwell existed in. And now, because the man's blackened soul was very close to transitioning, he was actually able to make physical contact with him.

With a devilish smile on his face, he slid his hand across Louie's lapel and straightened out his suit jacket. *"If I was you, I'd get this really nice, expensive suit that you have on, dry-cleaned. You'll look good in it lying in your casket."*

Louie tried to push Maxwell away from him; the only thing he touched was air. On top of that, his own momentum caused him to fall forward where he then landed face-first on the soot-covered soil. Frustrated, he promptly picked himself up, fully expecting that his adversary would have disappeared like the last time — but he hadn't. No sooner though had his eye's met his enemy's, his face met an oncoming fist. The punch to his right jaw knocked him straight back down to the ground.

That was twenty-five years in the making and had been well worth the wait. In fact, a sudden desire appeared; it was urging him to pick the asshole right back up and do it again and again and again. How appropriate that would be for Louie to get a little taste of what Maxwell had been put through. But a full-on assault on the man probably wouldn't sit well with Nefieti, even though he was fairly certain that the angel would understand why he had done it.

After dispatching the notion he had to obtain some semblance of revenge, Maxwell decided that for now, the one punch would have to suffice — only because he knew that Louie's eternal future was going to be accumulatively far worse than the single beating he could unleash on the man.

After allowing the pain in his face to subside some, Louie got up onto his knees; a blood and soot mix marked the exact spot where his face had just been lying. Since he had arrived here, he tried to stay in control of his emotions — but that was no longer possible. His now split lip incensed him — and he was determined to get even.

As he rose to his feet, he wiped the corner of his mouth with the back of his hand, and then declared with the utmost of belief, "You're fuckin' dead!"

"I already am, you idiot!"

In a fit of rage, Louie ripped off his suit jacket, slammed it down onto the ground, and then charged at his old adversary. Just when he was about to lay a shoulder into him, Maxwell disappeared. Louie ended up running right on through where he had been. It caused him to bellow at the top of his lungs in frustration.

Louie woke up startled. A moment later, he realized that he was sitting on the edge of his office sofa and still dressed from the evening before — except, his suit jacket was on the floor beside the couch and the back of his hand had a smear of blood. *'What the fuck?'* A few seconds later, he said to himself, *'How in the hell did I get here?'* Louie was baffled. The last thing that he remembered was having a drink in Madelyn's suite.

He wanted to search his mind for an answer, but the pain he was in would not allow that to happen; the right side of his face hurt like a motherfucker and a serious throbbing resided in his head. It wasn't the same type of a headache he had suffered through that came as a result of his Champagne binge back in Chicago; this one was much more intense than any he had ever experienced before.

He got up off of the couch and quickly realized that he had no balance. He immediately sat back down. After a few deep breaths, he slowly stood back up and then slowly made his way to his private bathroom. Not even thinking, he turned on the light; the pain in his head immediately intensified. He closed his eyes, waited a few seconds, and then cautiously opened them back up. The first thing he noticed was his busted lip; at least it wasn't bleeding any more.

After using a cold cloth on his face, he left the bathroom and made his way over to his synth-leather office chair. After claiming it, he realized that he still needed some time to regain his bearings. He thought about putting his head down on his desk, but he was afraid that Maxwell would pick that moment to return and assault him again while he was in such a vulnerable state. Instead, he decided that it was best he just grin and bear it.

As much as he could use a large cup of sim-caf at that moment, he didn't want to get up and make a fresh pot. Luckily, he remembered stashing a Baby Bull (Red Bull's version of a 5-hour energy drink) in his desk drawer the day he had moved into Antonio's old office. So he grabbed it, pounded it back, and then picked up his vid-phone — he wanted some answers and Madelyn could provide them. Just as he was about to dial her room though, Zhin and Nicoli arrived; he promptly invited them to come on in and take a seat.

"You don't look too good this morning, boss. And... what happened to your lip?"

"I really don't know! Last night was very strange, to say the least."

Those words caused his curiosity to want to learn more. However, Zhin decided that it was best to just get down to the business at hand, as that was what was important. "Since today is our last weapons deal, do you want us both to go and pick up the goods now and head straight up to Muskegon?"

"No. Nicoli can go and get the truck himself and then he can bring it back here. There's no reason for you two to go up there any earlier than we have to."

Without being asked, Nicoli got up and left the office; Zhin sat there a little unsure as to why his boss had sent his associate, the man whom he had quickly become friends with, to pick up the merchandise all by himself. It's not like he wasn't capable of such a menial task, but he felt that an unnecessary risk was being taken by picking up a vehicle loaded with firearms and then driving it back into the heart of the city. "You sure that's a wise thing to do?"

"I'm not worried." After a moment's pause, he asked Zhin to put on a fresh pot of sim-caf. Once a cup was brought to him and his associate had returned to where he had been sitting, Louie said, "I kept you behind because I have a favor to ask." He savored the first few

255

sips he took; at the same time, he could feel the Baby Bull begin to kick in.

Although he was still far from being his usual self, he got up out of his chair and slowly made his way over to his safe. Upon opening it, Louie removed an unsealed document from within and brought it back for Zhin to see. "I chose you to be my number one for a reason... and you have so far shown me all the confidence and dedication that I knew you would. Therefore, I now entrust you with the knowledge of what is written in these personal and private documents, as well as the responsibility that goes along with it. A day will come where I will need you to follow the instructions that accompany these and then fulfill my wishes. Will you do that for me?"

"Of course I will, sir."

Louie then handed the instructions to Zhin so that he could read them first and then understand what would be asked of him. Once he was finished, he quickly scanned over his boss's personal document; a document that revealed a secret he long ago suspected, but never before felt the need to verify. At that moment, he drew a conclusion. It was speculative, but it seemed apparent that his boss had suddenly become scared of his own mortality. What other reason would there be for him to share this kind of heavily guarded secret with him?

There had even been a time in Zhin's life where he doubted that his own existence had any sort of significance — but that questioning did not last very long. Because of all the years he had spent disciplining his mind, he was able to use that skill to dismiss that uncertainty. What also helped was the gift he believed he was given at conception, the ability to have a resolute comprehension of one's own imperceptible forewarnings. That was what had allowed him to be in concurrence with what Louie now thought was soon to happen to him.

Once he received the document back from Zhin, Louie handed his associate a copy of the combination to his safe. Right after he did this, he polished off the last of his sim-caf. He still felt like shit. So instead of getting himself another cup, he decided that an old-fashion hair-of-the-dog was what he now needed, so he went over to his wet bar and, disappointment enveloped him. He was out of Walker's Club.

Easily, he could have mixed something else; a Black Russian or a Screwdriver perhaps, but it just wasn't what he wanted.

Having to settle for a refill of sim-caf after all, Louie returned with it to his desk. Just as got there, his vid-phone rang; the ring was extremely loud and painful. When he answered it, he saw that it was the leader of the Muskegon Militia calling him — and the man did not look happy at all. "Mr. Collins. What can I do for you?"

"You can explain to me why your recent weapons shipments have all been confiscated shortly after they were delivered."

"Who says I know why? And if I did, how is that any of your business?"

"Let's just say that if you don't give me an acceptable explanation, then our pending deal tonight is off."

Louie was not at all happy that the word had somehow gotten out about the recent confiscations. They weren't his fault by any means. How could he be blamed for that? "I can't give you an answer. But I can assure you that steps have now been taken to eliminate any possibility of that ever happening again." If it did happen again, Louie simply did not care because this was going to be the very last shipment the D.U.O. would ever deliver anyway.

Mr. Collins took a moment, leaned out of visual range, and whispered into the ear of another person who was in the same room as he. He then came back into view and said, "Our business deal is still on, but only if you accompany the delivery. I want you to be here to make sure that nothing will go wrong tonight."

Louie had thought that his days in the field were over, but he understood that this was a circumstance that warranted him being present. Besides, it seemed fitting that since he had been on so many of them in the past, that he be there during the last one — for old time's sake. "Ok. I'll see you tonight."

Louie disconnected his call and then pounded back half of his fresh cup of sim-caf. "If you don't mind, Zhin, I'd like to be left alone for a while so that I can rest and try to get rid of this massive headache I have."

"Of course. I'll be in my office if you need me."

Briefly, right after his associate had left, Louie thought about going back over to his wet bar and grabbing himself a beer but then thought better of it — alcohol and his rapidly increasing age apparently no longer liked to co-exist. Instead, he picked up his vid-phone and called Madelyn's room. Surprisingly, she failed to answer. It was unlike her to be out of her room so early in the morning, so he just assumed that she too was as hungover as he was and that she was probably either still sound asleep or taking a long cold shower.

Accepting those as being possible reasons, Louie finished off the rest of his sim-caf and then went back over to his couch, stretched out across it, and shut his eyes. If he just happened to fall back asleep, he was ok with that happening, knowing that Maxwell Banks had told him he no longer was going to pay him an unwanted visit.

Before the first dozen sheep could jump over the fence, even with all the caffeine in his system, Louie was out like a light.

The following morning, Sabastian was awakened by the sound of his vid-cell ringing. He looked at the display, sat up on the edge of the couch, and answered it. It was Captain Swilling.

"Good morning, sir. What can I do for you?"

"Nothing. I just wanted to pass along some news." After a longer than normal silent pause, he began. He started off by letting Sabastian know that he had just finished debriefing the U.C.I.C. (Union Criminal Investigation Command) concerning everything he knew pertaining to the stolen weapons that had been recovered. He then informed him that, with all of the information obtained as a result of the S.N.A.F.U.'s combined sting operations, they were subsequently able to trace where the seized weapons had originated from; the Monmouth County depot in New Jersey.

After taking another moment to ensure that his facts were straight, the captain continued with his update. He told Sabastian that when the MP's went to investigate this further, they learned that the depot's longtime shipping clerk, Petty Officer Carey Sperron, had shown up for work yesterday, only to unexpectedly leave just a few minutes later, never to return. When the surveillance tapes were checked, it was discovered that two suspicious men had snuck onto the grounds, entered the storage warehouse, and then the man's office. Shortly thereafter, the three of them left together. "You're not going to believe this Sabastian, but those two individuals were the same ones who had used that city vehicle to deliver the stolen weapons to the United Arab League."

It should have, but the captain's information didn't surprise or even shock him one bit. What it did do though, was allow the feeling of success to wash over him. What had been missing for decades, had just been handed to him; the irrefutable proof that linked the Detroit Underworld Organization to the thefts of Union military weapons. "So then.., I can assume, Captain, that the D.U.O. has either kidnapped or moved this man to an undisclosed location in order to hide him from us?"

"It's possible, but... I think they're beginning to clean house."

"What makes you think that, sir?"

"The New Jersey State Police received a report late yesterday that the video surveillance system at a local meat processing facility had recorded a rather large object being snuck onto its grounds by two unknown men. They then proceeded to deposit that object into one of their refinement vats."

"That could be anything."

"I know, but... When the MP's went to speak with the petty officer's wife, she showed them the letter she had just received from her husband. He didn't admit to what he was involved with, but he did confess to leading a secret life. After that, he apologized to his family and told them he would not be returning home."

After a brief moment of thought, Sabastian said, "Then it certainly looks like Zhin and Nicoli killed the petty officer and brought his body to that facility to get rid of it."

"I agree. Unfortunately, the video surveillance system that the facility has dates back to the late twentieth century. For some reason, they are still using an analog tape recorder. And because of this, there is no way to know for sure if it was them or what it was that was being disposed of."

"I hope that the police are not going to dismiss this as being nothing more than two random locals trying to get rid of a dead farm animal?"

"The MP's aren't going to let them. Until it can be determined exactly what was dumped in the vat, the assumption is that it was a human body."

"You'd figure that they would already know the answer to that by now."

"They don't. Just like when you make homemade soup, the boiling water in the vat will soften the skin and meat, causing it to fall away from the bone. In order to determine if it was a body, the vat has to be completely drained, and then its entire contents sifted through."

"I would not want that job; tons of meat and tons of bone to separate."

"Neither would I. Hang on a second..." The captain placed Sabastian on hold, returning about three minutes later. "I just got an update on what's going on there. They have been able to verify that there was a human body inside the vat."

After a few seconds of expected pondering, Sabastian said, "Whether or not those remains do belong to Petty Officer Sperron, I would appreciate it if you could let me know." While silence was then shared between them, he sat there and argued with his thoughts. He really wanted to ask his former commanding officer a question — but it was one that he really had no right to pose. However, his better judgment was atypically being overruled by his desire to know — only because he felt just as responsible as Captain Swilling for what had happened in Dearborn. "Sir, um.., have you heard anything pertaining to our unsanctioned actions in Dearborn?"

"Not yet. There is an inquiry scheduled a week from today. I was only told that my report, along with the U.B.I.'s, as well as the ones from the missions in Tijuana and Puerto Rico, were all still being reviewed. Once that has been completed, a decision will then be made concerning my capabilities to aptly command the unit. Until then, I have been relegated to my desk."

"Your ability to lead the S.N.A.F.U. should not come into question."

"Thank you for the vote of confidence, Sabastian, but the unauthorized mission that subsequently resulted in the death of Sergeant Fraisure is really all the board of inquiry needs to request that a court marshal take place. If that happens, whether or not I am found to be liable for what happened to Ben, per the jag officer I have already spoken to, my career would basically be over. In fact, there is a good chance that my pension will be taken away as well."

To Sabastian, that revelation was a bunch of bullshit. Had they not done what they had, another heinous act of terrorism would have taken place, today, on domestic soil. That right there should be all that was needed to overlook the fact that protocol was not followed and that a good man had, unfortunately, lost his life in the process. In his mind, the ends justified the means. "I should be back in Texas in a few short days. I would be more than willing to speak on your behalf if you wish?"

"I appreciate your offer. I will consider it and then let you know what I decide."

After a few more bits of relatively trivial information was exchanged, Sabastian ended his conversation with Captain Swilling and walked out to the balcony. He had to be careful where he stepped because there were still quite a lot of smaller shards and slivers of glass on the concrete floor that he was unable to 'sweep up' the day before — he already had enough of it stuck in the treads of his new shoes.

Sabastian stood there, inhaling the freshness of the morning air. He had actually hoped to catch another glimpse of his mother, but he knew that she wasn't about to visit him two days in a row — there was no need for her guidance and advice at that moment.

For the first time ever he felt confident and in control. No longer were there any bits of T.J. Burelli within him. He felt completely like Sabastian Banks; like the man he was born to be. There was no questioning that his past had played a significant part in him becoming who he now was — and he was grateful for that. But now that he has had an opportunity to see his parents, and experience the love that they both have for him, a wondering of 'what if' was now there. Had they not been taken away from him, what would his life have been like? Undoubtedly, his path would have been much different. Even so, Sabastian had to believe that it would still lead him to where he was now.

When he went back inside the apartment, he saw Jerrelle sitting there on her old couch with an inquisitive look on her face; he could never get anything past her. He may be able to withhold information from her at times, but she always knew that something was going on. "So.., who were you talking to?"

He spent the next few minutes giving Jerrelle a recap of his conversation with Captain Swilling. Once Sabastian was done with that, he inquired on whether or not there was a sim-caf place anywhere nearby. Surprisingly, she volunteered to go. As soon as she went into her bedroom to change though, his vid-cell rang again. Jerrelle promptly stopped her forward progress; her need to know took precedence at that moment. "Hello?"

"It's me, Madelyn... And I can't speak long." Just because she had decided that she wasn't going to use the palmtop in her suite to make her call, didn't mean that she could be careless. Until she knew what was going to happen next, she decided it was best to not be that far away from her suite in case Louie wanted an explanation as to what had happened to him. For that reason, she chose to go down to the Cadillac Club room to make her call. It wasn't a private setting like she would have preferred, but she trusted the individual whose vid-cell she was now using to not throw her under the bus.

Other than Louie, Madelyn had spent more time with this person than anyone else. Jasmine was her name, and she had been the one who had given her basic bartending lessons in her suite during the few weeks in which she had been recovering from the visual remnants and emotional scars that came as a result of her being sexually assaulted. "I have found out something that I think you'll be interested in."

Jerrelle made her way over to her friend's side and listened. Within a matter of only a few minutes, her earlier opinion pertaining to Sabastian's girlfriend's decision to stay behind enemy lines had been solidified. Her unwavering trust in this person, however, would not yet be given — after all, Madelyn had participated in the attempt to kill her best friend. However, there comes a time when faith has to be given and one's own misgivings have to be ignored. This information that she had acquired for them, was exactly what they needed to slice the throat of the Detroit Underworld Organization. Therefore, Jerrelle was willing to allow this woman, who had stolen her friend's heart, the opportunity to prove herself.

When she had finished telling Sabastian what she had learned, he thanked her and then he asked her to pack her bags, as he now felt that there was no need for her to stay there any longer. At first,

Madelyn was hesitant to do what was being asked of her, believing that she was still useful where she was, but after a few moments of contemplation, she realized that her main goal had already been achieved. Her reason for remaining behind enemy lines was to only gather information, and that was what she had done — she just never thought that she'd be able to get everything that was needed in one night.

A part of her was scared about leaving. She had prepared herself to remain where she was until Louie's madness had come to an end. However, anything can happen between now and then, and there was no guarantee that when Sabastian's and Louie's paths crossed again, it would all end then. At that point, the chances of Madelyn's betrayal being discovered would all but be guaranteed. She undoubtedly would be killed because of it. Sabastian was right. There was no reason for her to stay where she was any longer. The risk was just too great.

Out of the blue, he handed his vid-cell over to a surprised Jerrelle. She was one of those individuals that preferred to have a face-to-face conversation with someone she really didn't know instead of having one over the phone — she was also someone who didn't like to be put on the spot. "Cloe told us that if we ever needed a favor..."

With Sabastian's vid-cell now in her hand, she was finally able to get a good look at the woman who her friend had become enamored with — and it was easy for her to see exactly why he had become smitten. To Jerrelle, Madelyn was one of those stereotypical fantasies that most men would dream about. She wasn't though, going to pass judgment on her based solely upon her looks. After all, she had found a way to acquire some great information about the enemy. For that reason, she had no other choice but to acknowledge that Madelyn was something other than just some expensive eye-candy.

Without needing to be told what it was that Sabastian was asking of her, Jerrelle informed her that she had a friend who could keep her hidden and safe until everything was over. She then gave her the address to The Cough Inn. After that, she hung up Sabastian's vid-cell, handed it over to him, then took out her own and called Cloe to ask her for that favor. "Done! Now what?"

Sabastian did not reply. He just sat there in thought. If everything went as he hoped it would, the pain of the past would finally be put to bed. Strangely, an old, but not at all famous movie quote came to him at that moment. In a low, yet still clear enough of a voice to be heard, and in a revised manner that he felt was appropriate, he said, "That will be my father's final joke, I guess. A man tells his stories so many times that he, in turn, becomes the story. They will thus live on after him. Unfortunately, the final chapter will become his immortality."

Sabastian has been known to convey an unnecessary metaphor from time to time. But what he had just conveyed admittedly baffled Jerrelle. However, instead of asking him to explain in laymen's terms what it was that he just said, she decided to simply ignore it. *'I honestly don't know, but I have to believe that Sabastian's occasional bout of unexpected, odd narrative must be a trait that he inherited from his father?'*

Deciding that her confusion wasn't going to result in her failure to miss something important somewhere on down the road, Jerrelle said, "I'm going to go and get changed, then go and get us some sim-caf and something to eat."

"Sounds good. And while you are doing that, I'm going to call the governor and tell him what we now know."

Sabastian's call to the governor didn't go quite as he had hoped it would. Knowing that there wasn't a snowball's chance in hell that he would be able to get the S.N.A.F.U. to come back to Michigan on another unauthorized mission, he had hoped that the governor would be able to convince the U.B.I. to send a few agents his way to back them up tonight. Unfortunately, Christopher had informed him that, although the bureau was appreciative of what Sabastian and his ex-military brethren had done; providing them with the proof that the U.A.L. was indeed a terrorist organization, the Muskegon Militia had yet to do anything to warrant any reason to be placed on their list of potential threats.

Christopher had no reason to doubt Sabastian's claims but reluctantly had to tell him that there was nothing he could do to help.

Even if he made a call to the Muskegon Police Department and informed them of what was suspected, they probably wouldn't do much more than just send out a patrol car to check over the property that the militia owned and see if they were up to no good.

Sabastian was disappointed that he wasn't going to get any state or federal assistance, but he understood why they would be reluctant to participate. This now left him with a rather large dilemma — how to appropriately handle the golden opportunity they now had.

Besides himself and Jerrelle, the only person whom he knew that he could get on such short notice to help him was Sharice — but that was only if she hadn't yet left the Union. Maybe it was time for him to reach out to some of his father's former police brethren, the ones who were with him and had survived that day when the Tuckerman's Warehouse blew up. The only problem Sabastian saw with doing that, was that after all these years, they may not wish to become involved. All but one of them was retired from the force and probably content to just sit back and enjoy the years they have left.

When Jerrelle returned from her food run, Sabastian briefed her on the conversation he had with Governor White and then explained his predicament. Unexpectedly, she just told him to only worry about tracking down his cousin and that she would make a few phone calls and try to get them some backup. That assertion made Sabastian feel a little better about his chances tonight, although deep down inside, he wasn't sure that he was okay with dragging any more outsiders into his mess. The last time that he allowed someone he did not know to volunteer to help, a tragedy came from it He surely did not want to have another unnecessary death weighing on his conscience.

By the time he had finished his breakfast and sim-caf, he was able to track down Sharice. Luckily for him, his cousin had just wrapped up whatever it was that she had been in Cleveland for and was about to head to the airport to go back home to England. Without hesitation, she agreed to help him with what he wanted to do and stated that she would be in Detroit within the next three to four hours. Sabastian would have loved to have his 'brother', Richard Atwater here helping him with this as well, but he knew it would be impossible for that to happen. During his earlier conversation with Captain

265

Swilling, he learned that his friend had submitted a formal request for escort duty so that he may have the honor of accompanying the body of Ben Fraisure back to his hometown of Jacksonville, Florida. That revelation caused Sabastian to become consumed with pride.

Although he was not going to be alone and doing what needed to be done, he admittedly was nervous. So long as Louie Mazotti did not have any surprises there waiting for them, the odds should not be overwhelmingly in the enemy's favor. However, knowing the D.U.O. as well as he did, it pretty much was guaranteed that once they got to Muskegon, they were going to end up finding something there other than what was expected. And how they handled that, would surely be the determining factor as to whether or not their objective was accomplished.

About an hour after Jerrelle had called Cloe, her friend sent her a message, letting her know that Madelyn had arrived safely at her bar. Sabastian was thankful for this news, as it gave him one less thing to worry about. Now, all that he had left to do was to try and figure out a way for the three of them to accomplish what had to be done without putting each of their lives in jeopardy.

For Jerrelle, she felt that this was going to be a far greater challenge than what she and Sabastian had so far taken on — mainly because the Muskegon Militia was an unknown entity. If time was on their side and they could do some extensive research on them beforehand, any uncertainty that might appear would be nominal. But because things were the way they were, their instincts, training, and experiences would have to solely be relied upon. Some luck would be needed as well, otherwise, this whole situation that they were about to embark on, could end up turning into one rather large clusterfuck.

Jerrelle really wished that Bai Lin was still here in Detroit so that she could be a part of this. At least then, she'd feel more confident with their chances of success. But her sister was back home in Japan, and by the time she would be able to catch a return flight to the Union, what was supposed to go down tonight, would be over.

Right after she disconnected the last of the calls she had made, Jerrelle huffed in annoyance. There were still a few individuals in the area that owed her a favor, but none of them had been willing to put their life on the line. They all felt that, in exchange for the absolution of their debt, what was being asked of them was worth far more than what each had still owed. For that reason alone, they all turned her down — including Chorister Black.

Conceding defeat, Jerrelle looked disappointingly across her near-empty living room. She was just about to inform Sabastian of her inability to recruit some help when a knock resonated on her front door. Before she could answer it, Sharice did.

Never before in her life had she seen a set of twins that big; they took up nearly the entire hallway. "Can I help you?"

"You can let them in. I know them." Why the Laperriére brothers were now standing outside her front door, certainly baffled Jerrelle. She looked over at Sabastian, hoping that maybe he knew — but he didn't. Only after a few minutes of uncertain silence had passed did that implicit light bulb then turn on in her head — all because André was wearing a t-shirt with a woodland scene on the front. Written underneath it were the words '*I don't kill for the thrill, I kill for the grill!*' "Do I need to ask why you boys are here?"

"Nope!" Henré emphatically stated; a cheeky grin appeared on his face right afterward.

André then said, "Shortly after Madelyn arrived at The Cough Inn, she told us what was going on, so we thought that we'd come and give you a hand."

"Yeah, it's the least we can do.., seeing that we owe you for removing the garbage from our neighborhood."

Sabastian looked at the twins and said, "You two don't have to do this. The loose ends are our responsibility to tie up."

"We know. But we both feel as though we need to make things right between us and Jerrelle because of all the years of crap we were forced to give her."

"Your help with this is greatly appreciated," she declared. "Let's go."

They left the apartment and piled into Henré's van. His beautiful custom, vintage vehicle was a 1971 Ford conversion that had an extended box and a second rear axle. Its paint scheme was metallic fleck; the kind of finish that appeared to change color as you passed by it: from dark purple, brown, dark green, charcoal, to black. It was really hard to determine exactly what color it was. The interior of it contained a real hardwood floor, and the inside walls and ceiling were done in synth-suede. Not counting the two captain's chairs up front, the van had four swivel, synth-leather, over-sized bucket seats in the back. It also had a thirty-two-inch flat screen to keep those in the rear of the vehicle entertained. Undoubtedly, the ride across the state appeared as if it was going to be a very comfortable one. Notwithstanding that, Jerrelle's pending comfort level promptly increase even more when she noticed the six Winchester hunting rifles that were vertically mounted in a rack up against the inside of the back doors.

By late afternoon, they had arrived in Muskegon. Madelyn had told Sabastian that this evening's transaction was scheduled to take place around nine. That left them with slightly more than a two-hour window to get ready.

Henré parked his van at the Muskegon Creek Hunting Lodge; a place that everyone else soon learned him and his brother had stayed at on several occasions over the years. Their apparent familiarity with the area thus became another advantage to this mission that they otherwise would not have had if the twins had not volunteered to be a part of it.

After checking their supplies and quickly reviewing the plan that they had devised during the drive, the five of them left the back parking lot of the lodge and began their long trek through the woods to where the exchange was supposed to take place. What actually awaited them, they could only assume.

For Sabastian, he was surprised the ambiguity that should exist with him, did not. More than likely it was because he finally felt as if he had the upper hand. Supposedly, he was dead. Therefore, there should be no assumption whatsoever that he might actually show up, or that he would become the reason that this arms shipment, like the others, would be stopped or seized.

9

The sun's low rays were slicing through the woods; the end of another day was drawing near. They estimated that about a half an hour of natural light was left. Even so, there was nothing for them to do but wait. If for some reason their target just happened to show up before darkness took over, the element of surprise they hoped for would undoubtedly be a lot harder for them to achieve.

Sabastian and his group were scattered around the perimeter of the area that Madelyn had said would be the site of tonight's deal; a clearing that was roughly the same size of an average county schoolyard. On the property sat only one structure; a two-story log cabin that was rather large in size and situated near the northern edge. Though there was no clear indication, Sabastian was fairly certain that this building wasn't used by anyone as a permanent residence. No one would know this though, as the entire property was very well kept — which also led him to believe that it probably wasn't left vacant for any length of time. *'This must be the headquarters for the Muskegon Militia,'* Sabastian thought, as he continued to get the lay of the land.

On the complete opposite side of the open area from where Sabastian stood, was Jerrelle. His cousin was positioned between them at the direct opposite end of the clearing from the cabin, and both André and Henré were set back on either side of the open pathway that led to the property.

"Hey, Sab! I really hope that this is the right place," Jerrelle said. Inside her ear was an invisi-bud; a two-way earwig communicator that was nearly invisible and was wirelessly linked to a vid-cell, just like an early generation Bluetooth device would be. "Knowing our luck, this place actually belongs to some backwater moonshine maker with an itchy trigger finger who thinks that his cabin is now surrounded by the local sheriff and his band of hick deputies."

"Too bad you didn't bring your Camero. Isn't that the kind of car they used to use in the 'good ole' days to run shine?"

"That was a Dodge Charger, and my car blows the General Lee away… in looks and with what is under the hood."

"I don't see nor do I smell a still anywhere nearby, so I doubt that this place is owned by Uncle Jesse," André said, with a bit of intended sarcasm.

"I'd at least like to see a deer," Sharice said. "I've never seen one before in person."

Jerrelle would prefer not to see any animals of any kind. She would be the first one to admit that she was a bit different than most people, but she also had a strange phobia that no one knew about. Oddly, she loved all reptiles, but all other wild animals she wanted to be nowhere near — hence to say that she was not at all comfortable with being in a place that doubled as a creature's natural habitat. "I have no desire to see Bambi up close and personal."

Unlike where the others were positioned, Jerrelle luckily didn't have to stand in the forest and wait for something to occur, as she had come across an old tree stump to sit on that was about ten meters back from the edge line — so she claimed it. Had she taken a moment to check out her surroundings before contently plopping her ass down, she'd have realized that there was a small ant colony on the ground not far from its base — at least, the ants wouldn't eat her alive.

The peacefulness of where she was, kind of reminded her of the Byakko Gardens. Though it was much different than that place, it still had a relaxing effect on her. Maybe, once she settled into her new life in San Antonio, she would venture out and find herself a similar place to those gardens where she could go whenever she needed to relax — so long as no wild animals called it their home.

In the city, she knew what her surroundings were and her senses were tuned into those nuances. She could recognize almost any sound she heard and her intuition usually never failed her. But out here where she now was, she felt completely out of her element. There were different sounds and sensations surrounding her in these woods that were unfamiliar and somewhat confusing — and her not knowing what it was that her ears would lock onto, allowed her mind to draw an abundance of baseless conclusions.

While her mind kept producing those crazy thoughts, a startling sound resonated from directly behind her. At first, she thought that maybe it was one of the others trying to scare her, but when she turned around, she saw nothing. Unsettled, but determined nonetheless to not let the unknown become the foundation for any sort of humiliation, she turned back around and continued on with her watching of the clearing.

Less than two minutes later, she heard a series of rustling sounds. She believed that whatever was responsible for that, it was moving in her direction. At that moment, she really didn't care how silly she might look; she jumped up from her seat and in one fluid motion, raised her rifle. After a few seconds of searching, she finally saw what had caused her unsettled nerves to dance. She felt like a total fool — but at least no one else had seen that a white-tailed squirrel, moving from tree to tree, had been the cause of her angst.

Now completely annoyed with herself for being so skittish, Jerrelle lowered her rifle and returned to her stump. Just as she was about to sit back down Henré's voice piped through her transmitter. "Hey, everyone! I think that we are about to have our long-awaited company."

"What makes you say that?" Sabastian asked.

"I can hear a low rumble and I can see some unnatural light bouncing through the woods off in the distance. I'm gonna back up a bit to make sure that I don't get spotted if indeed there is a vehicle headed toward the clearing."

"Ok."

Patiently, they waited and wondered if what Henré suspected was going to turn out to be true. Sure enough, in less than a minute's time, everyone could see a rather large off-road vehicle approaching the clearing. After breaking the perimeter of the woods, it stopped about fifty feet from the log cabin. Its engine was then turned off but its overhead searchlights were left on — this was probably done in order to help illuminate the area.

A few seconds after the vehicle's arrival, an outside light on the cabin turned on. Simultaneously, six identically dressed men walked out the front door; each was wearing grey, black, and green camouflage pants, and a solid black t-shirt. In their hands, they held a weapon of their choice. Obviously, they were all members of the Muskegon Militia.

271

"Those guys just look like a bunch of weekend warriors."

"Don't judge a book by its cover, Sharice. Though they all probably do hold down normal jobs, we have no idea what their backgrounds are."

This group was an unknown entity. Unsuccessfully, Sabastian tried to do some research on them during their trip across the state, but other than the evolution of how they came to be as an organization, no records of any kind could be found that documented their involvement in any illegal activity. Therefore, just like they had initially foreseen, they were going to have to assess how much of a problem the group was going to be once they saw what they would have to deal with, and then make a decision accordingly.

They hadn't come here tonight with the intent to stop the transaction that was taking place — what they had come here for, was to put an end to the madness. However, with what Sabastian was now looking at, he feared that they just might have wasted a trip. Yes, the three main players in the newly revamped D.U.O. had all come here today with a truck full of weapons to sell, but there were six extremists that may not take too kindly to a long-standing conflict being settled on their turf. The last thing that Sabastian wanted was to be added to someone else's enemy list.

Stepping forward from within the group of six was an averaged sized man; it was the same man who Louie had briefly spoken to earlier in the day. His hair was buzzed back, beard neatly trimmed, and he had a tattoo on his left forearm of a soldier in a tattered uniform carrying a bayonet rifle over his shoulder that had a torn American flag dangling on the end of it — the identical tattoo that everyone else in the militia had. "I'm glad you made it, Mr. Mazotti. Your presence here has done a lot to prove just what kind of businessman you are. Thank you for doing this."

"You're welcome, Mr. Collins. If you would please head on over to the truck, my associates will show you the merchandise that we have brought. If everything meets your satisfaction, then we will complete the transaction."

He and two of his men headed over to the off-road vehicle. Once there, Zhin opened up the back tailgate to freely display its contents. After a few minutes spent checking to make sure that everything they wanted had been brought, Mr. Collins returned to where Louie was waiting; his two men subsequently headed over to where the rest of the militia were gathered. "Everything is as I expected it to be, Mr. Mazotti. I see no reason why we can't complete the deal."

"Excellent! So... where would you like these weapons brought to?"

As this was taking place, a sharp, but somewhat faint noise caught the attention of Nicoli. He promptly whispered something into Zhin's ear for which he received a nod in agreement. He then turned about-face and walked directly into the woods; his right hand resting firmly on top of his sidearm.

Until he knew for sure whether or not something was going on, Zhin decided that it was best to put a halt to this transaction. So he promptly shut the back tailgate of the off-road vehicle and then at a fast pace, made his way over toward where Louie was standing. It certainly wasn't what he was supposed to do, but he decided that this situation called for him to be right there by his boss's side. Yes, the merchandise was being left unprotected, and he was probably overreacting, but as far as he was concerned, the most important thing was to ensure that the personal request his boss had just bestowed upon him did not come to fruition this soon.

Wanting to get a much better look at what was going on, Jerrelle shifted from her position over to the left a few yards because there had been an old outhouse near the edge of the wood line that was preventing her from having a clear, unobstructed view of the off-road vehicle. Unbeknownst to her though, she was completely unaware that she had stopped right beside a well-hidden, offset leg hold, illegal bear trap. Luckily, she never stepped into it. But as she squatted lower so that she could get a clearer view underneath some long branches, the butt end of her rifle touched the trigger mechanism and set off the trap, ripping it out of her hand in the process, and locking her rifle in its jaws. 'Fuck!' she cursed under her breath.

Jerrelle yanked on her rifle in an attempt to free it, but it didn't budge. Immediately, she realized that it was going to be impossible to regain the use of her weapon. If she had all the time in the world, she would have found a way to free it, but out of the corner of her eye, she happened to notice some movement inside the clearing — Nicoli was now headed in her direction. That left her with only one choice. She had to bait and run.

She knocked over her useless rifle onto the ground and then haphazardly swept a few leaves over it, trying to camouflage it as best as she could. Then, she vacated her position and began to make her way deeper into the woods. The only thing she could think of to make sure that the rest of her team was not discovered was to force Nicoli to embark on a manhunt — so that is what she did.

Only seconds into that decision, an unexpected, yet satisfying thought came to her. Not only was she doing her part in order to protect her friends, but once she led the man far enough into the woods, an opportunity just might present itself for her to pay back that son-of-a-bitch for the attempt on her life. It wasn't that she had secretly planned on doing this today, but her dim-witted mistake may end up turning out to be the gift from her that Nicoli was never going to forget receiving.

After only a few steps deeper into the woods, her thoughts switched to an unexpected realization. Not thinking that she'd need it, Jerrelle had left her handgun back in Henré's van. This now meant that, other than her own two hands, she was left with only one thing to defend herself with. And although she was very comfortable using it, having the security of a backup weapon would have at least made her feel a bit more at ease.

As she was reaching down to her sheath in order to remove her honor blade, she told everyone over open links, "We have a problem. It looks like Nicoli may have spotted me. I am going to lead him deep into the woods and hope that he thinks I am alone."

"Ok," Sabastian replied. "Be careful... and get back here as soon as you can." Contingency plans are needed quite often while on a mission; usually, they have to be drawn up and then executed on the fly. He had hoped that such a thing wasn't going to be needed but knew better than to expect that their initial plan was going to go off without a hitch.

Because Jerrelle was now being forced to handle a potential situation all by herself, that inadvertently left them with one less person to deal with. Even so, it didn't really help their odds, as they were still outnumbered, two to one. In Sabastian's mind, they needed a distraction of some kind in order to grab the militia's attention; one that would, in turn, leave Louie alone and out in the open. A small window; that was all he needed. "Hey, André! Do you think that you can sneak up to the cabin and create a diversion of some kind?"

"Absolutely!"

"Sharice.., I need for you to shift over to the left flank and take over Jerrelle's spot."

"Ok."

Sabastian's confidence seemed to waver. He was suddenly unsure if what they were doing was a mistake or not. If he only had his military brethren with him, then he would have no worries at all. But he didn't. He only had his cousin, a bouncer, and a cook with him. It's not that he didn't trust them; it just strangely felt as if he was on his own.

After taking a moment to dispel those negative thoughts, Sabastian reviewed their situation in his head. During his tenure with the Special North American Freedom Unit, he had gone on a few missions before in which the odds were slightly worse than what they now were and they had prevailed. This situation was really no different. No clear reason could be found that might cause them to fail. He couldn't let those who believed in him, down. He had a legacy to fulfill — and on top of that, a yearning to finally remove the longstanding burden from the shoulders of his father's old friend.

As Zhin arrived next to his boss, he did his best to not give off the impression that something was wrong. With the utmost of respect given, he first apologized to Mr. Collins for the interruption. Then, he pulled Louie off to the side so that he could speak to him privately. "There's a possibility that we are being watched. Nicoli has gone into the woods to verify it."

Not wanting to risk their deal going south, he kept this troubling information to himself. If Mr. Collins were to learn of this potential problem, Louie feared that the man might decide to back out of their agreement.

"Is everything all right?"

"Yes.., everything is fine," Louie said assertively, but not abrasively either.

"Really? Mr. Collins questioned. "Then where did your other associate take off to?"

Zhin chimed in with the excuse. "If you must know, he has had a bad case of the runs all day. He went into the woods to find someplace private in order to answer nature's call."

To Mr. Collins, that explanation seemed rather lame — considering that there is an old outhouse just beyond the ridgeline. Then again, Louie's associate would not have known that because it was evening and it wouldn't be all that visible from where he had been inside the clearing. Therefore, he had to concede to the possibility of it being the honest truth. And even with the knowledge he had of the recent D.U.O. weapons shipments being confiscated shortly after their delivery, he didn't think it was fair to use that in order to validate a suspicion that something might be going on.

In order to try and sort through everything that was flooding his thoughts, Mr. Collins excused himself, turned his back to Louie and Zhin, and lit a cigarette. After only a couple of puffs, he decided that he was still going to extend his trust; it was what both parties had to do in order for this deal to be completed.

Needing not to finish off his smoke, he dropped it to the ground, put it out with his foot, and turned back around. He looked directly at the head of the D.U.O., then at his associate; neither one of their dispositions had changed. *'Hum? Maybe they are telling the truth? Then again, honesty is a trait seldom possessed by someone in the type of business they are in.'*

After discarding his negative thought, Mr. Collins said, "Ok. My men will help your associate unload these weapons and then bring them into the cabin. Will you follow me over there so that I can give you the money that we agreed upon?"

"Of course." Two steps forward were all that Louie and the head of the Muskegon Militia had taken when someone yelled out a series of profanities. Zhin's eyes nearly popped out of his head when he saw what he had never expected to ever see in person during his lifetime — a bear had wandered right into their meeting place unnoticed and was now blocking the entrance to the cabin. Mr. Collins, not fearing the creature, continued his forward progress. Louie and Zhin, on the other hand, chose not to go any further than where they already were.

––––––––––––––––––––––––––––– ◯◯ –––––––––––––––––––––––––––––

Sabastian stood there behind his blind and found it difficult not to laugh. André had called and told him that his initial idea was to start a small fire at the rear of the cabin but then changed his mind when he noticed the fresh bear tracks. That gave him the idea to take the bags of garbage from the three refuse containers lined up out back and spread a trail of the trash from the paw marks to the front of the cabin. After doing that, he decided to toss the remainder of it onto the porch. Minutes were all it had taken. From out of the woods, a rather large brown grizzly bear appeared. It then followed the rotting trail and parked his plump, furry ass exactly where André had hoped it would.

While the animal was blocking the entrance to the cabin and garnering everyone's attention, Sabastian gave the order to move in. The majority of the members of the militia were showing signs of being nervous; some even looked as if they were only a mere few moments away from being in a full-blown panic — and that uncertainty is what had provided them with the opportunity they now had.

Exactly like when the twins would hunt, they stealthily snuck up behind their targets, all six members of the militia, and locked both hunting rifles onto their heads. "Drop your weapons!" ordered André.

Louie and Zhin both had seen the brothers come out of the woods but hesitated barking out a warning. They could easily have prevented what was happening but chose to do nothing. If this was another military sting, he didn't wish to be associated with the evidence that was still loaded on the truck. So he looked at Zhin and said, "Do it!"

Louie's associate reached into his pocket and pulled out a remote detonator. They had come here with a truckload of weapons; they weren't about to let someone other than their clients leave with the merchandise, so they wired up the truck.

Immediately, Sabastian recognized what was in Zhin's hand; he could not let the man blow up whatever it was that he was planning to. Sharice recognized the situation as well, so without having to even discuss it, both of them quickly left their positions in the woods and moved in, weapons aimed and locked. "It's over, Louie. It's time for you to pay the piper for what you have done."

He just stood there, shocked at first that the man whom he had thought he killed in Chicago, had somehow survived. But then he started to laugh; he followed that up with reverent applause. "I'm impressed, Sabastian. Not only have you cheated death, but you ended up making a move that I would have never in a million years, expected. You deserve a pat on the back for that one."

"Unlike you, I don't need to gratuitously boost my ego each time I successfully pull the wool over your eyes."

That declaration brought forth a previously dismissed thought. And upon review, everything suddenly made sense. It had been Sabastian all along, and not Casper who had been responsible for the raids on all those weapons shipments. He was after all, a trained military man and undoubtedly used his connections to subsequently help him with it. "Who's the bitch with you? I've never seen her before."

Sabastian turned his rifle around and slammed the stock right into Louie's already bruised right jaw; he dropped instantly to the ground and his lip split right back open. If that insult had been directed to Jerrelle instead of his cousin, then he would have just let his old friend handle it herself, but Sharice was his blood and he had to protect his family's honor. "She is my cousin... and you should be thankful that it takes more than an insensitive remark from an asshole, like you, to set her off."

Sharice looked over at her cousin and could see a definite change in him. In less than two month's time since she had first met Sabastian, he had morphed from being an unsure, somewhat timid young man, into a passionate and fearless individual with a drive and determination that would not allow anything or anyone to ever get in his way.

Remembering all of the stories that she had ever been told by her mother about her uncle Maxwell, Sharice could now easily anticipate what kind of man her cousin was destined to become. She felt proud to be related to him. In fact, she was all but certain that his rapid evolution was going to somehow influence her in a very positive way. "Since my cousin and I now have you in a very compromising position, I would suggest that you show our family the respect that is long overdue." Sharice then cracked a smile, not because she was more than willing to stand beside Sabastian at that moment, but because she was willing to do so for the remainder of her life. "Although my side of the family has been excluded from this war, I hereby officially declare my involvement to help restore the honor of the Banks family name. You..." she looked directly at Louie, "...are very lucky that I have not been a part of this until now. Otherwise, I would have, even with the oath that I took the moment I became an agent with the B.I.A., put a long-ago deserved bullet into your head."

"However," Sabastian interjected, "since I am not willing to let my cousin ruin her distinguished career over a piece of shit like you... And since I currently am no longer serving in our Union's Military, I will not hesitate to cross that line if either of you thinks about doing anything stupid to try and save your sorry asses." Although his focus was on Louie more than it was Zhin, Sabastian could see that the Asian man was starting to get an itchy finger. "If you even think about blowing up whatever it is that you've wired, I won't hesitate to castrate your little boys." He then lowered his rifle and briefly aimed it at his implied target.

"Wow!" Louie said, "You most certainly have changed. I never thought that you would have developed such aggressive tendencies. I always knew that I brought out the best in people."

"You are right, Louie. I have you, along with Sal and Antonio, to thank for making me who I am today. But your time as a free-spirited, narcissistic bastard is over. Drop that detonator, Zhin, and then you and your boss place your hands on your heads."

As they were about to comply with Sabastian's request, a shot rang out. It took a moment for everyone to realize that they were all okay — except for the bear. Someone had shot it dead.

In a moment of uncertainty, everyone began to wonder who had done the deed, but before an answer could be had, another shot rang out. This time they had all seen that it had originated from inside

the cabin. Panic consumed the clearing. Those in the militia didn't
care that there were still two rifles pointed at their heads; they all
scattered for cover and took off in different directions toward the
woods.

André and Henré could have just let them all go, but their job
was to secure the area. If they didn't do that, any one of those
members of the militia could potentially become a problem for them,
Sabastian, or his cousin. Therefore, the brothers together decided to
follow them and do what they were very good at — tracking.

This was supposed to have been a controlled setting in which
no one was supposed to get hurt, other than maybe the enemy. Yet, an
unexpected set of circumstances was quickly manifesting itself into
what was turning into a very dangerous situation.

Right after the second shot had taken place, Sabastian's
military instincts took over. Louie had become irrelevant. He spun to
his left and immediately observed his surroundings, focusing in on
where the gunshot had come from and preparing himself to shoot back.
Sharice had done the same; her police instincts had immediately told
her to locate the threat and protect her cousin. But then she realized
that Zhin was now making a run for the woods. She made a choice at
that moment, only because she knew that Sabastian was a well-trained
soldier and leaving him alone would not be that big of an issue. "I'm
going after Louie's associate."

He acknowledged his cousin while keeping his eyes focused
straight ahead as she left. After a few seconds, and not seeing anything
that might tip him off to the position of the shooter, he removed his
gaze from where it had been and looked over at Louie. He was
surprised that the man had not run for cover. Instead, the head of the
D.U.O. was sitting on the ground and clutching his wounded right leg.

It was a cold-hearted thought. Even so, Sabastian just could
not help but feel that a little poetic justice had been served. A bullet
right between his eyes would have been better, but sometimes you just
have to take what you are given.

With his adversary now seemingly incapacitated, Sabastian
returned his focus to the cabin. Just as he did, he saw a man exit it; a
man who looked as deadly as the weapon he carried. He didn't
recognize his face but knew almost immediately that the man was not

part of the Muskegon Militia. His hair was long and tied back and his face had seen far better days — too many pits and scars existed to fix with plastic surgery. The man's rather tall body was sculpted, but not overly large in size. He also sported a tattoo of bloodied black roses on his right forearm — the exact same tattoo that Sabastian had seen once before, on Vladi Chemzot, the former head of the Communist Revolutionary Assembly Party.

'Why is a member of the C.R.A.P. here?' he thought. This didn't quite make sense to him. But then that old saying suddenly popped into his head, 'The enemy of my enemy is my friend'. Whether or not that was true in this instance was yet to be determined. And the only way that he would be able to find that out was to face the approaching man, who appeared to be on a personal mission.

Sabastian looked attentively at the Serbian. His weapon, though not aimed, was probably ready to be fired if it became necessary.

"You don't have to worry about me, Mr. Banks."

"Ah.., I see that you know my name. What's yours?"

"My name is Uri Drakonna, and I am the new leader of the Revolution, no thanks to this lying bastard." Without wavering, he pointed his rifle in the direction of Louie.

"So.., I take it that the D.U.O. has fucked you over as well?"

"Until this day, I never understood why my predecessor had trusted them as many times as Vladi had. And the last time he did, it had cost him his life. This here asshole tried to convince me that you were the one who killed him... and he almost succeeded. Yet, there was something about what he had told me that did not seem right. So.., after doing a little investigating of my own, I learned that his words were nothing but a bold-faced lie. He said that the weapon used to execute our leader, and my mentor belonged to you. In actuality, it belonged to him." Uri motioned at Louie with his rifle.

"It may have been my gun, but it was Sabastian who pulled the trigger."

"You are the epitome of a Wolf in sheep's clothing," Sabastian stated. "No one is fooled by your claims of innocence."

Uri could not help but chuckle inside as he ordered Louie to stand up. Of course, he refused to comply. After being smashed in the face with the butt end of a rifle and now being shot in the leg, he just felt like staying right where he was. But Sabastian wasn't about to let him sit on the ground in protest, so he grabbed him by the collar of his shirt and hauled him upright. Louie cried out in pain; no one felt any sympathy for him.

"I always thought that you were smarter than this? The Muskegon Militia vehemently refused your offer to do business and then surprisingly, they call you back and tell you that they suddenly had a change of heart. When did you become such a pushover? "

"Business is business, Uri. You never ask why, nor do you deny whoever comes knocking on your door. When an opportunity is there to strike a good deal, you don't dismiss it, even if there is a risk attached."

"Well, that just proves you have never had a vacuum cleaner salesman come to your home," Sabastian sarcastically said.

"If I am at fault for anything, it was for believing that you were going to leave us alone so long as we stayed out of your territory."

"You should know better than anyone to never take someone at their word when you know you already screwed them over once before."

"How much did you pay the militia to lure me here tonight?"

"I didn't have to pay them anything. Mr. Collins owed us a favor from a few years ago, so I asked him to arrange for a weapons buy and then demand that you accompany its delivery."

Without having to be told, Sabastian knew exactly what Uri's intentions were. One part of him wanted to stop what the man was planning on doing because he wanted to get his own deserved justice for what Louie and the D.U.O. had done to his family. Yet, something inside was advising him to step aside and let the events that fate had apparently put into motion, happen as they should.

"Are you just gonna stand there and do nothing, Sabastian? Is it not obvious to you what's going on here?"

"It is. But as far as I am concerned, Louie, you just need to put on your big boy pants and face this problem all on your own."

"I have a bullet in my leg! It's not as if I can run for my life."

Sabastian looked at Louie and said with the utmost of seriousness in his voice, "My father couldn't defend his self either when you tied him to a chair and beat him half to death then buried his broken body in cement. I'd say that karma has chosen this to be the day in which she takes from you what she is owed."

Uri cocked his gun and looked over at Sabastian. "If you want, I could give Louie a head start… so that it's somewhat fair?"

"He doesn't deserve your empathy."

"Fuck you both!" Louie then hobbled a few steps toward Sabastian and said, "Your father would have stepped in and stopped this so that he could continue to play the game and try to win it on his own terms."

"I hate games. I never wanted to play this one in the first place. I quit!" Sabastian put the safety back on his rifle, hung it over his right shoulder, turned about-face, and began to walk away. "I'm going home."

Louie started yelling at Sabastian, calling him every derivative of the word coward that he could think of along with whatever profanity he could mix in with it. After exhausting every ounce of abhorrence he had, a realization hit him — Maxwell's prophecy was about to come true after all. He had been warned, but the arrogance Louie had, refused to allow him to listen. Had he, things might have turned out differently. Then again, he had walked his chosen path for thirty-some-odd years. Apparently, its end was located right here in Muskegon.

When Sabastian was about twenty feet away, he heard the kill shot — and then he heard Louie hit the ground. Sabastian didn't even turn around to verify the fact that the man's life was now over. He just kept on walking. When he was just about a meter away from the off-road vehicle, he stopped. A lot of things were going through his mind. He turned his head left and looked out into the woods. As he stared aimlessly at them, he wondered if his decision to allow Louie to be executed was the right one. The man was far from a saint and undoubtedly had to pay for his assortment of sins and crimes, but turning his back on a helpless man was something that he had never done before — not even during his time in the service. The burden of the debt that was owed to his family, sat squarely on Louie's shoulders. Unfortunately, there had been no clear-cut answer as to how he should have paid it.

To some, it may appear as if Sabastian had taken the easy way out and washed his hands of his anointed responsibility by allowing someone else to do the deed for him, but no affirmation had officially been handed to him stating that he had to be the one who ended the madness. What only mattered was that it was finally over.

After allowing his conscience to accept the results, Sabastian turned his focus away from the woods and looked over to where he had been. Uri was already gone and Louie was lying dead on the ground. His surroundings suddenly felt much different than it had just a few minutes ago. The night was well upon them; the temperature, however, seemed to be rapidly dropping. Then again, what he was experiencing might very well be the transference of an evil soul from the real world to its final destination.

An unexpected chill ran suddenly down his spine; an unknown noise then echoed from right behind him. Sabastian promptly turned about-face and looked at the edgeline of the woods. Simultaneously, his rifle came off his shoulder, as did its safety, and he placed it in a position to fire. Even with the illumination provided by the off-road vehicle's overhead lights, he still really couldn't see all that clearly.

After a few tense seconds had gone by, three figures emerged from the trees. Thankfully, Sabastian was able to recognize who they were: Sharice, Henré, and his hobbling twin. He exhaled in relief, lowered his gun, and walked toward them.

"So, what happened?"

"Unfortunately, Zhin got away. Thankfully, I stumbled upon these two, or I probably would have gotten lost myself."

Sabastian walked over to the off-road vehicle and opened up the tailgate. He hadn't done this to get a curious look at the merchandise that Louie had brought with him; he just wanted to give André a place to sit. Even so, the brief glance he took at the weapons packed in the back of the truck was enough for him to feel happy that these had not ended up in the hands of the Muskegon Militia.

André gladly took up the offered seat; his brother was clearly concerned about the wound, even though it was only a deep gash in the upper thigh. Sharice had her own concerns — and that's why she said to her cousin as she gave him the detonator, "I believe I know why this was in Zhin's hand."

No explanation was needed from his cousin, as her belief became his. The previous raids, combined with the evidence that was in the back of this off-road vehicle, were all that was needed to put the D.U.O. out of business for good. Louie couldn't risk the weapons being traced back to him. Had this deal gone south, he had planned on destroying them. Thankfully, Zhin hadn't gotten a chance to blow up the truck.

"What's going on here?" Jerrelle asked as she stepped beyond the perimeter of the woods and into the clearing.

At first, Sabastian had thought that she too had been injured, but Jerrelle quickly made it known that the blood on her clothes was not hers. "Are you sure you are okay?"

Jerrelle took a moment and looked herself over. She knew that Nicoli's blood was on her, but she had no idea just how much — she now understood her friend's concern. "Yes.., I'm fine."

Relieved that everyone had survived this ordeal, Sabastian encouraged Jerrelle to enlighten everyone about her expedition into the woods. With a smile on her face, she let it be known that she had led Nicoli on an extensive wild goose chase in which she double-backed several times until the man became utterly confused. At that point, she sprung her trap.

"Did you kill him?"

"No. As much as I wanted to, I felt that restraint was the best course of action for me to take at this time. I instead, decided to leave him with an everlasting gift." Jerrelle held up her honor blade to show everyone that it was also covered in blood. "I left a nice collection of well-placed gashes all over his body that even Freddie Kruger would be envious of. Nicoli will never look the same."

"And now he knows just how hard it is going to be to kill you."

"Yup! But that's not going to stop him. If anything, I just gave him more motivation than ever to try again."

While that conversation between Jerrelle and Sabastian was taking place, Sharice decided to leave the area of the vehicle and head over to where Louie had been. To light her way, she used her vid-cell. What she saw when she got to where the dead man lay, she expected. Even so, she wasn't sure how she felt about it.

Upon her return to the truck, she made an inquiry with her cousin, "Was it really necessary to kill Louie?"

"It was not I who pulled the trigger. Uri Drakonna of the C.R.A.P. did the deed. It was he as well who had shot the bear."

"What the hell was a Serbian nationalist doing here?" Sharice asked.

"Louie had killed their former leader, Vladi Chemzot. He was here for revenge. This whole thing was set up by him."

Jerrelle looked over at the bear on the front porch of the cabin; her biggest phobia lay dead there. She knew that her fears were unfounded, but her mind immediately chastised her for taking a hasty tour through the woods. *'I can only imagine how many wild carnivorous animals that call this forest their home were actually considering me to be their next meal?'*

Knowing that any sort of weakness being shown would all but destroy the reputation she had built, she took a few therapeutic breaths and then said to her friend, "Um… Sab?" Are you disappointed that it was not you who got to pull the trigger?"

"Actually… I'm not. I mean, I should have been the one to put an end to it all, but I chose not to."

"Well, now that it's over, I guess the only thing left to do is for you to turn this whole damn mess over to the authorities," Sharice not so subtly stated.

"Yeah, that's going to be fun explaining to them what happened here. I'm glad that responsibility is yours and not mine," Jerrelle sardonically pointed out.

Sabastian didn't respond to his friend's comment, even though she was correct. Instead, he walked over to the driver's side door of the vehicle and looked through the open window. Luckily, he saw that the keys were still in the ignition. He then said to Jerrelle, "Do you still have that bomb sweeping app on your vid-cell?"

"Yes.., why?"

"Can you sweep the truck?"

"Why do you want her to do that?" André asked.

Sabastian held out his hand, displaying the detonator Zhin had dropped and Sharice had found.

André leaped off of the tailgate; he winched in pain but kept on moving as far away as he could, as fast as he could. His brother laughed. So did Jerrelle. Even Sabastian could not help but chuckle. Yes, it was mean to laugh at someone else's misfortune, but when it comes to friends, times like these are hard to refuse — and even though the Laperriére brothers were not yet considered to be that to him, Sabastian had a feeling that at least a mutual respect was now there.

Once Jerrelle had completed her sweep of the vehicle, found the bomb, and then helped Sharice to defuse it (and remove the twelve bars of C4 from the constructed device, of which they put in the back of the truck with the weapons), Sabastian invited everyone to hop in. It was going to be a tight fit for the five of them, but it was better than walking the two-plus miles back to where the van was parked.

About ten minutes after Sabastian and his ragtag bunch had left the area, Louie's two associates returned. Nicoli was in rough shape; his body looked to be just as wounded as his pride. Stupidly, he had fallen for one of the oldest tricks in the book — and that was why Jerrelle Dakota Robinson had nearly carved him up like a Thanksgiving turkey. Numerous times, she stabbed each of his legs, had nearly sliced off his right nipple, and had left a series of parallel gashes right across his abdomen. Across his face, she also gave him a four-inch slice that without a doubt was going to turn into a nasty scar. But that wasn't all, as a fairly deep cut also lay right across the entire small of his back. He looked as if he had just wrestled a hardcore, deathmatch.

Needless to say, all of his wounds were going to take a lot of time to properly heal. Time, however, wasn't needed in order for him to think of the best way to get his revenge. Her pending death was already a guarantee. There was no need for him to think of a creative, satisfying way for that to occur. The next time their paths crossed, a simple bullet will suffice.

With Zhin's help, Nicoli stepped passed the dead bear and into the cabin. From there, they walked into the kitchen area. After gingerly taking up a seat in an old wooden chair, he was left alone so that his associate could search the place for some medical supplies. If there wasn't anything that could be used to clean and dress Nicoli's wounds, he'd all but be screwed because a good many of them didn't look like they would stop bleeding on their own. Thankfully, Zhin found the needed items in the upstairs bathroom cabinet.

After his injuries had been tended to, he again was left alone. Nicoli was uncertain as to what it was that his associate was up to, but once he saw him carrying the two kerosene heaters into the middle of the cabin, he had a pretty good idea. "We need to erase the evidence of what has happened here — and I don't give a shit about this beautiful place." Zhin then opened up the front door and began to drag the dead bear inside. Nicoli would have helped, but he was in no shape to do anything physical.

Although the animal weighed more than four times as much as what Zhin did, he was able to draw on his mental discipline and summoned the strength he needed. Once it was inside, he walked back out the front door and returned about five minutes later with Louie draped over his shoulder. He then laid his body down beside the bear, took off his own blood-covered shirt and pants, and threw them next to Louie — Nicoli followed suit and did the same with his torn and bloody clothing.

Once they both cleaned up and had changed into new shirts and pants; clothes that Zhin had found in one of the upstairs bedrooms, he poured the kerosene around and on top of both the bear and Louie. "Under normal circumstances, I'd rather give Louie a proper burial instead of carrying out a funeral pyre, but we need to destroy any and all incriminating evidence. We have to continue to make the authorities believe that the D.U.O. is trying to tie up all of its loose ends and trying to remove itself from any connection to its past weapons thefts. If we are successful in doing that, then that should buy us enough time to quietly rebuild this organization into the empire that Louie and his predecessors had envisioned."

"And how are we going to do that when neither of us has been around long enough, nor have earned the right to take this over and continue it."

"Before we came here, I was given explicit instructions in case something like this was to happen. It will be a long while before the D.U.O. can resurface and reclaim its position, but when it does, we will both be a big part of something that is right now, beyond our imagination. We just have to be patient and wait until the time is right."

After asking Nicoli to get up off of his chair and to leave the cabin, Zhin used the barbecue lighter he had earlier found out back next to the hibachi and set the cabin on fire. He then joined his associate outside.

After making their way to the mouth of the pathway that led up to the militia's encampment, they stood there in remembrance, watching the cabin become engulfed in flames and their former boss become one with the ashes.

After a couple of minutes, Zhin and Nicoli turned around and walked away from the area content. Because of how far away they were from any emergency services, by the time they arrived, nothing would be left of the cabin, and the bodies of the bear and Louie would be burned beyond recognition — which is exactly what they wanted.

He knew that it was his responsibility to inform Governor White of everything that had just taken place, but by the time they had arrived back at the lodge, Sabastian had decided that a late-night call wasn't warranted. It wasn't like the U.B.I. was immediately needed to go to the Muskegon Militia's base camp and arrest everyone; there probably wouldn't be any members of the radical group there anyway. Zhin and Nicoli would also be long gone, right along with Louie's dead body. The illegal arms that the D.U.O. had gone there to sell, they were already in Sabastian's possession. Therefore, the only thing that should still be there in the morning was the dead bear.

Besides, good news in the morning was what Sabastian thought the governor really needed to hear — the knowledge that the last remaining senior member of the Detroit Underworld Organization was no longer walking on the earth. That should make his day, right along with easing the burden of guilt he has lived with for far too long.

When he did make that call, right after breakfast, Sabastian's presumption had turned out to be correct. And although Christopher had surprisingly not uttered any sort of words to let him know just how happy he was that the last black mark from his days as a police captain had finally been erased, he could sense that a huge weight had immediately been lifted off of the man's shoulders.

There was one more thing. To Sabastian, it was very important. Even so, he felt very uncomfortable having to ask something of his father's old friend. It wasn't a personal favor; he just wanted a little assurance. Under any other circumstances, he was certain that Christopher would happily oblige any request of his. The problem with this one though, was that the governor would have to use the power of the office he held and pull some strings. Sabastian honestly didn't want to put him in that sort of position, but — it's not like the man had not done that sort of thing before.

What he didn't want was for Christopher to feel pressured into saying 'yes' based solely upon who Sabastian was. If his request was refused, then he would leave well enough alone. However, the ride back to Detroit was then going to be a very stressful one. And knowing his luck, he'd get pulled over and end up with an overzealous trooper with an itchy trigger finger and aspirations to be perceived amongst his peers as a real hero.

What he could have done was just unload the weapons from the back of the off-road vehicle and left them behind for the U.B.I. to deal with. At least then, they would have had much more room for the ride back to the hunting lodge. But doing that would have given the Muskegon Militia or Louie's two associates, time to claim the weapons before the feds even got there. The logical thing for him to have done was to drop them off at the nearest Muskegon Police Station, but these weapons had originated in Detroit — it simply made sense to him that they went right back there so that the police could take possession of them and determine if any of them were connected to other crimes or cases that were still open.

Surprisingly, Christopher had no issue with doing what was being asked of him. He understood and agreed with Sabastian's reasoning. So after he disconnected his call, he contacted the state police in order to notify them of the pending transfer of confiscated weapons to Detroit. Then, he made sure that the entire trip there would not be impeded in any way at any time.

While this had been taking place, Sharice used her limited medical knowledge to inspect and then re-treat the wound she had haphazardly bandaged up on André's leg the night before. Luckily for him, she was certain that a few stitches and some antibiotics would suffice, as his injury was probably no worse than the nastiest kitchen knife cut he ever sustained while working at his job.

By nine a.m., they had begun their journey back to Detroit. Sabastian drove the off-road truck, and Henré drove his van with his brother, Jerrelle, and Sharice inside. There was room for at least one person to ride shotgun, but no one wanted to ride back to the city in the truck. It's not that anyone was purposely shunning Sabastian, but they all had decided to rib him a bit, each claiming that they did not wish to be associated with someone who was transporting stolen weapons across the entire state. And even though they were aware that he was supposed to have been given an unhindered ride back, each of them acted as if they were not at all convinced of that fact.

Surprisingly, André chose to ride in the back of his brother's van, claiming that he wanted to have more room and be able to keep his injured leg elevated — which then left the front seat open. And even though there was plenty of room in the back of the van for everyone else, Sharice chose to sit in the front passenger seat. If Jerrelle didn't know any better, it appeared to her as if Sabastian's cousin had claimed that seat because she wanted to get to know Henré on a more personal level. And if that was indeed the case, then she had no doubts whatsoever that Cloe's doorman was soon going to become a very lucky man.

Upon their arrival at The Cough Inn, Jerrelle immediately got into the passenger side of the off-road vehicle. Judging by the conversation and flirtation that took place during the drive back, she highly doubted that Sharice was going to join them — and she was right. Though Sabastian's cousin's given reason for staying behind could be the truth; her mother had an old contact in the area that she wanted to touch base with before she left for home, Jerrelle wasn't all that gullible. She knew the real reason why, as it was far more obvious than what the real use of the old store across the street had been.

What Sabastian honestly wanted to do before they left was take a few moments, go inside the club, and check on Madelyn — but the illegal weapons had been in his possession for way too many hours already. He had a responsibility and he had to follow through with that before anything else.

Unfortunately, it was still going to be some time before that load of weapons was taken off of his hands. The reason for this extra delay was that they first needed to swing by Jerrelle's apartment in order to pick up her car.

As Sabastian was pulling into the parking lot, his heart literally stopped. Outside of Jerrelle's apartment building were two police cruisers. He had no idea why they were there, but his unfounded thoughts were saying that the cops were there waiting for him.

She looked over at her friend with a similar dumbfounded look, only to clue in a moment later once she had seen a police officer exit her, now ex-apartment building with its manager. "They're here for me. You want to use that intellect of yours and go find out why?"

"What makes you think that they are not here for me?"

"Because you have a free pass until you deliver the weapons. I, on the other hand, have a reputation that is etched in stone."

Although he was a little leery about leaving Jerrelle alone with the illegal weapons, Sabastian exited the truck. He then cautiously made his way over to where there were a few nosey bystanders. Once he arrived, he struck up a conversation with a middle-aged woman who was cradling her pet cat — to Sabastian, this woman seemed like the kind of person who just needed to know everything about everyone who lived in the apartment complex.

Five minutes later, he returned to the off-road vehicle, relieved in a sense, but worried at the same time. "The manager called the police once someone reported to him that they noticed your balcony glass door was gone."

"What? Do they think that someone broke into an empty apartment?"

"According to the cat lady, that is what was first expected. But once the police entered your place and found the spent casing on the floor, right beside your old couch, they had no choice but to treat it as if a crime had been committed."

"Shit... I never bothered to police my brass after I shot out the glass door 'cause I was buzzing and 'cause I was leaving."

"Well, you can't very well exit this truck now and go get your car without being seen." Sabastian held out his hand.

Jerrelle didn't want to do this. Only once had she ever relinquished the keys to her fully restored classic car, and that was to her sister — and only because Bai Lin was blood and the car had originally belonged to their father. But she knew that she didn't have any other choice at that moment; she had to let Sabastian drive it. So she grudgingly handed him the keys and then slid over into the driver's seat of the off-road vehicle.

Being careful that any curious eyes didn't see him, Sabastian made his way over to her Camero, slipped seamlessly into it, and then drove off — Jerrelle followed closely behind. A few blocks away, she pulled out and passed him, then braked. It forced him to stop the car, right in the middle of the road. She then promptly got out of the truck, walked back to her car, and opened up the driver's door; a word did not have to be spoken for Sabastian to understand what she wanted.

He was disappointed; he also could not blame her for not having any desire whatsoever to finish the drive to their intended destination in a truck full of illegal weapons — seeing that the law was just at her old apartment building and presumably, wanting to question her. But this was her baby and he'd honestly feel the same way if the Camero had belonged to him. Still, it was nice to feel what it was like behind the wheel, albeit briefly, of a seventy-five-year-old, mint-conditioned muscle car.

After switching vehicles, they proceeded to the Detroit Police Headquarters in the downtown corridor. Thanks to an arrangement that Governor White had made, Sabastian was to meet up with Captain Stratton. At that point, all responsibility of the weapons would be removed from him and his life could finally begin to be somewhat normal — if it was at all possible?

By late afternoon, it was all done. The off-road vehicle and its load were in the hands of the police and they were on their way back to The Cough Inn. He was not physically exhausted, yet Sabastian decided to just lie back in the passenger seat of Jerrelle's car and close his eyes. A lot had happened to him since he was temporarily recalled into active duty, but he never imagined that it would eventually lead him to the doorstep of his family's enemy. All the years that his father had dedicated himself to trying to stop the D.U.O. and its operation, now seamed in some twisted sort of way, all worth it.

If Maxwell Bank's death hadn't taken place, then would the chain of events that followed it, ever have happened in some other fashion? The answer to that question was unattainable. More than likely, Sabastian would still be living his life right now as Terrance Burelli Jr. Then again, fate would probably find a way to lay down just enough breadcrumbs in order to snag his curiosity. Once that happened, it would only have been a matter of time before he would discover who he really was, and the path that he was supposed to walk.

Inside, he was smiling. With the help of his friends, family, and others who volunteered their services, the Detroit Underworld Organization was finally dealt its long-deserved crippling blow. Still, he felt a small hint of sadness. Two good people had died during all of this: Helfred Nemchieve and Ben Fraisure. Even he and Jerrelle had come close to losing their lives on a few occasions. Was it all worth the risk? The end result would be 'yes'. But in hindsight, this vendetta that his father had chosen to embark on should not have been handed down to him. Then again, Sabastian should have been smart enough to not embrace it in the first place.

A few blocks before they arrived at The Cough Inn, his thoughts were transferred toward Madelyn. She had come into his life faster than a tsunami slamming the coastline of some small Asian country. She had swept him away and left him to try to survive the predicament she had wittingly placed him in. But she also had caringly thrown him a lifeline and was there afterward to help him achieve his goal. His relationship with her so far was unusual and confusing, but it also felt completely right. Parts of his mind were searching for just one clue that would indicate whether or not she was going to become his Achilles heel. But it was his heart that was speaking louder than the doubts — right along with his mother's words. *"You must be able to fully absolve her of her affiliation with Louie Mazotti before you can truly love her the same way she loves you."*

While in route to Muskegon, some internal reservations had surfaced — but Madelyn had done exactly what she said she was going to do. And because she had, no legitimate reason could be found for him to harbor any sort of ill will toward her. She had to be forgiven for her past decisions and choices. What's ironic about the whole thing was that Sabastian had been in a similar situation. He had been a victim of circumstance, all thanks to Terrance Burelli. His 'father' had done things that all but guaranteed him a one-way ticket straight to hell. But in the end, after it had come to light, Sabastian was still able to reserve a small corner in his heart for him because Terrance had tried to make things right. And because he was willing to forgive his 'father', it was only fair that he do the same for Madelyn.

As soon as Jerrelle's car pulled up to The Cough Inn, he jumped out of the passenger seat and headed directly into the club — he could not wait to throw his arms around her and give her a kiss. But neither of those things could happen. "Um... Where is Madelyn?"

André stood there with a cane in his hand; he really didn't need it, but he wasn't about to squander an opportunity to draw sympathy from the ladies. He also didn't wish to be rude, but Sabastian's question wasn't his to answer.

As Jerrelle made her way to her friend's side, Cloe came out from the kitchen. The moment she saw Sabastian, she walked right behind the bar and asked him to take a seat. Instead of pouring him what was surely going to be a much-needed drink, she handed him a letter. "It's from Madelyn." Discreetly, she then encouraged Jerrelle and André to follow her into the kitchen so that Sabastian could have some privacy.

Unsure as to why she had left him this, he took a moment and contemplated. Those doubts that he thought he had been able to successfully bury in the back of his mind, promptly resurfaced. It was then that he came to an unfounded conclusion. Madelyn didn't love him after all.

"Dearest Sabastian

Meeting you has forever changed my life. Up until now, I had never thought that someone like me truly deserved to find happiness — and that is what I know I have found with you. You also have given me the motivation and the strength that I have been looking for to repair the damage that I caused to my own family a long time ago. You set out on a journey to discover who you were and to make right what had wronged your family, and now I must do the same.

Throughout my youth, I was all but convinced that both of my parents hated me and that was why they had resorted to the abuse of many kinds of substances. I rebelled against everything they asked of me and did everything that I could to validate what I believed. I look back on that now and I can see that my unyielding resistance to their authority was what had caused many of their problems, not they who had caused all of mine.

When I was eighteen, I had fully convinced myself that I knew what was best for me, so I left my family behind and ventured out into the world; a world that I was nowhere near ready for. And it didn't take me long to realize that I knew nothing. Being out on my own was ten times harder than I ever imagined. Yes, I could have gone back home, but I had caused so much damage to my family that I felt it was impossible; that they would just slam the front door in my face and forget that I ever existed.

Like a lot of people, I have numerous regrets. The choice I made to embark upon a career as a prostitute though is not one of them. I did what I felt I had to do in order to survive. Now, the time has come for me to do what I should have done long before now. I must go home. There, I intend to do everything that I can to try and rebuild a relationship with my family.

I hope that you can understand my decision to do this. But I also want you to know that I am deeply in love with you, Sabastian, and I will come back to you after I have achieved my goal.

Please be patient and wait for me so that you and I can walk that same path together, forever.

Love, Madelyn"

Sabastian set the letter down on the bar top and took a moment to again banish the returning doubt. If anything, this letter had just solidified how Madelyn felt about him. And it also had touched an area in his heart that he didn't know existed; he had unknowingly changed her life for the better just by walking into it and being who he was.

He smiled at that thought, but at the same time, he felt a little selfish because Madelyn wasn't there with him at that moment. He would have at least liked to have her tell him what she had wanted to do in person, but there was so much magnetic pull between the two of them that it would have been difficult for either to not grab onto the other and forget that the world around them even existed. Not only that, but there would be an internal want on his part to suddenly protect her. Undoubtedly, Sabastian would have tried over and over again to convince her that she needed him to help her through this, even though he knew that he had no business being a part of it.

He picked up the letter and re-read it to himself. He could not doubt the sincerity in her words, and he fully understood her desire to heal the wounds that she had inflicted. For that reason, Sabastian had to do what Madelyn asked him to do — be patient and wait. She loved him as much as he admittedly loved her — and that love would one day bring them back together. But until that day happened, he had to let her go and get on with his own life; a life that no longer revolved around the D.U.O. or the military.

A few minutes later, Cloe, André, and Jerrelle came out of the kitchen. As Sabastian was folding the letter and placing it back into the envelope, a pint of beer 'magically' appeared in front of him.

"Is everything all right, Sab?"

"I guess... Madelyn decided to go back home to Chicago to try to rebuild a relationship with her estranged family."

"Well.., that's a good thing, isn't it?"

"It is. We all need to have our family and friends by our side. I understand why she is doing this, but the selfish part of me wishes that she were still here."

Jerrelle moved over to her friend and placed her arm around his shoulder at the same moment that Cloe placed a pint of beer in front of her. "I was too stubborn to let Helfred know what my true feelings were for him, and now I can never tell him how much I had really loved him. I can see it in your eyes that you feel the same way for Madelyn. I think you should call her, but only to let her know that you support her decision and that you are only a phone call away if she needs you. She will know for certain then that you feel the same way about her as she does about you."

Sabastian nodded his head in agreement. "Since when did you get a degree in psychology?"

Jerrelle expelled a halfhearted laugh as she glanced over at Cloe, then back to Sabastian. "No degree is needed. It's just women's intuition."

After sliding a beer down André's way, Cloe looked at Sabastian and said, "I only had a chance to speak with her for about an hour before she left, but I too could see how conflicted she was about what she knew she needed to do and what she wanted to do. Jerrelle is right. Just be there for her. If she needs you, she will call. And when she is ready, she will come back to you."

Sabastian took a healthy sip of his beer and stayed quiet in thought. After another sip, he removed his vid-cell and sent his cousin a quick text — her rental car was still parked at Jerrelle's apartment building and he thought that he should give her a heads up about the police being there. Five minutes later, she had yet to send back a reply. "Hum? Sharice usually responds to my messages right away. It's odd that she hasn't."

Jerrelle and André had a look on their faces that was hard to mask — and Sabastian quickly noticed it. "If there is something going on with my cousin that you both are aware of.., I would appreciate it if you would kindly share it with me."

"Um… She didn't actually go to where she said she was going."

"Then where is she?"

"We don't exactly know for sure," André said. "She and my brother took off shortly after we got back into town."

Jerrelle smiled. What she had earlier predicted, now certainly seemed to be the case. However, it wasn't her place to suggest that the two of them had gone someplace private to get it on. Sharice was unquestionably a beautiful young woman, and she wouldn't blame Henré one bit for wanting to move beyond just being mere acquaintances. After all, Jerrelle had once mentally undressed her out of pure curiosity. "They are both adults, and where they go and what they do is none of our business."

Sabastian didn't know what to think. On one hand, he was upset that Jerrelle had failed to inform him she suspected something was going on with his cousin and André's brother. On the other hand, he was not Sharice's keeper; she was a grown woman, and her choices are hers alone to make. If what was being implied, turned out to be true, at least he could take solace in the fact that Henré appeared to be an honorable man. If he turned out not to be, Sabastian was certain that Jerrelle would do him a solid favor and kick the giant man's ass.

Upon their arrival at Jerrelle's apartment later that evening, no evidence that the police had been there was visible — at least, not out front. Nevertheless, she didn't want to risk being seen entering the building, so she walked around to the back of it and then shimmied up the same tree that Sabastian had. Once she was onto the balcony, she cut the police tape that stretched across the boarded-up broken patio door, pried it open, and entered her apartment. The initial plan was to have stayed there one last night before they both headed to Texas, but there was a chance that the place was being watched. Just because Jerrelle was innocent of the assumption that had been made, it didn't mean that she could ignore it and hope that it would go away. Doing so could potentially ruin the fresh start she planned on making.

While she was breaking down her bed so that it could be taken with her, Sabastian drove the rental truck around to the backside of the apartment building. He then got out of the vehicle, opened up the rear doors, and waited for Jerrelle to pass her bed over the balcony railing.

"Give me a second," she said after the last of her bed was in Sabastian's hands. "I'll be right down." Except for the tattered couch, her old apartment was now completely empty. Before she left though, there was one thing that she wanted to do. She took the lid from the bucket of chicken she and Sabastian polished off the other day and wrote a detailed note on it. When she was done, she left it on the sofa cushion; it explained exactly what happened to the patio door, along with the information stating that she had tucked five hundred dollars in-between the cushions to help pay for its repair. Her reason for doing this was so that when her ex-landlord came back in the apartment to fix it, he would not be near as angry with her for the damage she caused.

Also, she hoped that on her behalf, he would tell the police the truth so that any pending charges waiting to be laid against her would not be.

After shimmying back down the tree, she noticed that Sabastian had already loaded her bed into the van. She smiled, thanked him, and then walked back around to the front of the complex to get her car. Even though they were under the cover of darkness, there was still a chance that someone with curious eyes might have seen them. So long as it wasn't the damn cat lady that was being her overly nosey self, Jerrelle was confident that no one would say a word.

As much as she was eager to leave Detroit behind for good, it was late so they met up down the street at the Motel 6. The next morning, right at the crack of dawn, they were both ready for what was going to be a very long day. By the end of it, Jerrelle was certain that she was going to be exhausted — but being tired as a result of her move would be a small price to pay. Her old life would officially be left behind, and for the first time ever she was looking forward to what the future held.

It was what the Fates had long ago determined. Yet, there was a part of her that was still mad at them because she had not been allowed to be a part of her son's life. Having been taken away from Sabastian when he was just a baby was the hardest thing that a mother had to accept. It wasn't until she had a chance to finally see what her son had become that she realized her death was a necessary sacrifice. Had she not died when she did, her precious little crown jewel would have become somebody else and not an individual who was destined to achieve greatness.

And now, as she sat there on the sofa in a manifested apartment that existed within a fallen angel's realm, looking at the real-time image of her son that was being provided by an ancient item, an Apollo's Stone, Sylvia could not be any prouder. All on his own, Sabastian had found the path that he was destined to walk. Along with that, a long life filled with happiness seemed to be in the not too distant future.

A bit of sadness was there though. Not because her recent visit had been far too short, it was because she was unable to be there for Sabastian during what surely was going to be an emotionally difficult time. He had won over Madelyn's heart, but something more important was taking precedence. As a mother, Sylvia fully understood why this decision had been made, why this woman had felt the need to go back home to Chicago and make things right between her and her family. No ill will could be harbored toward her for that. There was no denying that her son was a strong-willed individual. In time, he would be fine. And in time, Sylvia wholeheartedly believed that the stars would align and Sabastian and Madelyn would end up together, forever.

"Keeping an ever-watchful eye on your son again?"

Though that voice did not belong to her husband, Sylvia smiled anyway. "I missed twenty-five years of his life, Nefieti. And knowing that our time here in this place will be coming to an end soon, I just want to take with me as many memories as I can."

"I can't blame you for that. So.., where is your husband?"

"He is in the bedroom sleeping. Now that Louie Mazotti is no longer alive, and after last night's 'celebration', Maxwell needed some rest."

"Has he forgotten already that he is dead and does not ever need to sleep again?"

Sylvia could not help but crack a mischievous grin as she invited Nefieti to take a seat. As he made himself comfortable in the lazy boy recliner, it dawned on him why Maxwell was apparently tired. "Ah.., you two…"

"And that is why we would appreciate it from now, until the next aperture opens up, that you would at least knock before you enter our apartment."

"Have you already forgotten that this is my realm and that this 'apartment' is not real? If I choose to show up here without the courtesy of a knock on the door, I can."

"Then you may end up catching my wife and I doing something that should be kept behind closed doors. I mean.., I've always fantasized about having an audience, but I don't believe that my wife would be too keen on it." Maxwell stepped into the living room area, looking revived. For the first time in a very long time, a fervent bounce seemed to be in his step. "The netherworld may be run by you, but as long as my wife and I are here, we consider this our home. So like my wife has already asked, please show us both a little common courtesy when you decide to come and visit us from now on."

"Ok… Seeing that you are not going anywhere anytime soon, I guess that is the least I can do."

"Wait? What do you mean? We had a deal. The two of us would like to leave and spend our eternity together in heaven."

"We did have a deal. And even though you did what was asked of you, you did cross the line on multiple occasions."

Maxwell could not deny that, even if he wanted to. "I will admit to bending a few rules, but I got the job done. Therefore, I should be rewarded, not punished."

"Think of it more like a reprimand."

"It's the same thing."

"That's all in how you look at it."

"Am I staying here too, or am I going back when the next aperture opens up?"

"So long as your husband is here, Mrs. Banks, you are welcome to stay."

A smile of genuine contentment appeared on her face. Although she was looking forward to spending eternity with Maxwell in heaven, where they were really wasn't all that bad.

He was happy that Nefieti was going to allow his wife to stay, but there was a part of him that wanted to walk right up to the angel and punch him in the nose for going back on his word. But this wasn't earth; this was the angel's realm and Maxwell had no leverage here whatsoever — at least, not right now. In all honesty, he was nothing but thankful that he had been given the opportunity to keep watch over his son, torment his enemy, and be allowed to go through all of it in the company of his wife. "So then.., since I am not going anywhere, am I to assume that I will be given another task?"

"Yes."

"What is it and when?"

"As of now, I do not know either. But if everything progresses the way that it is believed, then your pending task will be even more important than the last one."

Not wanting to make an assumption of any kind, Maxwell straightforwardly asked, "We're going to be waiting for a while, aren't we?"

"That again, I do not know. But I would rather you already be here when the time comes than have to get on my knees and beg in order to get you back here."

"Ah... What exactly did you do to piss off your ex-boss?"

"Nothing! He just hates me, and I have no love for him."

Though fucking with someone else's life was something that Maxwell would thoroughly enjoy, staying right where he was in Nefieti's Netherworld basically meant that he was the angel's puppet. He hated the idea of him essentially being a 'prisoner' with no rights or say whatsoever. It was easy for him, though, to see why Nefieti was reluctant to send him and his wife on their way. Right after he had 'haunted' Louie for the first time, Maxwell had a sneaking suspicion that this whole thing wasn't going to be a 'one and done' type of deal. And now that he knew for sure that the angel intended to keep him around, he needed to find out what his end game was before he agreed to let this 'relationship' continue on the way it was. The last thing he wanted was to be at Nefieti's beck and call for all of eternity.

"Is there nothing that you can tell us?" Sylvia asked.

Nefieti was hesitant to say why he was keeping Maxwell around. His reason for doing so probably wouldn't surprise the ex-cop. His wife though — "Um... Louie has a son."

Sylvia's jaw literally dropped to the floor. "Are you serious?"

"Yes. He was born twenty years ago."

She looked at Maxwell and could see that he was not reacting to this unexpected revelation the way he should be. For that to happen, she had to conclude that he already knew and, for reasons she just could not fathom, chose not to inform her. For the first time since she could remember, she was angry with her husband.

"I have no problem keeping an eye on the little shit. And if I see that he is even contemplating follow in his father's footsteps, I will then..."

"You won't do anything! You can't do anything anyway, as the stone won't allow you to even find him."

"Why not? I saw him before."

303

"That is only because you were watching Louie at the time. As of now, Marco Santori-Mazotti is not a threat. He is a normal college student with a goal and a dream. However, if things unfold the way the Fates suspect they will, he will become heavily influenced and his soul will then turn. If that happens, his path will undoubtedly cross with your son's. Only then will you be able to watch and keep an eye on him whenever you want."

Maxwell did not like that provision. He had just assumed that once Louie Mazotti was killed, Sabastian would be able to freely walk his destined path. Now, there appeared to be another possible threat in which Maxwell could do nothing to stop it before it became viable. "So... I am to sit here on the sidelines, wait, and hope that this bastard son of Louie's does not follow the same path as he."

"Yes."

"You're in tight with those immortal sisters, are you not? Can you not find out for sure what the boy's path will be?"

"No. They don't even know. As of now, his destiny is uncertain. You see, at the moment of conception, multiple paths are laid out for an individual. Over time, as people grow, as things happen, as individuals come into their life, or individuals are removed from the picture, potential outcomes are then eliminated. As of now, there are three potential paths that Marco Mazotti could take. And I'm sure you don't want to hear this but.., I honestly think that he will venture on down the same road as his father, as there is much more of Louie in him than his mother."

"How strong of a chance is there that he will do that?" Sylvia asked.

"If I were to guess, I'd say that there is a seventy percent chance."

"Is there a chance that he won't be just like his father?"

"There is.., but I highly doubt it, Mrs. Banks. The Mazotti family line is far from saintly."

"Which means in all likelihood, he will become a heartless bastard," Maxwell stated, with the utmost of conviction.

"We don't know that, Max. He could be the exception to the rule."

"That's doubtful, dear." He then looked over at the angel and said, "I need for you to make an exception and allow me to go back to earth so that I can start to manipulate the boy's life in a way that will prevent his lineage from coaxing him over to the dark side."

Sylvia grabbed her husband's arm and turned him so that he was looking at her face and its unyielding expression. "Just because the Apollo's Stone is a tool that allows an individual to manipulate the laws of the universe, doesn't mean you have the right to use it in order to assure that history does not repeat itself. You have always been a man of integrity. Had you known that Louie's son existed when you were still alive, I don't believe that you would have used him as a pawn in order to defeat the D.U.O. or to gain the needed leverage in order to locate our son."

"I, uh… I don't know? Maybe? Sometimes you have to think like the enemy in order to bring them down, Sylvia."

"And that is exactly why Louie kept his son's existence a secret," Nefieti stated. As you know, he lived in a world that made him many enemies. It would have been a foolhardy thing for him to let his son's existence become common knowledge. Doing so would be the same as handing the enemy the key to a crane with a wrecking ball and letting them freely destroy the headquarters of the Detroit Underworld Organization. As much of a bastard as the man was, you cannot blame him for doing what he did."

Maxwell had absolutely no compassion for Louie Mazotti, but he certainly understood the man's reason to hide the existence of his own son. It's what he should have done in order to protect Sabastian.

He took a moment and walked around his 'apartment'. He needed to think. Sylvia was right. Even Nefieti was right. It was only Maxwell's determination to protect his son that was the basis for his suggestion that he prematurely cut off the head of the snake before it actually matured enough to strike. But that was not who he was — he had integrity and he had morals that he never once had compromised.

After coming to terms with what now seemed to be inevitable, Maxwell returned to the same spot that he had vacated. Louie Mazotti was dead; his death was going to have a profound effect on the man's son. Without a doubt, it was going to be the catalyst that influenced Marco to step off of his current path and merge with the same one that his father had taken. And when that happened, Maxwell needed to be ready to deal with it. "How long am I going to have to wait here until it is known exactly what path Louie's offspring decides to take?"

"Again, I do not know." To ensure that Maxwell didn't try to find a way to manipulate and bend the rules again, Nefieti turned his right palm upwards, closed his eyes, and a second later, the Apollo's Stone appeared. He then placed his other hand over it and spoke in a language that sounded ancient. "I have put a restriction on the stone. Between now and the events expected to one day take place, you both are only going to be able to watch your son. I cannot risk that you, Max, will somehow find a way to warn him in advance of the existence of Marco Mazotti. If it is at all to occur, their paths must cross naturally. Once they have, the stone will then return to its full capabilities."

"I know my role here. I would never take advantage of the privileges I have been given."

"Really? Correct me if I am wrong, but did you not already admit to me that you have no problem bending the rules in order to get the job done."

Maxwell hated it when his words got thrown back into his face. And though what had just been articulated was not done so with the intent to wound his pride, it was clear that a message was being sent. "I did, but... had I followed the supposed rules, it would have been impossible to complete my assigned task. You're smart enough to know that; it is why you never stepped in and stop me."

Nefieti let out a light-hearted chuckle; Maxwell's retort was just as accurate as his declaration had been. "I didn't stop you because... no one else, alive or dead, could ensure that Louie Mazotti stayed on his destined path. But..."

"But what?"

Nefieti got up from his seat and walked over to where Maxwell was standing, looked him in the eyes, and said, "You are not supposed to be able to make contact with a corporeal being."

Maxwell could not help but feel a rush of satisfaction. For the first time ever, he had crossed right on over the line — but barely. And whether or not it was justified, he simply could not resist the opportunity that had presented itself for a little payback. Louie's face meeting his fist had been long overdue. "He deserved it."

"That's not the point. It is supposed to be impossible for you, a dead you, to be able to have any kind of physical contact with a living being."

"The impossible is only a certainty because a decision is made to not search for a solution." Maxwell held out his hand; Nefieti returned the Apollo's Stone to him. "It took me quite a while to learn how to use this otherworldly object for something other than it just being a looking glass." Maxwell paused for a moment as he brought the stone to life. "With patience and determination, I slowly began to understand what this is fully capable of.., which included what laws of the universe I could bend and break with its help."

"You need to show me how you did this."

"I'll make you a deal... I'll show, but only if you allow me to keep watch over my son's new potential enemy."

Nefieti hated it when all the cards didn't fall in his favor. It had been many millennia since he had to negotiate for anything. That day, he was the one who wanted something. And even though in the end he got what he asked for, it still felt as if he did not get enough.

How in the hell did this happen? The angel was always in complete control of his realm. Then again, it should not have surprised Nefieti one bit that Maxwell had somehow found the 'cheat codes' and used it to his advantage. That punch, as impossible as it should have been, was what had helped to ensure that Louie Mazotti walked his fated path right to its very end.

Before he mulled over the offer made, the angel froze time in his realm — only because he didn't want the ex-cop to interrupt him. The Apollo's Stone, an item, though not indigenous to the Netherworld, has been in his possession for thousands of years — how could he have not known that it was actually capable of something thought to be impossible.

This revelation; it certainly changed the game. Because a dead person could now make physical contact with a corporeal being, it was all but guaranteed that they would use this ability to either satisfy a personal vendetta or gain some semblance of revenge. Not only could irreparable damage to the natural course of humanity's evolution be caused as a result of their actions, Nefieti would probably be held responsible as well.

So that such a possibility never came to fruition, the angel needed to learn and then understand how physical contact is achieved. Only then, could he apply a safeguard to the stone. In the future, if he were to determine that circumstances were warranted, he simply had to unlock that capability.

After spending roughly ten minutes trying to think of a justifiable way to deny Maxwell's request, Nefieti decided that it was best to let him win this round. He could have just played the 'Boss card' and forced him to reveal the secret, but he had a long-term plan for the ex-private eye and he wanted to keep a good working relationship with him.

The instant he unfroze time, the angel replied, "I cannot do what you are asking. As I said, the Apollo's Stone will not allow you to watch over Louie's son until his path crosses with Sabastian's. However.., I will permit you to use the stone to keep watch over Louie's two associates, as they have already crossed your son's path."

"But watching them will do what for me? Bore me with mindless Lug-head activity?"

"For as smart as you are, you can be a blatant idiot sometimes."

Sylvia couldn't help but chuckle at that one.

"Once Zhin Wi and Nicoli Nemchieve cross paths with Marco, it will then be pretty clear as to what path he will take. From that moment forward, you will be able to keep tabs on Marco through them. And only if and when his path finally crosses your son's, will you then be able to watch him without having to watch the others."

Maxwell didn't have to contemplate over the offer made. Although it wasn't exactly what he would have liked, it was acceptable. He could be unwilling and blatantly refuse it, then hope he would be able to figure out a way to get what he wanted. But there was no guarantee that he could figure out a way to keep an eye on anyone he so chose; he admittedly had gotten lucky when he figured out how to make physical contact with a living being. Therefore, he said, "We have a deal." He then extended his hand in order to solidify the agreement. Nefieti reciprocated.

Once that was done, the angel extended his left hand upward; it came to rest on the side of Maxwell's head. What he was doing looked very similar to that of a mind-meld; a technique the Star Trek character of Spock would use in order to link his thoughts with someone else's.

After a few seconds of searching through Maxwell's memories, as intrusive as this was, Nefieti found the key to understanding how to unlock the previously unknown ability that the Apollo's Stone had. It was surprisingly straightforward — for an immortal as old as he.

Long before he had brought the ex-private eye to the Netherworld to take on such an important task, he had utterly dismissed the long-ago affirmation made that Maxwell Banks had the potential to become his near equal. It's obvious now that Nefieti's belief had been wrong. For a onetime mortal to have figured out what he had, it meant one thing — that Lachesis was right.

This whole ritual really didn't need to take place, as the angel could have easily probed Maxwell's mind right after he froze time instead of striking the deal he had, but it was always a lot easier to work with someone when they didn't harbor any kind of ill will toward you because you had done something to them without first asking their consent.

Satisfied with what had just taken place, Nefieti left the manifested apartment without any other words being spoken. This surprised everyone. Even so, the angel's abrupt departure was unreservedly welcomed.

Before her husband had a chance to say anything, Sylvia got up and headed toward their bedroom. With her back to him, she then said, "It looks like we are going to have a lot of free time on our hands." She then began to strip out of her clothes as she made her way down the hall. By the time she had arrived at their bedroom door, her undergarments had created an implied barrier on the floor in front of the threshold.

"So long as Nefieti doesn't make any more unannounced appearances, I am game to explore every bit of... I mean.., maximize the free time we have until I am needed again." Maxwell was in no rush; he knew what would be waiting for him. When he had finally caught up to his wife, all but his underwear had been removed. As he was about to step over the pile of clothes that 'blocked' the entrance to their bedroom, Sylvia placed her hand up against his bare chest. With a wry smile on her face, she lightheartedly pushed him back into the hallway. She then swiped the clothes on the floor into the room with her bare feet and said, "You don't get to sample any of what's going to be waiting in here until you apologize." She then closed the door.

Stunned, Maxwell stood there nearly naked, unsure as to what had just happened. It wasn't until a few uncomfortable moments went by before he realized why his wife was playing hard to get — she was still somewhat pissed at him for not sharing the knowledge of Louie's son's existence. "I'm very sorry for not telling you about Marco. So... how long am I going to have to stand here in my Jimmies?"

Sylvia did not answer him right away; she wanted to make him sweat. "Um... I'm thinking until our first grandchild is born."

"Are you kidding? You can't be that mad at me?"

Slowly, the bedroom door opened back up. Sylvia stood there buck naked; an impish grin was on her face. She then reached across the threshold and unapologetically grabbed the top band of her husband's underwear. Her grin immediately became an anticipating smile, as Maxwell appeared ready and willing to make up for his lack of better judgment.

Epilogue

A legacy can be built using many different methods. It can come as a result of dedication and hard work that in turn, allows a goal or a dream being achieved. Being an upstanding individual with integrity, just being loyal, respected, and even admired can also attain it. Another way it can happen is by proxy, wherein one's birthright allows them to continue on with what had already been established and then they take it to the next level. Sometimes though, a legacy is so tarnished, it seems as if nothing can be done to salvage or repair the damage — not even by someone oblivious to the disreputable history left behind.

If an individual does happen to possess that sort of unwelcomed knowledge, distancing themselves from the past is easier said than done. An attempt can certainly be made to do that and hope it one day does not rear its ugly head. Chances are though that it will be discovered, no matter how much of an effort is made to erase that history.

What's most difficult to do, yet could end up becoming even more rewarding, is to first accept the responsibility of what those who came before you, had done. Then, do everything you possibly can to rebuild and rewrite that legacy, starting from the ground up, in your own respected image.

Friday, May 23rd, 2036

Mirella Santori had kept herself busy all day cleaning her house, as she wanted it to be spotless when her son returned home from college. It wasn't a special day or anything, but something inside of her had encouraged her to do this.

All throughout the day, she kept on thinking about Louie. She had not heard anything from him nor had she received a 'support' payment since he had returned to Detroit last September. And because of this, worry had become a daily part of her life. Over the years, long periods of time had gone by without any conversation or notification between them, but never had it been as long as this.

She didn't want to consider the possibility, but it was beginning to look as if that day had finally come. Louie's lifestyle had caught up with him. Although Mirella didn't know this for a fact, to her it seemed to be the only logical explanation for his lengthy absence from her and her son's life.

The last time Louie had been in Chicago, Mirella hoped that his stay would have been much longer than it had. Admittedly, she still had deep-rooted feelings for him after all those years and had even thought about letting him back into her life in a more intimate capacity. Fear though was preventing her from doing that. Firmly, she believed that if the truth were to ever be learned, her nearly perfect world would forever be ruined.

The last time she had seen her son's father, he had stormed out of her house — and she blamed herself for that. He had been right. She still didn't trust him to keep his promise. If she had, he'd probably still be in Chicago, and the unsettling thoughts that Mirella was having about him now no longer being alive, would not be there.

The lack of contact from Louie had also begun to immensely affect her son. The entire school year had come and gone and the usual motivation that Marco would normally have at the beginning of it, slowly disappeared as the months came and went. By Christmas, he had begun to show some signs of being depressed. On the first day of April, her son had mentioned that he was thinking about packing up his bags for the summer and taking a trip to Detroit to try to find his 'uncle'. At first, Mirella thought that Marco was just kidding, but then she quickly realized that he was quite serious. That intent of his did not sit well with her at all. It caused her to panic. She didn't know what to do. She needed Louie at that moment more than she had in a very long time. Yet, he had dropped off the face of the earth. His phone at his office had long been disconnected, his vid-cell was no longer in service, and he hadn't returned any of her dozens of e-mails and v-mails.

She didn't know exactly how she had managed to do it, but she was able to somehow convince her son to give up on his crazy idea of going to look for his 'uncle'. Now, she just needed to figure out a way to verify what had happened to Louie without actually going to Detroit herself to get those answers.

By mid-afternoon, Mirella had the majority of the main floor of her home cleaned. Before tackling the upstairs though, she decided to take a short break. As she was about to go into her kitchen to get a Coke-XG (an energy drink), her doorbell unexpectedly rang. Her selfish thoughts immediately went to Louie. She hoped that maybe he had finally decided to show the world that he was still alive and that he had returned to Chicago to see her and her son. But she knew what the chances were of that happening. Just because she had been thinking about him, didn't mean that he was suddenly going to show up on her front porch.

Disappointment immediately settled into her body the moment she opened up the door to her home as standing there, dressed in an expensive three-piece suit, was a man of Asian descent. Mirella knew that she had never seen this person before in her life and his appearance this particular day immediately conjured up her curiosity. He was only slightly taller than her, yet for some reason, she really didn't feel very nervous about his being there — even though she could easily see that this Asian man had an intimidating presence about him.

Mirella tried to think of a legitimate reason as to why this individual would be knocking on her front door. She could tell that he wasn't a salesman, a businessman, a lawyer, or even one of Marco's professors. What she was fairly certain of though, was that this man was someone of importance. "Can I help you?"

"Are you Mirella Santori?"

"Um... Yes, I am."

The stranger then handed her a long box and an envelope. "Louie Mazotti has entrusted me to make sure that I personally deliver this to you."

Mirella cautiously accepted the delivery from the stranger, but before her brain would allow her to ask any questions, he respectfully bowed his head, said good day, turned away from her, and then walked back toward an awaiting limousine.

She stood there puzzled and wondered for a moment why Louie had sent this stranger to her home. She remembered him telling her in the past that he had never once told anyone about his life outside of work and he had never dared to tell anyone about their son. *'Why would Louie send this man, who I have to assume works with or for him, to deliver something to me instead of bringing it to me himself?'*

After closing her front door, she went directly over to her sofa and sat down. A tear escaped her left eye; she wiped it away. Her heart was starting to break — but now was not the time for sorrow to consume her. She needed to gather her thoughts and reel in her emotions. Until she read the letter that was in her hand and comprehended everything that it said, she needed to refrain from drawing a conclusion.

She set the box down on the coffee table and then nervously opened up the envelope — she prayed that her fears were not about to come true. However, she only needed to read the first sentence of the letter to realize that it had.

"Dear Mirella,

If you are reading this letter, then life as I have known it is no longer. Before I met you, I had been content to exist in a world so few could even fathom or understand. It was only when our paths crossed that my whole perspective on life had changed. Up until that point, I never knew that I too had a place in my heart reserved for a soul mate... and it was you who had found it, you who had gained passage to it, and you who claimed it. You are, and will always be the only one that I will forever truly love.

I also want you to know that I do not harbor any resentment toward you because of your insistence to keep the truth from our son. Although you know that I did not agree with your decision, I cannot fault you for the reason behind it. Had you accepted me for who I was and what my chosen life had been, things certainly would have been different and our son would have undoubtedly grown into someone other than what he is today. So for that, I am thankful.

314

However, now that I am gone, I feel it is only fair that Marco is no longer kept in the dark, as I know that you will never come clean for fear of losing him forever. Secrets can come back to haunt you in the worst way; that I know from experience, as my entire life was based solely upon them. You have had twenty years to do this and have refused. I am truly sorry, but by the end of this day, my son will know who I really was because I have made arrangements for this revelation to take place. He has a destiny to fulfill; one that will take him down a path that I wholeheartedly believe he was born to walk.

Love eternally, Louie Mazotti,

Sept. 25ᵗʰ, 2035 "

Mirella set the letter down on top of the box. At the same time, she did not want to accept the cold hard facts. Her soul mate, the love of her life, a man who deserved the trust and respect she was too scared to give him, was never coming back. *'This letter is eight months old. Louie had to have had a forewarning of his pending demise.'*

She took a moment in order to let her thoughts sort themselves out. She knew that this day would eventually come — even though she selfishly hoped that Louie would be the honorable man she had met all those years ago and forever abide by her wishes. Fate apparently, wasn't going to let her win.

She didn't have to open up the accompanying box because she knew that there were a dozen roses inside. Louie would always send her some on the anniversary of the first day that they had met. And although today wasn't that day, she knew that there would never be another one. She cared deeply for him because of his thoughtfulness, generosity, and caring nature. Yet, she now hated him more than she had ever hated anyone else because he decided to break his promise.

She sat there trying to control her own emotions but found it impossible to do so. Tears freely flowed down both of her cheeks. Her world was on the brink of disaster — and there was nothing that she could do to prevent it from happening. Her own self-interest was the catalyst for this; it was about to cost her everything. The only thing left for her to do was prepare herself as best as she could for the pending shitstorm and then try to figure out a way to clean up the rather large mess that was going to be left behind afterward.

—————————————————— ☉☉ ——————————————————

Most students look forward to the last week of school. For Marco, he just did not want to be there anymore. He didn't hate school; his mind was simply somewhere else. His uncle, the man who was the closest thing that he ever had to a father, had not been heard from for more than eight months. He wasn't sure why, but his apparent disappearance had affected him more than he thought it should. Something deep down inside of him made him think that the worst had happened. Yet, there had been no word, no clues of any kind to indicate whether or not that was the case.

Desperately, Marco wanted to go to Detroit and try to find him, but he also had no desire to go against his mother's wishes. The last thing he wanted to do was cause her more unnecessary stress, even though she too was desperate to learn whether or not his Uncle Louie was all right.

Although it had already been tried, unsuccessfully, he didn't think it would hurt to try again. Once his very last exam was completed today, Marco was going to use every conventional and unconventional method he could think of in order to find him. Repeated phone calls, v-mailing, e-mailing, texting, an old fashion handwritten letter, a missing persons notice placed in the paper, and even a posting submitted on every single social media platform there was, would be used. It didn't matter to him that his mother had used some of these same dead-end methods already, or that his uncle's picture was going to be put out there for the entire world to see. What mattered to him was that he was found. Yes, Marco knew that Louie Mazotti had always been a private man and preferred to never have his image made public, but he just didn't care.

While walking across the campus, en route to his second last exam, he stopped at the same stone bench he always did every day before this particular class. He set his backpack down on top of the bench, opened it up, and took out a pack of clove-flavored cigarettes. He had only started smoking them a few months ago. He didn't know why he had chosen this brand, but he surprisingly found that they

316

helped him to relax. He didn't need to smoke them all the time, but the exam that he was about to write was for a class in which the professor, for some unknown reason, appeared to have it out for him. Marco did not know why, but the man, right from day one, got under his skin and drove him up the wall each and every time he had to endure another one of his unconventional lectures. This quick fix of nicotine is what he felt he now needed before he had to suffer through what surely was going to be his most difficult exam of the year.

When he looked at the time on his vid-cell, he noticed that he still had a few extra minutes before he had to leave and face the bullshit that awaited him. After taking a few long, unhealthy drags in an attempt to finish off his smoke, he looked casually across the campus grounds; his eyes directed him to, and then locked onto something that wasn't normally seen at an institute of higher learning.

Approximately one hundred feet directly in front of him, pulling up to the curb, was a dark charcoal colored limousine. Curiosity enveloped his thoughts, as he knew that only city buses, cabs, or Uber drivers would drop off and pick up students at the main entrance to the campus. *'Either some rich kid and their parents are here to take a tour, or a celebrity of some kind must be here to receive their honorary degree,'* Marco thought.

Once the vehicle had come to a complete stop, a very distinguished, yet fierce-looking Asian man, exited. He took a brief moment, pressed and straightened out his suit with his hands, and then began to walk in Marco's direction.

Normally, he wasn't afraid of anything. Many times in his brief life he had to step up to the plate and defend himself or even someone else who did not have the ability to. But this individual was causing trepidation to grow with each step that he took. Even so, Marco wasn't about to let his nervousness show, so he casually unzipped his spring jacket and took it off. Just in case he had to fight, he wanted nothing to restrict him.

"Marco Santori? My name is Zhin Wi, and I am a friend of your father's."

Confusion instantly enveloped him. "My... father's?"

"Yes! And I'm sure that you have a lot of questions about him." Zhin handed Marco a letter. Then, with what appeared to be a genuine smile on his face, said, "I suggest that you read what's inside this envelope and then take a few moments before making a decision. What that will be will then determine whether or not all those questions that you have about your father, get answered." Zhin then turned around and headed back to the awaiting limousine.

He wasn't actually doing it, but Marco was essentially scratching his head. That apparent 'friend' of his father's had just dropped the biggest surprise he had ever had into his lap. He didn't know what to make of it, only that the answers that he had been searching for his whole life were supposedly within reach.

His initial instinct was to just follow the Asian man, but he had been instructed to first read what was in the envelope — so that was what he was going to do. Intriguingly, Marco looked at the unopened letter. He then took a second and thought. Although he could not even begin to fathom what was written inside, he now believed that he held in his hands that long sought after first, all-important piece of the puzzle.

When he finally felt ready, Marco opened up the letter, while at the same time, trying to keep his expectations at bay. It was difficult, but he knew that he had to stay focused on what was written because he did not want to skip past anything that could be important.

"Dear Marco,

I know you have always felt that your life would have been a lot different had your father been a part of it. Well, I was. Right from the beginning, I was there… just not like any father would normally be.

Before you were born, I made a promise to your mother that I would keep my identity a secret from you because she was afraid that the knowledge of my existence would change you and what she had felt you were destined to become. And although my belief was not the same as your mother's, it turned out that she was right. If you had always known who I was, then you would not have become the man that you are today. So for that, I am grateful. However, I feel that the time has now come for you to finally be made aware of my identity. The only problem with me telling you this is that, due to circumstances

318

beyond my control, I am not physically able to be there for you: to guide you, to love you, and to be a father to you.

The life that I have chosen to live, the life that your mother insisted I keep hidden from you, is a life in the world of the criminal underground. For thirty years, I was a fully-fledged member of the Detroit Underworld Organization. My affiliation with them also meant that I had to be willing to accept whatever consequences came with the territory. Including, the day in which I would have to pay the piper.

With what you have so far read, I'm sure you have already figured out that I am no longer alive. Do not be sad and please do not be angry with your mother, as I was as much a part of that decision to keep you in the dark as she was.

Now, you have to make a life-changing decision all on your own. If you want to continue on with the way things are, then stop reading this letter right now, burn it, walk away, and forget what you have so far read. If you wish to find out more about me and the life I have lived, then get inside the limousine that awaits you. But just so you know… If you choose the latter, if you really want to know who I was and the world I was immersed in, you must unreservedly give up everything that you cherish and have. Once you take the first step on down that road, there will be no going back. You will be in it for the remainder of your life.

Do not do this if your only desire is to acquire the answers you have forever sought. You have to fully commit yourself to the same kind of life that I had in order to get those. I know that this is a very tough decision. And whichever one it is that you make, I want you to know that I will not be disappointed.

In closing, there is only one thing left that I need to tell you. And that is I have always, and will forever love you, my son.

Your father,

Louie Mazotti."

Marco lowered his head in disbelief. The man whom he had admired and loved like a father was actually his own flesh and blood; a man whom he now knew was no longer alive. *'Why did you keep that a secret from me? I don't understand the reason behind that decision?'* Marco looked at his vid-cell and realized that he was now very late for his exam — but he really didn't care. He had just found out the most shocking news he had ever heard in his twenty years of existence. His uncle, the man whom he had loved and adored, was actually his real father; a father that he now will never be able to tell just how much he had always loved him.

Marco raised his head and stared out across the campus, while at the same moment, doing everything that he could to hold back the tears that wanted to freely flow. It was difficult, but he found a way to keep his emotions in check.

After a few deep inhalations of the cool afternoon air and a brief look over at the awaiting limousine, he glanced down at the now wrinkled letter in his hands and thought, *'Should I forget that Uncle Louie is my real father, or should I take the biggest step in my brief life and get inside the limo that awaits me?'*

After a moment of uncertainty had passed, he used his hands and his body to smooth out the letter as best as he could, folded it, and placed it back inside the envelope. Marco then rose up off the stone bench, grabbed his spring jacket, and was about to take that first step toward a new life when one of the few close friends he had, walked up to him. "Hey, Marco! Are you not late for Professor Ireton's final exam?"

"Yeah… and I don't care, Lucy. Something has come up that I have to deal with."

"Like what?"

"Let's just say that things are about to drastically change." Marco leaned in close to his friend, Lucy Islington, and gave her a goodbye hug. He had always had a thing for her and had even convinced himself that this coming summer was going to be when he would finally get up the nerve to move past the 'just friends' relationship that they had always had. Now, he was saying goodbye to her — maybe forever.

Turning away from Lucy, Marco intently walked toward his awaiting future. Once he got inside the vehicle, Zhin was sitting there at the far end of the back seat with a contented smile on his face. Up near the front of the vehicle, occupying that seat was another man; he was much larger and unsurprisingly, even more intimidating than the Asian. Notwithstanding that, the man also sported a rather nasty scar across the side of his face. "Hello, Marco. My name is Nicoli."

He looked back over at Zhin; he was still a bit hesitant about taking this uncertain journey — but inside, he knew that this was what he needed to do. So as he sat down, he said, "Which one of you is going to tell me how my father died?"

Nicoli removed a bottle of Walker's Club from the limousine's wet bar, poured himself, Zhin, and Marco a glass, and then smiled. "We have a long drive ahead of us to Detroit. By the time we get there, that, and all of your other questions will be answered."

Through the window of the limousine, as it began to leave the grounds of the University of Chicago, Marco looked at Lucy. She and the life that he had known were forever being left behind — right along with everything else he thought was in his future. Strangely, he wasn't at all sad. He was instead, at ease with the unknown. An unimaginable world awaited him. And whether or not he was ready for it, he was going to welcome it with open arms.

About the author

       Steven F. Deslippe was born in Canada on September 24th, 1966. He grew up in a rural community, right next door to his grandparents' farm, just outside of the town of Amherstburg, Ontario.

       Farming wasn't of interest to him; however, music was. Beginning in late 1987, and lasting for fifteen years, Steven worked as a disc jockey, playing music and emceeing weddings, parties, dance clubs, rock clubs, and gentleman's clubs. It was during this time period where he discovered a passion for reading and writing — both of which he admittedly did not like, nor was very good at when he was younger.

       As the years went by, both of these skills greatly improved — the result of this dedicated hard work, now forever captured in each book that he writes.

Social Media

Facebook
https://www.facebook.com/Author.Steven.F.Deslippe.Official/

Goodreads
https://www.goodreads.com/author/show/16559506.Steven_F_Deslippe

Youtube
https://www.youtube.com/channel/UChXnJAOrOEv0vnWNdQWJbqQ

Contact

sdeslippe@sympatico.ca

*** Other releases ***